The
Green Man's
War

The Green Man's War
Juliet E. McKenna

WIZARD'S TOWER

Wizard's Tower Press
Rhydaman, Cymru

The Green Man's War

The Green Man - Book 7

First edition, published in the UK November 2024
by Wizard's Tower Press

Paperback ISBN: 978-1-913892-90-6

Cover illustration and design by Ben Baldwin
Editing by Toby Selwyn
Design by Cheryl Morgan

No AI tools were used in the creation of the text or cover art
of this book.

http://wizardstowerpress.com/
http://www.julietemckenna.com/

Contents

For my fellow authors
who support me with their friendship
and sustain me with their books.

Praise for the Green Man Series

I'm here to be your good bookfriend and express my own quiet but fervent enthusiasm for this contemporary folkloric fantasy series. You should take the plunge, the water is fine if full of terrifying naiads and nixes. — Imyril on *There's Always Room for One More*

The series of Green Man novels goes from strength to strength, bringing a modern fantastical sensibility to traditional folk tales and things that go bump in the night. — Ben Jeapes on Goodreads

Praise for The Green Man's Heir

Finalist for The Robert Holdstock Award for Best Fantasy Novel, the British Fantasy Awards 2019

"... any way you look at it, the book is a delight from start to finish. [...] It's one of my favorite books so far this year." — Charles de Lint in *Fantasy and Science Fiction*

"I read this last night and thoroughly enjoyed it, more please!" — Garth Nix on Twitter

"I really enjoyed this novel!" — Kate Elliott on Twitter

JULIET E. MCKENNA

"Juliet McKenna captures the nuances of life as a stranger in a small town in much the same way as Paul Cornell does in his splendid Lychford series, with the local gossips, the hard-pressed police, the rampaging boggarts and rural legends come to disturbing life. Thoroughly enjoyable; a UK fantasy author branching out (oh god, sorry for the inadvertent and terrible pun!) and clearly having a great time doing it. Highly recommended." — Joanne Hall

"So far up my street it could be my house." — K.J. Charles on Goodreads

"*The Green Man's Heir* is a thoroughly engaging, at times almost impossible to put down, tale which, despite besides its titular character, is peopled with an impressive array of interesting and intriguing women." — *The Monday Review*

"After a stumbling start, I found myself unable to put down *The Green Man's Heir*. If you're looking for a book to read on your summer holiday, then this is it." — Charlotte Bond via The British Fantasy Society

The Green Man's Heir is a straightforward fantasy story, with a lively pace and characters who wonderfully come alive. It starts as *Midsomer Murders* set in the Peak District but with added supernatural element and turns out to be the book you won't put down because you enjoy it too much." — *The Middle Shelf*

"I hope this turns into a series. I'd love to read more about Daniel's adventures." — N.W. Moors in *The Antrim Cycle*

"And she has absolutely nailed it. This is a complete and utter joy." — S.J. Higbee in *Brainfluff*

"I'm certainly on board for reading more such novels." — Paul Weimer in *Skiffy and Fanty*

"Brilliant concept, compellingly told" — Virginia Bergin on Twitter

Praise for The Green Man's Foe

Finalist for Best Novel,
the British Science Fiction Awards 2020

"I loved *The Green Man's Heir*, and while I expected to thoroughly enjoy *The Green Man's Foe*, I did not expect it to be even more satisfying than its forerunner. Which was foolish of me, I admit – I should know by now that McKenna is more capable of outdoing her previous tales in a series." – *The Monday Review*

"If you've read the first book then I'm pretty confident you're going to love this one, and if you haven't read the first one then you need to remedy that straight away." – Naomi Scott

"This is one of my outstanding reads of the year." – S.J. Higbee in *Brainfluff*

"*The Green Man's Foe* is a great addition to what is becoming a great series. I was entirely caught up in it for a couple of days. It is a must read if you have enjoyed the first one, and a great reason to start on this series if you have missed it." – *The Middle Shelf*

"*The Green Man's Foe* is a tasty serve of mystery and myth that has done quite enough to cement this series as one I'll be reading and cheerleading for from now on." – Imyril at *There's Always Room for One More*.

"What I loved reading this tale is how genuinely real McKenna makes the story feel." — Matt at *Runalong the Shelves*

Praise for The Green Man's Silence

"These Green Man books provide a wonderful blend of British folklore and ordinary people trying their best to make the world — or at least their corner of it — a better place. The characters are likeable, while the mythical creatures are earthy, dangerous, and full of that Sense of Wonder that makes fantasy such a pleasure to read. Recommended." — Charles de Lint, *Fantasy & Science Fiction*

"Highly recommended for fantasy fans who are looking for well-written fae adventures with a difference." — S J Higbee in *Brainfluff*

"This is undoubtedly one of the best books I've read this year and I thoroughly enjoyed it. I can hardly wait for the next book!" — *The Monday Review*

Praise for The Green Man's Challenge

Finalist for Best Novel,
the British Science Fiction Awards 2022

"I don't usually review every book in a series, but I'm so taken by this one by McKenna that I want to keep touting its virtues so that people will, I hope, buy each one of them." — Charles de Lint in *Fantasy & Science Fiction*

"Wowee! That was one hell of a ride. A fantastic ride, both the main tale and the bonus short story at the end." — Pers at *Goodreads*

"It is also a delight to read a novel written by someone who knows her genre so well and works at finding different ways to exploit its tropes. The threat in *The Green Man's Challenge* is a giant: the hero doesn't have the strength to match the foe, so other ways must be found, ancient knowledge must be discovered again. By doing so, McKenna consciously subverts the expectations of a certain kind of fantasy: no lone hero, no unbelievable physical prowesses, no amazing powers (political or supernatural)." — *The Middle Shelf*

"Ms McKenna has a glorious sense of place" — Jacey Bedford

McKenna has brilliantly utilised the likes of the giant figures cut into chalk hillsides and some of the numerous folk stories around hares to add to her intriguing Brit rural fantasy tale. — S.J. Higbee in *Brainfluff*

Praise for The Green Man's Gift

"If you've enjoyed the previous Green Man books, then you'll enjoy this one without a doubt. If you haven't read them yet... What are you waiting for?" — *The Middle Shelf*

"The Green Man's Gift [...] is another excellent tale in one of the most interesting contemporary fantasy series around." — *Runalong the Shelves*

"As ever, McKenna writes an absorbing, utterly compelling tale." — *The Monday Review*

Highly recommended. You could start here, but I recommend you do yourself a favour and read the whole lot in order. — Jacey Bedford

Praise for The Green Man's Gift

Winner — Best Novel, the British Science Fiction Awards 2024

"It's a great place for new readers to test themselves and I suspect many of those who do will rush rightly to read the rest. The Green Man series continues to be one of the most engaging and fascinating series in our current fantasy landscape and is strongly recommended!" — *Runalong the Shelves*

"There's a real sense of peril in this one, with a genuinely scary villain with interesting motivation." — KJ Charles at *Goodreads*

"Juliet McKenna is pushing the bounds of her world and it shows no signs of growing stale." — Ben Jeapes at *Goodreads*

"another story full of adventure and incident in this superb series. Very highly recommended for fans of fantasy in a contemporary setting filled with creatures from British folk-lore" — *Brainfluff*

"... how rich and complex McKenna's world is. Actions have consequences and unintended ripples that threaten secrets and long established status quo." — *The Middle Shelf*

"Dan Mackmain is a fascinating character in his own right, but he's only half the story: the other half being the depths of British folklore..." — *The Monday Review*

Chapter One

I'd been wondering what was going to happen. Without being too obvious, I'd been watching the other people setting up their stalls for this bank holiday weekend's craft fair. Who was going to cause the problem I'd been sent to sort out?

It was going to be something that only someone like me could handle. My dad's an ordinary, mortal man, but my mother is a dryad, a tree spirit. My greenwood blood means I can see threats that most people dismiss as fairy tales and folklore. I know that dangerous creatures and other beings who don't live in the everyday world still lurk in out-of-the-way places. But I'd arrived at this Northamptonshire rare breeds farm bright and early, and I hadn't seen anything unusual. Until just now, when four men in grimy overalls stormed in through the barn's tall double doors.

The leader was yelling, menacing. 'Stay where you are! Nobody move! Keep your mouths shut and no one gets hurt!'

I stood very still beside the cloth-covered table I'd been allocated. Everyone else did the same. This threat was real. The man in charge, the first one into the barn, was holding a billhook. The two who followed him were armed with a pickaxe and a heavy-duty mattock. Any one of those tools would cave in some have-a-go hero's skull. I could tell none of these men would hesitate. I've met killers before.

Billhook guy headed straight for a jewellery seller who had been setting up opposite my woodwork stall. The silversmith was in his mid-fifties, with greying hair pulled back from his thin face into a ponytail. He wore chinos and a short-sleeved pale blue shirt. I put him at no more than five foot ten, and skinny with it.

Billhook guy leaned across his table and grabbed him by the throat, quick as a cat catching a bird. The jewellery seller was too frozen with shock to even think about dodging. Bill-hook guy pulled him close and whispered something in his ear. My hearing's better than most, but I couldn't work out what the bastard was threatening. Nothing good. The silver-smith's legs gave way when billhook guy let him go. He collapsed onto the chair behind his table. As the stranger waved the tool in front of his face, the silversmith's white-rimmed eyes followed the gleaming steel.

The last of the gang who came in through the door had a sledgehammer in one hand and a big square shopping bag in the other. One of those heavy-duty, stiff-sided bags that people fill with jars and tins and then wonder why they can't lift them out of their supermarket trolley. He tossed that towards the silversmith's table and turned to stare at me.

I spread my hands slowly and held them up level with my shoulders. I tried to look unthreatening, but that's not necessarily easy. When I'm not solving mythical mysteries, I manage a private estate's woodland, as well as doing repairs and maintenance around the properties. It's mostly outdoor work with a fair amount of heavy lifting, and that builds muscle. I'm also six feet four and I buy my clothes in XXL sizes. It wasn't a warm day, even for the first weekend in May, so I was wearing a hoodie over my T-shirt, and that made me look even bigger.

Sledgehammer guy was barely five foot eight, but he was stocky and solidly built. Not young, not old, dark-haired with a tanned and weathered face. How old was he? I decided I didn't care. He could do me some serious damage if he swung that hammer at my ribs or my knees. I couldn't get out of his reach with the barn's solid stone wall behind me. I didn't move.

At least I could see over his head. A twenty-something couple had been setting out organic soaps and hand creams on the table next to the jewellery seller's. They'd been wondering how the weather forecast might affect potential sales. The app on the woman's phone predicted sunshine and showers with the possibility of thunderstorms just about anywhere. No great surprise for a UK bank holiday weekend.

'Excuse me, sorry, can I just...?' The jewellery maker squeezed past them, coming out from behind his table.

The organic soap couple retreated. The silversmith picked up the shopping bag. He was so scared he couldn't stop shaking. Snatching necklaces, bracelets and earrings off his stall, he showed them to billhook guy before dropping them into the bag. Each handful landed with a slithering thump, loud in the tense silence.

The white-haired lady to the soap couple's right, my left, made glass ornaments. She'd been sitting down when the robbers arrived. Her face was expressionless as my eyes met hers for a fraction of a second. I realised I couldn't see her hands below the edge of her table. Was she dialling 999, keeping her phone out of sight? If she was, she'd better have it on mute.

I looked away so sledgehammer guy wouldn't start wondering what I was looking at. I wasn't convinced a phone call would be much help. No one in the barn was saying a word. A 999 operator would have to be telepathic to work out what was going on. I remembered reading about a way to let emergency call handlers know you can't talk. I should look that up and sodding well remember it. Did the glassmaker know that sort of thing?

How long would it take the cops to get here? News stories about emergency services focus on towns and cities where response times are measured in minutes. It's different in the countryside. More police stations close every year. Unsurprisingly, rural crime is soaring. Expensive farm equipment and vehicles are stolen by organised gangs and shipped abroad.

·I didn't want to think how long it might take for an ambulance to get here, so I really hoped no one was stupid enough to try to intervene. No one was moving a muscle at this end of the barn, but I couldn't look past the central threshing floor without moving my head. I wasn't going to risk that. Sledgehammer guy was shifting from foot to foot as he stared at me. He was definitely on edge. It wouldn't take much to tip him into bloody violence.

'And the rest.' Billhook guy threatened the silversmith with the sharp steel again. 'Everything that's under the table.'

Sledgehammer guy glanced over his shoulder to see how the heist was going. I snatched a quick look down the barn, past the tall doors that reached to the rafters on both sides. In days gone by, they would stand open to let the breeze winnow the chaff from the grain on the threshing floor. The farmyard doors were the only ones open today. I saw a guy selling pottery looking at the closed outer doors. I hoped the 'Fire Exit Only, This Door Is Alarmed' signs convinced him he had no chance of getting out that way. Not before the closest robber floored him with that pickaxe.

Sledgehammer guy turned back to scowl at me. I stared past him, not reacting. My arms were getting tired with my hands held up. My right forearm was also stinging. It's a few years since I was slashed by a hostile hamadryad, and those scars are fading. The narrow white lines are only really noticeable when I get an outdoor worker's summer tan. They still warn me when something uncanny and dangerous is around. Unfortunately, I still had no idea who or what these thieving bastards might be.

I tried to think about something else. Were they brothers? I reckoned they shared a distinct family resemblance. They were much the same height, wearing dark grey overalls which I guessed they'd dump as soon as they left, to make any descriptions of their clothes useless.

Had anyone outside realised something was wrong? I listened for someone raising an alarm. All I heard was a shouted query in the distance about plugging in power leads. Someone else was bitching about mobile phone reception for taking credit card payments. The gates wouldn't open to the general public till ten o'clock this morning, and it wasn't even nine yet.

'Hurry up!' Billhook guy stepped back. The white-faced jewellery maker dragged a second plastic crate out from under his table and emptied it. Little black boxes, silky red drawstring pouches and Ziplock plastic bags slithered into the shopping bag.

'That's everything?' Billhook guy used his free hand to rip the cloth off the table, to check nothing else was under there. I still couldn't place his accent.

The man by the door with the mattock said something I didn't catch, but he was obviously warning the others. Sledgehammer guy looked around again. His mate with the pickaxe took a couple of steps towards a jewellery seller at the other end of the barn. She was tiny, wearing a long black dress, with purple hair that matched her lipstick and eyeshadow. If she was next on their list, there was nothing I could do.

I'd have to take that sledgehammer off the short-arse in front of me, then get past his mate with the mattock. No chance. My mother's a dryad, but that doesn't give me superpowers, not really. A dryad's daughters take after their mothers and live for centuries in the unseen world alongside normal life. I'm tall and strong and hardly ever get ill, but I'll grow old like my dad.

Billhook guy called out. I realised I hadn't misheard mattock man guarding the door. Whoever these thieves were, they weren't speaking English between themselves. The bloke with the pickaxe turned his back on the tiny Goth and hurried over to his cousin, or his brother.

Billhook guy stepped close to the silversmith and said something else I couldn't hear. Then he punched him brutally hard in the gut. The poor sod didn't see that coming and went down like a sack of spuds. Organic soap bloke yelped, startled. I braced myself.

Billhook guy wasn't interested. He grabbed the big bag of loot and headed for the exit. Pickaxe guy followed him with mattock man close behind. Now I heard startled shouts. Sledgehammer guy was the last to leave, walking backwards and watching me and everyone else until he reached the door. Then he turned and ran.

The glassmaker hurried over to the gasping silversmith, who was lying face down on the flagstones. She helped him sit up. 'Slow breaths, in through your nose and out through your mouth. That's it.'

Organic soap bloke had his phone to his ear. 'Police, please.'

I left him explaining what had happened and went outside. The daylight was dazzling, and I shaded my eyes with a hand. A bald, bearded man in a hi-vis waistcoat hurried towards me. His lanyard and badge said he was staff. 'What on earth is going on?'

'One of the jewellery sellers has been robbed.'

'Oh my good God.' He didn't waste time asking more questions, but hurried past me into the barn.

I didn't go after him. I wanted to know where the bastards had gone. They had to be the reason I was here. A man and two women by the paddock fence in front of the old farmhouse were gesturing and exclaiming.

'Did you see that?'

'Who on earth were those people?'

I looked around. Visitors hoping for a nice day out bought their tickets and came into the farmyard through the long low building which used to be the milking parlour. That's what the display board said, with black-and-white photos of a line of cows' backsides. The wooden five-barred gate beside it was open at the moment, so stallholders could bring in stock from the car park. With so many people milling around out there, I couldn't believe the thieves had gone that way. For a start, no one was lying on the gravel with a lethal head wound.

I went over to the people staring across the paddock and out towards the fields where visitors could see the rare breeds. 'Those men just now. Which way did they go?'

'What? Sorry?' The man's pale apron advertised an artisan bakery with big brown letters and a sprig of wheat logo.

'Those men robbed a jewellery seller in the big barn. Where did they go?' I asked a bit more forcefully.

The woman not wearing a bakery apron was listening. 'I saw them go past the Tamworths. They must be heading for the bridleway. Is anyone hurt? I'm a first-aider.'

'He took a nasty punch to the stomach.' I wasn't sure how bad that could be, or what she could do about it.

'I'll see if he's okay.' She broke into a run, heading for the barn.

'What's happening now?' the baker lady asked me, wide-eyed. 'Will we still be opening up?'

'How should I know?'

Since I couldn't see anyone wearing hi-vis, I headed for the tea and coffee stall beside the farmhouse. That was already open for business when I'd arrived. The brisk man behind the counter was pouring more milk into insulated jugs while his partner filled a wicker basket with packets of sugar and stuck wooden stirrers into a pot.

'What's going on?' The older man put down the milk. 'Tea?

'Yes, please, the biggest cup you've got.' My travel mug was still by my chair in the barn. I told them about the robbery. The brisk man dropped a teabag into a recyclable cup and filled it from the hot water urn. His partner offered me their credit card reader and I paid with a quick tap. 'Any idea where I can find a steward?'

'Try the farmhouse kitchen?' the older man suggested.

'Now we know why they went rushing off.' His partner grimaced. 'We're going to be stuck here until the police say we can go. I'll grind some more beans.'

'Thanks for this.' I added milk to my tea and left them to it. Other stallholders were starting to realise today wouldn't be going as planned and were coming over to get a drink.

Before I reached the kitchen door, the stewards came hurrying out of the farmhouse with their hi-vis vests flapping. I recognised the woman I'd spoken to earlier, when she told me where to park my Land Rover. 'Excuse me, can you—?'

'Sorry, no, not just at the moment.' She stepped around me, not even looking at my face.

Okay. I went to sit on the low wall between the yard and the farmhouse's vegetable garden. A grey tabby cat stalked between the rows of potato plants. It paused, looked at me, and went on its way to disappear under a flourishing rhubarb patch's leaves. I drank my tea and watched one of the stewards close and padlock the five-barred gate. There was no sign of any vehicles moving in the car park. Groups of traders clustered around the stewards. Waving hands made it clear they weren't happy about being told they couldn't leave.

Anyone wearing hi-vis was going to have a very bad day dealing with angry people demanding answers. The rare breeds farm people were facing a nightmare. A lot of traders would be demanding refunds if this whole weekend was a write-off. I hoped their cancellation insurance was watertight. The estate where I work, Blithehurst House, is a small private stately home. It's open to the public, and I've been involved in special events there, to bring in extra income.

The sun had come out. Flowers in the borders edging the lawn were scenting the breeze. Blackbirds tweeted in the apple trees, so the cat must have gone somewhere else. I heard cows lowing out in the fields. I wondered about going to find the bridleway the not-bakery woman had mentioned. No, that could wait. The cops would want to talk to everyone who had been in the barn. If I wasn't around, they'd take a closer interest in me, and not in a good way.

The police turned up before too much longer, announcing themselves with a quick burst from a siren. Two squad cars pulled up on the other side of the five-barred gate. Four coppers in uniforms, stab vests and Batman utility belts came into the yard through the milking parlour. They started going from one knot of people to the next. One of them went back to a car and fetched some blue-and-white tape to stop anyone going into the barn.

I stayed where I was. I had my phone and my credit card reader in the side pockets of my combat trousers. My cash box was still in my Land Rover out in the car park, with the smallest pieces I make, like honey-dippers and light-pulls, which are the things most often nicked by everyday thieving bastards. I didn't think the cops would be stealing the lathe-turned wooden plates, bowls and candlesticks off my table.

A bit later, more police cars and a van turned up. People in white hooded overalls went into the barn. I didn't think there was going to be much evidence for a forensics team to find. No blood had been spilled, and the robbers hadn't touched anything they hadn't taken with them, apart from the cloth on the silversmith's table.

A while after that, a dark blue Škoda arrived and two coppers in suits who had to be detectives went straight to the barn. They had a quick chat with the white overalls' leader in the doorway and took a look inside from there. One of the forensics team handed over a box of stuff and headed for the bridleway while the plain-clothes officers and the craft fair stewards went into the farmhouse. The jewellery seller was still in there, as far as I could tell.

It wasn't long before the man in the dark blue suit came out of the farmhouse's front door and looked around the yard. As soon as he saw me, he snapped his fingers to get a constable's attention. After a brief conversation, the detective went back inside. The heavy-set constable headed my way. His expression told me he'd been around the block a few times, even if he wouldn't have been moving very fast carrying that much weight.

'Mr Mackmain, is it?' He looked at the business card in his hand. 'Daniel Mackmain?'

'That's me.' I'd put a wooden box of those cards on my table.

'We need to take a witness statement. If you'd follow me?'

'Fine.' Once the cops had what they wanted, I could go and find that bridleway. Maybe seeing the robbers' escape route would give me some idea where they might have gone. Hunting the bastards down had to be why I was here, even if I didn't know what they were up to.

Still, I didn't hurry after the constable. I had to decide what I was going to say. I wasn't going to lie, obviously. That would be stupid, especially since they had to have looked up my criminal record by now. But I sure as hell couldn't tell them the whole truth. No police officer was going to believe I'd been sent here by the Green Man.

Chapter Two

I dropped my empty teacup into a recycling bin by the door as I followed the heavy-set constable into the farmhouse. We walked past rooms with historical displays and went into a wing that visitors wouldn't see. The police had set up their operation in what looked like a classroom for school visits or staff training. Two folding tables with metal chairs were next to each other. The woman in the dark grey suit sat at one, talking quietly to a younger man in uniform. He was busy using a laptop with a portable printer beside it. The detective in the navy-blue suit sat at the other table, looking through a heap of flyers and business cards.

'Mr Mackmain.' He smiled and waved a hand at the empty chair on my side of the table. 'Please, take a seat. Thank you for bearing with us. First things first, can you give us your current address?'

In other words, they wanted to see some ID. I got out my wallet and handed over my driving licence. As I sat down, I wondered what the police computer had to say about me these days.

'Thank you.' He passed the photocard to the woman in the grey suit. 'Please, can you tell us what happened here this morning? Everything you can remember.'

'Right.' I had no idea what anyone else was saying, but my version was short and to the point. The lad with the laptop typed up every word.

The detective in blue nodded when I stopped talking. 'You've never seen any of these men before?'

'Never.'

'Do you come to many of these craft fairs?' the lady detective asked as she handed back my driving licence.

'I used to. Not for the past five years or so, since I started working at Blithehurst House.' I could guess why she was asking. I hadn't seen anyone here from the days when I'd been a regular on the craft show circuit.

'My girlfriend and I are talking about moving in together. That's going to be expensive, so I've started earning some extra cash at weekends again.' Not that it was any of their business, but I needed these cops to hear me saying something that would ring true.

I could hardly tell her I'm looking for tree spirits isolated in remnants of old woodland where they've lived for centuries. Dryads can see straight away that my mother must be one of their sisters who fell in love with a mortal man. That's usually enough to get them to talk to me. Some craft fairs give me the excuse I need to get onto private land where I've been told a dryad is living. The money I make helps pay for diesel, food and overnight stays. The Green Man doesn't cover expenses.

This weekend was different. The Green Man had turned up in my dreams three nights ago. He'd shown me this place. I'd been standing here in the farmyard with him, beside a table stacked with the wooden things I make. Treen, they're called, if you want to be accurate. The Green Man had laid his hand on my shoulder. His emerald gaze told me I had to come here. There was no point in arguing.

'You made a last-minute booking, I believe?' The detective in blue took his turn.

I wondered if I was a witness or a suspect now. 'I saw the craft fair advertised and rang up on the off-chance. I got lucky. They'd just had a last-minute cancellation.'

I had no idea how the Green Man had managed that. Stalls at these fairs can be fully booked up months in advance. I would have come here as an ordinary punter if that was my only option, but being on site as a trader would give me a lot more access.

'Some of the witnesses said the robbers seemed to think you might try to stop them.'

The detective in blue wasn't exactly asking a question, but I could see he wanted an answer.

I shrugged. 'They looked ready to drop anyone who gave them trouble. I was just the biggest bloke in there.'

The cops must have looked me up on that laptop before they called me in. They'd know I had taken a spade off one of a gang of badger baiters who'd been threatening my dad. I'd broken the arsehole's arm with it. That mistake had landed me in court.

The detective in grey had already moved on. 'Some witnesses thought these men spoke a foreign language. Did you hear anything you recognised?'

'No, sorry.' I wanted to ask if anyone had suggested what that language might be. I didn't. These cops didn't need to know I was interested in the thieves.

The detective in blue studied the photographs on one of his flyers. 'You did these wood sculptures?'

'Yes.' The photographer Blithehurst uses for publicity stuff had taken a really a good picture of the armoured knight I'd carved from the stump of an ancient sweet chestnut, struck down by a storm. I'd done the owl for an arboretum where an old Cedar of Lebanon had to be felled before it started dropping branches on visitors' heads.

The detective looked at me, expectant. I had no idea what he wanted to know.

'They're getting more popular,' I explained. 'Especially where a big stump will be a nightmare to dig out.'

He turned the flyer over. 'Price on application. How much would that be?'

'It depends. How big the job is. How long it'll take me. How much detail the customer wants in the carving. If I'm working on site and the risk assessment says I need safety fencing, that's an extra cost. There's insurance, wear and tear on my tools, somewhere to stay if I'm working away from home.'

I used my hands to indicate a piece about a metre tall and the same wide. 'If I can take the timber back to my workshop, I can do something small for about a thousand. Something man-sized carved on site? Five grand, maybe more.'

People in the market for this sort of work won't ever notice a cost-of-living crisis.

The detective in grey looked impressed. 'Do you do many of these?'

'I've got three commissions lined up. I want to get them done by the end of the year. That should bring in about twelve thousand. Gross,' I added. 'Before expenses and tax, and my boss takes a cut if she needs to hire someone to do my work at Blithehurst while I'm away.'

That should answer the question they weren't asking. No, officer, I'm not the inside man for this gang, telling them who's worth robbing at craft fairs, because I need the deposit for a house. I can earn that without risking prison.

'If you remember anything else, please let us know.' The detective in grey handed me a card with her contact details. 'Even if it seems insignificant. People often recall something later on, once they're over the shock of being in an armed robbery.'

Armed robbery? I supposed that's what this had been. If you'd asked me yesterday, I'd have said that meant thieves with guns. I leaned forward, ready to stand up. 'Can I go?'

'Yes, thank you.' The detective in blue smiled briefly. He was already looking at another business card.

28

As I left the farmhouse, I decided I needed a pee. The toilets were in what used to be a stable. As I headed that way, I saw four teenagers wearing generic yellow hi-vis vests duck behind the building. The way they were looking around, to be sure they hadn't been seen, made me suspicious on general principles. Right now, anything suspicious was worth following up.

Stopping a few metres before I reached the stable block, I took out my phone and looked at the screen, tapping it a few times. The teenagers were keeping their voices down, but like I said, my hearing's better than most, thanks to my mother's blood. The breeze shifted and I caught the sickly-sweet scent of a vape. That explained why they needed somewhere to skulk. The farm had 'No Smoking' signs everywhere, specifically including e-cigarettes.

'I'm telling you, they had horses waiting. That's how they got away.' A lad's voice cracked with indignation.

The girl wasn't having any of it. 'You're telling me no one noticed four horses left tied up out there, saddled and bridled?'

'Three horses, if you must know,' he retorted. 'And they were in the field on the other side of the bridleway and only wearing halters. No one's going to look twice at that, are they?'

'Clever.' One of the others was reluctantly impressed. 'No way the cops could chase them.'

'Riding bareback? Must be gyppos. Fucking thieves.' The last lad's voice was thick with contempt.

I went to use the Gents. I wondered if there was anything to his theory apart from knee-jerk prejudice. The other lad was right about using get-away horses being a smart move. No number plates for the cops to look up. No tyre tread patterns to match to suspect vehicles. Good luck to the white overalls trying to work out which set of hoof prints to follow.

Was that just a clever plan, though, or was something else going on? The Green Man had sent me here. That must mean the everyday world was going to collide with something or someone far from ordinary, and not in a good way.

Walking away from the Gents, the smell of fried onions made me realise I was hungry. I'd been up since sparrow-fart this morning. It was a two-hour drive to get here and I needed time to set up when I arrived. Breakfast back in the Peak District was a distant memory. I headed for the barbecue stall by the farmhouse scullery door. The chalk board offered burger or sausage in a bap with options on onions, salad, relish, mustard or ketchup.

While I was queueing, I thought about the robbers some more. What if they hadn't turned up with guns just to avoid being sentenced for firearms offences as well as robbery? Those tools had wooden handles. Maybe they didn't like handling metal? Maybe they hadn't escaped by car for the same reason. Maybe they had at least one foot in the world that people like me can see. Maybe more than one foot.

Then I saw the silversmith heading through an arch in the wall surrounding the farmhouse's orchard. He was carrying a packet of sandwiches and a can of Coke. Sod it. I'd lose my place in the burger queue if I went after him, but if I didn't, I might not get another chance to talk to him. I followed, ducking my head to get through the low arch. He sat at a picnic table in the shade of a gnarled apple tree. There were a few other people around, but no cops. Good.

The jewellery maker was carefully tearing his sandwich packet open. He glanced up when he realised I was coming to join him. 'If you don't mind, I'd rather—'

'What did they want?' I sat down opposite, sideways on the wooden bench attached to the table.

'Sorry?' He pretended not to know what I meant.

He didn't know that wasn't going to work. Those fairy stories about creatures who cannot lie but who know when someone's lying to them? My mother's one. Her blood means I can tell when someone's bullshitting me. It also means I'm a really crap liar, which is why I had to answer the cops as truthfully as I could without telling them things they didn't need to know.

'They were looking for something. That bloke with the billhook, he checked everything you dropped in that bag.'

The silversmith stared at his uneaten sandwich. 'No, you're—'

I leaned towards him. 'If they came here on the off-chance, they'd have robbed that girl at the other end of the barn first. She's half your size. Come to that, they wouldn't have turned up first thing. They'd wait for the end of the day and steal everybody's takings. Enough people still pay in cash to make that worth their while, and they wouldn't have to fence a big bag of stolen jewellery that's going to be all over the news.'

The silversmith looked sick. 'Is that what you told the cops?'

I moved my feet in case he was going to throw up. 'No.'

He stared at me. I shrugged.

'I could be wrong. Either way, it's up to you to tell the cops what you want them to know.'

He heaved a sigh. 'You're not wrong, but I haven't got a bloody clue what's going on.'

Bugger.

'He said something to you, though,' I persisted. 'The one in charge. Before he hit you and they left.'

The silversmith glared at me, suddenly hostile. 'How is any of this your business? Who the hell are you, anyway?'

'Daniel Mackmain. Dan.' I found a creased business card in one of my pockets. I put it on the table, holding it down with a finger so it wouldn't blow away. 'I don't like bullies and I don't like getting threatened by some arsehole with a sledgehammer. I don't like seeing someone else's hard work being stolen by a bunch of pricks. And no, I don't particularly like coppers. Once they get an idea in their heads, they're like a terrier with a rat. They won't let go and they won't look anywhere else. That's sod all use if you're innocent.'

But the silversmith was looking past me, towards the gate in the orchard wall. I twisted around and saw a woman with long brown hair twisted up in a bun coming towards us. She wore a farm staff T-shirt underneath her red hi-vis waistcoat.

'Mr Mackmain,' she said breathlessly. 'The police say we can open the gates at two o'clock this afternoon. Tomorrow and the Bank Holiday Monday can go ahead as planned. There will be officers on site, but they say it is highly unlikely that anything like this will happen a second time. I hope you're going to stay?' She couldn't hide her anxiety.

'Yes, I'll be here for the whole weekend as planned.' Apart from anything else, I wouldn't get a refund on my hotel room if I went home today.

'Mr Tanner? I know you've had a dreadful experience, but I have to ask. Will you want your table tomorrow?'

'No.' The silversmith got up and walked away.

'I'm so sorry. Are you all right?' Flustered, she hurried after him. 'Is there anything I can do?'

He walked faster, ignoring her. He'd left his packet of sandwiches and can of Coke. I waited, but he didn't come back. I popped the can open and drank the Coke. If he did reappear, I'd buy him another one. Somehow I didn't think he was going to, and I was thirsty.

I still had no clue what was going on. That said, Mr What-ever-His-First-Name-Was Tanner had pulled that business card out from under my finger before he walked away. He could look me up online. My name wasn't going to bring up hits about anyone else, even with search engines so crap these days.

He'd find the news stories and realise why I steer clear of the cops. It wasn't that long ago that I'd been the prime suspect when a girl was found dead in the Peak District. I'd been cleared, but mud sticks. Hopefully he'd read the other stories about me saving a kid from drowning a year later. With luck he'd decide I wasn't the dangerous loner the Derbyshire cops had been so keen to lock up.

Would that convince him to talk to me? I had no idea. I finished the Coke and got up. I tossed the can into a recycling bin as I left the orchard and dumped the uneaten sandwiches in a general waste bin. Then I went to get a burger.

Chapter Three

By Monday lunchtime, this craft fair was going to prove there's no such thing as bad publicity. Yes, a lot of the first rush of people on Saturday afternoon had come to see a crime scene. They were shit out of luck. By the time I'd eaten my burger, the police were starting to pack up. I got asked to read and sign my statement, which was all fine, and I was given a Victim Support leaflet in case I wanted to talk to someone later on.

When the white overalls team finally left the barn and we were allowed back inside, the silversmith's table was gone and the other stalls had been shifted along to fill the gap. When the Saturday afternoon ghouls realised there was nothing to see, they went away. Business got back to something like normal.

Sunday and the bank holiday were a whole lot busier. Stories about the robbery on local news and social media must have reminded people about the craft fair. Since the weather stayed pretty crap, having a day out where there was shelter if it rained made sense. I was glad I'd paid for the all-you-can-eat breakfast at the chain hotel where I was staying, and decided to get my money's worth. I barely found time to grab a cup of tea for lunch on either day. Ordinarily, I'd have booked a cheaper local B&B, but I'd had no choice, so I'd had to pay last-minute bank holiday prices.

With an hour and a half left before the fair would be closing on Monday, the glass ornaments lady had sold out and gone. The organic soap couple didn't have much stock left. When a lull meant I could get a quick coffee, I fetched my reserve box from the Land Rover. These pieces hadn't turned out as well as I'd hoped, so I wrote bargain prices on Post-its and spread everything out across the table.

I'd have to spend a good few evenings and days off in my workshop before I could book a dealer's table anywhere else. That was just to make straightforward stuff like bowls and plates. Carving the birds and animals that people like takes a lot more time. I was thinking about that when movement caught my eye. The organic soap couple waved awkwardly as the silversmith came into the barn. He smiled, but he didn't go over and talk to them. He turned to me.

'Daniel. Hi.'

'Call me Dan. Everyone does.' I offered my hand and tried to look friendly.

'Nicholas Tanner. Nick.'

'Good to meet you.' I felt a nervous tremor in his hand-shake and tried a grin. 'I mean, the circumstances could be better, obviously.'

He smiled for about half a second. 'Obviously.'

'What can I do for you?' I might as well get to the point.

'Have you got to head home once you've packed up?' He tried to sound casual and failed. 'Do you have time for a pint?'

'I can do that.' Hopefully I'd still get home tonight, but that would depend on what he had to say.

That was okay. I'd rung my boss on Saturday evening to let her know what was going on. Eleanor Beauchene understood the Green Man would have a good reason for sending me here. There was a dryad's son seven generations back in her family tree, though she's the only one out of her brothers and sister and a whole load of cousins who can see anything out of the ordinary. Finding out I can see and hear the things that really go bump in the night was one reason why she gave me a job at the family's ancestral manor house.

'I'll see you later, in the car park.' Nick Tanner walked away.

I watched him reassuring the soap couple that he was fine, just a bit bruised. He did a quick circuit of the stalls in the barn, telling people yes, he'd been on the phone to his insurance people. He'd be talking to a loss adjuster. No, the police hadn't caught the robbers. Apparently, it was early days in their enquiry.

One of the farm staff must have seen him arrive. The woman in hi-vis from the orchard appeared. She hurried over to offer Nick a cup of tea, or coffee, or would he prefer something else? A cream tea? He glanced my way as they walked out of the barn. This time he grinned for at least a whole second.

'How much is this?' A young man with a long red beard and a cheerful baby in a sling on his chest picked up an apple-wood bowl.

'You can look, but don't touch.' His wife or girlfriend held their little girl's hand as she peered at a carved curled-up cat that would fit on her dad's outspread palm.

I told him, and he said they'd think about it. I said that was no problem, and sold a pair of candlesticks to the next customer. The couple with the baby and the little girl came back to buy the bowl and the cat as the stewards were announcing the car park would be closing in half an hour. Would everyone please make their way out through the farm shop, and thank you very much for coming.

The other stallholders looked knackered but satisfied. Despite the weekend's disastrous start, I'd taken more money than I'd expected. As an added bonus, I didn't have much to carry back to the Landy. I was putting the last boxes in the back when I saw Nick Tanner coming across the car park.

'Still on for that pint?' He tried to smile, but he was too on edge to be convincing.

'Absolutely. Do you know somewhere good nearby?' He should do. He was a local. Once I knew his surname, I'd found his business after a bit of an online search on Saturday evening. He worked out of a unit in a cluster of small workshops on the edge of a village not far away. Eleanor said she'd do a bit more digging, but she hadn't rung me back, so I guessed she hadn't unearthed anything significant.

He nodded, relieved. 'The Elm Tree. It's not far. You can follow me.'

'Right.' I closed the Land Rover's back door and watched him head for a two-seater compact Fiat van. I'd have to fold myself up like a deck chair to get into that.

He flashed his headlights when he saw I was ready to go in the Landy. We joined the line of cars heading for the gate. He signalled left and I followed the little Fiat along picturesque country roads. Most people only see Northamptonshire from the M1 driving north or south, or taking the A roads east and west. They're missing out.

After a couple of miles, Nick Tanner turned into a pub car park by a three-way junction with a triangular patch of grass left over from the days of horse-drawn carts with lousy turning circles. I pulled in beside him. The car park wasn't anywhere near full. Maybe we'd hit a lull before the evening trade, or people were saving their pennies at the end of the long weekend.

As I got out of the Landy, I couldn't see any elm trees in the hedgerows. I wondered when the last of them had died off. Decades ago, most likely. It would be nice to see disease-resistant hybrids reclaiming the countryside. Elm's good for turning on a lathe, and occasionally, I get hold of some pieces that have been salvaged from an old house or garden shed. Back in the day, elm was used for building, furniture and tools. Handles for pickaxes, sledgehammers and billhooks.

As we went into the pub, the barman greeted Nick with a brief wave while he served other customers. So he was known here. Did he think he might need backup? I wasn't offended. He didn't know me, even if what I'd said in the orchard convinced him we should talk.

'What can I get you?' he offered.

I looked at the beers on tap. 'I'll have a pint of the best bitter, but let me get these. I've had a better weekend than you.'

Nick could hardly deny it. 'Okay. Thanks.'

A blonde woman in an Elm Tree apron put down a tray of glasses and slid behind the bar.

'Two pints of best, please, Donna.' Nick managed a fairly normal smile.

'Right you are.' She looked me up and down as she pulled the pints. I could tell if I put a foot wrong, I'd be out on my ear.

I paid for the beer with a tap of my bank card and followed Nick to a corner table. He heaved a sigh as he sat on the padded bench and took a long drink. I had to stop myself downing my pint in one. It had been a long day. Hell, it had been a long weekend. But I was driving. I'd better look at a menu if I got the chance.

Nick put his glass down. 'You were right. Those pricks were looking for something specific. Necklaces. I don't know what's going on, I swear, but a week or so ago, I bought some broken jewellery from a silver scrap dealer. I've been thinking about making a weeping willow tree. An ornamental piece, you know?'

I didn't, but he waved that away before I could say so.

'I thought I might as well use broken chains rather than make them from scratch. Anyway, that bastard said they wanted their stolen necklaces back. I told him I didn't know what he was talking about. He told me to hand over everything I had or he'd hook out my eyes.'

38

His voice shook. Nick had believed that threat was real. I could also hear he wasn't being entirely honest. I wondered if the robber had been able to hear that. Maybe he'd seen the evasion in Nick's eyes that I was seeing now. Maybe this dealer had a habit of handling what turned out to be stolen property. Maybe Nick was a bit too relaxed about buying scrap silver without asking awkward questions.

'Before he punched me—' Nick stared into his half-empty glass. 'He said – he said they would give everything they took back if I could find their stolen necklaces. He sounded like he meant it.'

'Can you do that?' I took another sip of beer.

'No.' He grimaced. 'But I might know who could.'

Now we were getting down to it. 'But?' I prompted.

'When the cops took me back to my workshop yesterday, the place had been trashed. Someone had broken in. They must have gone there first on Saturday morning. If I'd been a bit later leaving, they'd have caught me there, on my own.' That thought made him shudder.

'You're sure it was them?' Though I didn't think it would be anyone else.

'Clear as day on the CCTV.' Nick heaved another sigh. 'There was paperwork all over the floor. That must be how they knew I'd be at the craft fair. The thing is, if they found the invoice from Hayley, the scrap silver dealer, that could lead them to her.'

Nick was genuinely scared for her. 'I've tried ringing a couple of times, but no one's answering any of her numbers.'

'You haven't told the police?' I knew the answer to that before I asked him.

'I don't want to drag her into this mess if she's got nothing to do with it. Now the cops have finally left me alone, I want to check that she's okay. But what if she isn't? What if—?'

He didn't have to lay it out. Nick wanted someone with him who was big enough to get a billhook or sledgehammer off one of those bastards and scare the shit out of them for a change. Someone who wouldn't insist on calling the cops. Someone who might have something useful in his Land Rover like a heavy-duty wheel brace to even the odds.

He was still hiding something, but his fear of coming face to face with those robbers again was absolutely real. I finished my beer slowly, to give me a few moments to think. It was a fair bet that detective in the grey suit knew she wasn't getting the whole truth from Nick. She'd be looking into his business contacts, but she couldn't do that on a Bank Holiday Monday. First thing tomorrow morning would be her first chance to make some phone calls.

So we should be able to check on Hayley this evening without the cops turning up. But, worst-case scenario, what if we found her pinned to the floor by a pickaxe? The more frustrated these robbers got, the more dangerous they would be. I didn't want to be caught at a murder scene, even with an explanation. Withholding information from the cops had to be obstruction of justice or something that would land me in court.

On the other hand, if I didn't do this, I could guarantee the Green Man would be back in my dreams tonight, and he wouldn't be pleased. And where else was I going to find some clue to explain why he'd sent me here?

I put down my glass. 'Okay. Let's go.'

'Really? Oh, mate.' He was breathless with relief.

'Come on.' I stood up. 'Let's not piss about if you think she could be in trouble.'

'Right.' Nick stayed close as we walked out to the car park. He kept his voice down. 'There must be something wrong. Otherwise she'd have called me back, don't you think?'

'Unless she went away for the weekend and turned off her mobile for some peace and quiet.' I got my keys out of my pocket. 'If you know where she lives, let's try her home first. If those pricks did find an invoice with her workshop address, she's probably okay. But you should warn her she's likely to find she's had a break-in tomorrow morning.'

'Oh, yes, right.' Nick looked stressed again.

'Okay. I'll follow you.' I nearly asked him to text me the address. Then I realised there were no phone calls or messages to link the two of us. Best to keep it that way.

'It's about half an hour from here.' Nick headed for his Fiat.

Thankfully, he was an easy driver to follow, never going too fast and indicating in plenty of time whenever we reached a turn. His friend Hayley lived on the edge of a village, in a spacious 1980s dormer bungalow with newer white uPVC windows and a matching lever-locking front door. The house was brick-built with a brown tiled roof and a garden big enough to sell off half as a building plot. There was a double garage on the right-hand side, but a grubby green Renault was parked on the gravel drive outside the front porch.

Nick pulled up beside the Renault. I parked the Land Rover on the road and got out. I resisted the temptation to look around for CCTV. If there were cameras, I could do fuck all about them. I'd also look shifty as hell if the cops checked the video later and saw me trying to spot surveillance. So far, I couldn't see any windows with twitching net curtains, which was good. There was a neighbourhood watch sign bolted to the nearest lamp post, which wasn't. If there was nothing to find here, I wanted to leave before some random dog-walker came along.

Nick was ringing the front doorbell. No answer. No shit. He turned to me and spread his hands in a 'What now?' gesture.

Everything looked fine at the front of the house. I thought about getting the wheel brace out of the Landy, but that would be a pain in the arse with my craft fair stuff stowed in the back. More to the point, if a neighbour did ring 999 and the police sent armed response, I didn't want to be holding something long and metallic in dim light.

I walked over to the Renault and rested my hand on the bonnet. The engine was stone cold. There weren't any lights on inside the house and the daylight was fading. This didn't look promising. 'Let's check the back.'

'Right.' Nick went around the left-hand side into the massive garden.

I followed. There were no broken windows, or any sign that someone had tried to force the door. I looked at the ornamental trees that lined the edge of the garden on the other side of the neatly mown lawn.

'Nick? Take a look at the garage, will you?'

'Okay.'

As soon as he turned his back, I walked over to a healthy young rowan. Sometimes I can learn things from trees. Specifically, I wanted to know what might be lurking around here. Creatures that someone who isn't a bit more than ordinarily human wouldn't be able to see. I gripped a thickish branch and murmured under my breath to the tree, 'Please, if you don't mind.'

It never hurts to be polite. I got a swift sense of everything living in that garden and out along the edge of the farmland beyond. Trees, plants, birds and a few small mammals stirring as dusk approached. Nothing else. No robbers, and that was a relief. On the other hand, when was I going to find out something actually sodding useful?

'Someone broke into the shed.' Nick came back across the lawn. 'What is it? Did you see something?'

'Hang on.' I'd just seen movement in one of the dormer windows. 'There's somebody in the house. Up in that bedroom.'

I had no idea who or what that might be. As far as dryad radar goes, buildings and anything inside them are just blank space.

'Where?' Nick squinted, but he couldn't see anything with the sunset reflected in the glass. He took out his phone and tapped the screen. 'Let me try— Tina? What's going on?'

He broke off to listen to the woman who'd answered. 'Okay. See you in a minute.' He ended the call and looked at me. 'She's coming down.'

'Front or back?'

'Oh.' He looked blank. 'I'm not sure.'

A moment later, I saw someone in the kitchen. A moment after that, the back door opened. A woman in her fifties backed away to let us come into a utility room between the house and the garage. She wore stretchy leggings and a loose sweatshirt. Her short spiky hair looked like she'd just got out of bed. She also looked like she'd been in a fight, and she hadn't won.

'Tina?' Nick was horrified. 'What's happened? Where's Hayley?'

'In – in hospital.' Tina pressed the back of a bandaged wrist to her mouth as she leaned against the sink unit. She was trying not to cry. Not just to answer Nick's questions. Crying would pull horribly on the three stitches in her split lip. She had a nasty black eye as well, swollen almost shut.

She drew a shuddering breath. 'I tried to get upstairs and hide, to ring the police. But they chased me. One of them kicked in the bathroom door and threw me down the stairs.'

'When?' I asked. 'When did this happen?'

Tina fought back the threat of tears, confused by questions from a complete stranger. 'Friday. Friday night. We were coming in from the garden when four men jumped over the back fence. They forced us into the house.'

I glanced at Nick. 'Then this wasn't your fault. They followed the trail from Hayley to you.' And this was where they'd got those tools to threaten traders at the craft fair.

Nick rubbed a nervous hand over his face. 'I don't know if you've seen any news—'

'He kept yelling.' Tina stared into the distance, reliving the nightmare. 'Where was the scrap silver we bought? He wouldn't stop shouting. The same thing, over and over. Hayley said, she told him, there's nothing here. He didn't believe her. He said he'd break her hands if she didn't tell him the truth. He started pulling her fingers out of their sockets, one by one. She was screaming, so I told him. She melts down the scrap as soon as she has enough. She gets rid of the solder and muck and casts it into silver sheet and wire. That's when he lost it. He punched her so hard he knocked her over. Her head hit the wall.'

Tears trickled down Tina's cheeks as she focused on Nick with her unswollen eye. 'She was unconscious, but he kept on kicking her. I swear, he was going to kill her. I said – I said we'd sold some scrap necklaces to you. I told them where to find your workshop. I'm sorry, but I had to do something. I mean, you wouldn't be there on Friday night and there'd be other people around in the morning.'

'How badly did they hurt her?' Nick looked as if he was going to be sick.

Tina swallowed hard and sniffed. 'They're saying the concussion is the worst thing. Then there's, you know, her hands. I heard about the craft fair—'

'That doesn't matter.' Nick shook his head. 'You did the only thing you could.'

I interrupted. 'Did someone from the hospital tell the police you'd been attacked?'

Tina nodded. 'I told them what I could on Friday. They're coming to see me again tomorrow. I came home to get some sleep. The doctor gave me some pills.'

That explained why she was a bit vague. That was a pain, because I had more questions and I needed answers tonight. I guessed the detectives who had come to the craft fair hadn't known about this first attack on Friday night. They'd sure as hell know about it by now. Once they'd spoken to Tina tomorrow, they'd have a whole lot more questions for Nick.

'Where does this scrap jewellery come from?' I needed to find out as much as possible as fast as I could.

'Auctions. House clearance firms. We advertise online, and we have arrangements with some second-hand and charity shops.'

Those pills must be wearing off. I could see she was starting to wonder who the hell I was.

'Did the robbers ask you about that?'

'No.' She turned to go back into the kitchen. 'I'm going to make some tea.'

'Let me do that. You should rest.' Nick's glare warned me not to ask her anything else. 'And I don't think you should be on your own. I'll stay here tonight.'

'Good idea,' I agreed, even if I reckoned Nick was offering so he didn't have to be on his own.

I moved to stop him following Tina as she switched on the kitchen light. 'I'm really sorry about your friend, but now you know what's happened. I'll be on my way. Lock the doors and windows and keep your phone ready, but I can't see those bastards coming back. They must know what they want isn't here.'

'Right.' Nick tried to look as if he believed that.

'You had better tell the cops everything. Say you were in shock before. That's why you forgot the one who punched you said he'd give your stuff back if you could find what they were looking for. How are you supposed to contact him anyway?' I asked as casually as I could. 'If you found their necklaces?'

'They said they'd contact me.' Nick looked towards the sound of a running tap filling a kettle.

'Then the police can tap your phones and set up some sort of trap.' I didn't think there was much chance of these robbers calling Nick though. They must have realised he didn't have what they wanted. So where the hell would they go next?

'Right. Well, thanks. I appreciate you coming with me.' He offered me his hand.

I shook it. 'No problem.'

I left quickly, hearing Nick lock the back door behind me. Now I had a bit more information, I had a few ideas about how to approach this puzzle from a different angle. I needed to talk to Eleanor and make some calls.

Right now, though, I needed to concentrate on following the satnav's directions as I drove away. I also needed to stop somewhere for dinner since I hadn't had a chance to eat at the pub.

Chapter Four

I got home late, went straight to bed and slept very well. Those robbers had no reason to come after me. If sledge-hammer guy had sensed I was a bit different, if they had found out who I was, he and his mates would still have to find my cottage deep in the Blithehurst woods. They'd find more than they were expecting. A black shuck roams the estate, and the local dryads are not to be messed with.

I didn't hurry over getting up and having breakfast. I'm not on the Blithehurst staff rota now. Officially that's because managing the woodland is a full-time job. Unofficially, it's because Eleanor and I and a few other people have things to do that take up most of my spare time. After putting my toast plate and mug in the dishwasher, I walked up to what had once been the dairy yard, supplying milk, butter, cream and cheese to the Tudor manor house. The old brick outbuildings are used for storage these days, and I've converted the dairy into a workshop. I'd parked the Landy in the yard last night.

No one else was around. The house and grounds were closed to visitors today, though the garden centre and cafe would be open, next to the main car park by the road. I took everything I'd taken to the craft fair out of the Land Rover. Then I sat down and updated my records on my laptop with the weekend's sales. I bagged up notes and coins to go to the Post Office to be paid into my bank account, now the last local branch had closed. More than rural cop shops are going extinct.

Once I'd done the admin, I checked the milk in the workshop fridge. That was still good, so I made a pot of tea and rang my mate Aled. He can see the local spirits in the woods and mountains where he lives in North Wales. His grandfather's great-grandfather had been a coblyn's son. That adventurous Welsh earth spirit had been friends with a miner who'd been killed in a rockfall. The coblyn had come up from deep underground to make sure his friend's widow and kids were okay. One thing led to another, and apparently no one had counted the months between the miner dying and his wife's last baby being born. Like me and Eleanor, Aled had grown up wondering if he'd ever meet anyone else like him. Like us, he'd kept his mouth shut to avoid ending up on a locked mental health ward.

These days, I'd have to stop and think before I could say how many people I know who can see the uncanny. I can thank the Green Man for that, so I can't complain if he expects a few favours in return.

Aled answered his phone on the second ring. He was as cheerful as usual. 'Hiya, Dan. How was your weekend?'

'Pretty good. How about you?' Aled makes jewellery. He has a workshop in a crafts and cultural centre in Snowdonia, or, as I keep trying to remember to call it, Eryri.

'Good and busy,' he said with satisfaction. 'Work on the farmhouse is coming on nicely too.'

'No unexpected surprises?'

'Not so far. Fingers crossed.'

We weren't just talking about dodgy wiring or dry rot or any of the other things that can turn up in a house renovation. As far as the trustees of Canolfan Meilyr are concerned, Annis Wynne had simply been an ancient old lady who'd owned the farmhouse next door to their craft and cultural centre. When she had died this past winter, they'd been very surprised to learn she'd left the property, its contents and the derelict slate quarry behind it to the centre in her will. Her solicitor had explained she'd had no immediate family.

Aled and I knew the truth. We really hoped none of Annis's more distant relatives turned up. Dangerous things live

48

in the shadows in the deep dark woods and the hollow hills. Creatures from folklore. From the original stories full of blood and terror, not tidied-up fairy tales for kids.

'Well then, what can I do for you?' Aled knew I wouldn't be calling just to chat.

'Are you on your own?' I didn't want anyone overhearing this conversation.

'Yes, Daisy's got the day off. It'll be quiet after the bank holiday.'

'Right.' I told him about the robbery, and about the attack on Nick Tanner's friends.

'That's nasty,' Aled commented. 'But I reckon you're right. They don't sound like common or garden thugs.'

'So what are they?'

He took so long to answer that I checked my phone to see if I'd lost the signal. Mobile reception's always a problem out in the woods, but it's usually okay by the house.

'You are kidding me, right?' Aled sounds very Welsh when he thinks I'm being an idiot. 'You're telling me you haven't read every story about swan maids you can find?'

I didn't answer, because he was right. My girlfriend, Fin, is a swan maid, like the rest of her mother's family. I've read every myth I can find about people who can turn into birds. There are more of these legends than I ever realised, from right around the world.

'The Children of Lir in Ireland.' Aled was still talking. 'Their ability relied on silver necklaces instead of their feathers.'

Yes, I knew that story. 'These arseholes didn't feel like swans to me.'

'They're nasty bastards, I grant you,' Aled commented. 'But what else could they be?'

'I was hoping you could tell me.' I drank some tea.

'Best way to find that out is to find them, isn't it?'

'How do we do that?' I'd already thought about going back along the robbers' trail of destruction and violence. 'They didn't ask where Nick's friend got her scrap silver. I think they knew who had stolen their necklaces. They wanted to know who'd got hold of them next. And there's no point asking anyone who sold scrap silver to Hayley about necklaces I can't even describe.'

Especially when the police were bound to be following that lead. I didn't want to get in their way.

'As far as finding these necklaces goes, I'd say they're buggered.' Aled doesn't often swear. 'Once a batch of scrap silver goes into a crucible and gets cast into something else, you might as well try taking the eggs out of a cake.'

I didn't want to be the one telling them that. Not after what they'd done to Tina and Hayley.

Aled went back to his original point. 'You need to talk to that Irishman. Connor, isn't it? Fin's sister's friend.'

'Right.' The Irishman's name was Conn. I hadn't noticed him wearing a silver chain around his neck, when he was a human or a swan. To be fair, we had been busy trying not to get killed on a Welsh mountainside in the pitch dark.

'Let me know what he says,' Aled said briskly. 'So, are we done? Anything else?'

'No, that's it. Thanks.'

I ended the call. Fuck. I'd really hoped Aled would give me a different lead to follow.

Conn, the Irish swan shifter, had been Fin's older sister's boyfriend. He had refused to get involved in the last situation the Green Man sent me to sort out. Real life isn't like the movies, with everyone dropping everything to band together and save the day. People like us keep our secrets and keep our heads down. That's the only way to stay safe.

Besides, Fin had told me Conn and Iris had split up after a hell of a row. Iris blamed Fin for that, don't ask me why. They had barely spoken for months, even after their sister, Blanche, gave them a bollocking for being so stupid. I stayed well out of it. When I was a kid it was just me, my dad and my mum. So no, I didn't want to call Iris to ask for Conn's phone number.

I wondered what Eleanor would say. She'd be in her sitting room in the manor house this morning, after working the long weekend. No, she deserved her day off, even if she was probably doing paperwork. Besides, we've both read every one of the books on myth and folklore that had been added to Blithehurst's library by generations of Beauchenes. That Irish myth was the only mention of silver necklaces she would recall.

I could go for a walk around the estate's woods, to check on the hazel coppicing and the Christmas tree plantation. Except I'd done that last week. There was no reason why anything would have changed. Plus, there was every chance Blithehurst's dryads would turn up. They would want to know where I was heading next to find another of their sisters, and how soon.

Trees across the country have been badly stressed by the way the seasons are getting screwed up. Woodlands are battered by once-in-a-decade winter storms turning up four times in a month and a half. Dryads are sending each other oak seedlings and saplings to reconnect their territories. To be accurate, they're giving the little trees to me and telling me where to take them. I'm clocking up a lot more miles than usual, and that's not just getting expensive in diesel. There's wear and tear on my old Land Rover, and I'll need new tyres before the next MOT. I'll be lucky if that's all the annual service turns up. Refusing isn't an option though. An angry dryad will make your life one bad luck crisis after another.

I didn't want to talk to the Blithehurst dryads just now. I left my phone on the table and went out to my store. I keep interesting pieces of fallen wood that I find around the estate, as well as assorted thick, flat blanks for my lathe. I could get a stack of wooden bowls and platters roughed out today. I chose some blanks, found the chuck I wanted, adjusted the tailstock and spun up the first piece to check its balance.

The blank wouldn't stay put. After the third time it slipped, I gave up. I kept remembering Tina's battered face, and thinking about Hayley ending up in hospital. Scrolling through my phone, I found Iris's number. I texted her, asking for Conn's number. If she wanted to know why, she could call me.

I left the phone on the table and went back to my lathe. This time, I had the wooden blank secured on my first try. I fetched my safety visor and dust mask, and my phone pinged with a message. Iris had sent me a number starting +353. No message.

I took off my mask and leaned against the battered oak table I'd salvaged from the manor house's cellars. I wondered about texting Conn and asking him to ring me, but I couldn't tell if this was a mobile number or a landline. I decided to just call. If he didn't pick up, I could leave a message.

'Hello.' Conn's deep voice sounded wary and curious in that single word.

I waited for him to ask how I'd got his number. He didn't. 'Do you have a minute to talk?'

'A minute's all you'll need?' He sounded sceptical.

'Probably not.' Maybe this was a bad idea. I realised I had no clue what Conn did for a day job. Whatever it was, he drove a Mercedes. Assuming that had been his car I'd seen in Wales.

Conn laughed, though he didn't sound particularly friendly. 'I can spare you ten minutes.'

I talked fast. For the second time that morning, I explained what had happened at the craft fair, and at Hayley the silver dealer's house.

'So what do you want from me?' That was definitely a challenge.

'Could these robbers be Irish swans?' I asked bluntly. 'Hunting stolen silver necklaces?'

He didn't answer. For the second time, I checked my phone to see if our call had dropped out. It hadn't. Assuming he was still listening, I went on.

'I didn't get any sense they were swans. If you know different, if you have any idea what's going on, someone needs to do something. If the next person these arseholes go after ends up dead, the cops might find out they're more than they seem. That could make trouble for us all.'

Conn didn't argue. 'Who else have you told about this?'

'No one.' I corrected myself quickly. 'Apart from Aled in Wales. To see what he knew about the scrap silver trade. No one else.'

'Your boss Eleanor will need to be told, and so will Finele.' Conn was thinking this through, sounding grim. 'But no one else, human or otherwise. Do you understand? Especially not those wise women you were working with in Wales. I cannot have them sticking their noses in where they don't belong. Do I have your word on that?'

'Yes.' Conn could hear that I meant it. I was sure Eleanor and Fin would agree.

There was another long pause.

'I might be able to find out something. I'll be in touch.' Conn ended the call.

Fair enough. I went back to work. I'd just pulled my safety visor down when my phone rang. The voicemail kicked in before I'd got my visor and dust mask off, but I rang Fin straight back.

'I thought you'd be busy today.' I'd planned to talk to her this evening. Fin's a freshwater ecologist, working with her sister Blanche. They've been consulting on a farm rewilding project in Shropshire, off and on for the past eighteen months. Local people had been invited to come and take a look at what was going on over the bank holiday weekend. Today was meetings in a local hotel's conference room with council officials, various interested organisations and the groups who'd been making complaints.

'Our presentation went well. The photos of cute beavers helped, but explaining how many hundred cubic metres of floodwater the mature habitat will hold back definitely got people's attention. A couple of the anglers didn't look convinced when we told them how fish get around beaver dams, but I think the others were listening. The insect guy was very good, and he stuck to pictures of butterflies and bees, not spiders. He was funny, which is always a plus, and he had a great waistcoat with beetles on it. But someone should have told the nice birdwatcher lady that PowerPoint bar graphs and pie charts are as dead as the dodo. We're on a coffee break, so I'm stretching my legs. Why did you want Conn's number from Iris? She's just texted me.'

Now it was my turn to go silent for so long that Fin thought she'd lost her signal.

'Dan? Are you still there?'

'I'll tell you if you want me to, but Conn's made me promise only you, me, Eleanor and Aled know what's going on. Do you want the whole story, or do you want to be able to tell Iris I haven't told you why I needed to speak to him? And Blanche as well.'

Fin's other sister would be somewhere close. They were working on the rewilding together. They've run BFW Environmental from their flat near Bristol for nearly eight years now.

'Oh.' Fin took a moment to think that through. 'Has this got something to do with where you went at the weekend?'

'Yes. There was a robbery at the craft fair.' Fin would find that news as soon as she went looking online. Blanche would do that too.

'It has something to do with the reason the Green Man sent you there.'

That wasn't a question, and I was glad about that, because I still had no clue why he'd done it. 'Yes.'

'And you won't be lighting the rabbit signal?'

She was asking about contacting the wise women. That had started as a silly joke one evening when we were watching a Batman film. I know wise women transform into hares, but 'rabbit signal' had stuck. It came in useful if other people were around. Anyone hearing us mention witches would definitely have questions.

'No.' I didn't know why Conn insisted I keep the wise women out of this, though I could make a guess. They're organised and effective, and once they decide they know what's best, they'll go right ahead and do what they want without asking anyone else, or even telling them.

'This is very mysterious.' Fin was somewhere between amused and frustrated. 'I assume this means you won't be coming over this weekend?'

That was what we had planned. Fin and Blanche would be staying in Shropshire for the rest of this week for discussions about the rewilding project's future with the family who owned the farm.

'No idea. I'll ring you as soon as I know, one way or the other.'

'Right.' Fin knew as well as I did how unpredictable the challenges the Green Man threw at me could be. Unpredictable and dangerous. 'Whatever's going on, be careful.'

'I will be,' I assured her. 'Anyway, I'm glad your day's going well.'

'It's definitely nicer than measuring sewage pollution and agricultural run-off in rivers.'

I heard the smile in her voice. 'No shit.'

Fin laughed. 'In every sense.'

'Hopefully I'll see everything for myself this weekend.' I'd seen photos, but that wasn't the same.

'Fin! It's time to go back in.'

That was Blanche's voice, some distance away.

'I'd better go. I'll call you this evening,' Fin said quickly. 'Love you. Bye.'

'Bye.' I looked at my lathe. Then I called Eleanor instead.

'How was your weekend?' she asked at once.

'Eventful. Can I come over and tell you about it over a coffee?'

'That sounds good. I'm just checking the attics after the weekend weather. Give me ten minutes to finish up and I'll get the kettle on.'

Now torrential rain and strong winds are becoming the new normal, old houses are vulnerable. The slightest damage has to be caught early before a leak or a crack means disaster.

'Is there anything for me to take a look at?' My dad grew up doing DIY before anyone called it that. He taught me how to do most repairs and maintenance, before I trained as a carpenter and joiner.

'No, everything looks fine. See you in a bit.' She ended the call.

I stuck my phone in my pocket and found my keys. I put my laptop away in one of the cupboards, locked up and checked the yard doors were secure before I left. Even when the house and grounds are closed, some people think 'Private' and 'No Entry' signs don't apply to them.

I took the path that cuts through the hedge and the ornamental trees that one of Eleanor's forebears planted to hide the dairy yard from the house. I found Eleanor in the modern kitchen which isn't on the manor's visitor tour. I carried the tray of coffee into the library, and she brought a packet of chocolate biscuits.

I told her everything. Eleanor can keep a secret. She had to, growing up. She told me once she'd overheard her parents discussing her imaginary friends. They assumed it was a phase she would grow out of. If she didn't, they agreed they would get her professional help. So Eleanor stopped talking about the mysterious women she met in the woods. She'd been alone with her secret until the Green Man brought me to Blithehurst.

He brought me here to get rid of a monster, and it did its damnedest to kill us. We won, but I took a hell of a beating. Working for the Green Man gets fucking dangerous at times. If the absolute worst ever happens to me, I trust Eleanor to break the bad news to my dad. She knows where I keep my will, and she and Fin are my executors as well as Dad.

By the time I finished telling her about my weekend, Eleanor was as mystified as me. 'What happens now?'

'As soon as I know, I'll tell you.'

Someone needed to know where to start looking if I followed some lead to find these robbers and I didn't come back.

Chapter Five

Conn called me back three days later. 'How long does it take you to get to Rhyl?'

I was talking to the dryads out in the Blithehurst woods. I interrupted before he could say anything else. 'I'm with Asca, Frai and Etraia right now. I'll have to check and let you know.'

I really hoped Iris had told Conn that dryads can listen in to mobile phone calls. Did Iris know that? I couldn't remember if I'd ever told her. Did Conn know the Blithehurst dryads' names?

'Call me back.'

My phone went dead before I could answer him, so I stuck it in my pocket.

The oldest of the dryads, Frai, narrowed her autumnal copper-coloured eyes, suspicious. That wasn't unusual. She's been living here since before the Normans arrived, so she has plenty of reasons not to think much of humans. When she's pretending to be one of us, she looks like a white-haired little old lady who can tear a teenager to pieces with sarcasm for doing something she doesn't like.

'An Irish man?' Asca, her daughter, was politely curious. When she's mingling with tourists, she looks like a woman in her forties, dressed like someone photographed for *Country Life* or some other magazine for the rich. She clearly wanted to know more about my phone call.

Etraia didn't say anything. She rarely did. A dryad's eyes are one solid colour, without iris or pupil. Etraia's gaze was the pale yellow-green of early spring leaves. She was the youngest of the three, and I had no idea what to call their relationship.

When I'd first arrived here, I'd met Frai, Asca and Sineya, who was Asca's daughter. But Sineya had left Blithehurst. She went to live in a remnant of ancient forest in the Cotswolds. Frai still blamed me for that. Etraia had appeared here not long after I'd fetched a seedling oak from Sineya. Did that make her Sineya's daughter? They looked about the same age, able to pass as twenty-somethings when the gardens were full of visitors. I couldn't see a family resemblance though. Something a lot more complicated was going on.

'Daniel?' Asca prompted.

'I didn't see any sign of dryads at the rare breeds farm or in the local area.' I shrugged. 'Let's wait for Zan to tell us where I should go looking next.'

Asca raised her eyebrows at me. Dryads can't lie, but they're experts at not answering questions they'd rather dodge. I'd learned that skill from her and Frai, and Asca knew it.

'Have you seen Zan recently?' I asked before she could ask me outright what was going on.

'No.' Frai sniffed with a dismissive waft of her draperies. Since I was the only one there, the three dryads looked as if they had strolled off a vase painted by some ancient Greek who'd gone down to the woods one day and got a big surprise. 'Sylphs.'

That was hardly fair. We're only able to find dryads in widely scattered remnants of ancient woods because Zan is willing to see who might be where. Air spirits can travel hundreds of miles in the blink of an eye. They can also be as fickle as the British weather. If Zan got bored and went looking for entertainment elsewhere, the dryad networking project was screwed.

'I should get back to work.' I deliberately didn't ask if there was anything else the dryads wanted.

'Indeed.' Asca's dark green gaze told me she wasn't finished discussing that phone call.

'Make yourself useful then.' Frai vanished. So did Asca and Etraia.

I headed for my workshop, though my cottage was closer. Dryads can choose to be completely invisible, even to people like me. If Frai and Asca were really curious, they weren't above listening in on a private conversation. They rarely come close to the manor, though, and I can count the times either of them has come to the dairy yard on the fingers of one hand. They wouldn't set foot in my workshop. Dryads keep well away from iron and steel. Fairy tales are right about that.

I didn't only want them kept out of this mystery. Thankfully, I was sure that Zan would be wherever Blanche was today. Fin and I have no idea what might happen when or if their fascination with each other fades. Calling sylphs unpredictable is like calling a tornado a bit of bad weather.

Right now, the most important thing was ringing Conn back. Where the hell is Rhyl anyway? When I got to the workshop, I took out my laptop. It turns out Rhyl's a seaside town on the North Wales coast. I zoomed out to see more of the online map. If Conn was taking a ferry to Holyhead from Dublin, meeting there made sense. Assuming he was driving, not flying.

I checked times and distances and called him back. 'Rhyl should be a couple of hours' drive for me, maybe closer to three if the traffic's bad.' Peak tourist season was still a couple of months off, but plenty of people without kids in school go on holiday in May, before the late spring bank holiday and half-term week.

'Can you be there for one o'clock tomorrow afternoon?'

'Yes, unless something comes up.'

'Let me know if it does, as early as you can. Use the central car park. I'll call you when I arrive.' Conn ended the call as abruptly as the last time.

Keeping conversations that brief was a good way to avoid questions. I checked ferry times online. That timing made sense if Conn was catching a boat around eight in the morning. I rang Eleanor.

'Hold on a second, Dan. I'm in the middle of a stack of bug traps.'

'Right.' I waited. Any sign of silverfish, carpet beetles or clothes moths in the manor house, and whatever it is gets obliterated.

'Okay. Go ahead,' Eleanor said a few minutes later.

'There's nothing you need me for tomorrow, is there?'

She got the hint. We had discussed the possibility of the dryads listening in on our calls more than once. 'No.'

'I should be back by the evening.' Then I realised I couldn't be sure about that. 'I hope so, anyway.'

'Text me when you get there, and drive safely,' Eleanor said calmly. 'Let me know when you're heading back.'

'Will do.'

Then I rang Fin to tell her I wasn't coming to Shropshire for the weekend. She was disappointed. So was I. We both knew there was no point bitching about it though. Not with the Green Man involved.

I stayed in my workshop for the rest of the day, and I wasn't only hiding from the dryads. As well as making my own stock for craft fairs, I keep the Blithehurst shop and garden centre supplied with treen and wooden gifts as well as hazel hurdles. When someone's in the market for an expensive addition to their garden or patio, they can buy one of my solid oak benches.

I had steak and chips in the closest pub for dinner. I had an early night. I didn't sleep particularly well.

Waking up well before my alarm went off, I decided to get on the road. Saturday would be changeover day for anyone who was on their holidays. The later I set out, the more chance I'd get stuck in a traffic jam. The local roads were still quiet as I cut across country to pick up the M6. I followed the M56 towards Chester and took the North Wales Expressway along the coast. The traffic got busier, but everything kept moving. Taking the exit for Rhuddlan and Rhyl, I followed the satnav's instructions to the central car park.

I drove along street after street of 1930s semi-detached houses with bay windows and arched porches that could have been anywhere in Britain. Crossing the railway, I saw green hills in the distance, and the sky brightened in that way that tells you the sea's ahead. Big modern stores had replaced older industrial buildings and the jobs that went with them. Then I hit a one-way system trying to keep traffic flowing around the pedestrianised heart of the original town. Like everywhere else these days, plenty of empty commercial premises were for rent. There were more than enough places for tourists to eat, though, and more nail salons, hairdressers and phone shops than I thought a place this size could need.

A final right turn took me onto the West Parade. I took the first exit off a roundabout with a clock tower and a floral display and drove under a wide footbridge. The central car park was underground with some spaces cordoned off, which was a bit unnerving. I parked and paid-and-displayed for a couple of hours. Hopefully that would be long enough, as long as Conn got here when he'd said. Coming up into the open air, I saw cranes along the shore. Major civil engineering was happening on this seafront.

I walked the other way. Young couples with little kids were enjoying the beach. I saw a toddler looking thoughtfully at a handful of sand. Its mum intervened just before the kid tried a taste test. Fin's mum, Helen, had mentioned grandchildren the last time we'd visited her. Not dropping an unsubtle hint, just in passing. Fin said she'd been hoping Iris and Conn would start a family, but it didn't look like that would happen. Did Fin want kids? Did I? We'd never discussed it. Maybe we would once we'd worked out how we could move in together. Maybe not.

I had some time before Conn was supposed to arrive. I found a coffee shop on the High Street. Getting a pot of tea and a sandwich, I used my phone to read about the plans to update the local coastal defences. Sea walls built a century ago aren't enough to stop flooding and erosion these days.

I suddenly remembered I'd promised to text Eleanor to let her know where I was. I did that, and was thinking about having a blueberry muffin with my last half-cup of tea when Conn rang.

'We're here and I can see your Land Rover. Where are you?'

'Not far. I'll come to you.' This wouldn't be a conversation for a crowded cafe.

Walking back to the car park, I wondered who he meant by 'we'. I soon saw he wasn't with either of the two men or the woman who had come with him to Eryri. The stranger waiting with him on the footpath was about six feet tall with a cheerful round face and thinning sandy hair, though he looked younger than me. I wouldn't fancy my chances of tackling him on a rugby pitch. He was solidly built, wearing Crocs, khaki shorts and a green T-shirt, with a grey nylon backpack slung on one shoulder.

Conn wore trainers, jeans and a well-worn black leather jacket. Fin and her family are blonde, but the Irishman has dark hair and intense brown eyes. I hadn't noticed the permanent crease between his eyebrows before, but I'd only met him once, and at night.

The stranger offered me his hand with a smile. 'I'm Alexander. Good to meet you.'

He was Scottish, which was a surprise. I'd been expecting another Irishman. There was also something faintly familiar about him.

'I'm Dan.' I shook his hand and looked at Conn.

'Let's walk.' He headed for the seafront.

Alexander grinned at me as we followed the Irishman. Sometimes, a crowd can be the best place to find some privacy. There were plenty of people about, but no one was interested in us. Locals were enjoying their weekend and visitors were making the most of their time at the seaside. Conn found an empty stretch of railing to lean on, looking out over the lazy waves. I saw the tall white spikes of wind turbines offshore, and wondered what sylphs thought about them.

'So, you're curious about silver necklaces, Dan.' Alexander didn't look at me though. He was watching Conn. 'I'm not surprised, after what happened last weekend.'

So Conn had told him. Good. That saved time.

'You know the stories about swan maids kept captive because their feathers were stolen.' The Irishman gazed out to sea. 'My ancestors decided to do something about that. Don't ask me who first thought of enchanting silver necklaces or who discovered how to do it. Nobody knows. These things were never written down. I can tell you who was involved though. My people asked some cunning men for help.'

'Right.' Now I understood why he'd insisted the wise women stayed out of this. They weren't the only humans who'd been communicating with the hidden world of dryads, naiads and the rest for centuries. Cunning men had their

64

own links with the uncanny. Wise women generally stayed in their villages to help the locals. Cunning men travelled around, offering assorted services from lifting curses to curing sick animals and taking out people's teeth. Aled's ancestor, the coblyn's son, had been one.

Seventeenth-century witch-hunters hadn't been interested in their differences. They saw them all as evil and condemned them to be burned. Today's wise women blamed the cunning men back in those days for running away to hide, leaving their foremothers to torment and death. The cunning men who survived believed wise women had betrayed their brothers to the witch-hunters, to save their own skins. From what I'd heard, there was some truth on both sides, as well as exaggeration, misunderstandings and lies.

When the flames had died down and the smoke cleared, the wise women who were left rebuilt their networks with cut-outs and fail-safes like a paranoid spy ring. Cunning men disappeared completely. Until recently, the wise women had assumed they were dead and gone. Now both sides knew the others were still around. Mutual hostility and suspicion were back with a vengeance.

I realised why Alexander looked familiar. 'I'm guessing this is where you come in?'

I'd met a group of cunning men in a remote Scottish village on the Argyll coast. That wasn't where they lived full time. Hazel, the wise woman who'd been with me, suspected they had a hidden refuge out in the Hebrides. We did learn that group were friends with selkies, who are a bit more than ordinarily human and can change into seals.

Alexander nodded. 'My kin chose not to get involved. Keeping a sealskin safe can be a pain, but no one's going to mug you for it. We knew of others who were interested though. We knew certain cunning men wanted to learn how to change shape themselves. They traded their skills in fixing uncanny powers into tokens for secrets some were willing to share.'

I knew for a fact that whatever those cunning men learned had been passed down to the present day. The men I'd met in Argyll could turn themselves into big black cats. I hadn't noticed them wearing silver chains, but I hadn't got that close, whatever shape they'd been in.

'So where do I find these swans who have lost their necklaces?'

'No,' Conn said quickly. 'None of us are involved.'

Alexander shook his head as well. 'My guess is your robbers are kelpies.'

I pictured the dramatic steel sculptures I'd seen near Falkirk. 'Water horses?'

'Strictly speaking, they're no' the same thing.' Alexander wrinkled his nose. 'Horse is a form a kelpie can take, but there's a wee bit more to it than that.'

'Isn't there always?' Conn murmured.

'Kelpies are creatures of shadow,' Alexander quickly explained. 'They lay claim to deep, slow stretches of old rivers. Places where they can lure folk into the water to kill them.'

'Like a nix?' I'd met one of those, and it had been an utter bastard.

'Yes and no.' Alexander tilted a hand. 'Nixies are solitary and they like lakes and lochs. Kelpies run in packs, or at least, they used to, when there were enough of them around. Nixies can look human when they choose to. Kelpies can be horses or men.'

I was starting to remember the stories that inspired those massive statues. 'When they're horses, when people try to ride them, the kelpie gallops into the water and drowns them.'

66

'That's right.' Alexander nodded. 'And when they're horses, their silver chain becomes part of a halter. When they're men, it'll be a necklace. If they lose their silver chain, they're stuck in the shape they're in at the time.'

I saw where this was going. 'So these robbers didn't escape from the craft fair on horses just so police cars couldn't chase them. They were all kelpies in one form or the other.'

Still leaning on the seafront rail, Conn turned his head. 'So who stole their necklaces? And why? How did they even manage to do that?'

'Why did they sell those chains as scrap silver to be melted down?' I answered my own question. 'To trap those kelpies in the forms they were in.'

'Looking for revenge, mebbe?' Alexander speculated. 'Kelpies drown folk to eat them. Maybe this gang picked the wrong victim.'

'And whoever did this knows who and what they're dealing with,' Conn observed. 'We need to know who they are for that reason alone.'

This finally explained the Green Man's interest. I wondered how the hell I was supposed to track down four men and three horses hiding somewhere in rural central England. I couldn't see how I could ask Zan for help. However much I insisted this was a secret, the sylph was bound to tell Blanche, just for a start. When I refused to answer her questions, she'd most likely ask Hazel what she knew. I couldn't have that. I had to be the one to decide when and if to involve the wise women. Apart from anything else, I wouldn't get anything out of any cunning men I knew if I pissed them off right from the start. If I had to go to the cunning men. Was there any alternative to asking them?

'Do you know any kelpies?' I asked Alexander. 'One who might be persuaded to talk to me?'

'Oh, no.' He shook his head, emphatic. 'We keep well clear. Kelpies are killers, and they're not fussy about what's on the menu.'

Great. So if I did find the craft fair robbers, I'd be out-numbered by creatures who would see me as lunch. Would the ones on two feet armed with hammers be more danger-ous, or the ones with four legs and hooves?

'What about naiads?' The river spirits I'd met would have plenty to say if kelpies were hunting humans along their rivers.

Alexander shook his head again. 'Sorry.'

'Talk to the cunning men,' Conn advised as he took out his phone to check the time. 'If there's nothing else we need to discuss, I'll catch the next ferry back.'

He'd given up a whole day to have this short conversation face to face. He really must not trust phones. 'Thanks for your help. I appreciate it.'

He nodded before glancing at Alexander. 'Do you want a lift anywhere?'

The Scot shook his head. 'I'll make my own way back. It's a lovely day for a swim.'

He must have his sealskin in his backpack, I realised. He could carry that in the water with the straps in his mouth.

He grinned. 'I wouldn't say no to an ice cream first.'

Conn put his phone away. 'I can spare five minutes for that.'

'My treat.' I saw a kiosk and started walking.

'So, do you follow the football?' Alexander asked once I'd bought three cones.

I shook my head. 'I watch a bit of rugby. The internation-als.'

Conn grinned. 'I'm sorry for your troubles.'

We ate our ice creams as we went back along the seafront. Alexander stopped where the path divided. 'Conn knows how to reach me, if you've anything else to ask.'

'Let me know what you find out.' Conn wasn't asking. That was an order. 'And keep what we've told you to yourself.' He walked away.

'Safe journey.' Alexander followed the other path along the shore.

Down in the gloomy car park, Conn's Mercedes drove past the front of my Land Rover as I stuck my key in the ignition. Before I started the engine, I texted Eleanor.

On my way back now. Look up kelpies.

As soon as I'd hit send, I wondered if dryads could read text messages as well. I'd better remember to ask my mum.

Eleanor texted back before I'd left the car park. I sneaked a quick look at my phone. *Come over for dinner so we can talk.*

Fair enough. I tossed my phone onto the passenger seat and looked both ways for other vehicles. There was no sign of Conn's Mercedes as I reached the roundabout, but that was hardly surprising. We were heading in opposite directions.

The drive back was straightforward. Motorways can be surprisingly quiet on Saturday evenings. By the time I'd got home, parked, had a pee and walked up to the manor, Eleanor had found a stack of references in Blithehurst's library and online. She's got a history PhD, so she knows how to do research. She had confirmed everything Alexander told me.

'A halter would usually just be rope or leather, but I guess this silver token could look like a lip chain, or maybe a stud chain.' She turned her laptop around on the library's low coffee table, to show me what the horse on the screen was wearing.

I'd take her word for it. Plenty of photos around Blithe-hurst show Eleanor and her brothers and sister on ponies as kids. I've sat on a horse precisely once, when I was sixteen. One of the volunteers at the nature reserve where my dad's the resident warden invited me to an open day at their riding stables. I'm sure it was a very nice horse, but it had been sodding enormous. The thought of falling off and hitting the ground at any speed convinced me I wasn't built to be a horseman.

I poured myself more tea. 'But why wear a halter at all? If that can be pulled off and leave them in the shit?'

Eleanor was drinking a gin and tonic. The manor house was peaceful with the day's visitors gone. The library would have been like this when she'd lived here as a kid with her family.

'Kelpies want to lure people towards them. Make them think they've found a horse they can ride. A halter says that, for a start. A fancy halter with a bit of chain? That says a valuable horse has got loose. The owner might be offering a reward. That would be easy money in days gone by, don't you think?'

'That makes sense,' I agreed.

'So who are you going to ring?' Eleanor looked at me over the rim of her glass. 'The cunning men or the wise women?'

'I'll text Iain to start with. Kelpies are Scottish, after all.' I had no idea how the old cunning man had got my mobile number, but he'd sent a message to wish me a happy Hog-manay. He knew where I lived as well. He'd proved that by sending me an unlabelled bottle of very good whisky. All things considered, I didn't want to get his back up unless I really didn't have a choice.

'What are you going to say?'

'That we need to talk? That I would like to talk to him,' I corrected myself. Politeness would work better with the old man. 'Should I say I need to know about some stolen silver necklaces?'

'That should make him curious enough to ring you back.' Eleanor put her glass down and rubbed her eyes.

'You look knackered. Do you want to go out for a curry? I'll drive,' I offered.

'You're on.' She finished her drink. 'Send that text while I get a jacket.'

I messaged Iain. While I waited for Eleanor to come back, I looked up at the library's ceiling. The medieval carved panels had been installed when this Tudor house had been built to replace the original fortified manor down by the river. The panels had come from the old chapel there. Eleanor's stubbornly Catholic ancestors had sheltered renegade priests who celebrated Mass in the library.

The panels themselves weren't religious. Medieval craftsmen had carved wreaths of fruit and flowers, with birds and animals here and there. I was convinced one of those carpenters could see a bit more than most. What the guidebook called a wolf's head looked like a black shuck to me, and I had found several sprites. Carvings of the Green Man's face made from oak leaves looked down from each corner of the room.

Sometimes those carvings show me or Eleanor a glimmer of the bright emerald light that gleams in the Green Man's eyes. That tells us we're on the right track. I couldn't see anything this evening. I'd have to see if he turned up in my dreams to tell me I was getting this wrong.

Chapter Six

The tree branch smashed through my bedroom window at fuck knows what o'clock. I was out of bed and looking for something to fight back with before I was anywhere close to awake.

'Daniel! You have to come with me!'

'Zan?' The sylph appearing right in front of me did nothing to slow my racing pulse. 'What the fuck are you doing?'

'Get dressed! Now!' This pale figure with vivid blue eyes could be male or female, wearing a long tunic or a short dress. If I hadn't recognised the sylph's anguished voice, I wouldn't have known this was Zan. After the day we'd first met, I'd always seen them disguised as a human.

'Why?' I sat on the edge of the bed and switched on the bedside lamp. Broken glass glittered on the floor. 'And couldn't you fucking knock like a normal person?'

Though as I said that, I realised a sylph wouldn't touch the iron door knocker I'd bought at a craft fair. Still, Zan had sodding knuckles.

'I tried. You sleep like a log, dryad's son. Move!' Zan was getting frustrated. 'Fin and Blanche need your help before their beavers' dam is destroyed.'

I reached for my underpants and the combat trousers slung on the bedpost. I still wasn't fully awake, but I tried to make sense of what Zan was saying. 'What's happening to the beavers?'

I picked up my phone. A blast of scorching air knocked it out of my hand.

'You have no time for that!'

'Zan, listen to me. It's a two-hour drive to the farm.' Doing my best to sound calm and reasonable, I got dressed as fast as I could, dragging a sweatshirt over my head. 'Let me call Hazel. If she can contact some wise women nearby, they can help a whole lot quicker than I can.' I sincerely fucking hoped so.

Zan shook their head, emphatic. 'No. You must come. I'll take you.'

'Hold on!' I backed off as far as I could, though that trapped me in the corner of the bedroom. 'Let me get my fucking boots on.'

I tried to see a glass-free path to the door. I'd be no use to Fin or anyone else with my feet cut to shreds. Zan flung out a pale hand. Shards of glass and the oak branch crashed against the skirting board. Zan's eyes had darkened from sky blue to thunderous cobalt. I grabbed some socks and hurried out into the hall. My work boots were by the door. I got my socks on, shoved my feet into my boots and—

The sylph grabbed my shoulder. I've been carried from place to place by dryads, and that's weird but bearable. Being swept along by a naiad's eerie power had been a whole lot more unpleasant. The sylph's freezing cold touch was infinitely worse. Everything around me went white. I felt so light-headed I thought I was going to pass out. I couldn't breathe. I couldn't see or hear. I didn't know which way was up. My arms and legs were numb and useless, except for vicious pins and needles shooting down to my fingers from Zan's brutal grip.

My feet hit solid ground. Zan let go. I collapsed onto my hands and knees. I could hear commotion in the distance, but that would just have to wait. My head was pounding, and I concentrated on not throwing up. The night air was damp with a marshy green scent. I felt soft wet mud and crushed plants under my fingers. Water chuckled faintly close by.

Somewhere further away, I could hear loud splashing and cracking.

When I was reasonably sure I wasn't going to be sick, I sat on my backside to lace up my boots. As I tried to see what the fuck was going on, a swan swooped low overhead, flying into the darkness in front of me. I scrambled up and followed it as fast as I could through the scrubby woodland. There was no moon to help me see what I might trip over or fall into. A moment later, I found Fin standing in a clearing.

She stared at me in disbelief. 'How the hell did you get here?'

'Zan.' I was relieved to see her, but I was furious with the sylph. I was eighty-odd miles from home without my wallet, my phone or any transport. Plus, we'd left my cottage with a smashed window any fucker could climb through. Hell, a burglar wouldn't even need to risk that. I hadn't had a chance to lock the fucking door.

'Same here,' Fin said grimly. She was wearing stretchy leggings and a loose T-shirt. She didn't even have shoes on.

So I wasn't the only one Zan had dragged out of bed. 'What's happening?'

'Some loose horses have got into the big beaver pond. They must be panicking, but I don't know what do.' Fin was trying to stay calm but her voice was tense. 'They're trashing the beavers' dam, and if one of the stupid things injures itself, I have no idea how we'll get it out of the water.'

'Where exactly are they?' My eyes were starting to adjust to the near-darkness. 'Where's Blanche?'

'Trying to scare them off. We both were, not that it was doing any good. When I saw you, I thought you must be their owner, come to round the damn things up. I can't think where they could have come from.'

Now I could see shadowy shapes splashing around in a broad stretch of water. I heard ominous splintering but no other noise. I don't know much about horses, but I'd have expected a bit of neighing.

With a glimmer of white feathers, another swan swooped close to brush a dark shadow's head with one wing. The shadow reared up, teeth snapping, trying to bite her. I thought horses chose flight over fight if they could when something unexpected got in their face. An angry swan, for instance. Besides, as I ran my fingertips along my forearm, the four raised lines of my scars prickled like a nettle sting.

Fin took a step towards the chaos. I grabbed her arm.

'Wait. Where's Zan? Can you get Blanche back here as well?'

Fin shook off my hand, but she stuck her fingers in her mouth to give an ear-splitting whistle. I saw Blanche fly around in a wide arc with her long white neck outstretched as she turned towards us. I breathed a little bit easier. Swans are big birds, but they're not built for a fight like this, what-ever people say about their wings breaking someone's arm. They're just not that manoeuvrable, and the worst feet made for paddling will do is land a nasty slap.

Blanche arched her wings to slow her speed. Her black feet spread out wide. She touched down and ran across the grass for a few metres, wings flapping to shed her momen-tum. The bright light I see when someone changes shape flared and she was human again, wearing a crop top and pyjama shorts.

'Dan?' She stared at me, startled.

That could wait. 'They're not horses.' And I didn't believe for a single fucking minute that this was some coincidence.

Fin didn't waste time either. 'What the hell are they then?'

Zan appeared and answered her. 'Creatures of shadow.'

'They're kelpies,' I clarified.

'What are they doing here?' Fin was completely confused.

'I have never seen their like before.' Zan was intrigued.

That threw me until I remembered we'd met Zan on the Jurassic Coast in Dorset. Why would a sylph from the seaside recognise a monster that lurked in remote Scottish rivers? That didn't get Zan off the hook though. 'Can you carry them away from here? Dump them somewhere else?'

'No,' Zan said as if that should be obvious. 'I am of air and light. Why do you think I fetched you?'

'There must be something—'

'What are you talking about, Dan?' Blanche was close to losing her temper.

I explained as fast as I could. 'They're kelpies, shapeshifters. They can look like horses or people, but they're not the least bit human. Three of them are trapped in their horse forms. There'll be four others somewhere close. They'll look like men.'

The bastards must have been watching Nicholas Tanner. They must have seen me with him. Dryads and naiads can tell I have greenwood blood, so I guessed the kelpies could too. How the fuck had they linked me to Fin though? And why attack her work here? Never mind. That could wait. I needed to know where the kelpies stuck on two legs were hiding. I looked around for a tree so I could find them with dryad radar.

Any one of those willows should do, but I couldn't see well enough in the darkness to work out the safest way to get to them. I remembered Fin saying the beavers dug holes and tunnels that sometimes collapsed and helped expand the wetland. None of us needed a broken ankle right now.

'There are five horses in the pond, Dan,' Blanche insisted.

'And no others nearby.' Zan was certain. 'Not in any form.'

What the fuck? If they were right, this must be a different mob of kelpies. 'Are they wearing anything on their heads? Did you get close enough to see?'

'Those headstall things people use to get hold of them.' Blanche was still talking as if these were ordinary horses.

'If we can get those off a couple of them, they won't be able to change shape. That should force them to talk to us.'

Even in the gloom, I saw both swan maids found this idea repellent.

'Do you want to stop them wrecking your work here or what? There isn't another way.'

Fin still looked appalled. 'How do we avoid getting trampled to death while we're trying to do that?'

That was a very good question. Okay, new plan.

'I'll get a halter off one of them to start with. Zan, be ready for me to throw it to you. When they realise attacking me won't get their silver chain back, they'll have to negotiate.' I sincerely fucking hoped so anyway.

'What do we do?' Fin demanded.

'Distract them. Same as you were doing before.' She and Blanche had to be safer as swans. That was a plus as far as I was concerned. If I was going to have any chance of literally pulling this off, I couldn't be worrying about Fin getting hurt. 'Come on. Let's do this.'

Blanche and Fin transformed in a flash of light. Zan vanished. I waited for a moment until my eyes got used to the darkness again. Then I walked towards the pond, testing my footing with every step through the tussocks of grass and bracken.

I hoped the beavers were hiding somewhere safe. The kelpies were still busy trashing the dam. The closest not-a-horse gripped a thin branch with its teeth. It shook its head like a dog with a rat, trying to wrench the wood out of the dam. It had already ripped out several sizeable lengths. The kelpie beside it was stamping, determined to force a hoof behind a lower layer of interwoven branches. They didn't even glance my way.

Two more were trampling down the edge of the pond on the far side, churning the water into mud. The last one stood on the bank close by, looking up into the night sky for swans. They were all wearing halters. So they definitely weren't the kelpies who'd robbed the craft fair. What the fuck did they want?

The closest kelpie saw me. It plunged through the water, charging towards me, neighing and whinnying. Trying to convince me it was just a horse? Try again, pal. It reached the edge of the pond and reared up, but it had miscalculated the depth of the water and the steepness of the bank. It was going to have trouble getting out.

Maybe so, but the other ones in the water had seen me now. The kelpie that had been keeping watch on the far side galloped away upstream, with its long, shaggy mane and tail streaming behind it like flickering shadows. I guessed it knew where to cross the stream and circle around behind me. I'd be lucky to see it before it attacked. Its hide was black as the night.

The first kelpie managed to fight its way out of the water. The others found an easier bit of bank and scrambled up onto the rough grass as well.

'Okay, it's all right, calm down.' I backed off, trying to sound as if I thought they were just ordinary horses.

To be honest, I'd expected they would be bigger. The closest one was barely a metre and a half tall at the shoulder, with a round belly and thick, stubby legs. Size doesn't matter, I reminded myself. Even an ordinary pony would be big enough to hurt me if it wanted to.

I heard swan wings overhead. The kelpies kept on watching me, which was a dead giveaway. I took a couple of steps towards the closest one and stretched out a hand, trying to sound calm and reassuring.

'Where've you come from then? Let's get you back to your owner before you hurt yourself.'

The kelpie let me get almost close enough to reach for its halter. Then it shook its head and trotted off. A moment later, it stopped, looking back with its ears pricked. Just a tubby little horse, playing games before it let itself be caught. Right.

The others stayed where they were. I tried to keep half an eye on them as I walked after the one that had moved away from the pond. A swan swooped out of the darkness, coming up behind the kelpie. It turned its head, and I covered the space between us in a couple of long strides.

The kelpie tossed its nose up, backing away. It was expecting me to try grabbing its halter. That's what anyone trying to catch a horse would do. Wrong. I reached past its head and wrapped my arm around its neck. I grabbed a handful of mane just in time. The kelpie reared up, taking me off my feet. It tried to shake me off, shrieking with fury.

My weight dragged the creature down. As soon as its feet hit the ground, the kelpie lowered its head, trying to bite my thigh. That was just what I wanted. I managed to shift my feet so its teeth slid off my leg as I dug my free hand into the coarse mane behind its ears. Hooking my fingers behind the strap, I pulled as hard as I could. The halter came loose.

'Zan!'

The kelpie screamed as I yelled for the sylph. I had no idea if Zan had heard me. I threw the halter into the air anyway, more sideways than upwards. A pale shape caught it, though I couldn't tell if that was Zan or a swan.

The kelpie wanted to shake me off, to charge after whoever had its treasure now. It was bucking and rearing, twisting its whole body in every direction. All I could do was hold on. I had no chance of finding my footing. The others had arrived now, neighing and jostling me. This bad situation was getting worse. If the one I'd got hold of shook me loose and I ended up on the ground, this whole maddened mob could trample me into a bloody smear on the grass.

As it was, I was already bleeding. My fingers were tangled in its mane and I felt the coarse hairs slice through my skin. It was no good. I couldn't hold on. I tried to push myself away from the beast. My boot soles skidded on the trampled, muddy ground. I just about managed to stay upright as the frantic kelpie disappeared into the darkness.

Something kicked me hard in the back of the knees. A heavy blow landed between my shoulder blades. I fell forwards, barely getting my hands down to avoid breaking my nose or my jaw on the ground. An arm tried to wrap itself around my neck. One of the kelpies was trying to strangle me, man to man.

I pressed my chin to my chest and hunched my shoulders. Gripping my attacker's elbow with one hand kept his arm where it was, pressing against my jaw. I dug my other fingernails into the skin between his finger and thumb. That forced his grip to relax just for a second. That was long enough. I grabbed his thumb and ripped it backwards against the joint as hard as I could.

The kelpie screeched and tried to wrench his arm away. I loosened my grip just enough for him to think he could pull free. That let him roll me over as he stood up. Now I was flat on my back, but I still had hold of his arm, forcing him to bend forward. He planted his feet on either side of my hips, and I saw him raise his free hand in a fist, ready to smash my face in. I couldn't see his face in the darkness, but his breath as he panted was foul.

I reached up and under his chin. My arms were longer than his. I closed my bleeding fingers around a metal chain. He was already throwing himself backwards as he realised what I was doing. Too late. As I let go of his arm, he lost his balance. The necklace broke as the kelpie went sprawling and I kept hold of it.

I got to my feet just before the others arrived. Two still looked like horses, baring stained teeth and ready to bite lumps out of me. The other three could have been the brothers or cousins of the men who'd robbed Nick Tanner at the craft fair. Their faces were twisted with rage.

I backed away, showing them the broken chain dangling from my fist. 'You can have this back when we've talked. And the halter.'

They could hear I was telling the truth. They hesitated. White light behind me told me Fin and Blanche had arrived to back me up.

'Just listen,' Blanche yelled. 'For one bloody moment.'

'We just want to talk,' Fin pleaded. 'I swear, we won't keep—'

The kelpies charged. So much for solidarity among shapeshifters.

A solid wall of wind-blown sticks and vegetation slammed into the ones on two feet. They were knocked right over. The kelpies on four hooves staggered backwards. A swirl of wind gathered up the debris and hammered them with it again.

All we felt was a gentle breeze as Zan appeared beside me. The sylph couldn't carry these kelpies away, but they had other ways to help us.

81

Chapter Seven

'Enough!' I yelled at Zan. The barrage of greenery subsided.

The three closest kelpies looked warily at us, getting slowly to their feet. They swapped uncertain glances. The one who had tried to strangle me stepped forward. I could tell it was him because his thumb stuck out at an odd angle, broken or dislocated. He didn't give a toss about that.

He gestured at the halter wrapped around Zan's wrist. 'Gie that back, and aye, we'll talk.'

His accent was so dense, I could barely make out what he said. He was Scottish, obviously, but I had no clue whereabouts they could have come from. I could tell he wasn't lying, but he wasn't saying nearly enough to convince me they wouldn't attack us as soon as they saw a chance.

I raised my hand and shook his silver necklace. The kelpie's eyes followed every twitch of the thick, heavy links, and his uninjured hand reached out for it. As soon as he realised what he was doing, he clenched his fist and scowled.

I rattled his chain again. 'If you want this back, you have to swear, all of you, that you won't attack us again. Not now, not ever. Swear never to come back here. Give us your word that you'll leave without doing any more damage to anyone or anything here. Do that, and I promise we'll give you your – your property back when you've answered our questions.'

Fin and Blanche echoed that assurance as they came closer. 'We promise you'll get your things back.'

'Once we're satisfied with your answers,' I added quickly. 'Then we'll let you go on your way and we won't come after you.'

Had I covered every possibility, or was there some loop-hole in my conditions that the kelpies could exploit? I saw they were looking at the sylph.

'Zan?' I didn't just want them to agree with me here and now. I haven't met anyone better than sylphs for getting around the intended meaning of some agreement while sticking scrupulously to the actual words.

Zan's chilling smile reassured me. 'You have my word. As long as I am satisfied.'

I could see the kelpies saw that as a threat as well as a promise.

'Aye,' the first one muttered. The other two mumbled some sort of agreement.

I shook my head. 'Not good enough. Say it, all of it.' In these situations, the only way to stay safe is to nail down every word.

The kelpies glowered but said... something. With their accents, I couldn't be certain they were repeating what I'd said. The two in horse form whinnied. I don't speak horse. I glanced at Zan.

The sylph nodded. 'They have bound themselves in agreement.'

'Thank you.' I still watched out for sudden moves. 'Why did you come here tonight? How did you know these women are friends of mine?'

The closest kelpie looked at me, open-mouthed. 'How'd ye ken...? Yon maids...?' His words trailed off and his gaze drifted to the chain in my hand.

It's not only dryads who avoid giving answers by meeting questions with questions. Fuck that.

'Don't piss me about. I was there when your friends attacked the silversmith.'

The kelpies stared at me, men and horses alike. Whatever I had expected, it wasn't this utter bemusement.

Zan glowed brighter so we could see each other more clearly. That just made the kelpies' confusion more obvious. 'They have no idea what you mean,' the sylph observed.

'Nor do we,' Fin said crisply at my side.

Oh, shit. No, she still didn't know what had happened at the craft fair.

'What the hell's going on, Dan?' Blanche stood next to the sylph.

Zan looked at me with piercing, unblinking blue eyes.

I tried to decide what I could say, at the same time as still technically keeping my promise to Conn, more or less. I spoke to the kelpies again.

'I know what – who you are, because I met seven of your kind last week. None of them could change their form because these had been stolen from them.' I raised my hand with the dangling chain. 'They robbed a man they thought might have been given their silver. They'd already attacked a woman while they were trying to find what had been taken from them.'

That was true, as far as it went. I braced myself for questions that would be a lot harder to answer. None of the kelpies said anything. They just looked terrified. Terrified and exhausted. Seeing them by Zan's merciless light, I realised the dirt on their hands and gaunt faces wasn't just mud from tonight but ground-in grime. Under their dark, ragged clothing, two of them weren't much more than skin and bone.

Unless this was some cunning deception, to make us think they weren't a threat. Alexander had warned me that kelpies were killers. That's why the selkies avoided them, and there couldn't be much a fully grown seal was afraid of, short of orcas.

84

One of the skinny kelpies spoke up, trembling. 'Did they find the siller?'

I guessed he meant silver. 'No. We think it's been melted down.'

One of the horses shrieked. It reared up and retreated, shaking its head. The man-shaped kelpie who'd said nothing so far collapsed to his knees. He buried his face in his hands, and his shoulders shook as if he was crying.

'Do you know them?' Fin was concerned. 'Are they friends of yours?'

'We know of them.' The kelpie who'd fought me struggled to get out the words.

'Why did you come here?' Blanche was getting impatient. 'Why wreck this place?'

The kelpies glanced at each other. Two of them shrugged, but no one spoke.

'You will only get this back when we're satisfied with your answers,' Zan reminded them, holding up the halter. 'I can leave here whenever I wish, and you'll never see this – or that necklace – again.'

Everyone could hear that was no idle threat. The kelpies looked at each other. Somehow, they made a decision. The ones still in horse form walked up to flank the three on two feet.

'We were sent tae wreck the work of yon twa maids.' The one whose chain I was holding looked me in the eye. He spoke slowly and clearly. 'We will tell ye who sent us when our kin are made whole.'

That was his last word, no doubt about it. What the fuck was going on? I tried to think this through.

'Whoever sent you here, is that who stole those chains from your kin? The ones who I met last week. Has this thief threatened to do the same to you? If you don't do what they want?'

The kelpies stayed stubbornly silent. That was as good as a yes for me. I also realised I had just told them that the mysterious bastard who had sent them here would absolutely follow through on that threat to destroy their necklaces. I wondered what the desperate kelpies who'd robbed the craft fair had refused to do.

'Who makes these chains?' I tried my hardest to sense something, anything, that was unusual about the silver I was holding. I didn't feel a flicker.

The kelpies didn't answer. Now I was getting annoyed. It was the middle of the sodding night. I was cold, tired, stuck in the middle of Shropshire, and the hand I'd cut on the kelpie's mane was stinging like a bitch. 'Then how are we supposed to help you?'

'We dinna ken.' The second kelpie forced the words out. That was the truth, but I couldn't tell which question he was answering.

The leader gave him a filthy look before turning to me. 'Ye knew enough tae tek tha' frae me. Ask whoever tellt ye tha'. Ye ma, was it?'

So he could tell I had greenwood blood. What did that mean? Before I could decide, Fin slid her hand into mine. She was shivering. It was time to wrap this up. We were getting nowhere, and I needed to talk to the others without any kelpies listening in. I chose my next words very carefully.

'I have no idea if we can find out how to help your friends who have been robbed. There may be no way to replace what they have lost. You cannot blame us if that's simply impossible. *If*—' I really stressed that word '—we learn something that might offer some hope of restoring what has been stolen, how do we let you know?'

The lead kelpie's gaze slid to Fin. 'We can watch—'

'No you won't.' I didn't like that predatory glint in his eyes.

'No, you won't.' Zan's swift agreement sent a chill down my back. 'I can find you, now we have met. If you have word for my friends, whistle and I'll come to you.'

I saw that really unnerved the lead kelpie. Good. 'I want your word that you won't come near us,' I said quickly. 'Not any of us, or our families or friends, until we send Zan to find you.'

The lead kelpie spat on the grass. 'Aye.'

Zan tossed the halter towards him. The kelpie snatched it out of the air and threw it to one of the others. He held out his uninjured hand towards me, palm up. I walked forward to give his broken necklace back. I did think about asking if I could keep a few links from it, just for a little while. I really wanted to see what Aled might make of it. Maybe his coblyn blood would sense something useful for us to know.

The kelpie scowled as if he knew exactly what I was thinking. No, that wasn't going to happen.

'Get out of here,' I told him. 'Now.'

One of the others was putting the halter I'd grabbed onto the bareheaded horse. The kelpie instantly twisted into a knot of shadow darker than the night. Another man stood with the group. The last kelpie shifted into human form as well. They swapped silent glances and walked away.

'Where do you think they'll go?' Blanche asked uneasily.

'I can follow and see,' Zan offered.

'No,' I said quickly before the sylph disappeared. 'We need you to take us home. I can't walk back to Blithehurst from here.'

'Take us back to our rental,' Fin said firmly. 'Dan has some explaining to do.'

I was going to suggest that could wait. I didn't get the chance. The dark night turned cold and white. Thankfully before I could feel suffocated, I was in an unfamiliar kitchen.

Blanche switched on the overhead lights. 'I'm glad we decided against staying in the hotel.'

She was trying to make a joke, but her voice was shaking. From the shock of what had just happened or from the cold? Her long legs were splattered with mud. Fin was equally filthy. I looked down at my boots and trousers. So was I.

'Showers,' Fin said with feeling. 'We'll feel better when we're warm and dry.'

I wanted more time to think this through. 'I have to get back to Blithehurst. I can shower there.'

Fin shook her head. 'Not until you've told us what the hell is going on.'

'Not unless you're planning on walking,' Blanche agreed. 'That's right, isn't it, Zan? You can go and see where those creatures have gone now. Come back here when you know where they're hiding, so we can talk.'

'My lady's wish is my command.' The sylph was gone before I could protest.

Blanche got a first aid kit out of a kitchen cupboard. 'Let's get some plasters on that hand, Dan, before you bleed over everything.'

'Let me wash it off first.' I turned on the cold tap at the sink and held my hand under the running water. I used a piece of paper towel to wipe away the blood and mud. The horsehair had cut deep into the outer edge of my palm as well as slicing the lowest joint of my forefinger. It could be worse. No one had got kicked in the head. 'Where are we, exactly?'

It was a decent kitchen. The cooker and fridge and the marble worktops weren't top of the line, but they weren't dirt cheap either. Durable was the word that came to mind.

Fin was getting towels out of a tumble dryer. 'In a holiday let about three miles from the farm. We got a bargain because someone cancelled at the last minute.'

Blanche sat on one of four chairs around the small table. She opened up the first aid box. 'Dan. Your hand.'

I sat down and rested my forearm on the table, palm up. 'How did Zan wake you up?'

'Ringing the doorbell.' Blanche uncapped a bottle of blue liquid and wetted a cotton wool ball. 'Why do you ask?'

'Never mind.' I hissed as she swabbed the cuts on my hand.

'Don't be a baby.' Blanche smeared antiseptic cream on the cuts and covered them with sticking plasters. 'This is a bit of a waste, since these'll get wet in the shower, but I don't want you dripping blood on the carpet and costing us the damage deposit.'

I wasn't surprised by her priorities. 'Thanks.'

'Whatever.' Blanche got up and took a towel from the laundry basket. 'I'll take the first shower.'

She went through the door to the living room as I turned to Fin.

'How did Zan know what was going on at the farm?'

She folded the last towel. 'Sylphs don't need sleep as such, so when Blanche has dozed off, Zan generally goes off to do their own thing. Let's just be thankful they like watching the beavers when they're out and about in the night.'

'Will the beavers come back to the pond?' I hated to think the kelpies had chased them away for good.

'Let's hope so. They're very good at repairing storm damage to their dams in the wild. You can put your clothes through a quick wash with mine while I'm in the shower. They'll be dry before you need to leave.' Fin stripped off her muddy leggings and pulled the loose T-shirt over her head. Bundling the dirty clothes up, she shoved them into the washer.

Then she grabbed a towel and left the kitchen wearing only the downy white feathers that give her family their shape-shifting ability and complicate their lives in all sorts of ways these days. If Fin had a doctor's appointment that might mean stripping off, she had to think about more than having decent underwear on. She had a lockbox where she would put her feathers for safe-keeping, and I guessed her family did the same.

I thought about that as I untied my sodden boot laces. Did someone who wanted to force a swan maiden to become an unwilling 'wife' have to get hold of every single one of her feathers? If so, that would be quite a challenge. I'd have to ask Fin, because I couldn't recall a fairy tale that said anything about it.

Something else occurred to me. Even if the would-be rapist only needed a certain percentage, gathering up enough to tip the balance would be a damn sight more difficult than snatching a single chain. I wondered if Conn and his people regretted whatever deal their ancestors had made with the cunning men. I remembered what Alexander had said about not getting mugged, and reckoned the selkies had made the right decision.

I heard the shower running as I took off my muddy clothes. While I was wrapping one of the towels from the dryer around my waist, the water upstairs stopped. Blanche came into the kitchen as I was finding the washing machine's fifteen-minute programme on the dial. She was wearing flowery blue pyjamas.

'Laundry liquid's under the sink.' Blanche opened a cupboard and took down three mugs. 'Tea or coffee?'

'Tea, please.' I wanted to be able to get at least some sleep when I got back to Blithehurst. As I found the detergent, I saw the night sky was growing pale through the kitchen window. I closed the washing machine door and switched it on. 'Where's the bathroom?'

'Straight ahead at the top of the stairs.' Blanche filled the kettle at the sink.

I followed the dirty footprints. I always wonder why anyone buys pale carpet, especially for a rental property. At least my feet were clean, thanks to my boots and socks. I knocked on the bathroom door and the shower paused for a moment.

'It's not locked,' Fin called out.

She was rinsing foam out of her hair as I went in. I took her towel off the heated rail and held it ready as she stepped out of the bath.

'Thanks.' She gave me a quick kiss before she left. That improved my night.

I showered quickly, dried off and went downstairs wearing the damp towel. I still hadn't worked out what I was going to say. As I reached the bottom step, I smelled coffee and heard Blanche talking in the kitchen.

'—sodding vandals. No one can say different. No one was there to see what really happened.'

'We'll have to be as surprised as everyone else. That won't be easy.'

Fin and Blanche were sitting at the table. Fin was dressed in jeans and a pale yellow cotton sweater. 'I've put your clothes in the dryer. There's tea in the pot.'

'Sit down and spill.' Blanche shoved the last empty chair out from under the table with one foot. 'What's going on, Dan?'

Zan was back and sitting opposite her. As far as the every-day world was concerned, Blanche's boyfriend was a lean, shaven-headed man much the same age as her, with vivid blue eyes and light brown skin.

'Give me a minute.' I peeled the soggy plasters off my hand and binned them. Since the cuts weren't bleeding, I de-cided to let them dry for now. I got myself a mug of tea and leaned against the worktop. 'It's like this.'

I told them the whole story, including Conn's insistence that I keep my mouth shut. 'Please, don't tell anyone else about this, not yet. Not your mum. Not anyone. I'll tell Conn what's happened here tonight, so he understands I had to ex-plain what's been going on to you two, but it's a safe bet he'll want you to keep what he told me to yourselves.'

Fin and Blanche nodded, but the sylph wasn't listening. Zan gazed out of the window. 'Shall I go in search of those kelpies who have lost their magic?'

'No!' Blanche said sharply. 'Don't do anything like that until we tell you there's something we need. Promise me.'

Zan was startled by her insistence. 'Very well.'

Fin broke the awkward silence. 'So what are we going to do now?'

The dryer stopped. I went over to fish out my clothes. Everything was still a bit damp, but I didn't care.

'I have to get back to Blithehurst. I need to tell Eleanor about tonight as soon as she's up and about. I need to check my phone as well. If Iain's called or answered my text, I'll let you know what he's said. Then we can decide what we should do next.'

'Do you think the cunning men will know how to replace those kelpies' stolen chains?' Blanche clearly doubted it.

'If he does, do you think this Iain will tell you?' Fin was equally dubious.

'No idea. We won't know until we ask.' I didn't imagine for a second that the old cunning man would share whatever he might know unless there was something in it for him and his group. I was already wondering if I could force some answers out of him by saying I'd go to the wise women instead.

That wasn't an idle threat. If the cunning men wouldn't talk, I had to find someone who would. I had to know who or what could threaten two different mobs of kelpies like this. I needed answers from the kelpies themselves. Why had they been sent to wreck the rewilding project? Specifically, to wreck Fin and Blanche's work on the farm? Coincidences happen, but I didn't believe this was one for a second.

Blanche yawned and stood up. 'I'm going to grab a nap before my alarm goes off. See you later, Dan.'

Once she'd left the kitchen, I threw the damp towel on a chair and got dressed. 'I'll ring you as soon as I have anything to tell you.'

Fin nodded, still sitting at the table. 'At least you don't have to drive home after a night with no sleep.' She put down her mug and came over to give me a hug. 'Love you.'

'Love you too.' I was about to tell her I was looking forward to seeing the farm rewilding when we were free of other distractions when Zan took my hand.

The kitchen vanished. The trip back to Blithehurst was just as vile as my first experience of travel by sylph. The only good thing was it seemed shorter. I staggered and managed to stay on my feet when I felt solid ground under my boots. I was outside my cottage. I focused on the fresh scent of the woodland and the cheerful dawn chorus.

'See you.' Zan vanished.

As the threat of a headache receded, I noticed two things that hadn't been here when I left. A massive black shuck was lying underneath my broken bedroom window, dozing with its muzzle on its paws. Good luck to any burglar trying to get past that.

Also, a Toyota 4x4 was parked beside my Land Rover. I walked over. Someone was sleeping inside, with the driver's seat tilted back as far as it went. Someone solidly built with dark wavy hair, wearing jeans and a black sweatshirt. The last time I'd seen him, he'd been wearing a kilt. Peter's a bit younger than me, in his late twenties, but he's one of Iain's closest allies.

I knocked on the driver's door window. Peter woke up with a start. He saw me and pressed a button, but the window didn't move. He opened the door instead of turning the key in the ignition. 'Good morning, Daniel.'

'Come on in.' I stepped back to let him get out of the vehicle. 'Long drive? How was the traffic?'

Peter stood beside the Toyota and stretched his arms over his head, taking a deep breath in. 'Give me a minute.' He bent double and touched his toes, breathing out.

So he wasn't going to tell me where he had come from. 'You could have gone inside and slept on the sofa,' I pointed out. 'The door's not locked.'

Peter grimaced. 'I don't think your watchdog would have allowed that.'

The shuck lumbered to its feet as he spoke. Its deep-set eyes glowed red as it hunched massive shoulders and its hackles bristled. I felt rather than heard its low warning growl. Peter's hiss of unease behind me sounded distinctly cat-like. I wasn't surprised he had decided to spend the night surrounded by metal.

'Come on in.' I walked towards the cottage and the shuck retreated.

Peter started talking as soon as we got through the front door. 'Iain says you have to—'

'I'm going to bed for a few hours.' I raised a hand to stop him saying anything else. 'Then I need to tell Eleanor what happened last night. You're welcome to stay and hear what's been going on. Have something to eat if you want, then you can come up to the manor with me. That's the deal. Take it or leave it.'

I heard the shuck's muted growling outside.

'Okay.' Peter didn't look happy, but he didn't argue.

'Help yourself to whatever you can find.'

I went into the bedroom and dropped onto my bed fully clothed. I didn't even take my boots off. There was still broken glass on the floor.

Chapter Eight

I woke up hungry and thirsty and I needed a pee. I sat up and noticed the oak branch was gone. Someone had cleared up the broken glass too. Peter must have decided to make himself useful. To put me in his debt? Where was he now?

I could hear birdsong through the broken window. It was a nice sunny day outside. I checked my hand. The cuts were healing cleanly, so I decided not to bother with more plasters. I changed into fresh clothes and went to find my unexpected visitor.

Peter was sitting on the sofa reading a thriller from my stack of library books. As he closed it, his smile was a bit strained. 'Good morning. That's to say, good afternoon.'

'I'll be with you in a minute.' I went to use the loo, washed my face and cleaned my teeth. I used the time to think.

When I came out of the bathroom, Peter had put the kettle on. 'Tea or coffee?' he asked.

'Tea, thanks. And thanks for sweeping up that glass.' I went to open the fridge. 'Sausage sandwich? Bacon and eggs?'

'Whatever you're having yourself. And you're welcome, about the glass. I did think I might wake you up,' Peter remarked, 'but you do sleep sound.'

'Like a log, as you might say.' I guessed he'd hoped I'd stir so he could start asking questions. I turned on the electric ring under the frying pan.

'How did that happen anyway?' he asked casually. 'The broken window.'

'Later.' I left the pan to get hot and took a loaf out of the bread crock. 'I need to update Eleanor, and I don't want to have to say everything twice.'

'Fair enough.' He didn't look too happy about that, but he didn't argue.

I cut four thick slices off the loaf and raised the knife. 'How many for you?'

'Two will be fine. Iain said you wanted to talk about some silver necklaces?' Peter poured hot water into the teapot.

He'd had a good look around while I was asleep. I could see he knew where everything was. I cut a couple more slices and buttered the bread. Then I laid six rashers in the hot frying pan and washed my hands. 'I'll give Eleanor a call and ask when she can see us.'

I reached for my phone, but it wasn't in the thigh pocket of my trousers. I remembered Zan knocking it out of my hand last night. I hoped the damn thing wasn't broken. 'Hang on.'

After looking under the bed and everywhere else, I found my mobile hidden in a fold of the duvet. I rang Eleanor as I walked back into the kitchen.

She didn't waste any time when she picked up the call. 'Have you heard from Iain?'

I looked at Peter, who was turning the frying bacon over with a fork. 'He's sent a friend to see me. We're having something to eat. I've got more news that he needs to hear as well. When's a good time for us to come up, so we can talk?'

'Five o'clock? I can hand off the last tour of the house to Abigail.' Eleanor was curious, but she couldn't ask questions. I could hear visitors' voices in the background.

'Fine. We'll see you then.'

'She can't find the time any sooner?' Peter moved the frying pan off the heat. 'Iain seemed to think whatever you need is urgent.'

'It is, but Blithehurst is a business and Eleanor has to keep it running.' I put my phone down and took plates, mustard and ketchup out of the cupboards.

'What network are you on?' Peter asked, frustrated, as he made himself a bacon sandwich. 'I haven't had a bar of signal since I got here.'

'Reception comes and goes. You'll be fine up at the house.' I sat down and started eating my own breakfast/lunch. 'You can help me mend that window this afternoon, if you like.'

'No problem.' He still wasn't happy, but he was trying not to show it.

We finished eating and I found the steel tape I keep in the kitchen odds-and-ends drawer. Measuring up didn't take long. Not having double-glazing in the cottage meant I could easily replace a single pane. I had some battens in the work-shop that would do for new glazing bars.

I put the tape back in the drawer and found the keys to the Landy and my wallet. 'I'll go and get the glass.'

'I'll come with you.' Peter picked up his phone.

As we walked out to the Landy, I thought the shuck had gone. Then I saw darkness shifting under the trees. The shuck wasn't alone. Etraia leaned against an oak tree, watching us intently.

'You have some interesting neighbours,' Peter commented as he fastened his seatbelt.

'You get used to them.' I didn't think his lack of a phone signal was a problem with his network's coverage. Dryads don't only listen in on mobile calls. They can screw up reception completely.

When we reached the estate's back entrance, Peter got out to open and close the gate without me having to ask. We drove on in silence. I waited. I didn't think he'd come with me because he didn't want to be left on his own in the cottage with the shuck around. At least, that wouldn't be his only reason.

'Is there really nothing you can tell me?' he pleaded when we pulled up at some traffic lights.

'All right.' I made it sound as if I was doing him a favour. Actually, I'd realised he might as well know about the kelpies attacking the silversmith before we talked to Eleanor. That would save time all round.

When I'd finished telling him, Peter didn't comment, though he couldn't hide his shock. I didn't mention Conn or Aled. I told him about the legends Eleanor had found when I'd asked her to look for stories about silver chains. If he assumed that was how we'd made the connection with kelpies, that was down to him. I hadn't told any lies.

While I was waiting by the glazier's counter for my glass to be cut to size, I glanced through the window. Peter had said he'd wait in the Landy. I could see he was on his phone. That was fine. With any luck, Iain might know something useful that Peter could share.

Before we went back, I made a quick stop at the DIY store to buy a doorbell. Nothing fancy, just one with a plastic button that a sylph or anything else that didn't like iron could press. Installing that and mending the window took us most of the rest of the afternoon. I wasn't in a hurry.

I didn't see Etraia or the shuck again. That didn't mean they weren't close by and staying unseen. I hoped they were. Then I could be sure nothing else was lurking in the shadows.

When it was time, we walked up to the dairy yard so I could put my tools away. I took Peter along the path that cuts through the hedge and the ornamental orchard. We walked around to the front of Blithehurst House.

'This is some place.' He stopped on the gravel to admire the manor.

He's right. Blithehurst's not huge but it is impressive. The limestone masonry has weathered over the centuries to soft grey or gold, depending on whether or not the sun is shining. The two floors have tall leaded and mullioned windows which look out over ornate gardens at the front, and across the valley to the wooded pastures on the other side of the river at the back. The steep roof has russet tiles which run down to fake battlements along the tops of the walls. Those are purely for show. This house was built to impress, not to be defended in battle.

The Roundheads had thought that meant they would easily seize the house from Eleanor's Royalist, Catholic ancestors in the English Civil War. They were in for a surprise. The dryads got them so thoroughly lost that they never arrived. Not that any of the attackers could know what had really happened.

Visitors with tickets for the last guided tour of the day were waiting outside the monumental front porch. A short, wiry woman came out through the weathered oak door. Abigail was a former teacher who'd taken voluntary redundancy, and some school's loss was definitely Blithehurst's gain.

'Welcome to the ancestral home of the Beechen family.' She smiled as the visitors clustered around her. 'Please, do follow me.'

Peter glanced at me. 'Beechen? It says on the website—'

'It's spelt Beauchene because the family came over from Normandy with William the Conqueror. The locals turned that into Beechen centuries ago. And that's Eleanor.'

As the last of the tourists went inside, my boss came out through the front door. Peter looked surprised. Eleanor gets that a lot. She's a couple of years younger than me, five ten, and she wore the same blue uniform polo shirt as Abigail. Most visitors assume she's just another member of staff. You'd think some would see the family resemblance with the portraits in the gallery, but people can be very unobservant. Spending most days on her feet keeps her fit, and she's tied her long dark hair back in a plait or a ponytail as long as I've known her.

'You must be Peter.' She offered him her hand.

'Hello.' He shook with a smile.

She looked at me. 'So where do you want to talk? Shall we have a coffee up in the cafe?'

I didn't need to explain to Eleanor that we didn't want to be overheard by someone we couldn't see. 'We're fine. We had a drink before we came up here. Shall we use your sitting room?'

She nodded. 'Come this way.'

We followed her across the front of the house and around the corner to a narrow terrace overlooking the gardens running down to the original manor's ruins beside the river. Eleanor unlocked the plain door with the 'Staff Only' sign. That opens into the kitchen corridor with the old servants' hall. That's the staff break room these days. Eleanor unlocked the door to the back stairs and locked it behind the three of us. The servants' stair took us up to a door directly opposite her private apartment. She relocked the door once we were inside.

Peter was clearly surprised. 'You take your security seriously.'

'You can put a sign on a door saying "No Entry" in twenty languages, and someone will still try to open it.' Eleanor put her keys on the mantelpiece next to the softly ticking clock. 'Please, take a seat.'

She gestured at the two-seater sofa facing the bay window. Peter sat down. Eleanor went to her usual chair at the table in the bay. Books and files flanked her laptop.

I leaned against the dark oak–panelled wall opposite the fireplace. 'I've told Peter about the robbery at the craft fair, and about the stories you found linking kelpies with silver chains.'

Eleanor's nod told me she understood what I was leaving out. 'You said you had more news?'

'Last night was eventful.' I told them what had happened in Shropshire.

The cunning men already knew about Fin and Blanche. Even so, Peter's eyes widened when he realised a sylph was taking such a close interest in their lives. He couldn't hide his astonishment when I repeated the kelpies' ultimatum. They'd only tell us who was threatening them if we found a way to replace the stolen silver chains.

'First things first,' Eleanor said firmly. She looked at Peter. 'What can you tell us about them? What are we dealing with?'

He took a moment to think. 'For a start, those ones at the craft fair, I'd guess they were speaking the Doric between themselves. That's an old dialect from the North East – the North East of Scotland, you understand. Some say it's a language in its own right. That fits with what we know of the kelpies that are left.'

'How many is that?' I wanted to know the chances of another attack.

'Fewer and fewer. That's as much as I can say.' Peter spread his hands, apologetic. 'They've been in decline for the past couple of centuries. This last hundred years or so have been dire for them. You've read that they eat the folk they drown? These days, most folk won't even try to catch a stray horse. They wouldn't know how. If someone who can ride does have a go, as soon as the kelpie gets them into the water, well, most people can swim nowadays. Not many hikers go out on their own, and if they do, they'll have a mobile phone or a smartwatch or one of those electronic maps for walkers.

Something with a GPS. As soon as an alert confirms someone hasn't checked in, the police or mountain rescue turn out. There'll be helicopters searching, specialist divers if there's a chance someone's gone into deep water. Kelpies won't want to be within a mile of that much activity.'

I thought about the ones I'd met last night and their gaunt faces. 'Are you saying they're starving to death? How does that work, if they're creatures of shadow?'

'Oh, they are,' Peter assured us. 'Or at least, they were. Something changes when a creature that's not of this world starts hunting mortal prey. Shedding living blood gives them a solid presence here. You know that, I take it?'

He waited for us both to nod before he went on. 'That's as much as most of these creatures want. If they eat more than a few of their kills, though, they begin to crave mortal flesh. The more they eat, the more they become bound to our reality. That's a one-way street.'

Eleanor raised a hand. 'That sounds like the warnings against eating or drinking anything you're offered in fairy-land. Are you saying that cuts both ways?'

'So it would seem.' Peter nodded. 'Kelpies don't starve as such, but they'll fade to no more than a shadow of themselves if they go without fresh meat for long enough.'

I definitely didn't want predators like that anywhere near Fin and Blanche. Especially the ones I'd seen who clearly weren't half-starved. 'The ones who attacked the craft fair were fit enough to cause plenty of trouble. What are they eating?'

'The ones who still thrive live on roadkill. Deer, mostly. They will eat the odd hiker, if they get the chance,' Peter admitted. 'There's no way for us to know if they've come across them dead or alive. People go missing in the Highlands every year.'

Eleanor leaned back in her chair. 'Where do these silver chains come in? What's the story there?'

Peter hesitated. 'I must have your word not to share what I tell you with anyone.'

I wondered how he'd react if I told him just how many people had said that to me in the last ten days. But he wasn't going to say anything unless we agreed. I knew Fin wouldn't like it, but she'd understand I had no choice.

I shrugged. 'I promise.'

Eleanor nodded. 'I promise.'

'Thank you.' After a moment, he went. 'A long time ago, more years than anyone can count, a few canny men and women realised we share this world with various spirits of wood and water, of the air, the earth and the shadows. Those first cunning folk found ways to work with the unseen world and those who live there. They bargained with the uncanny folk, to find what was lost, to cure sickness and to solve other problems. They became acquainted with selkies and the like. Some of the cunning men had more dealings with the shapeshifters than most. As time passed, my forebears envied their ability more and more. They were willing to trade their skills for whatever a shapeshifter might want in return, if they could find one willing to share some secret knowledge they could use to do the same.'

Eleanor was doing a good job of looking as if this was news to her. This sounded to me like a story Peter had told before. More than once. Presumably new recruits to the cunning men's ranks wanted to know what they were getting into. I wondered what Peter had thought the first time he had seen someone turn into a big cat.

He went on. 'The selkies weren't interested in making a deal, so the cunning men asked the kelpies. They learned the kelpies were jealous of naiads and dryads, and those who live in the hollow hills. The folk who could use their allure to overcome a mortal's natural caution. They saw humans wouldn't hesitate when they were entranced. They wouldn't even notice they were walking straight into danger. Kelpies wanted to draw their prey closer by charming travellers, but creatures of shadow have no such power.'

He paused for a moment. 'A skill some cunning folk devised long ago was a way to bind a tiny fraction of a willing spirit's power into an object. Cunning men sold these things as talismans to ward off evil, as amulets to bring good luck or to keep people and their property safe. These worked by drawing on that surrendered power to do what was needed. Some cunning men sold love charms to those keen to woo a reluctant bride or groom. Those held a little of a naiad's or a dryad's allure.'

I had so many questions. What did the naiad or dryad get out of making that sort of deal? How willing had their cooperation been? And Peter was talking as if this stuff was in the past. I was willing to bet some cunning men were still selling date-rape spells. I also noticed he hadn't mentioned the Irish swans. Fine by me. I wouldn't mention them either. They must have a different story, but that could wait for another day.

Peter raised a hand, though neither of us had said anything. 'That's as much as I can tell you. Anyway, back then both sides realised they had something the other wanted. They came to an agreement and the deal was done. The power to lure mortals was bound into silver chains, along with the kelpies' ability to shapeshift. That's the only way it would work. No one knows if the kelpies realised that at the time. We don't know if those cunning men warned the beasts what would happen if they lost their talismans. But they should have realised there's always a price to be paid.'

I wondered what gaining the power to turn into big cats had cost the cunning men. Was there still a price they had to pay? I wondered what deal the wise women had made, and who with, to be able to turn into hares.

Eleanor got straight to the point. 'How do we get new necklaces made, to get rid of these kelpies? How do we find whoever – whatever – is threatening them, and forcing them to do who knows what?'

'And why did they go after Fin and Blanche? And what do you want from us,' I asked bluntly, 'before you'll help?'

Peter hesitated. 'Nothing, as such.'

That wasn't a lie, but 'nothing as such' was vague enough to mean anything. The same as 'that's as much as I can tell you' could be interpreted in a lot of different ways. I wasn't going to let him get away with that.

'Can one of the cunning men who answers to Iain make new talismans for these kelpies or not? If not, do you or Iain or one of you know someone who can? Or where to find out how to do it?' I hoped I'd covered every angle to stop Peter dodging a straight answer.

Eleanor nodded. 'If you can't help, why have you come here?'

Peter looked down at his phone. I expected him to say he needed to speak to Iain. Instead, he answered Eleanor's question.

'A few weeks ago, we found out that mobs of kelpies were travelling south. We didn't know where they were going or why, but it was obvious they were going to cause trouble. That's bad news to begin with. When Dan texted Iain, we had to find out what you knew. That's why I'm here.'

'How many mobs?' I demanded. 'How many kelpies?'

'Ten? Twenty? More? Do you want me to guess?' he challenged me. 'We honestly don't know.'

'Then tell us what you do know,' Eleanor said. 'How do we replace these stolen chains?'

Peter shook his head. 'We can't make these talismans ourselves, not any more. We might be able to find those who can, but you'll have to help me, Dan. I cannot do it without you.'

Every word of that was true. So was his regret, though that could mean several different things.

I folded my arms. 'I'm not agreeing to anything until I know exactly what you're asking.'

Peter didn't answer me. He looked at Eleanor.

'More secrets you can't share, I take it,' she said dryly. 'Can I at least know where you're going and how long Dan will be away?'

'Let me...' He looked down at his phone, typing quickly with two thumbs.

We waited. Out in the corridor, we heard Abigail escorting the last visitors of the day out of the picture gallery and back towards the main stairs. A few minutes later, Peter had his answer. He looked up.

'We have to go to the Borders. The Lammermuir Hills, not far from Berwick-upon-Tweed.'

'To do what?' I demanded.

He shook his head. 'I can tell you when we get there, but only you. Sorry,' he apologised to Eleanor.

She shrugged. 'If that's the way it has to be. How long will this take?'

'Shouldn't be more than two or three days.' He sounded fairly confident about that.

I was surprised. 'To get the kelpies' chains replaced?'

Peter's smile came and went so fast I could have imagined it. 'To see if we can find the – the folk who might be able to make such things. To find out if they'll agree to do it for a start, and then what the price might be.'

'Fair enough.' I had thought that sounded too easy.

He looked at me. 'If we set off now, we can get to Berwick by midnight. I'll drive—'

'No.' I wasn't going to risk being stranded without transport anywhere. 'We'll each take our own car, and we'll go tomorrow morning. I need a decent night's sleep first.'

Peter looked as if he wanted to argue. He didn't. That was good. Or was it?

'Can you find your way back to the cottage?' I asked him. 'I've got a couple of things I need to sort out in the workshop.'

'If you think yon black dog will let me in.' Peter was still uneasy about the shuck.

'Why don't I show you around the house?' Eleanor suggested. 'Dan can come and find us when he's done and then we can go out for some food. Just the local pub, the White Hart,' she told Peter. 'They're very reliable.'

'That sounds like a plan.' I walked over to take Eleanor's keys off the mantelpiece before Peter could suggest coming to the workshop with me. 'I won't be long.'

'Let's have a coffee,' Eleanor suggested to him. 'I don't know about you, but I've been talking all day.'

I left them to it. When I got to the dairy yard, I found an old steel toolbox and looked around for whatever I might need to complete some mysterious challenge. This wouldn't be the first time. On the other hand, those encounters had been so wildly different, it was hard to know what to take.

I found a torch and spare batteries, and collected an assortment of nails and screws of different lengths. A claw hammer, a lump hammer and a hacksaw as well as a couple of screwdrivers and chisels. Gaffer tape, paracord, glue. Some offcuts of wood to fill up the space I had left. Plastic bags and a handful of rags got stuffed into the corners.

Last but by no means least, I took the washing-up liquid bottle off the draining board and got a paper bag of sugar out of the cupboard beside the fridge. I keep a small jerry can of petrol in the Land Rover, even though it runs on diesel. If I'm ever stopped by a curious copper, I'll insist that's just in case I ever come across a stranded motorist. Honest, officer, I swear it.

I'd get a couple of empty glass bottles out of the recycling. You never know when you might want to make a Molotov cocktail. I dropped a box of matches as well as a throwaway lighter into the toolbox.

Then I rang Fin. 'How are you? How's it going?'

'We've spent most of the day clearing up. The beavers are all accounted for and there's no sign that they were hurt.' She sounded tired. 'We've just had a crisis meeting, and I think we've convinced the farm owners not to go to the local news-papers. At the moment, no one outside the project knows what happened. We'd like to keep it that way. We don't want any other yobbos getting ideas.'

She was saying that for someone else's benefit, not mine. I could hear voices. 'Where are you?'

'In the pub with some of the other consultants. Let me find a quiet corner and you can tell me about your day.'

I waited until the voices faded. I heard Fin put a glass down on a table.

'Go ahead,' she prompted.

I quickly told her what Peter had told us.

'Bloody hell.' I heard the ice in her drink clink as she took a sip. 'Do you want Zan to follow you tomorrow, to see where he takes you? Blanche should be able to convince them to stay out of sight.'

That was tempting. On the other hand... 'Probably better not,' I said reluctantly. 'That could screw things up with the cunning men, or whoever we're going to see. If they decide to be helpful, whoever they are.'

'I suppose so.' Fin wasn't thrilled, but she didn't press it. 'Keep your phone charged and make sure you've got your location switched on.'

'Will do. As soon as I know more, and as soon as I know what I can tell you, I'll call. I promise.'

'Be careful. Love you.'

'Love you. Bye.'

I ended the call and looked at my phone. I left the workshop and walked out of the dairy yard into the closest stand of trees. I was about to reach for a branch to try and locate one of the dryads when Etraia appeared. She wore a green tunic and leggings and looked ready to join a yoga class.

I held up my phone. 'Can you find one of these to trace someone who's lost?'

I'd never thought to ask if a dryad could sense a GPS signal.

'I have no idea.' Etraia looked intrigued though. 'I can certainly try.'

'Thanks. Can you do something else for me, please? The man who's visiting me, if he tries to leave in the night, can you stop his car working? Or get Frai or Asca to do it. And make sure he can't use his phone.'

As well as wrecking a mobile signal, a dryad can screw up a modern car's electronics spectacularly. Like I say, you really don't want to piss them off.

Etraia angled her head. 'You don't trust him?'

I grimaced. 'I trust Peter, but I'm not sure I can trust the men he answers to. They might tell him to do something different. To break our agreement.'

Peter had found out a lot today, and he'd passed that on. I didn't want the cunning men to decide they'd sort out the kelpies some other way, leaving me with a promise I'd made which I couldn't keep. Leaving Fin and Blanche to face the kelpies' retaliation.

Etraia thought about that and nodded. 'I can do that.'

She disappeared. As I walked back to the house, I wondered if she would be able to find my phone once I'd left in the morning. If she couldn't, and things did go tits up for some reason, I reminded myself a whole lot of dryads would be wanting to know where I was, if I left Blithehurst with Peter and disappeared. They'd want answers from the cunning men. I knew who my money was on.

Chapter Nine

After steak and chips at the White Hart, and a couple of pints since Peter was driving, I slept very well. The Green Man didn't send me any dreams, so hopefully we were still on the right track. I got up bright and early and heard Peter snoring in the living room. The sofa-bed must be a lot more comfortable than sleeping in his car seat. He didn't stir when I unlocked the front door. I could still hear him snoring as I locked it behind me.

I went up to the dairy yard and put the old toolbox from the workshop in the back of the Land Rover. Then I went up to the manor and found a couple of empty glass bottles in the kitchen there. I also left a note I'd written for Eleanor inside the cafetière. That guaranteed she'd see it.

Can you see if someone can get hold of Kalei? Maybe she or someone she knows can tell us more about these troublemakers. Maybe they can find them? Ask if someone can watch Fin's back.

That wouldn't mean anything to anyone else, in the unlikely event that someone on the staff found it. Only Eleanor knew that Kalei was the river spirit who considered the waters flowing through Blithehurst to be part of her domain. Maybe Asca or Frai could get a message to her. I wished I'd thought about enlisting the naiads sooner. Though Kalei came and went as and when it suited her. We didn't see her that often, and mostly only when she wanted something from us. Something like help getting rid of kelpies? I couldn't imagine any naiad I'd ever met wanting them in her river.

I went back to the dairy yard and drove down to the cottage. When I got out of the Landy, the shuck stepped out of the shadows under the trees. Its unblinking eyes were dull red embers in the morning light.

'I'll call you if I need you,' I assured the beast.

'You can do that?' Peter stood in the open doorway, wearing pyjama shorts. His yawn didn't cover his surprise at what I'd just said.

'Yes.' And the shuck wouldn't need a GPS signal to find me. I should have remembered that last night when I was talking to Fin. 'Do you want to shower while I make breakfast?'

'Thanks.' Peter went back inside. The shuck had already disappeared.

I cooked bacon, scrambled eggs and toast, and made coffee and tea. I also had questions for Peter as we ate. 'What's the best way to fight kelpies? If it comes to that?'

He shrugged. 'The usual. They can hide themselves in the shadows from ordinary folk, but not from the likes of you or me. They're bound close enough to this world that steel blades and fire can hurt them, even kill them. Some tales say they can be drowned, which is a bit of a surprise, but there you go.'

Maybe the naiads wouldn't need any help getting rid of them. Still, I'd pass on what he'd said to Fin.

'Is there anything you want to ask me?' I offered.

He thought for a moment, then shook his head. 'No, I don't think so.'

Eleanor had told him plenty about Blithehurst's history over dinner last night. More than the history the general public can read in the guidebook. She had shared selected highlights from her family's involvement with the dryads over the centuries. When she mentioned the monster that had brought me to Blithehurst, she kept that brief. Peter had nodded and the conversation moved on. He could see that was a sensitive subject. I'd been wondering if he'd want to know my side of that story now we were alone, but apparently not.

I washed up while Peter put the few things he'd taken out back in the holdall he'd brought in from his car. I fetched my overnight bag from my bedroom. I had packed as much as I'd want for a few days away. If I was gone any longer than that, I had my bank card and Berwick-upon-Tweed must have shops.

'Ready?' I asked.

Peter nodded, picking up his holdall. 'I need to get fuel.'

'We'll do that first. You can follow me there.' I held the front door open, and Peter went outside. I locked up. 'Can you give me a postcode for my satnav? In case we get separated once we're off the motorway.'

I half expected him to say he'd need to ask Iain first, but he nodded. 'I'll text it to you. Oh, there's one thing I meant to ask. Can you use your phone hands-free while you're driving?'

My Land Rover's far too old for things like that. 'No.'

'Best we don't get separated then. Let's decide where we'll stop for a break. Durham services okay?' He sounded as if he knew the route we'd be following.

'Fine with me.' I'm more familiar with travelling north up the M6. We could have done that to get to Berwick. There's surprisingly little to choose between the main two routes, if you compare distance and time. The chance of getting caught in bad traffic around Leeds or Manchester is always the luck of the draw. But if Peter wanted to go via Durham, I didn't have a problem. He'd put up with me making every decision yesterday, without getting his own way once. He hadn't given us the slip in the night, and we were going to have to work together. I could let him have this win.

Peter followed me to the nearest petrol station. We both bought fuel and snacks. He texted me, and I put our destination's postcode into my satnav. From what I could see, we were heading for the back of beyond in the Lammermuir

Hills. I didn't get a chance to look any closer before Peter started his engine.

I followed his Toyota off the forecourt. My satnav reckoned our best option was going north through the Peak District National Park and cutting across to pick up the M1 at the Barnsley junction. Apparently, Peter's satnav agreed. After Leeds, the A1(M) was busy, but the traffic kept moving, so that was okay. We stopped at the Durham services as agreed for a pee, a coffee and a sandwich. Peter was looking thoughtful as we walked back out to the car park, but he didn't say anything. Once we were past Newcastle, we took the A1 to Berwick-upon-Tweed.

I expected Peter to take the turning to follow the route around the town, across the River Tweed and into Scotland. That's what the satnav was showing me. Instead, he followed the signs for Tweedmouth. I lost sight of the Toyota twice in the afternoon traffic. I was searching ahead for somewhere to pull over safely, so I could use my phone to ask where the hell he was going, when I caught sight of the Toyota. I managed to keep it in sight until Peter turned into a Tesco superstore right on the edge of the town.

I managed to find a parking space and called Peter's phone. 'What are we shopping for?'

'This and that.' He sounded evasive. 'See you in there.'

By the time I reached the store's doors, he was waiting with a trolley. He had also come up with a better answer. 'We'll be staying somewhere fairly remote. We'll need to feed ourselves.'

'Fine.' As I followed him around the store, I wondered who he had spoken to while we were driving. Asking if I could use my phone hands-free had to mean he could do that in the Toyota. I was sure he hadn't been expecting to go shopping. For one thing, he would have told me earlier, at

Blithehurst or when we stopped at the services. For another, he didn't have any reusable bags with him.

Peter put some apples and a loaf of crusty white bread in the trolley, along with milk, butter, bacon, eggs.

'Pizza okay for tonight?' He paused by the chiller cabinet. 'Any preference?'

'Nothing with too much chilli. Shall I get a few beers?' I suggested as he chose a meat feast and a barbecue chicken pizza.

He nodded. 'Why not?'

I put some garlic dough balls in the trolley and went to find some local beer. When I caught up with Peter, winding up and down the aisles, he pointed to a jar of Fairtrade instant coffee and a box of tea bags.

'Those okay?'

'Fine.'

We carried on and Peter added a jar of marmalade, a box of sugar lumps and a packet of caramel wafer biscuits to our shopping. I was more interested in the other things he was stacking at the far end of the trolley. There was a second loaf of bread, sourdough this time, as well as a big pot of double cream, a jar of clear honey and a whole cooked chicken, ready to eat. I followed as he found the aisle that sold paper plates and cups. He picked up a packet of each, plain white, as well as some paper bowls, a paper tablecloth and a carton of single-use wooden cutlery.

'Are we having a picnic?'

'Sort of.' He wasn't looking at me again, and not just because he was trying to find something else.

'When are you going to tell me what we're here to do?'

'When we get there. Now, we need salt. Lots of salt.'

'You should have said before we left Blithehurst. We keep plenty to spread on the footpaths if there's a hard frost. I could have brought as much as you're going to need in the back of the Landy.'

With the last few mild winters, we'd barely needed to use the stuff. Peter didn't answer me, though, and not just because he was scanning the hanging signs that theoretical-ly told shoppers where to find what they wanted. He hadn't known before we left that he'd need salt for whatever we were going to do.

'Down there.' I pointed.

Six kilo-and-a-half bags of cooking salt were stacked on the bottom shelf. Peter put them all into our trolley. 'That's everything,' he said, relieved.

I wondered if the self-service check-out would object to someone buying that much cooking salt. It didn't. The mem-ber of staff who came to check we looked over twenty-five and could be allowed to buy beer gave the stack of packets a glance, but didn't say anything either.

Peter was quick to take the first shopping bag for the chicken, the cream, the honey and the sourdough loaf. I packed everything else while he added the paper plates and other party stuff to his bag. I put the salt back in the trolley as it was.

'I don't know if these bag handles are up to nine kilos of weight, and I'd rather not find out the hard way.'

'No,' Peter agreed.

He paid with a tap of his bank card and waited to get a receipt. I wondered if that meant the cunning men paid expenses.

Peter drew a deep breath. 'Right. Let's go.'

'To the place you gave me the postcode for?'

'That's right.' He pushed the trolley towards the door.

Peter loaded everything into the Toyota. We worked our way slowly out of Tweedmouth and drove for just over another hour. The roads got steadily narrower and the satnav gave up giving me route numbers at junctions. Now it just told me to turn into 'the lane'.

The Lammermuir Hills were old and gently rolling moorland covered with coarse grass and dense heather. Clouds scudding across the sunny sky dappled the gold, green and brown patchwork landscape. When the heather bloomed in the summer, those brown patches would be pink and purple. At least until grouse shooting in August wrecked the peace and quiet.

I passed signs to cycle paths, waymarks for walkers and directions to campsites. Though there wasn't much to indicate many people lived here year-round. The satnav had several castles marked, but when we drove by those sites, I saw a few remnants of weathered masonry, or a prehistoric earthwork. This would be a very different place in winter, bleak and exposed, even if really heavy snowfalls happen less often these days.

Countless rivulets carved paths down the slopes to join up and make larger streams. I guessed the locals would call those burns. I didn't see any flowing water big enough to interest a naiad. We passed a reservoir, but as far as I know, naiads ignore those. I hoped kelpies did as well. I didn't see many trees, so I didn't think I'd be meeting any dryads. The lack of trees would also mean I couldn't use dryad radar to see who or what was around, whenever we got to wherever we were going, to do whatever we were here to do.

Peter was going to explain as soon as we arrived. I'd had enough of not knowing. I was thinking about that instead of keeping an eye on the satnav when the Toyota turned into a rough track. I nearly overshot the entrance and had to wrench the steering wheel around to make it. We drove a short distance up the hillside to a long low single-storey house. The front door was just far enough off-centre to be irritating, like a picture hanging a few millimetres crooked on the wall.

A patch of gravel offered parking for two vehicles. I pulled up beside the Toyota, got out and pushed my shoulders back, lifting my chin to ease my stiff neck. This had been a long day of driving. Peter was looking at his phone. He walked over to a key box screwed to the whitewashed wall beside the front door and put in the code. I got my overnight bag and followed him inside.

'Is this a holiday let?' I knew at least one of Iain's followers rented out a cottage in Argyll. That was one of several ways he made money, and it gave him an official address for government paperwork, even though he was never really there.

'Sometimes.' Peter went to fetch his holdall and everything we had just bought from his car.

A fine layer of dust and a newspaper from early March on the dining table told me no one had rented this place over the Easter school holidays. From the chill, the storage heaters had been switched off since then. Still, I couldn't smell any damp despite that sticking front door. When I tried the nearest switch, the lights came on.

The furniture was clean and solid, even if it wasn't new. I opened a couple of cupboards and saw the plates and saucepans were a mix of styles and patterns. I guessed someone had inherited the place. They didn't want to live here, but they didn't want to sell, so they were letting it out. I was going to have to make that sort of decision myself one day.

I didn't want to think about that right now, so I checked the layout. This end of the building was now a large kitchen-diner-sitting room. To the right of the front door, a corridor ended at a window offering a spectacular view of the hills. The first of the three closed doors was a bedroom, so I left my bag on the bed. The next door along was the bathroom, which was a relief. I was glad to find loo roll on the holder and soap by the basin. The last place Fin and I had booked for a week away had expected visitors to bring everything short of their own lightbulbs.

When I came back into the living room, Peter was kneeling in front of the ancient cast-iron wood-burning stove. He was lighting a fire. 'This'll warm the place up. There's no point switching the heaters on. We won't be here that long.'

'You reckon?' I saw the teabags, coffee and sugar lumps by the kettle. I opened the fridge and the bread bin and found about half of our shopping. The bag with the paper plates and everything else was on the dining table. He'd stacked the bags of cooking salt beside it. 'What are we going to do?'

When Peter was satisfied the kindling had caught alight and the logs would follow, he closed the stove's front door. 'We're going to try to contact the brown men of the moors.'

'Who are they when they're at home?' I rinsed out the kettle, filled it and switched it on.

'Earth spirits. Like hobs, brownies, that sort of folk. Some call these ones delvers.' Peter came over and opened the jar of coffee. He found a spoon in a drawer. 'They live under these hills, and they have a particular interest in working with gold, silver and precious stones. They've been known to tell the people they're friendly with where to go looking for seams of ore that'll make them get rich.'

They sounded very like the Welsh coblynau Aled had told me about.

Peter was still talking. 'They also take an interest in what goes on up above ground. Someone who gets on their wrong side can end up lost in the hills for days. Sometimes they'll never find their way back.'

I believed him. I'd seen dryads and hamadryads do that to people. Frai and Asca call it mazing. 'What gets someone on their shit list?'

'Fly-tipping, causing a wildfire, generally trashing the place. Cruelty to animals makes them really mad, apparently.'

These delvers had that in common with dryads then. I found a couple of mugs in a wall cupboard. 'You think they could make new chains for the kelpies?'

'Old stories tell of them making magical gifts.' Peter spooned coffee granules into both mugs and poured hot water from the kettle. 'Rings, torcs, cups. That sort of thing.'

That sounded promising, but I suspected there would be a catch. I got the milk out of the fridge, added some to my coffee and passed it to Peter.

'Is there a particular cave where we can find them?'

Peter grinned as he picked up two lumps of sugar. 'No. We invite them to a picnic.'

'Seriously?'

Then again, I remembered the hob I'd met at Fin's mum's house in the Fenlands. We'd persuaded him to give us a hand over an evening of beer, bread and cheese, pickles and pork pies. He had other good reasons to help, but sharing that meal had been important.

'There's an old earthwork not far from here.' Peter opened the end cupboard. He took out an unlabelled bottle of the cunning men's whisky and put it in the bag on the table. 'We'll set out food and drink a wee bit before midnight, and wait to welcome them.'

'Okay.' I couldn't see any point asking what we'd do if they didn't turn up. 'You'll need a bread knife. Those wooden things won't get through that sourdough crust. Something to carve the chicken would be useful too. And a chopping board.'

'Good thinking.'

He found a couple of knives and a wooden bread board and added them to the bag. I checked my phone. I had one bar of signal and no chance of data. I looked up, and Peter shook his head before I asked.

'No Wi-Fi here. Sorry.'

'I can live without it.' I put my phone away. There wasn't any point in giving Fin or Eleanor half a story anyway.

'We can see if there's anything on telly. Or do you fancy a game of cards?' Peter walked over to a bookcase with games on the top shelf.

'Cards is fine.'

We played gin rummy to pass the time. I told Peter how I'd learned the game from my dad. He used to play with his mates at lunchtimes, when he worked in a local factory, before he took early retirement. Then he became a full-time site warden at the nature reserve where he'd met my mum. They set up house together, in the cottage Dad had bought and renovated. My mum spent a year or so convincing local people she was human before I was born. I didn't tell Peter any of that.

He told me the cunning men played a lot of cards because so many of the places where they met up were off the grid. They played for money, which sounded risky to me, having met a few of the others. A bit later, we shared the pizzas and dough balls for dinner. Neither of us had a beer. I wanted to be fully alert tonight. I guessed Peter had decided the same.

We didn't draw the curtains. Outside the window, the daylight slowly faded. Finally, Peter looked at his watch and put the playing cards back in their box. 'Time to go. What do you want to carry?'

'I'll take the salt, to start with.' Nine kilos may not sound that much, but I didn't know how far we were going. 'I'll let you know when I'm ready to swap.'

I fetched a couple of hessian carrier bags from the Landy and put three bags of salt in each one. Equal weight in both hands would make carrying the load easier. The sun was below the horizon by now, but I could see the horizon clearly enough and the sky was still bright in the west. Overhead, the first stars were appearing.

Peter led the way. The track we'd driven up continued over the crest of the hill. It dwindled into a grassy path. Peter didn't have a torch, but he had no trouble following it. Maybe he got the benefit of a cat's night vision without having to change shape. I could see where we were going thanks to my mother's blood.

We carried on walking as the last of the daylight faded and a glimmer of twilight lingered overhead. We were far enough north and far enough into the year for this to be as dark as the night would get. My arms were getting tired when Peter left the path. Now it was barely a suggestion of a line on the turf cropped short by sheep. It was hard to see anything clearly, and the first faint sliver of the new moon was no help.

'Watch your step,' Peter warned.

I realised we'd reached the earthwork he'd mentioned. The weathered bank and ditch were shallow enough for someone to easily walk right past them, even in the daylight. They were still a trip hazard in the dark. I followed close behind Peter as he circled around and found the entrance.

'What now?' I put down the heavy bags of salt.

Peter knelt in the centre of the grass and found the white paper tablecloth. He ripped open the cellophane. 'Get ready to weigh this down.'

The breeze would easily carry that off. The night was also cold enough on this exposed hillside that I was glad I was wearing my army-surplus coat. Still, it wasn't raining, and I wasn't going to say that out loud and tempt whoever or whatever might be able to summon a downpour around here.

Peter spread out the paper tablecloth, and I pinned down the corners with the whisky bottle, the honey, the big pot of double cream and the chicken, still in its packaging. As Peter set out everything else, I shoved wrapping and the plastic carrier bags inside the hessian ones. Littering wouldn't impress the delvers, from what Peter had said, and we were here to ask for a favour.

Peter got to his feet and picked up the first bag of salt. 'Now we pour this out in a circle, just leaving one narrow way in for the brown men. There mustn't be any other breaks in the line. Okay?'

'Okay.' This was a new one on me. 'Why?'

Peter sounded exasperated that I needed to ask. 'Because other folk besides the brown men of the moors live in these hills. Not all of them are friendly. If someone we don't want to have dealings with decides this invitation's for them, we want to be inside a barrier they cannot cross. We have to keep enough salt back to close up the circle completely,' he added.

'Right.' That was disconcerting. 'Have you done this before?'

'No.' Peter jabbed a corner of the bag of salt with the carving knife and walked away. Five paces or so from the tablecloth, he tipped up the bag and started to draw a line on the turf with the free-flowing salt. I watched as he walked slowly around the delvers' picnic. He had to bend almost double to stop the wind carrying off the salt before it reached the ground.

I wished he had mentioned this earlier. I could have calculated how much salt we would need to mark out a ring of any given diameter. A good, thick line. I'd rather not be setting up such a flimsy defence as this by eye in near-darkness.

A few minutes later, Peter stopped walking and straightened up. He looked back at the line and came back to pick up a second bag of salt. 'I think we're going to be fine. Do you want to start from the other end? Best get this done as quick as we can.'

'Right.' I made a hole in a bag of salt, dropped the carving knife onto the white paper tablecloth and walked to the other end of the line Peter had started.

'Shall we leave a metre gap?' I called out.

'That sounds about right.'

By my feet, the salt line gleamed more brightly than I expected. Was some cunning man's trickery at work? Did that matter? No. I started pouring out the salt, trying to work out how much to use. Too little and I could leave gaps in the line that we didn't even realise were there. Too much and we'd run out of salt before the ring was complete. If anyone was going to screw this up, it would be me. Unless it started raining.

It was hell on my back, but the next bag went faster, and Peter was already on his third. When the last pale trickle faded to nothing and I stood up straight, I could see we'd got it right. I had just enough salt left to complete the circle if we had to.

I stepped very carefully into the ring. Peter was kneeling on the edge of the paper tablecloth, setting out paper cups, each one standing in a paper bowl. He weighed them down with a double shot of whisky. Taking the top off the cream, he put the pot on a plate with a wooden spoon.

'Cut the bread, will you?' He opened the jar of honey and put that on a plate with a spoon.

I sliced up the sourdough loaf and split the bread between four plates. Peter took the cooked chicken out of its packaging and put it on a paper plate. He pulled the legs off, dividing them into a drumstick and a thigh joint. He carved thick slabs of breast meat and piled those onto a second plate. Then he looked around for something he could use to clean his hands.

'Here. Wet wipes.' I tossed him the packet I'd taken out of the glove box in the Landy and shoved in my coat pocket.

'Thanks.' He sat cross-legged on the ground, scrubbed the grease off his fingers and dropped the wet wipes into the rubbish bag. He tucked that inside the hessian bag where I'd put the empty salt packets.

I sat down on the other side of the tablecloth. 'So, what's next?'

'We wait.' Peter was watching the gap we had left in the salt circle.

Chapter Ten

We waited. The night was chilly but bearable. The breeze carried the reassuring scent of water and grass and growing things. Soft noises out in the darkness told me small animals were looking for food or mates or whatever mattered most to them. The night sky was darkest where the horizon merged with the shadowy landscape. Overhead, stars shone in the infinite depth of space you only see out in the country.

We waited some more. As time passed, the peace and quiet of this wilderness started losing its appeal. I shifted my position as quietly as I could, but my arse was numb and my back and legs were stiff. If anything leaped out of the darkness to rip us to shreds, I'd have to ask if I could do a few stretches first. Though hopefully the scars on my forearm would give me some forewarning. How much warning? I realised I'd never worked out how close a threat had to get before I felt its presence. I should do something about that.

How long would Peter sit here before he decided no one was interested in his picnic? No one out of the ordinary anyway. There had to be foxes around. One of those could scatter the salt with its brush or its feet as it came to investigate the smell of chicken. A badger would obliterate our circle, and I wasn't getting between one of those and free food. Badgers are solid and powerful. We might not even realise the salt barrier had been broken. A weasel or a stoat could sneak up and back off when it caught our scent without us knowing. A tree close by would have come in really handy. I could have used dryad radar to keep watch for wildlife.

Much more of this and I'd get serious cramp. Stretching out my legs, I flexed my ankles inside my work boots. I reminded myself that if something unexpectedly dangerous appeared, I could always whistle up the shuck.

That started me thinking about something else. The shuck was a creature of shadow, no question, but it didn't seem bound to this world like those kelpies. Did that mean it didn't eat people, however menacing it looked? At least, I corrected myself, that might mean the shuck living at Blithehurst didn't eat people. Myths of black dogs crop up right across Britain and far beyond. What might be true for one wasn't necessarily true for them all. It's only film and TV monsters that have to stick to some handbook of rules and regulations issued for their particular species.

That said, I'd read endless folk tales of brownies and pixies and similar earth spirits helping out in a house or a farm in return for bread and milk or cream or honey. The hobs in the Fens had been happy to share a meal, and that didn't do them any harm. I'd seen for myself they could vanish and flit from place to place as easily as ever.

'Peter. Why do you think eating human food doesn't give these delvers the same problems as the kelpies?'

The paper tablecloth rustled as he moved. 'I have no idea.'

But I could tell from his voice he was thinking about it now.

'None of this food or drink is anything they've hunted and killed for themselves,' he said a few minutes later. 'That could be significant.'

'That chicken didn't die of old age,' I pointed out, 'and I've met a hob who eats pork pies every chance he gets.'

'But chickens and pigs are raised to be eaten,' Peter countered, 'and someone else has done the slaughtering.'

Out in the darkness, a chuckle floated through the night.

'Hello?' Peter's voice tensed. 'May I ask, who's there?'

'May I ask who you were expecting?' Whoever answered him sounded amused, in a soft Scottish accent. I could understand every word, and that was a relief. This wouldn't be like dealing with the near-incomprehensible kelpies.

'We hoped we might speak with the men of the moors.' The shape in the near-darkness that was Peter shifted and the tablecloth rustled again. 'We have meat and drink to offer.'

'You say "we",' the voice said thoughtfully. 'But you two are not brethren.'

I cleared my throat. 'We're allies. Working together.'

'Aye, that's what allies do.' A short, stocky figure approached the entrance to our salt circle. 'You're a long way from home, son of the greenwood. What brings you to our hills?'

I don't know if we'd been sitting there for so long that the sky was starting to lighten or if the delver did something to make himself more visible. Either way, I could see he had a bushy dark beard, and long hair tied back in a braid. I couldn't see what he wore on his legs or feet, but his sleeveless jerkin looked like leather.

Like the hob I'd met in the Fens, his skin was deeply tanned. But the hob had been an earth spirit in a very obvious and literal sense. He'd had mud on his feet and his hands and matted in his hair. This delver's skin was as smooth as polished stone. Both had golden eyes, but the hob's gaze had gleamed like sunset. The delver's paler eyes had a distinctly metallic glint.

If we stood side by side, the top of the delver's head would be roughly level with my belt. I wasn't stupid enough to think I could take him in a fight. Even without whatever magic he could call on, his bare arms were muscled like a weightlifter's. Also, he'd brought backup.

A handful of figures roughly the same size and shape stood some way off. Maybe more than a handful. I couldn't get an accurate count while they kept moving about. They seemed to be talking among themselves, though I couldn't make out a word, and not just because of the distance. The delvers were doing something to make sure they weren't overheard. Whenever one of them glanced our way, their eyes glittered like fool's gold. Even working together, Peter and I wouldn't stand a chance against this squad.

So I was very relieved not to feel a thing from my scars. I also didn't see anything to be gained by pissing about. It was late and I was tired, cold and stiff. 'I've come to ask for your help.'

Before Peter could interrupt, I told the delver the whole story. Most of it, anyway. The important stuff, though I didn't share anyone's names. I didn't introduce myself either. That could come later. I didn't mention Conn or Alexander the selkie. I implied that my friend researching myths about silver chains had come across that obscure legend about the kelpies. Since kelpies belonged in Scotland, I had decided consulting the cunning men I knew was my logical next step.

'If the beasts are going to tell us who's forcing them to cause so much trouble, we have to try to find a way to replace the silver chains that have been stolen and most likely destroyed. My friend here—' I nodded at Peter '—tells me you might know how that could be done.' I was careful to avoid making any sort of direct request.

'Does he?' The delver's voice hardened. 'To answer your question, son of the greenwood, we can eat food such as you offer us here because we belong to this place, alongside the spirits of wood, water and air whom I assume you know. It's those who do not belong here who find themselves snared by their appetites and mired by hunger. They were lured out of the darkness where they should have stayed by deceitful promises from those lusting for power they could not come by honestly.'

So the delvers knew what the cunning men had done and they didn't like it. That explained why Peter had no chance of getting help from them on his own. I was trying to work out what to say next when he spoke up.

'I cannot undo the misdeeds of those who came before me. I can and will answer for my own actions. I am here to help my friend, no more and no less. This food and drink is offered to prove my good faith, without expectation or obligation.'

'So you say.' The delver didn't actually call him a liar, but his meaning was clear.

I interrupted before Peter could say anything. 'I – we – the Green Man and everyone caught up in this – we want to stop these kelpies hurting anyone else or causing any more damage. I want to find out who's behind this and stop whatever they're doing.'

The delver looked at me, not saying a word. His backup squad stood still and silent. I waited. So did Peter. I was ready for them to disappear. Eventually, the delver leader waved a hand. I saw he was pointing at the bread board and the knives.

'Put those blades beyond your reach, outside this circle.'

Since asking why risked him thinking I didn't want to do it, I got stiffly to my feet and picked them up. It was a relief to get some blood flowing in my feet and legs. The delver squad watched me intently. I walked to the opposite side of the circle, as far away from them as I could get. Reaching out across the salt, very careful not to disturb the pale line, I threw the knives at the turf, hard and point first. The blades stuck into the ground.

'Now, close up this circle.' The delver leader was still only talking to me, so Peter didn't move.

I used the last of the salt to join the ends of the pale line on the grass. The sky was definitely growing lighter. I could see the delver support squad weren't happy about this. Some were arguing with emphatic gestures. But their leader had helped himself to a slice of sourdough bread, and he was using a wooden spoon to cover it with cream and honey. Peter still hadn't moved.

I stayed where I was, to avoid looming over the delver. I waited for him to finish eating. Swallowing his last mouthful, he licked his lips and his fingertips. I wondered where the wet wipes had gone. We should have bought some paper napkins in the supermarket. The delver sipped a tot of whisky, nodded with approval, and drank the rest. I wondered if Peter was going to point out that was the cunning men's work.

The delver looked thoughtful, and I realised he didn't mind me seeing he was considering what to say next. That was interesting, though I couldn't decide exactly why.

'Do you not think,' he said finally, 'that whoever is forcing these kelpies to do their bidding would know who might be able to replace what has been stolen and destroyed? Do you not think they would have already taken steps to prevent you securing such help?'

Shit. We'd come all this way to learn that whoever was behind this bollocks, they were one step ahead of us. The delver looked steadily at me.

'Do you not think they would have threatened those who could have helped you as mercilessly as they have threatened those kelpies? That seeing their baleful assurances of vengeance fulfilled would be a compelling warning to refuse you any aid? Even those not involved would see their wisest course is not to anger whoever lurks in these shadows.'

Make that two or three steps ahead of us. Fuck.

The delver picked up one of the untouched paper cups of whisky. I expected him to drink it. Instead he came over and handed it to me. 'You look like a man who could use a drink.'

He walked back and helped himself to another tot, or I supposed it was a dram since we were in Scotland. He was still ignoring Peter.

I took a sip. I don't usually drink whisky neat, but this was silky smooth, aromatic and warming. I saw the delver looking at me, expectant. I thought about what he had just said. He'd sounded like a lawyer in some TV cop show, making sure a client didn't technically confess by starting every admission with 'hypothetically speaking'.

I looked at the ring of salt surrounding us. Did that mean whoever was behind this couldn't hear what the delver had said? Maybe, maybe not, but regardless, the delver had offered me a major gesture of trust. He had let me close this circle with him inside with me and Peter. Without those knives within reach, because he wasn't stupid. The delvers didn't trust the cunning men, and that wasn't going to change. But I was here on the Green Man's behalf, and I was starting to think the delver wanted his – my – help.

'If whoever made such threats could be found,' I said cautiously, 'and if steps could be taken to make absolutely certain they couldn't do any such harm, would it be reasonable to hope we might be able to get the help we are looking for?'

The delver took a moment to answer. 'If such a menace was to be lifted, it would be reasonable to expect any interested parties could have that conversation in due course.'

I unravelled that and wondered why he didn't just say, 'You might very well think that, but I couldn't possibly comment.' Peter had said the delvers took an interest in what went on above ground. Given the way their leader was talking, I was starting to think they spent a fair bit of time around the people who visited these hills, staying unseen and unheard.

Peter raised a hand. He was still sitting down on the turf.

The delver looked at him, still unfriendly. 'You have something to say?'

'If the silver chains that have been stolen or destroyed could be replaced, perhaps that could be considered restoring a balance that has been disturbed?'

I wasn't sure exactly what Peter was saying, but the delver tilted his head, considering this. He studied the young cunning man, then reached for the last dram of whisky and handed it to him.

'I'll drink to that.'

Peter raised the paper cup. 'Slàinte mhath.'

I don't understand Gaelic, but I know that one. 'Cheers.'

I drank the rest of my whisky, which made me unexpectedly light-headed for a moment. We'd eaten those pizzas hours ago. It was a good thing neither of us would be driving back home tonight – this morning – whatever the hell the time was.

'Very well,' the delver said briskly. 'I'll bid you farewell for now. If you would be good enough to make a doorway?'

This time he did look at Peter as he gestured towards the pale line of salt.

'Of course.' Peter stood up, and the turf where I'd closed up the circle turned blurry.

A very specific breeze carried off a metre or so of salt and scattered it high in the air. The delver didn't move, though, and his backup squad was walking towards us.

Peter saw them too. 'Will you accept our hospitality?'

The delver shrugged. 'Since you have offered, it would be ungracious to refuse.'

Peter nodded. 'You're welcome.'

There was more going on under the surface of that conversation too. Fine. I could ask Peter if I needed to know.

'Thank you for your time,' I said to the delver leader. 'I hope to see you again.'

He nodded, but he didn't answer me. Was that because the circle was open? The other delvers were close enough to hear as well. They wore leather jerkins like their leader, and leggings that reached to their knees. Thinking about the family portraits in Blithehurst's gallery, Eleanor would probably call them breeches. The delvers were barefoot, and one tapped his toes on the turf, impatient for Peter and me to leave.

I picked up the bag of rubbish and everything else. Stepping over the salt circle, I retrieved the knives I'd stuck in the turf. I could see the delvers watching me warily. I didn't look directly back at them. Best to avoid anything that might seem like a challenge.

Peter was waiting at the entrance to the earthwork. I joined him and we walked away. Finding the path to take us down off the moor was easy enough now the morning sky was getting brighter. I looked back just once, to make sure we were out of sight of the circle.

'The delvers like to see balance restored?' I glanced at Peter. 'Does that mean they want everything to stay the same?'

'There's more to it than that.' He stuck his hands in his pockets as we walked. 'They accept change is natural, and I don't just mean the passing seasons and things like erosion that they see going on around them. They have no problem with people farming the land or mining for metals. They're artisans themselves. What matters is how things are done. Sustainable farming is fine, and so is following a seam of ore by digging a tunnel to extract it with minimal impact. What pisses them off is opencast mining or industrial farming that exhausts the soil before poisoning it with weedkiller and fertiliser. Time was they would fight back by breaking tools and machinery. These days they've retreated to places where they know they won't be bothered.'

'You know a lot about them.' Did that mean he had some idea what the sodding hell was going on?

'Considering how much they dislike us, you mean?' Peter shook his head. 'There's more to that as well. Delvers don't mind cunning folk using magic for useful, restorative things, like healing a broken bone, or curing an infection. Finding something that's been lost is restoring a possession to its rightful owner. Finding someone who's run away from a violent marriage or an abusive parent? That's not okay with them. They believe those situations are an offence against the natural order in the first place.'

'Was there something specific a cunning man did to really piss them off?' Apart from making a deal with the kelpies to gain the power to change shape. That had to be what the delver leader had been talking about.

'Possibly. Probably,' Peter admitted. 'Who knows? We don't. You have to understand how much of our history has been lost. And back in the day, different groups of cunning men were following different traditions. They might work together from time to time, on their own or in groups, but they wouldn't necessarily share what they knew. When a cunning man died, a lot of their secrets died with them, especially if they didn't have an apprentice. Barely anything was written down. Keeping records or notes on rituals was too risky, even for a healer. Anything on paper could be twisted and used against them. Unless they were rich and well connected. Then the rules were different.'

'No change there then,' I commented.

'The delvers don't only disapprove of us, you know,' Peter added. 'Your friend Hazel wouldn't be any more welcome than I was up there. A hedgewitch lifting a curse means another one had cast it first. Helping a childless couple to conceive would be doing a kindness. Giving a second husband or wife an heir to disinherit an older child who'd lost their parent, that's spiteful. The delvers know wise women did things like that, and they have long memories.'

'Right.' I had no problem believing some wise women could behave as badly as some cunning men. And this wasn't all in the past. The Green Man had sent me after a couple of arrogant pricks trying to use arcane lore to get rich quick by dominating and manipulating people who had no idea what was going on, or by compelling spirits like hobs and sylphs to obey them.

We walked on until I saw the long low roof of the house ahead. 'What now?'

'We get some sleep?' Peter yawned. 'Then try to think who or what could be threatening delvers as well as kelpies.'

'And what the hell do they want?' I was getting fed up with hitting dead ends.

'Maybe working out their end game will show us who's behind the curtain,' Peter suggested.

'Perhaps.' I didn't share his optimism.

We got back to the house and we both went to bed. The thick curtains in my room kept out most of the daylight, so I slept well enough. I was still pissed off when I woke up. I wanted to get back to a normal routine. I'm not sodding nocturnal.

I checked the time on my phone. Just after midday. If I set off inside the next hour or so, I should reach Blithehurst in time to eat dinner at a sensible time. Assuming I didn't get a whole load of messages telling me something drastic had happened as soon as my phone found a decent signal. I really hoped that didn't happen.

A door opened and closed, and I heard the shower running. I got up and went to put the kettle on while I waited for my turn. I had just come out of the bathroom when we were both surprised by a knock at the door.

'I'll get it.' Peter opened the door. It was sticking again. If I'd put a plane in my toolbox, I could have sorted that out.

No one was waiting outside. Peter picked up a cloth bundle from the step. He closed the door and brought it over to the table. What looked like half an old bedsheet had been knotted around something. Peter untied it and we saw the empty whisky bottle, the used paper plates and cups, wooden cutlery and everything else we had left up at the earthwork. The cream and honey had been eaten, and I couldn't see any chicken bones.

'Let's hope,' Peter said cautiously, 'this means we have a deal.'

Chapter Eleven

We ate breakfast and washed up. I rinsed a plate under the tap and passed it to Peter. 'What now?'

'There's no more to be done here.' He dried the plate. 'The delvers aren't going to tell us who's threatening them. So how do we find that out for ourselves?' He was asking me, himself and the entire universe.

I sponged egg off the second plate. 'I'd ask the wise women.'

Peter wouldn't like that. Tough. The cunning men had survived by heading for the hills, every one for himself and travelling light. The wise women had gone to ground. Keeping their heads down, they'd watched each other's backs and found ways to be the first to hear any rumour of witchcraft. When one of them had to run, the others helped her hide.

Paranoia about magic had faded. Getting in touch with each other got easier, from the invention of telegrams onwards. The wise women's early-warning system became a network to share news of clashes between the everyday world and the things that go bump in the night. They got very good at shutting down trouble and convincing ordinary people that nothing in folklore or fairy tales could be real.

Peter took the plate. 'Could you give me a day or so to see if Iain will agree, please?'

He didn't sound optimistic, and neither was I. On the other hand, I knew the wise women's network in Scotland was limited. 'Okay. Ask Iain to send someone looking for kelpies who haven't come south. See what they know. There has to be some lead we can follow.'

'Let's hope so.' Peter started drying the cutlery.

'Ask anyone else who might know something.' I started scouring the frying pan. 'Selkies, mermaids. I'll see what the dryads and naiads have to say.'

But we weren't looking for a needle in a haystack. We didn't even know where the field the haystack was in might be. And Iain's authority over the cunning men only went so far. He could ask them to help us, but he couldn't make that an order. They weren't a democracy.

'Right.' Peter opened the fridge. 'Do you want to take these beers with you?'

He'd paid for them, but I wasn't going to argue. 'Okay. Thanks.'

We emptied the fridge and packed up. I put my overnight bag in the Landy and took the rubbish bag to the bin by the lane. Peter put the key back in the lockbox. I got settled in the Landy and told the satnav to take me home.

Peter followed me down the track in the Toyota. He turned right onto the lane after I turned left. I drove along the narrow moorland roads until I reached the A68. Then I followed the A7 towards Carlisle, where I'd join the M6. That was the plan, anyway, if I ever got through the endless sodding roadworks.

My mobile started ringing not far from the motorway. I let it go to voicemail. The last thing I needed was a fine and points on my licence for taking a call when I was driving. I didn't want to get into an accident either. My phone rang again though, and a third time. A few minutes later, the phone told me I had a text. And another text. This couldn't be good.

I saw a safe place to stop and pulled over. I turned off the engine and checked my phone. Three missed calls from Eleanor, and two texts saying 'Call me AT ONCE'. Shit. Had something happened to Fin? Fin and Blanche? Otherwise

Blanche would be calling, wouldn't she, or Iris? Wouldn't Zan have turned up?

My heart was pounding as I returned Eleanor's call. 'Hi. What's—'

'Daniel, good.' She spoke over me, crisp and official. 'What time do you think you'll be back?'

'Some time between seven and eight, depending on the traffic.' I heard Eleanor repeat that to someone else. At least two people were with her.

'Tomorrow morning will be fine,' one of the voices said.

'We open at ten o'clock.' Eleanor was still speaking to them. 'Daniel? Come up to my office first thing tomorrow. The police want to speak to you.'

What the fuck? 'Is there some problem?'

'We'll save any questions for tomorrow,' the second voice told Eleanor firmly.

Good luck with that. I'd ask what this was about as soon as I got back to Blithehurst.

'How did you get on?' Eleanor asked me. 'With the wood sculpture commission?'

'Oh, right. I think I can do something with it. It depends on the client.' I stopped talking before I said anything too definite.

'Good. I'll see you in the morning. Have a good journey.' Eleanor ended the call.

I sat in the Landy by the side of the road, staring at my phone. Eleanor hadn't ever spoken to me like, well, the lady of the manor before. That's not how she treated any of the staff. And why did the police want to talk to me? Was this about the craft show robbery? If it was, why wouldn't Eleanor say that?

I called Peter. He spoke loudly over traffic noise.

'Dan? Is everything okay?'

'I need an alibi. Eleanor called. The cops want to see me tomorrow.'

'What about?' Peter was as startled as me.

'No clue, but something's up. Eleanor told them I've been away looking at a possible commission for a wood carving. If you look at the Blithehurst website, you'll see—'

'Aye, I know, like yon knight. Leave it with me.'

He ended the call, and I stared at my phone some more. I wondered how much interest the cunning men were taking in me, if Peter knew about my carving of Sir Graelent.

I turned the key and started driving again. If he didn't get back to me with a cover story, I'd ring Hazel first thing. The wise women would be able to help. I'd have to tell her what was going on, but that was going to happen sooner or later. If the cunning men didn't like it, that was their problem. Though one way or another, I'd end up in somebody's debt.

I got onto the motorway, but I couldn't stop wondering what the fuck the cops wanted. I stopped at the Tebay services to calm down before I caused a pile-up. I had a pot of tea and a piece of chocolate cake, and bought some cheese and bacon and sausages from the farm shop. The downside of making that stop was hitting rush hour traffic from Preston to Knutsford. It was well past eight o'clock before I got back to Blithehurst.

I parked in the dairy yard and walked up to the house. The front entrance was dark, and that was odd. Eleanor usually leaves the porch light on when the house is closed, to tell any passing prowler someone is still inside.

The motion-sensor lights lit up the gravel as I went around to the side door. Warning beeps that told me the alarm was set. I hurried into the staff room and entered the code to shut it down. Eleanor didn't need me calling out the security firm by mistake. She must have gone out for the evening if she'd switched the alarm on this early. I walked through the hall and the dining room to the bottom of the main staircase. The house was silent. I retraced my steps and looked into the library. Specifically, I looked up at the ceiling. I didn't see a glimmer of the Green Man's presence. Did that mean everything was fine?

I tried to ring Eleanor. My call went straight to voicemail. I didn't leave a message. Resetting the alarm, I locked up and left. Going back to the dairy yard, I deleted the history on my satnav. Now no one would be able to prove where the Land Rover had or hadn't been from that. Better safe than sorry. Then I got my bags and the beers out of the passenger footwell and walked down to my cottage.

It was a mild night and the woods were peaceful. The shuck wasn't around, and I didn't see any of the dryads. I put the beers and everything else in the fridge. Then I went to bed. It wasn't late, but I was knackered. I'd done a shitload of driving in the past two days, and let's be honest, a Land Rover isn't the ideal vehicle for long journeys. I'd been up half the night twice this week as well. I set an alarm on my phone to give me time to check in with Peter, eat breakfast and have a shower and a shave before I had to talk to the cops.

It took a bit of finding, but I wore my Blithehurst staff polo shirt up to the manor in the morning. I got there at five to ten. In the hall, Abigail was checking the velvet ropes that keep sticky fingers off the glass-fronted china cabinets and away from the ornaments on the mantelpiece. Those little posts get nudged out of place every single day.

I went up the main stairs, apprehensive. Eleanor hadn't called me back, but at least Peter had been in touch. The weight of my phone in my pocket was some reassurance.

In the upstairs corridor, I knocked on Eleanor's sitting room door. 'Miss Beauchene?'

'Come in.'

I opened the door and saw Eleanor in her usual seat in the bay window. Between her and the door, two upright chairs had their backs against the wall, facing the fireplace. Two coppers in uniform were already waiting for me. The woman closest to the door was about my age. She had short dark hair and shrewd brown eyes. The other woman was older, with grey hair brushing her shoulders.

Eleanor was talking to her. 'As you can see, we haven't spoken since yesterday. I spent the evening and the night at my parents' house. They will confirm that none of us saw Daniel.'

The one with grey hair handed back her phone. 'Thank you.'

'Mr Mackmain. Good morning.' The younger officer got to her feet. 'Please, take a seat.'

That meant I'd be sitting on the sofa. Not my first choice, but I wouldn't be towering over everyone else in the room.

Eleanor got up from her chair. 'You'll excuse me if I lock the door. You wouldn't believe how often a visitor will try the handle. We don't want to be interrupted.'

She didn't wait for an answer before she walked over to turn the key. The grey-haired officer didn't look keen, but she decided to put up with it. I saw Eleanor's quick nod of approval at my staff polo shirt. Her expression also warned me that whatever was going on was serious.

The younger copper smiled at me as she checked her Batman utility belt for... what? A Taser? Pepper spray? Sitting down, I did my best to look harmless. I waited for someone else to say something first.

The grey-haired officer offered me her quick and meaningless smile. 'How would you describe your relationship with Eleanor, Daniel?'

Sorry, what? 'She's my boss.'

'But you're friends,' the older copper prompted.

'We're friendly, yes.' I couldn't work out what they wanted, so I told them the truth. 'Miss Beauchene's friendly with all the staff. She's a good boss.'

'You live on the estate, quite close by?'

That was barely a question. 'Yes.'

'And Eleanor lives in the manor. Do you socialise much when the house is closed?'

I was glad the grey-haired officer could see I was genuinely confused. I also tried to work out where the trap was. Because there was definitely a trap. I'd better not say anything someone else could contradict. Anyone who had ever seen us in the pub could tell the cops Eleanor and I were relaxed in each other's company.

'We go out to have dinner together sometimes, to the pub or for a curry. If there's estate business to talk about, or if one of us has had enough of eating alone.' I shrugged. 'We get on.'

The younger copper nodded. 'Why not? You're both single.'

That sounded like a throwaway line, but the grey-haired officer was watching me intently.

'No, I'm not. I've got a girlfriend. She lives near Bristol.'

'Is that where you've been for the past few days?' the older copper asked a bit too casually. 'How often do you see her?'

'As often as I can, and when I can't, I'm not screwing my boss.' I looked at Eleanor. 'What's going on?'

'Coercive control,' she said icily. 'According to some busybody who's rung the police with an anonymous tip-off to waste their time and mine.'

'If you don't mind, Miss Beauchene.' Annoyed, the grey-haired officer raised a hand to stop her talking.

I looked at Eleanor, incredulous. 'Excuse me?'

'Apparently you have some sort of hold over me.' Her sarcasm could have stripped paint. 'You get paid a ridiculously high salary even though you only work when you feel like it. I can't stop you going off who knows where, any time you want. You don't let me have other friends, and you keep me away from my family as much as you possibly can. You even stop me leaving the estate, apparently.'

I looked at the coppers. 'This is bullshit.'

Coldly furious, Eleanor continued. 'I told these officers this is complete nonsense yesterday. I explained your working arrangements and showed them your payslips. I have taken them through my diary and the amount of work needed to keep this business running. I wasn't aware it would be considered suspicious to spend what little free time I do have on my own with my books. I didn't realise it's compulsory to be part of a couple by a certain age. Apparently my word isn't good enough. Presumably I'm scared of your retaliation if I confess what's really going on.'

The police officers waited a moment to be sure she had finished speaking. I'd seen people underestimate Eleanor before. They don't do it twice. She can cut someone off at the knees with the unshakeable confidence people learn in expensive private schools. Her ability to find the weak points in anyone's argument, before she destroys them with razor-sharp words, comes from her history PhD, as well as a lifetime dealing with dryads.

The younger woman tried again. 'Miss Beauchene—'

'I have asked to see their evidence.' Eleanor was still talking to me. 'Obviously, they won't tell me who's been making these ridiculous accusations.'

I took my phone out of my pocket and looked at the grey-haired officer. 'I can give you my girlfriend's contact details. She'll tell you this is total crap. I've been away to discuss a commission for a wood sculpture. I got a text about it this morning.'

I tapped the screen to bring up the message and turned it towards them. However Peter had managed it, the Laird of Strathlearag thanked me for making the trip. He confirmed my initial quote was acceptable and suggested several dates his family would find convenient for me to start work, subject to my employer's agreement.

'A big Douglas fir came down in a storm last winter. He wants what's left carved into a unicorn.'

Obviously I'd deleted the texts between me and Peter where we'd come up with this idea while I was eating breakfast. He assured me the laird was a real person who would confirm the story if the police got in touch. I'd wondered if he was a cunning man, or someone who owed Iain a favour.

'Thank you, Mr Mackmain.' The grey-haired cop didn't reach for my phone. She and her colleague exchanged a glance. They were ready to leave.

I had a question before they went. While Eleanor was speaking, I'd been thinking. 'Did this tip-off come from a woman called Denise?'

'I'm sorry,' the older officer said quickly. 'Details of complaints are confidential.'

She wasn't fast enough. I saw a flicker of recognition in the younger copper's brown eyes. If she ever played cards, she'd better not try poker.

'Denise Hindlow?' Eleanor's anger found another gear. 'She's behind this nonsense?'

'We can't—'

The grey-haired officer raised a hand to stop her younger colleague speaking. 'Why would you think that, Mr Mackmain?'

Now I had to make an effort to keep my temper. 'Because she was always making up stupid shit when she worked here, especially about Eleanor. After she'd left, the restaurant got a load of bad reviews online, complaining about stuff that never happened, like a customer finding hair in their soup. But there were enough details regular customers would recognise, to make them think it was the truth. Ask any of the staff. Everyone thought it was her. Whoever's made up this crap about me and Eleanor, they know enough to put together a story that's just about believable for someone who doesn't know us.'

'The woman is a fantasist,' Eleanor said curtly.

The older officer turned to look at her. 'Why would she do something like this? Does she have some sort of grievance?'

I half expected her to say 'hypothetically speaking'. Neither cop was going to confirm or deny where this accusation had come from, but that didn't matter. We knew who we were talking about.

'If she does, she's invented that too,' snapped Eleanor. 'She handed in her notice and left of her own accord. I don't mind saying I was glad to see her go. That saved me the trouble of going through a poor-performance procedure to dismiss her. Her work was wholly unsatisfactory.'

'When was this?' the younger copper asked.

'About a year ago.' Eleanor started typing on her laptop. 'I can find you the exact date.'

'But you haven't seen her since she left your employment?'

'No.' Eleanor shook her head as she reached for her computer mouse.

The grey-haired officer looked at me. 'How about you, Mr Mackmain?'

'I didn't like her. She was always sticking her nose into other people's business and pestering me to sign up for stupid social media stuff. I stayed away from her as much as I could.'

'I meant, did you see her after she left her job here?'

Shit. I was going to have to be very careful. 'Just once.'

'When was that?'

Bollocks. What did this copper know?

'On Sophie Beauchene's wedding day last summer,' I said reluctantly. 'I saw Denise sneaking around, down by the castle. That's where the ceremony was going to be held, and the reception.'

'Did you speak to her?'

'Just a moment,' Eleanor interrupted. 'Dan, what are you talking about? Why didn't you fetch me when you saw Denise?'

She was genuinely angry with me. That should help convince these police officers I hadn't got a hope of intimidating her.

'I didn't want to spoil your family's day,' I protested. 'If Denise wanted to make a fuss to get attention, I wasn't going to help her.'

To be strictly accurate, the dryads had seen Denise first. They had sent her wandering around a distant bit of the estate, so mazed she didn't know where she was or what was going on. They only asked for my help to get her back to her car. They swore Denise wouldn't remember a thing. I hoped to fuck they were right.

'She left using the public footpath.' I gestured through the window towards the far side of the valley. 'I've no idea where she went after I lost sight of her.'

That was true as far as it went. Asca and Frai had helped me get Denise along the footpath to the road. I'd dumped her on the grass verge in the shade of her parked car. She'd been nearly unconscious with heat stroke. I had no idea where the ambulance or whoever answered the 999 call I made on her phone had taken her.

I'd assumed she had survived. I'd checked the local newspaper website for accidental deaths for the next few weeks and her name hadn't come up. That was a relief. I detested the woman, but I didn't want her dead. Not back then anyway.

'If she is behind this slander, there's something you should see.' Eleanor was hitting her keyboard hard and fast. She spun the laptop around to show the police officers the screen.

I recognised the photo of the derelict watermill on the Blithehurst estate. By derelict, I mean it's completely and utterly trashed. We keep it securely fenced off and the estate paths leading to it are closed. It's not even marked on the maps given out to visitors. I got up from the sofa to take a closer look at the writing across the top of the screen.

How Did Robert Beauchene Die? We Demand The Truth!

What the fuck? I barely managed not to say that out loud.

'She is a fantasist and a conspiracy theorist.' Eleanor sat back in her chair, folding her arms tight, as if that was the only way to hold in her rage. 'She maintains that some secret about my brother's death is being deliberately concealed by yourselves, the coroner's court and, of course, by my family. She set up this revolting website a while ago. Her name's not on it anywhere, but we retained an IT specialist who traced it back to her easily enough. We're taking legal advice on the best way to shut down the site and, if possible, take Ms Hindlow to court.'

As she was talking, Eleanor was writing on a notepad. She tore off the top page and handed it to the younger officer.

'That's our family solicitor, the partner who's dealing with this, and her direct number. Please contact her if you have any further questions. She will want full details of these unfounded allegations about Daniel and myself. I suggest you let the relevant department know to expect her call. Now, let me show you out.'

That wasn't a suggestion. Eleanor was telling these coppers their time was up with the authority of a bloodline going back a thousand years. Sir Graelent de Beauchene had been granted the manor of Blithehurst on condition he slaughtered the wyrm living in the swampy valley when the Normans arrived. Right now, Eleanor looked angry enough to draw her ancestor's sword, if it had been within reach. I wouldn't have got in her way.

'Thank you.' The grey-haired officer stood up. 'And thank you for your time, Mr Mackmain.'

'No problem.' I sat back down on the sofa.

Eleanor went to unlock the door. The coppers exchanged a glance, but neither of them said a word as she held the door open. The cops went into the corridor. Eleanor followed them out.

I locked the door and waited for Eleanor to come back. I looked at the laptop, but I didn't click through to read whatever that horrible website was saying. I wondered how much trouble we were in. Unfortunately, Eleanor and I really were hiding the truth about Robbie Beauchene's death. It hadn't been a horrible, tragic accident. He had been murdered.

Chapter Twelve

Eleanor didn't come back. I was wondering where she'd gone when she rang me. I hadn't seen her pick up her phone before she left.

'I need some air. Let's get a coffee from the castle.'

'I'll meet you there.' I left the manor and took the path down past the rock garden. The Victorian Beauchenes had planted that in the hole where their Tudor ancestors had quarried stone for their new house. Going past the herbaceous borders, I crossed the immaculately mown lawn to the ruins of Sir Graelent's fortified manor. It's got a moat and battlements and a twin-towered gatehouse, so everyone calls it the castle. The gatehouse is a cafe these days. When I arrived, Eleanor was talking to Sarah the manager.

'I know it's a pain, but if you could do a quick trawl of the main websites, I'd be very grateful. Our solicitor needs as much evidence of harassment as possible if she's going to make a case.' She turned to me as I crossed the footbridge over the moat. She looked stressed instead of angry now. 'I got you a tea.'

'Thanks.' I took the takeaway cup and nodded to Sarah. 'Morning.'

'Hi.' Sarah greeted me with a gleam in her eye. She'd never liked Denise. 'I'll let you know what I find, no problem. Right, no rest for the wicked.' She went back into the gatehouse.

'Do you want to sit in the wilderness garden?' That was the closest place I could think of to find some peace and quiet. With luck, anyway. There were plenty of visitors around.

Eleanor shook her head. 'Let's go up to the temple.'

We left the castle and crossed the lawn to the bridge over the river. The other side of the valley has been wooded pasture since the Middle Ages. These days, organic rare-breed white cattle graze there. The meat's another income stream for the Beauchene family trust. The cows ignored us as we walked up the long sloping path to the eighteenth-century Greek-style temple high on the skyline. It's more of a climb than most visitors expect when they look up from the bridge. I was glad to sit down on one of the curved marble benches and drink my tea.

Eleanor sipped her coffee, staring into space. Since no one else was up here, I looked around for the dryads. This is usually a good place to come to let them know we want to talk. Asca had been the model for the barely dressed statue of Venus on the circular temple's plinth.

'What's this about bloody Denise trying to gatecrash Sophie's wedding?' Eleanor asked after a few minutes.

I told her what had happened. I assumed we'd come up here because she guessed the dryads had been involved. Asca and Frai didn't show up to explain themselves though.

Eleanor listened, slowly drinking her coffee. 'Is that everything?'

'Not quite,' I admitted. 'I had a look at her phone. There were loads of photos of you and Sophie, and your mum and dad. She'd been stalking all of you. I did think about going to the cops, but I'd have to explain what I'd been doing with her phone. So I deleted them.'

There are advantages and disadvantages to having a dryad in your family tree. Those can be two sides of the same thing. Take the dryads' and naiads' allure which the kelpies envied. In my teens and twenties, I'd enjoyed being able to get girls I fancied into bed quickly and easily. Everyone had a good time, so no harm, no foul, right? I knew better these days. Eleanor and Sophie had grown up being pestered by

153

men who didn't want to take no for an answer. I'd assumed the Beauchenes' greenwood blood explained Denise's obsession with the family.

'Why didn't you—?' Eleanor shook her head. 'Because you didn't want to worry me. The same reason I didn't tell you about that disgusting website. You say you deleted those photos? Just from her phone? Did you have the option to delete backups in the cloud or on another device?'

'I don't think so.' I couldn't remember seeing anything like that.

Eleanor nodded. 'If we can come up with a good reason for the cops to look at her laptop, maybe she'll still have them. I'll need to convince Lucinda that I have solid grounds for suspicion... Our solicitor,' she explained.

'Can you hold off on that? Just for a bit.'

'Why?' Eleanor was getting her usual focus back. That was a relief.

'When did you first see that website about Rob?' I'd been thinking about that while I waited in the sitting room.

'Early April. Ben found it by accident.' Eleanor grimaced. 'He put the link up on the family chat. I wish he'd talked to me first. Anyway, Sophie came over, and she was able to calm Mum and Dad down. She got Lucinda on to it straight away. They've been friends since uni.'

'Right.' I don't know Sophie Beauchene very well, but she's a solicitor in Manchester. Ben's an architect, living in London.

'The thing is,' Eleanor said, frustrated, 'Denise only moved here when she'd retired. That was four or five years after Rob died. She never even met him.'

'But she'd been asking Sarah and the other staff what had happened to Rob, just before she quit. Don't you remember?' I'd done my best to ignore the bloody woman when she insisted on talking at me. Apparently, I hadn't tuned out everything she'd said.

Eleanor looked thoughtful. 'She was convinced there must be details only close friends and family had shared. I think she wanted to be in that inner circle. But she believed the coroner's report. That there'd been an awful accident.'

'So what's changed? Something must have happened. She got bored with posting those fake reviews after a couple of months. The last I heard, Sarah said she hadn't updated her stupid Blithehurst fan site for ages.'

Denise's obsession with the Beauchenes should have faded when she wasn't around the family any more. A dryad's allure is strongest when they're up close and interested in getting personal. I'd also hoped Denise waking up in an ambulance or in hospital, with no idea what had happened after she'd gone to Blithehurst, might have scared her into staying away.

'Why start shit-stirring about Rob's death now?' I kept coming back to that while I was trying to make sense of this. 'Why make up stupid lies about you and me, when anyone who works here will tell the police that's crap?'

Eleanor took the lid off her empty coffee cup and stacked mine inside it. 'I take it you have a theory?'

'You said it yourself. Dealing with this crap is wasting our time. Not only yours and mine. Fin and Blanche have got to clear up that damage to their beaver pond now. They've got to convince the farm rewilding people the "vandalism" was a one-off. If they can't, and some sort of security gets set up, that's going to be more hassle. You're trying to get that shitty website taken down, maybe taking Denise to court. Your mum and dad, and Sophie and Ben, are upset about Rob's death all over again, so that's something else you have to handle. I'm driving here, there and everywhere, trying to find someone to make silver chains for kelpies, so they'll sod off back to wherever they should be lurking. It's endless fucking distraction, and these things are serious, so we can't let any of them go.'

I took a breath to get a grip on my frustration. 'Like they say, once is chance, twice is coincidence, but three things? That's a pattern.'

'Perhaps.' Eleanor was willing to listen, but she wasn't convinced. 'So who wants to waste our time?'

'Someone doing something they don't want us to notice. It has to be something big, if they're putting this much effort into keeping us distracted. So it's something we'd try to stop.'

'But who could "they" be?' Eleanor asked the question I couldn't answer. 'What could they be up to?'

'No clue,' I admitted, 'but if I'm right, they've screwed up by getting Denise to cause trouble.'

'How so?' Now Eleanor was interested.

'We know who she is. We know where she lives. If she's moved, we can find out where she's gone.' Now I'd realised something screwy was going on, I was going to do something about it.

'Which gets us where?' Eleanor was still cautious.

'Denise was a pain in the arse when she worked here, but she wasn't stupid.' I had to give the woman that much. 'She'd have to know that setting up that website and telling these lies to the cops could land her in deep shit. This isn't putting up a few fake reviews online. Someone has persuaded her, and I don't think they're just a fast talker.'

'You think she's under some sort of influence?' Now Eleanor saw where I was going. 'That kind of control has to be maintained.'

'Right,' I agreed. 'Whoever's doing this will have to stay close, otherwise she'll come to her senses. So let's find out who's new in her life. See where she goes and who she meets. There has to be a good chance I'll see the bastard we're after.'

Eleanor pursed her lips. 'You're going to start stalking her? I'm not sure that's a good idea. What if she sees you? What if she calls the police?'

'I'll stay out of her way. Anyway, how am I breaking the law if I'm just seeing where she goes? If a cop turns up, I'll say I'm worried that she's a threat to you or your parents, now that I've seen that website.'

Eleanor wasn't convinced. 'Can you ask Blanche's friend, the sylph, to do it?'

I shook my head. 'They're too unpredictable.'

'They can disappear completely. You're not exactly inconspicuous,' Eleanor pointed out.

'I'll be careful. If Denise does notice me and makes a fuss, the police can give me a bollocking, or a caution if that's what it takes.'

Eleanor was still shaking her head. 'Finding out who's pulling Denise's strings won't tell you why they're doing this. If you're right, it's someone or something powerful and dangerous if they can scare kelpies and delvers into doing – or not doing – what they're told. If they are using Denise against me, starting with that website, they've been planning this for a while.'

'Which is all the more reason to put a stop to whatever's going on.' I'd had enough of being pushed around. It was time to push back. 'This is the only lead we've got, isn't it? We won't know if it'll take us anywhere until I at least see what she's up to for a day or so.'

'I suppose so.' Eleanor looked a bit less tense.

'How about I go over to her house this afternoon?' It wasn't even lunchtime. There was no reason to wait.

'Won't she be at work?' Eleanor objected.

'Has she got a new job? Has anyone contacted you for a reference?'

'No,' Eleanor said reluctantly.

'If there's no sign of her, I'll come straight back.' I stood up. 'Have you got her address somewhere?'

'It'll be in her file.' But Eleanor still wasn't convinced.

She glanced around. If the dryads had been listening to our conversation, they didn't show themselves. Eleanor started down the path towards the river. I followed. I did think about asking one of the pasture's oak trees to find out where Asca and Frai were. I decided not to. If they'd been listening, they had decided not to get involved. If they didn't know, and they disapproved when they found out what I was doing, I didn't want to give them a chance to stop me.

Thinking about how dryads can screw up a car's electronics, I walked faster to reach Eleanor's side. 'Can I borrow the Fabia? Denise might recognise the Landy.'

'Good thinking.' Eleanor nodded.

We went down to the business archive in one of the manor's locked cellars. The government says you have to keep financial records for at least six years. The dates on these fire-and-waterproof filing cabinets went back ten years, and everything earlier is kept at the Dower House, where Eleanor's parents live. Both attics are full of boxes of letters and account books from the generations before Blithehurst had to be opened to the public.

Eleanor knows where everything is. She found Denise's address in a folder for ex-employees' records. She held the sheet of paper up and I got out my phone to take a photo.

'Delete that as soon as you can.'

'I will.' I checked the writing was readable. 'Where are the Fabia's keys?'

'In the office at the garden centre.' Eleanor put the folder away and locked the filing cabinet. 'I'll walk up there with you.'

The manor's stable block had been converted into garages over a hundred years ago. When Eleanor and her brothers and sister had ponies, those lived at the Home Farm. When the family realised the only way to keep Blithehurst in the family was to turn it into a visitor attraction, the stables/garages became a garden centre, a gift shop and a restaurant. Janice the restaurant manager spared us a quick nod as we went through to the staff room, but she was too busy to come and chat.

Eleanor unlocked the key cabinet in the office behind the staff room and gave me the Fabia keys. 'Be careful.'

'I will. What are you going to do?' I could see she had something in mind.

'Janice should know Denise might start posting more fake bad reviews. Though it's not easy to get them taken down, even when you've got the facts to prove they're lies.'

I saw this crap was really getting to Eleanor. The sooner I found out who was pulling Denise's strings, the better. 'I'll be back as soon as I can.'

The staff car park is behind the stable block. The old silver Fabia originally belonged to Eleanor's mum. When she'd bought a newer model, this one became the Blithehurst staff pool car. Janice and Sarah used it to go to the Cash and Carry and stuff like that. I used it when I was doing odd jobs and maintenance on properties the family owned away from the Blithehurst estate. Eleanor said that was easier than paying us individual expenses and mileage.

The Fabia didn't have a satnav, so I checked my phone for the best route to Denise's address. She lived in a village that had just about been sucked into the outskirts of Macclesfield.

It was about a half-hour drive. I turned the key and drove out of the staff car park.

With no traffic to hold me up, I found her house easily enough. As soon as a few fields were sold with planning permission for houses, this would be a Macclesfield suburb. For now, though, it could still call itself a village. Either way, it would be a nice, quiet place to live. Post-war planners had left wide grass verges between the road and the footpaths along gently curving streets.

Denise lived in a cluster of brick-built 1970s houses with sizeable gardens. I vaguely remembered her boasting to Janice about the profit she'd made selling her house somewhere in outer London. She'd had some sort of government job, so I guessed she had a decent pension, to live here on her own. Part-time wages from Blithehurst wouldn't pay her bills.

Sticking strictly to the twenty-mile-an-hour speed limit, I was having serious second thoughts about coming here. Off the main route through the village, these streets weren't simply quiet. They were deserted. The big gardens meant each house had its own drive where the few cars I could see were parked. I'd stick out like a sore thumb if I pulled up to the kerb and stayed there, sitting in the Fabia. The best I could hope for was some net curtain twitcher coming out to ask if I was lost.

Worst-case scenario was someone working from home, looking out of their window and ringing the police to report a suspicious vehicle. I had no idea how fast a police computer would link the Fabia's number plate to Blithehurst, or how soon the news would reach this morning's coppers. When it did, I'd be in the shit.

I passed Denise's house. I assumed the newish white Ford on the drive was hers. If I'd ever known what car she drove, I'd forgotten. So that should mean she was in. I stopped at the T-junction, even though there wasn't any traffic, and checked the rear-view mirror to look at her front door. What was I going to do now though? I couldn't sit here blocking the road.

Just as I thought that, the two police officers who'd come to Blithehurst came out of the house. Fuck. They hadn't wasted any time. I watched them get into the Ford. So that was an unmarked police car. At least I caught a glimpse of Denise as she closed the door, but I was already pulling away.

I turned left because that was easiest. This road took me to the oldest part of the village. Terraces of smaller ironstone houses had front doors opening onto the pavement. I passed the solitary village shop, next door to The Stag's Head pub. Seeing the pub made me realise I hadn't had any lunch. Too bad. If I went into the pub or the shop, I'd be far too memorable.

Fifty metres or so ahead, I saw a middling-sized mid-Victorian church at the edge of the village. A sign just beyond it pointed to St Osmund's car park. I turned in there and found seven cars in spaces for five times that many. I parked at the far end, to put the Fabia behind as many other vehicles as possible.

I watched the road to see if the cops in the Ford drove past. They didn't. I wondered if they had come straight here after leaving Blithehurst, to see what Denise had to say about that horrible website. If they had, I wondered what she might do about that. I pulled up a local map on my phone. Those cops could have gone in any direction from Denise's house. Still, as long as I didn't see them, that meant they hadn't seen me. Maybe. Maybe not.

I thought seriously about going back to Blithehurst. Eleanor wouldn't say 'I told you so', however loudly she might think it. But if I did, I wouldn't only have wasted a couple of hours. Denise was at home right now. She'd just had a visit from the cops. If she was going to ring whoever was getting her to harass the Beauchenes, this could be my only chance to see who turned up.

But I had to get close enough to watch Denise's house. I couldn't see anyone believing I was strolling along these empty streets, just out for a nice healthy walk. Right, after driving through miles of picturesque countryside, ignoring umpteen paths waymarked for hikers.

There was also a Church of England primary school on the other side of the road. Going-home time would be around three o'clock unless a lot had changed since I was at school. Mums and dads turning up to collect their kids would definitely look sideways at a man on his own sitting in a car park opposite the school gates. So I had to be gone by then.

I zoomed in on the map and shifted it up and down and left to right. That would have been a sodding sight easier if the phone had a bigger screen and I had smaller fingers. St Osmund's had a sizeable graveyard with what looked like two public footpaths following old field boundaries on two sides. One path started from this road, which was unsurprisingly called Church Lane. It ran along the far side of the graveyard before heading for the centre of the village. About halfway there, it crossed another path.

As far as I could tell, this second path ran between the development where Denise was living and some curly cul-de-sacs built ten or twenty years later. The online map wasn't definitive, but it looked like houses on both sides had access to the old footpath. That would be a much nicer walk to the church, or to the village shop and the pub, than the main road.

Would one of those cut-throughs give me a less obvious place to stand and watch Denise's front door? There was only one way to find out. I got out of the Fabia and walked as casually as I could along the path. The graveyard was deserted, but I glanced at the gravestones. I'd say I was looking for

162

a particular name if someone appeared with nothing better to do than chat to a stranger. That would be easier if I could find a memorial I could actually read. These old stones were weathered into lichen-spotted illegibility.

I thought about using another talent my greenwood blood has given me. When I'm in a wood or out in the countryside, I can sort of fade into the background. Ordinary people can't see I'm there. I wasn't sure it would work when I had tarmac under my feet. Add to that, this graveyard didn't have any trees, and the neatly clipped privet hedge on the boundary was barely waist high.

Besides, I didn't know if doing something out of the ordinary would attract something else's attention. Eleanor sees the ghosts at Blithehurst, and she's got used to them showing her interesting bits of the house's history. She's welcome. I've met a couple of ghosts elsewhere, and even thinking about disturbing one here gave me the creeps. I walked faster.

As I left the graveyard, white lines and blue signs divided the path between cyclists and pedestrians. A few beeches and birches on the other side of tall garden fences might have been survivors from the original hedgerows, but I mostly saw ornamental cherries, maples and magnolias. A couple of gardens had pear, apple and plum trees grafted onto dwarfing rootstocks. Would dryad radar even work through a tree like that? I wasn't going to find out. None of the fruit trees were within easy reach, even with arms as long as mine.

Checking the map on my phone again, I got my bearings. The next right turn should connect this path to the street where Denise lived. Denise's house was on the opposite side of the road, a few doors down. I walked more slowly, cautious. Whoever owned the house to the right of this cut-through had only marked their boundary with a line of lavender bushes. No good for someone my size to hide behind.

I stopped moving as soon as I saw her front door. Unsurprisingly, it was closed. She also had those slatted wooden shutters that have got so popular in her front windows. I wasn't going to be able to see any movement inside. This really had been a waste of time.

I realised someone was coming up behind me. Kneeling to retie a bootlace, I glanced over my shoulder to see who was there. A middle-aged woman with grey hair, wearing trainers, jeans and a white waterproof jacket, stopped dead in the middle of the path. For a moment, I thought she looked familiar. Then she blinked and I saw she was only pretending to be human. Her blank eyes were cold and pale, as translucent as moonstone.

She was as startled to see me as I was to recognise her true nature. She blinked again. Yes, I really had just seen that. Oh, fuck me.

She spun around and ran off. That was even more of a surprise. As I stood there, too shocked to move, a bicycle bell echoed loudly between the houses. A young woman in black Lycra leggings, a yellow nylon jacket and a black helmet shot past me on a bike with a child seat over the back wheel. She was heading towards the school. It was time for me to go.

I didn't dare go down the path after the woman with the deathly cold eyes. Not on my own, and whistling up the shuck wouldn't help me, even if I could do that in this artificial landscape. I went the other way, past Denise's house. I didn't care if she saw me and called the cops. We had way, way bigger problems now.

There were more cars in St Osmund's car park. Parents looked warily at me. I ignored them, looking out for the woman in the pale coat. I couldn't see her, but that didn't mean she wasn't around. I could only hope she wasn't willing to attack me where she'd have to kill so many witnesses.

My skin was crawling by the time I reached the Fabia. I got in and hit the button to lock the doors. Shoving the key in the ignition, I took out my phone and called Fin.

'Pick up. Pick up. Pick up.' It took me a moment to realise I was muttering out loud.

She was talking to someone else as she answered. 'Sorry, just give me a moment. Hi, Dan. What's up?'

'How soon can you get here? You know that thing we talked about? That really bad thing? It's just happened.'

Chapter Thirteen

I waited for Fin to say something. I could still hear voices at her end of the call.

'I can be there by seven,' she said after a few endless minutes.

'I'll meet you at the back gate.'

'Okay.' Fin paused again. 'Who can I tell?'

Now I had to stop and think. 'No one. Just to be safe. For now.'

'Right.' Fin took a deep breath. 'Wow.'

'Yeah.' I knew how she felt.

'See you soon.'

I started the engine and drove away. I didn't go back to Blithehurst. I headed for Manchester and the Trafford Centre. I wanted to be surrounded by concrete, glass and steel. I'd have to time my journey back carefully, to allow for the rush hour, but this was one time when I wouldn't mind crawling along in a traffic jam. I'd be safe in a nose-to-tail line of cars.

When I arrived, I wondered how to kill a couple of hours. Going to see a movie would be a waste of money. I wouldn't be able to concentrate. I'd be replaying memories I would much rather forget if I sat in the dark and quiet, or what passes for quiet in a cinema, with people whispering and crunching nachos.

I needed distraction. I needed bright artificial lighting and lots of people. I went into the shopping centre and checked the store directory. I found the bookshop and browsed the shelves for a while. I bought a couple of paperbacks and went to the nearest coffee shop. I didn't feel particularly hungry, but sitting and reading a book was a good excuse for taking my time over a pot of tea, an egg-mayo sandwich and a blueberry muffin.

I had barely read the first chapter of the historical murder mystery I'd bought when my phone rang. I swiped the red button to reject Eleanor's call. Of course, as soon as I did that, I realised she'd ring back. I thought about resetting my phone to send calls straight to voicemail. No, that was no good. Fin might ring me. I quickly texted Eleanor.

Can't talk. Back around 7.30

I left my phone on the coffee shop table, screen up. A few minutes later Eleanor texted me.

OK

I felt guilty, but this wasn't a conversation we could have on the phone. It wasn't a conversation I had ever wanted to have with her. Since I was going to have to, I wanted Fin with me. I worked out when I needed to leave, to be at Blithehurst when she arrived. I had long enough to read a few more chapters of my new book, keeping half an eye on the time.

A member of staff came over several times to collect used cups from the tables around me. I didn't look up and I didn't take the hint. If they wanted me to leave, they could say so. They didn't. Sometimes it can be useful, looking like a man it's safest not to annoy. When I got up to leave, I took my tray back to the counter. 'Thanks.'

Walking out into the crowds of hurrying people, I couldn't remember where I'd parked. For a sudden, shocking moment, I couldn't even remember which door I'd come through. Realising I was standing right where everyone else wanted to walk, I told myself to get a fucking grip. I moved over to the wall and concentrated on remembering the shops I'd first passed. I checked the store directory. Now I knew where I was, and where I had to go.

The Manchester traffic was predictably awful. Things improved the closer I got to Blithehurst. Once I left the main roads, I could put my foot down, not that the ageing Fabia had much poke. I reached the estate's back entrance at a quarter past seven. Fin was already sitting in her car by the locked gate. She couldn't have been there long. If any of the staff had seen her as they were leaving, they'd let her drive in. But everyone had gone home by now.

Fin got out of her car. As I pulled up, she came over. I lowered the window and gave her my keys. She unlocked the gate, we both drove through, and Fin snapped the padlock shut on the chain again. She followed me to park in the dairy yard. I got out of the Fabia. Fin came over to give me a hug.

'What now?' Her voice was muffled against my chest.

There was no sign of the dryads, and that was a relief. They would have to know what I had seen, and soon, but I wasn't going to talk to them until I'd told Eleanor what had happened. She would need some time to deal with this news before she'd want to talk to Asca and Frai.

'We let Eleanor know we're here.' I took out my phone.

She answered the call at once. 'Dan? Where are you?'

'I'm back. Can we meet in the library?'

'Of course.' Eleanor didn't waste time with questions.

I looked at Fin as I put my phone back in my pocket. 'What did you say to Blanche and Zan?'

'That something had come up here. That they needed to stay put and keep watch in case the kelpies came back.'

'Sounds good.' I hoped that would keep the sylph out of our hair for tonight at least. I held out my hand. Fin managed a faint smile and we walked up to the manor together. As we went in through the side door, Eleanor appeared in the kitchen doorway.

'I've got the kettle— Oh, Fin. Hello.' Puzzled, she went with the easiest question. 'Tea or coffee?'

'Coffee, please.' Fin managed to sound as if everything was normal. 'I'll just use the loo.'

'You know where it is.' Eleanor went back into the kitchen.

She probably expected me to follow her. I went into the library instead. I stared at each of the oak leaf masks in the corners of the carved ceiling. The Green Man must know I'd found the enemy he was sending me up against. Now we needed some sodding help!

Nothing happened before I heard voices behind me. Fin pushed the library door wider so Eleanor could bring in a tray with tea, coffee, mugs, milk and biscuits. She put it on the low table and dropped onto one of the sofas. I sat opposite her with Fin, facing the library's tall bay windows.

'What is going on?' Eleanor was running low on patience.

'I saw who's got at Denise. It's a wyrm.'

Eleanor went so pale I thought she was going to faint. She drew a deep, shuddering breath. We waited. She breathed out slowly.

'You're sure? Of course you are. Stupid question.' She shook her head. 'Was it...?'

She couldn't get the words out. I couldn't blame her.

'It's not the wyrm that killed Robbie.'

This is the secret Eleanor and I are hiding about her brother's death. I'd come to Blithehurst for the first time when a wyrm was trying to get to an egg that had been buried here when the river flowed through a swamp over a thousand years ago. When Sir Graelent built his castle, the egg ended up underneath his great hall.

The Green Man had sent me here because that egg had been about to hatch. The wyrm wanted to make sure its spawn found an easy first kill to fill its belly with meat.

Once it left the shadows, the first newborn serpent dragon for hundreds of years would have been loose in the English countryside.

I have no idea if the wyrm had realised Eleanor and I were intent on stopping the wyrmling, or if it simply wanted us out of the way. That didn't really matter. In its human form, it seduced Robbie Beauchene to get access to Blithehurst. When it couldn't get into the undercroft beneath the castle ruins, the monster took Robbie to the disused watermill downstream from the gardens. It made him tear down the willow trees along the banks, throwing them into the water to block the river.

When the manor's grounds began to flood, Eleanor and I came downstream to find out what the hell was going on. The wyrm reverted to its serpent form. It demolished the old mill, trying to crush us under the rubble when we tried to rescue Robbie. He died, but we survived. The Beauchenes were devastated. Things were a hundred times worse for Eleanor. She had to lie about everything, to the police, to the coroner and the health and safety people.

After that, she was determined to see both wyrms dead. I wasn't going to argue. I did nearly end up as the wyrmling's first meal before I managed to hack it to pieces. The older monster came to kill us for that. I honestly didn't think we could beat it, until the dryads, a naiad and the Green Man turned up. Plus, Eleanor had loaded a box of shotgun cartridges with ball bearings. She fired those into the wyrm, at close range. That slowed the fucker down. But the wyrm I'd seen today was a whole new threat.

'It didn't expect to see me there. It couldn't stop me seeing what it was. I saw its eyes, clear as day.' I couldn't help a shiver.

'Could it have some connection with the one that killed Robbie?' Eleanor wondered, tense. 'Is it out for revenge?'

'Does that matter?' I didn't see it was relevant.

We were in serious trouble. Any wyrm we came across had been keeping its head down, and its eyes and ears open, for hundreds of years by now. We'd already seen this one knew enough about the modern world to go after the Beauchenes using the Internet and social media. But that wasn't a direct attack. I was still convinced it wanted us distracted. So what was the fucker really up to?

'You are absolutely sure that wyrm who attacked you is really dead?' Fin looked from me to Eleanor. 'You said the body disappeared.'

'It sank into darkness as such creatures do when they are mortally wounded.' Etraia's voice startled us. She stood in the library doorway, wearing jeans and a long, loose dark green shirt. 'Frai and Asca stood vigil as it faded to nothing. It is truly gone.'

'How—?' I managed not to ask a really stupid question. My mother had been in and out of the cottage where I lived with my dad when I was a kid. Just because the older dryads didn't come up to the house, that didn't mean they couldn't. I also realised I hadn't locked the manor's side door behind us. Shit.

'So this is a different wyrm.' Eleanor leaned forward and carefully pressed the plunger in the cafetière. 'And it knows we're on to it now. It knows we know it's got its claws into Denise.'

I could hear her tightly controlled anger. Well, I had been asking myself how badly I might have screwed up on the journey back here.

'We needed to shake things up. Hopefully now we'll find out what the sodding thing is up to.' That came out a bit harsher than I meant it to.

Fin's hand on my knee stopped me saying anything else. She got up from the sofa as Eleanor silently lifted the cafetière to offer her a coffee. Eleanor poured me some tea. Fin picked up both mugs and came back to sit beside me.

'Let's go through this from the start,' she suggested. 'Maybe we'll see something new, or get some idea what to do next.'

I was watching Etraia walking around the room. She studied the leather-bound books on the shelves before going over to the tall windows and gazing out across the valley towards the ornamental temple. When she looked up at the carved ceiling, fascinated, I did the same. There was no hint of an emerald gleam in any of those hollow wooden eyes.

'Can you and the others warn us if the wyrm comes here?' I asked her.

'Oh, yes.' She turned to reassure us. 'And we will do whatever we can to frustrate the creature.'

That made me feel a bit better about forgetting to lock the side door. I was about to ask if the dryads could alert Kalei, the naiad who comes to Blithehurst from time to time. She could keep a look out up and downstream. But a more urgent question occurred to me. 'It hasn't already been here, has it? You would have told us?'

Etraia shook her head. 'It has come nowhere close. We would know, or the shuck would have challenged it.'

'Then maybe it's not out for revenge.' Fin sipped her coffee. 'Didn't Peter say the kelpies had started moving south around the equinox? That would have been around the same time as that horrible website went up.'

She looked across the low table to Eleanor.

'Possibly.' Eleanor leaned back, cupping her mug in both hands. She looked a bit less cross with me.

Fin's eyes unfocused. 'The kelpies – the first lot of kelpies – they'd had their silver chains stolen before we knew anything was happening. And the delver said he and his people had been threatened before that, by whoever – whatever's behind this. To make sure they didn't even think about helping, if the kelpies came to them trying to get new necklaces.'

'Wyrms have long had dealings with those who work metal and gemstones beneath the earth,' Etraia observed. 'They seldom deal fairly with them.'

'I recall a few European myths along those lines,' Eleanor agreed dryly.

'I think two separate things are going on.' Fin looked around. 'Whatever this wyrm is up to, it needs the kelpies. It convinced them to go south by promising them some reward. Something they really wanted. It made sure it could force them to do what it wants, in case they had second thoughts, by threatening the delvers. So far, so good. Then something happened.'

She paused. We waited. Fin went on.

'The Green Man got involved. Maybe he found out something was up when this wyrm went through with its threat to destroy those necklaces. Maybe the kelpies went to someone else for help. Someone with a connection with him. Anyway, when he realised the kelpies would go after whoever might have their silver, he sent Dan to the craft fair. I bet if we checked with whoever sells scrap silver to that dealer, Hayley, someone would tell us a woman who looked like this wyrm sold them some broken necklaces.'

Eleanor raised a hand. 'Are you suggesting—?'

'No.' Fin shook her head. 'That would take ages and we don't have time to waste. Whatever this wyrm is planning, I think it's up against a deadline. That's why it's throwing anything it can think of at us now. Sending the kelpies to trash the rewilding project. Using Denise to make trouble for Dan.'

'You think it's panicking?' Eleanor didn't like that idea. I didn't either.

'I hope not.' Fin was uneasy too. 'But it hasn't got time to be subtle.'

'But we still don't know what the fuck it's planning.' I was so frustrated, I couldn't sit still. I got up and glared up at the carved masks. Not a flicker.

'It has to be something Eleanor knows about.' Fin put down her mug. 'Even if you don't realise it yet. This business with the website's the giveaway. You're the only one the wyrm wanted distracted from the start. It used Denise to set up that horrible website before it did anything else. It only went after the rest of us when the Green Man got Dan involved.'

Eleanor stared at her. 'I need a drink.'

She walked out of the library. We heard cupboards opening in the kitchen across the corridor, and the clink of glass. Etraia left the window and perched on one arm of the other sofa. Eleanor came back with a bottle of expensive whisky and four glasses.

'I'm not saying you're wrong, Fin, not in the least.' She sat down and started pouring. 'What you're saying makes sense, but I have no idea what this could be about. Nothing comes to mind. Not a bloody thing.' She was getting upset.

'Let's leave it till tomorrow,' Fin said quickly. 'Perhaps you'll think of something after you've slept on it. We can start asking around. Someone has to know something that'll give us a clue.'

Eleanor pushed two glasses towards us. 'Is this where we get the wise women involved?'

'Maybe.' I reached for the whiskies.

Eleanor realised she had poured four drinks and looked at Etraia. 'Do you want this? I didn't think to ask.'

'I don't know. Let's see.' Etraia was amused. She picked up the glass and breathed in the whisky's aroma. She took a sip. 'Interesting.'

Fin blinked and put down her own glass, still half full. 'I'd better have something to eat before I drink any more.'

'You're not driving anywhere.' Then I realised I hadn't actually asked if she was staying the night.

'Why are you here?' Eleanor looked at Fin, puzzled. 'Sorry, I didn't mean that how it sounded. You're always welcome, and not just when you're stopping me and Dan from having a blazing row. What brings you here today though?'

'Dan asked me to come.' Fin looked at me.

I emptied my glass. 'We've been thinking about dragons and wyrms for a while. You know every county has at least a couple of local legends about them. They're everywhere, or at least they used to be, back in days of old when knights were bold and all that. We know for a fact there are still some around. There was that one we had to deal with in East Anglia a few years ago. We can't assume we won't come across another one some time. If that happens, I want to be a damn sight better prepared. So we've been trying to find ways to kill them. Ideally, in some way that doesn't involve getting so close it can kill us first.'

I hadn't talked to Eleanor about this because I didn't want to upset her with memories of Robbie's death. But Fin and I had read every scrap of dragon myth and folklore we could get our hands on.

Eleanor stared at me, open-mouthed. 'Have you...?'

'We've come up with a plan,' I said cautiously.

Fin corrected me. 'Half a plan.'

I couldn't deny Annis Wynne's death had thrown a serious spanner in the works. 'Let's call it two-thirds.'

'What—?' Eleanor shook her head and poured herself another drink.

I looked at Etraia. 'If this is going to work, it has to be a secret.'

'That seems wise to me.' The dryad drank her whisky. 'If the wyrm gets wind that you have such a scheme, it will surely kill you as soon as it can.'

She put down her glass and walked out of the library. We sat looking at each other as we heard her go out through the side door. Finally, Eleanor broke the silence.

'I don't know about you two, but I don't want to go out to eat. Shall we see what's in the freezer?'

'Sounds like a plan.' Fin got up and collected the mugs and glasses.

She handed me the tray. I followed them into the kitchen. I put the mugs into the dishwasher and washed up the lead crystal tumblers.

Fin opened the cupboards. 'I can see tinned bamboo shoots and bean sprouts and hoisin sauce.'

Eleanor stood up holding a package of meat from the bottom drawer of the freezer. 'How about beef stir-fry with egg-fried rice?'

'Sounds good.' I was getting my appetite back. I got out a chopping board and a sharp knife. 'How many onions?'

We ate in the library with trays on our laps. We didn't mention the wyrm. Eleanor wanted to hear how the rewilding was going. Fin wanted to see the latest photographs of Sophie's new baby.

Then we told Eleanor how we had pieced together our plan to try to kill a wyrm without any of us ending up dead.

She told us about a few ideas she had come up with, in case it ever looked like she was going to have to face one again.

176

JULIET E. MCKENNA

Chapter Fourteen

I f we were going to kill this monster, we needed to get a lot of things in place. I rang Fin's cousin Will first thing the next morning, but it was three days before he got back to us. To be fair, what I was asking him to find wasn't going to be easy. I tried not to get too wound up while we waited. I did my best not to keep asking Eleanor if she had come up with any ideas about what the wyrm could be up to. We could only try to get everything ready before it made its move.

It was a week after I'd gone to Berwick when I got up at the crack of dawn to drive to East Anglia. This was going to be another long day. Travelling east–west across England towing a trailer meant using A roads, and the Land Rover would clock up at least another three hundred miles before I got back today. Still, I was relieved to finally be doing something besides waiting for disaster to strike.

The dot on the map where I was supposed to meet Will didn't have a name or a postcode. He had sent me an Ordnance Survey grid reference. I'd never had to put one of those into the satnav before, so that was something new. As I drove away from Blithehurst, I couldn't help feeling that was going to be the most straightforward bit of my day.

The journey there was every bit as tiresome as I expected. Once I reached the Fens, I still couldn't relax. I had to find my way along lanes with ditches on both sides deep enough to drown the Land Rover. Forget crash barriers; there weren't even hedges to stop a vehicle skidding off the pot-holed and crumbling tarmac. I drove slowly and carefully, conscious of the trailer behind me. At least I wasn't holding anyone up. I couldn't see any sign that traffic came out this way from one month to the next.

I'd been driving for nearly four hours when the sat-nav cheerfully informed me I'd reached my destination. I checked the time as I switched off the engine. Just after ten. Getting out of the Landy, there wasn't a house or a tractor, or anything moving, anywhere to be seen. It had been at least half an hour since I'd spotted a single sign of people in this flat, agricultural landscape.

The lane dead-ended where fields growing something leafy and green met an expanse of saw-edged sedges threaded through with ribbons of dark water. There wasn't a gate or a fence. The road just gave up when it reached a ridge of soil some optimist was hoping would hold back the winter floods. I climbed up to the top of the grassy bank, but anything lurking in the fen was hidden by the tall, feathery plants. If this had been a wasted trip...

'Hiya, Dan.' Will waved cheerfully as the sedges parted. He was sitting on the front seat of an open canoe. His girlfriend, Witta, sat at the back. She expertly paddled the boat up to a narrow grassy ledge where the water met the bottom of that side of the bank.

'Daniel.' She nodded and smiled. We'd met before.

I looked at Will. 'So?'

'We've found a couple of possibilities that no one will miss.' He got out of the canoe, careful not to slip on the long, coarse grass. 'You go with Witta and we'll show you.'

He saw me hesitating as he used the rope at the prow to hold the canoe still. 'Come on. Bend your knees. Get your centre of gravity as low as you can. Steady yourself with your hands on the sides and step into the middle, not the edge.'

I crouched down and got slowly into the canoe. 'How am I going to get the Land Rover—?'

But Will had already tossed the rope in after me and transformed into a swan. He ran along the top of the bank, stretching out his long white wings to take off.

Witta was laughing. 'Do you think they have any idea how funny they look doing that?'

'Probably not.' I twisted around as she sent the canoe surging through the sedge. 'Can I help?'

'You can make yourself useful with that other paddle, as long as you do exactly what I say, as soon as I say it.' She was completely serious now. 'One hand on the top, and the other one halfway down the shaft. Don't try anything you think you've seen on TV. Just use the paddle on your right-hand side and stick to a steady rhythm. I'll follow your pace. But wait until I've turned us around.'

'No problem.' I would do whatever she said. I can swim because I had to learn at school. I didn't want to have to prove that today, especially when I couldn't see what might be in the water.

Witta is more at home on the water, salt or fresh, than I – or any other human – was ever going to be. She's a nereid, the daughter of a river spirit and a merman. A lot of families who've lived in the Fens for generations have had regular dealings with the uncanny. Witta's had plenty of experience adjusting her outward appearance to pass as human. If anyone gets close enough to see the webbing between her middle and ring fingers, most visitors are too polite to mention it. She tells curious kids it's because her grandmother was a mermaid. They think that's a brilliant joke.

Once she had the canoe's nose pointing away from the bank, I dug the paddle in deep. The little boat cut quickly through the sedges. The tall plants rustled and waved overhead.

'Ease up, Dan,' Witta called out a few minutes later.

As the canoe slid into dense reeds, I lifted up the paddle and waited for her to tell me what to do next. We left the reed bed and reached a long narrow channel of open water. I couldn't see solid ground on either side.

Witta deftly turned the prow to the left and put us in the centre of the channel. 'Okay. You can put your back into it now.'

'Where are we going?' I concentrated on paddling with regular, even strokes.

'Look up. We're following Will.'

I did as she said and saw the swan flying on ahead. He soon banked and headed west. We reached a junction with another channel. These Fenland waterways big enough for boats are called lodes. Fin had told me that. The ditches that divide the fields are called dykes around here, and they drain into the lodes. The lodes take the water to the rivers, which carry it to the coast, where it flows into the sea. That was the theory, anyway, when men who saw nature as a challenge to be overcome had decided to turn the ancient marshes into farmland centuries ago. Silt had turned out to be a major problem, just for a start.

A bit further on and Will made another turn, then another. I guessed we were still technically paddling up a lode, but this one was barely wide enough for one of the punts tourists fall out of in Stratford-upon-Avon. Not long after that we reached a pool with a much taller, steeper grassy bank. We were surrounded by reeds, and I couldn't see any way to go further by canoe. I laid the paddle carefully down. I wasn't sorry to stop. Canoeing's harder work than it looks.

'Over here!' Will appeared on the top of the bank.

I saw a gap had been cut in the reeds below him. Witta drove the canoe's prow right up to the dark, sodden earth.

'Careful.' Will came down the bank on his backside. 'Throw me that rope.'

I did as he asked. Once he was sure of his footing, Will held out his other hand to help me. I gripped his wrist and concentrated on keeping my balance. I'm taller and heavier than he is, so if I went into the water, he'd be coming in too.

'Okay,' I said with relief as soon as I was on dryish land.

'This way.' Will was already scrambling back up the slope.

I followed him, using my hands as well as my feet. When I paused at the top, I realised this was a much taller bank than the one where I'd parked. These fields were a couple of metres below the level of the water where Witta was still sitting in her canoe. It's one of the weird things you see in the Fens. I had no idea where we were. I could see a long way in every direction, but there were no houses, no church spires, or any vehicles speeding along somewhere to show me a road.

On one hand, that was a good thing. I could see what I had come for lying along the edge of the closest field. As long as no one could see us, we shouldn't have to face an outraged farmer accusing us of stealing. Furniture makers pay good money for decent-quality bog oak. Coming here on the water to stay out of sight made a lot of sense. Driving a Land Rover towing a trailer over private land was asking for trouble.

On the other hand, I wondered how the hell Will thought we were going to get a piece of wood several metres long and weighing a couple of thousand kilos back to the Landy in a canoe. He was sliding down the far side of the bank to the field on his arse. I didn't want to drive back to Blithehurst in filthy trousers, so I did my best to stay upright as I followed him, digging my boots into the soft earth and grabbing handfuls of coarse grass to stop myself slipping. Once I was safely down, I walked across the dense black soil to join Will.

'There you go.' He gestured, triumphant. 'Plenty of choice.'

He was right about that. Seven substantial chunks of ancient tree trunks had been dumped at this edge of the field. The wood was as dark and dull as the earth it had been pulled from, to stop it wrecking a few hundred thousand pounds' worth of hi-tech modern farm machinery.

The longest piece had to be at least seven metres, with the suggestion of its lost root ball in the flare at one end. A couple of the others had stubby remnants of branches, and the smallest couldn't be less than four metres. They were all too long and too heavy for the trailer. I'd have to go back to the Landy with Witta and get my chainsaw and protective gear, assuming I found anything here that was going to be any use.

'Do you know when these were dug up?' I took a closer look at the nearest ancient tree. If these had been lying around through one of the wettest springs on record, they'd been repeatedly drying out and being soaked by the rain again. There was every chance this wood would disintegrate as soon as a tool touched it.

'The hobs unearthed these just yesterday,' Will assured me.

Seriously? Some farmer was in for a hell of a surprise. I reached down and touched the bark with a fingertip. 'Shit! This is yew.'

'Me? What did I do?' Will was confused.

'These are yew trees. Not oak.' I clenched my fist and waited for the cramps knotting my hand to fade. The images flooding my mind receded more slowly.

Yew trees have long memories. I'd found that out once before. These groves had flourished in a vast ancient forest covering the land in every direction. Then sea levels had risen, leaving the rivers with nowhere to flow as they carried the rain here from far inland. Their spreading waters had drowned these trees where they stood. The dead yews had fallen one by one, as peat bogs transformed the land around them. Animals, birds and insects had got to work until the trees' stubborn remnants finally sank into the waterlogged, acid soil. Decay couldn't touch them then.

When I'd told Fin the first thing we needed for our plan to kill a wyrm to have any chance, she told me what she'd learned about bog wood as a kid, growing up around here. Half-fossilised trunks and branches started to reappear when the fens were drained and ploughed. Right up to Victorian times, the locals used this hard black wood for household joinery or just for fuel.

Will was looking at me, concerned. 'Are you okay?'

'Give me a minute.' I was still stunned by the sights and sounds of the ancient forest. For a split-second, I had sensed every living thing that had been here for miles around all those aeons ago. It felt like dryad radar turned up to eleventy-one. I flexed my hand a few times as I remembered something else Fin had said. Not every bit of wood that's called bog oak actually is. It can be yew or birch, or even pine, drowned when the land flooded.

'We really do need oak.' Every reference Fin and I had found as we put our plan together had talked about bog oak. Even if some other tree would work, I wasn't going to risk experimenting. We'd get one chance at this.

I waited for Will to ask why. I waited for him to ask what we were really up to. He didn't. Fin had said he had been paying attention when she told him knowing our secret could put him and Witta in danger.

'Okay. Let's try the next lot.' Will flew off as a swan, leaving me to get back to the canoe on my own.

'No good?' Witta used her paddle to keep the canoe hard up against the steep bank as I made my way down to the water.

I didn't answer until I was safely back in my seat. 'Those were yew trees. We need oak.'

'Will said he had a couple of places to show you. Wait a moment.' Witta expertly spun the canoe around in the tight space and paddled us out into the narrow lode again. 'Okay, now you can help. Just do the same as before.'

I heard the rush of a swan's wings overhead as I picked up the paddle. Will circled and headed away. Witta steered the canoe and I paddled as fast as I could to follow him. It wasn't long before we saw him in non-swan form. He was waiting beside a sluice gate where a wide dyke drained into the lode. A little bridge carried the footpath that followed this much shallower bank across it. Witta held the canoe sideways on to the bank with her paddle and I got out.

'This way.'

I followed Will across a long field. Well away from the water, ancient black stumps and lumps of wood had been piled in a heap as high as my head. Some had already weathered into a splintery mess.

'The pieces the hobs found for us are over here.' Will walked quickly to the far end of the pile.

That was a relief. Anything recently dug up shouldn't have had time to deteriorate. Of course, this wood was still sodden, and that doubled its weight. I was hoping Etraia could do something about that when I got a suitable piece back to Blithehurst. Watching videos and reading up online, I'd found out that joiners working with bog oak could spend months drying out the wood in carefully controlled conditions. We didn't have time for that.

'Well?' Will looked at me anxiously.

'Let's see.' I braced myself and laid my outspread hand gently on the nearest twisted branch.

This was nothing like touching a living tree. Thankfully, it was also nothing like the shock I'd got from the yew. Something faint slowly stirred deep within the black timber. I caught a glimpse of majestic trees soaring up to a leafy canopy overhead. These oaks would have been twice the height of any I'd seen growing today. That fleeting memory of daylight faded. A momentary sensation of cold water seeping through my clothes and skin chilled me to the bone. It was so vivid I was surprised my palm wasn't damp when I took my hand away.

'This is oak.'

'Great.' Will grinned, relieved.

It might be oak, but I still needed to find the right piece. I walked alongside the heap, searching for a section of trunk that was about the right length and thickness. I pointed. 'Can you help me get that out?'

Will came over to help me haul a gnarled stump away from the new wood the hobs had added to this farmer's stack. 'Bloody hell. This stuff is heavier than it looks.'

'It really is.' I tried not to think how difficult it would be to carve.

We moved a few more pieces. I ran my hand along the bog oak I'd picked out. Nothing happened. That was a relief. I took a step back and estimated it was just under three metres. Good enough. I wouldn't have to use my chainsaw and risk getting someone's attention. That noise would carry a long way across this flat landscape. I pushed the black wood gently with my foot, to get some idea of its weight. We still had to get the bog oak onto the trailer. I could use the winch on the Landy, and I'd brought everything I'd need to make an A-frame, but this still needed thinking about.

'Well?' Will prompted me.

'This should work. Where's the nearest road? How close can I get the Land Rover?'

'Don't worry about that.' Will stuck his fingers in his mouth and gave an ear-splitting whistle.

A sylph appeared, pale and translucent. Looking me up and down with bright blue eyes, they didn't seem impressed. I didn't react.

'Right.' Will slapped the black tree trunk I had chosen. 'Let's get this back to Dan's Land Rover.'

'Why? What's it for?'

Another sylph stepped out of thin air. I recognised this one's voice.

'Zan? What are you doing here?'

'Watching your back,' the sylph said earnestly.

That was bollocks, for a start. Eleanor, Fin and I had discussed what Etraia had said, about the wyrm coming to kill us if it heard the slightest whisper we had some plan to attack it. We decided not to tell anyone else we thought we could kill a wyrm. Not until we knew what the monster was really up to. And Eleanor insisted we see if there was some other way to put a stop to whatever it was up to. None of us wanted to leave a wyrm on the loose, but that might be the safest option. In the short term at least.

Fin had explained as much as she could to Blanche. She told her we were making progress finding out who was causing so much trouble and why. She said sharing what we knew would put everyone in danger. They'd had that conversation sitting in Fin's car. Blanche didn't like it, but she'd agreed to accept it for the moment. More importantly, she'd promised not to tell Zan a thing.

The sylph could do plenty of useful things for us. Right now, they were supposed to be searching for kelpies who were roaming central England. But here they were in the Fens. The problem with sylphs – one of the problems – is they do get easily bored. I didn't think Blanche had let anything slip. Not knowing why Fin was staying at Blithehurst would have been enough for Zan to suspect there was something they weren't being told. They must have followed me here, staying invisible until their curiosity got the better of them.

Zan crouched down to peer at the bog oak trunk. 'What do you want this for?'

Will's sylph was scowling. 'If you have no need of my help, I'll go.'

'No, please. Your agreement is with me, and that still stands.' Will shot me an irritated look. 'Please take this to Dan's Land Rover for us.'

'It needs to go into the trailer,' I said quickly. A pissed-off sylph can cause a whole lot of trouble by creatively reinterpreting whatever they've agreed to. 'Please.'

'I can do that,' Zan said brightly.

'Nobody asked you,' Will snapped.

'I'm sure you could, but that's not necessary, thank you all the same,' I said to Zan.

I didn't want them pissed off either. We'd need their help with the plan later on, and that was something no one else could do. We'd explain when it wouldn't matter if the sylph couldn't keep it to themselves.

Zan's nose wrinkled, like a cat smelling something unpleasant. 'This wood is very wet.'

Will's sylph gestured. 'Not for long.'

Moisture clouded the air around the bog oak. Shit.

'I need the wood a bit drier than it is now, so thank you for that,' I said hastily. 'But it has to stay strong enough for me to carve.' Sucking the damp out of the log too fast would leave it cracked and crumbling.

Will's sylph looked at me, and swirling droplets hung motionless in the air. 'Why? What's it for?'

'I told you,' Will answered for me. 'We cannot say, not yet.'

'Then why should I help?' His sylph looked sulky.

Zan grinned. 'I can—'

'Have you told Blanche you've given up on the search you promised to do for her?' I interrupted. 'What do you think she'll say when I tell her you came here instead?'

Now Zan scowled. 'I am only trying to help.'

Give me strength. I managed not to say that out loud. 'Yes, I know, and thank you, but we need you to do other things. That's why Will asked his friend to help us.'

Will's sylph smirked. 'So we have no need of you.'

'We need you both,' Will said fast. 'Just in different places.'

Zan vanished. The local sylph laughed. Before Will or I could say a word, the world went white around me. A second later, I felt solid ground under my feet, and I heard a stomach-churning crash.

Blinking until I could see clearly, I realised I was back at the Landy. The bog oak had been dumped in the trailer, just about anyway. Half of the tree trunk stuck out over one side. I ran over and grabbed the end before a passing breeze could unbalance it, accidentally or on purpose. I'm sure watching me struggle to get this sodding great lump of wood back into the trailer would entertain an offended sylph no end.

I carefully eased the ragged end of the heavy log around. When the whole thing lay lengthways in the trailer, I started lashing it down securely. A swan landed nearby and turned into Will. He watched me tie a tarpaulin over the whole thing.

'Is it okay?' he asked, breathless. 'Honestly, sylphs.'

'Tell me about it. I think the wood's fine.' Testing the log with a fingernail, it still felt pretty wet. We'd just have to see. 'Thanks for everything, seriously. Thank Witta for me too.'

Though I wasn't sorry to get back here without doing any more paddling. My shoulders were going to feel that exercise tomorrow.

'I'll tell her.' Will nodded. 'Take it steady on the drive back, towing that much weight.'

'Absolutely,' I agreed. 'Right, I'd better get a move on. I want to get back ahead of the school run.'

Will stayed where he was. 'You will tell us, won't you, when you've done whatever you're planning? We had to promise the hobs we would tell them before they would agree to help.'

I should have expected that, and I could see Will was equally curious. Not that I could blame him. I'd have felt the same in his shoes.

'I'll explain as soon as I can.' I rechecked my last knot and hoped that was a promise I'd be able to keep.

'It's just – I'd like to be prepared. You know. In case.'

Will had been with us in Wales. He knew how dangerous my life could be. I knew if our plan did go horribly wrong, he'd be getting the letter Fin and I had agreed to write, to tell her family what had happened. I took my keys out of my zipped pocket and thought carefully about what I could say.

'It'll be more dangerous not to try.'

Before Will could ask me anything else, my phone rang. I expected Fin wanted to know how I was getting on. No, this wasn't anyone in my contacts, and I didn't recognise the number.

'Hello?' Some cold-calling spammer was going to regret this.

'Dan? Is that you? It's Dave here. Dave Fulbrooke.'

'Yes, hi.' I tried to stay calm, but my heart was beating faster. Dave Fulbrooke was my dad's friend. Why was he ringing me out of the blue? 'What can I do for you?'

'Are your mum and dad visiting you?' He sounded apologetic and worried at the same time. 'Or have they gone on holiday somewhere?'

He sounded dubious about that, and I couldn't blame him. We never went away on holiday when I was a kid, and my dad didn't go anywhere much after I'd moved out. People assumed we couldn't afford it. No one wanted to embarrass us by asking, so we didn't have to find an excuse that didn't involve my mum.

'They're not with me.' I fought to keep my voice level. 'Why do you ask?'

'I called round the day before yesterday, to see if your dad wanted a lift to the library. No one was in. That's fair enough, but I went over again yesterday and today as well. No one's answering the door. I tried your dad's phone this morning. His mobile, I mean. I could hear it ringing inside, and nobody picked it up. I know where to find the spare key, so I went in to do a welfare check.'

Dave wasn't apologising now. He'd been a copper before he retired. A good one. He'd spoken up for me as a character witness when I ended up in court. He was still talking.

'I mean, with your mum going to visit her cousins like she does these days, I was worried your dad might have had a fall. Neither of them were there, but there's food in the fridge and a pan of soup was left on the cooker. Not on the heat, but still, that's not like your dad. The car's still outside as well. I know your dad doesn't like to drive much these days, and they could have got a taxi, but if you don't know where they are, honestly, Dan, I'm worried.'

'Yes. Same here.' I swallowed to try to get some spit into my dry mouth. 'I'm in East Anglia right now. I'll come home as soon as I can.'

'I'd appreciate it,' Dave said. 'A missing persons report will be best coming from you.'

Shit. I really didn't need that complication. I cleared my throat. 'Right. Listen, Dave, I have to finish up a few things here, then I'll come down first thing tomorrow. I'll call you as soon as I get home.'

That was a lie. I hoped he didn't hear it.

'I'll be straight round,' Dave promised. 'As soon as you ring me.'

Which was why I'd be going down there tonight, as soon as I'd got this piece of bog oak back to Blithehurst. Whatever was going on, it must involve my mum somehow. I couldn't handle that with an ex-copper looking over my shoulder. Was this some sort of attack by the wyrm? My hand shook as I put my phone in my pocket.

'I heard,' Will said. 'What can I do?'

'I wish I fucking knew.'

Chapter Fifteen

Driving the Land Rover back to Blithehurst towing the weight of the bog oak forced me to concentrate. I couldn't worry about my dad while I was on the alert for other drivers not paying attention.

I'd done a training course on how to drive safely with a trailer ages ago. When I dropped out of university and got an apprenticeship with a joiner, his insurance company insisted. It's come in very useful. It never hurts to be able to put up your hand if a foreman needs someone to drive a works van with something on tow.

That instructor had told me to assume everyone else on the road was an idiot. My dad had said the same when he taught me to drive. I hadn't listened then, but I knew better now. Driving with a trailer means going more slowly than most people expect. That makes other drivers impatient. The dickheads will try to overtake the very first chance they get. They may think they can do that safely. What they don't realise is a Land Rover towing a heavy trailer won't stop nearly as fast as a Land Rover on its own. It doesn't turn corners in the same way either.

I really did not want to have to make an emergency stop to avoid turning an Audi or a BMW into a roller skate. Apart from anything else, I didn't want to have to explain what I was carrying in the trailer to a traffic cop. I kept as much distance as possible between me and the vehicles in front and used the gears to slow down in good time for junctions. Accelerating gently at green lights gave a couple of wankers the chance to put their foot down and flick me a V-sign as they roared away. I didn't give a toss. They could wrap themselves around an HGV coming the other way as long as they didn't block my route home.

By the time I got to Blithehurst, I had a splitting head-ache. The trip back had taken close to four hours. My neck and shoulders were so stiff it was painful to turn my head. Fin was waiting for me, sitting on the top rail of the estate's back gate. That improved my day a whole lot right then.

Fin climbed into the Landy's passenger seat once I had driven through. 'Will rang. He told me about your dad. I've told Eleanor. She says take as long as you need.'

'Thanks.' I gripped the steering wheel to stop my hands shaking. I was suddenly exhausted.

'I've packed a bag for you. It's at the cottage.'

All I could do was nod.

'Do you want me to drive you there?' Fin looked through the windscreen as the driveway took us through the trees. 'We can take the Landy or my car. Whatever you like.'

'I don't—' I swallowed hard. 'I think I'd better go on my own. If this is— If something...' I coughed and tried again. 'I don't want to give it another target. Whatever it is. If I need backup, I'll call the shuck. There should be other dryads around, even if my mum...'

I was really hoping Mum was missing because she had taken Dad somewhere safe. Anything else was too horrible to think about.

'All right.' Fin was still looking straight ahead. 'Be careful. Find out what's going on and ring me. Talk to us, me and Eleanor, before you do anything risky. Please, Dan. Promise me.'

'I promise.'

That was an easy ask. I'd expected Fin would insist on coming. I absolutely didn't want that. I wouldn't be able to focus on whatever had happened to Dad if I was worried about keeping Fin safe. The closer I'd got to Blithehurst, the more I had dreaded arguing about it. I wondered if she had been talking to Eleanor about the wyrm we had fought. How dangerous that had been. Maybe Fin didn't fancy facing the kelpies again.

That was a thought. Would the wyrm have been able to send kelpies after my dad? 'Can you check something for me? Look at a map and see how far the craft fair was from the nearest river where that first gang of kelpies could have been lurking. See if you can find any story that says how close they have to stay to water.'

'Do you want me to ask the cunning men?' Now Fin did look at me. 'You'll have to give me Peter's number, or Iain's.'

She sounded dubious. I felt the same, though I couldn't say why. I hesitated. Then I went with my gut feeling.

'Not yet. The same goes for the wise women. We need to know what we're dealing with first.' I glanced at her. 'I will be careful. I'll find out what I can. Then I'll call you.'

Fin still didn't look happy, but she nodded. 'How about Zan? Do you want me to call Blanche and see if they're willing to help?'

'Let's see what I can find out first.' I wasn't at all sure Zan would be in a cooperative mood after our encounter today.

'Okay.' Fin didn't have anything else to say.

Neither did I. I drove into the dairy yard, and Fin stood by the workshop door to watch as I manoeuvred the trailer into the far corner. She walked over as I unhitched the Landy.

'Can I see it?'

'I need to keep it under cover.' I began unlacing the tarpaulin. 'Can you tell Etraia I need it dried out enough to carve, without giving the game away?'

Fin and I had agreed we wouldn't even talk directly to each other about any element of our plan. There was no knowing who might be listening unseen.

194

'Of course.' Fin looked at the black wood as I pulled the edge of the tarpaulin back. 'Where will you be working?'

'In there.' I nodded at a door at the end of the yard. I'd cleared out an outbuilding that had once been used for storing cheese or something else from the dairy. A few battered shelves still clung to the flaking whitewashed walls. I'd also found a badly stained pine kitchen table in the manor's cellars. I hoped that would be sturdy enough to make a workbench.

I tied the tarpaulin down again. 'Have you found anything new?'

Fin had spent the week working in Eleanor's sitting room, scouring obscure bits of the Internet and Blithehurst's library. Wearing a staff polo shirt, no one paid her much attention as she went up and down the stairs with an armful of books.

If we couldn't slot the last piece of our plan into place, my journey today had been a complete waste of time. I didn't want to even consider that possibility. We knew what we wanted to do, and we knew it could be done. We just had to find someone to do it.

'Not yet.' Fin wasn't about to give up though. 'I'll keep looking while you make sure your dad's okay.'

I nodded. 'Will you do me a favour? Ask Eleanor if you can stay in one of the guest rooms while I'm away. If they're trying to pick us off one by one, you two should stick together. Warn Blanche. Tell her to keep Zan close.'

'I don't think that will be a problem,' Fin said lightly. Then she looked more serious. 'And yes, it makes sense for me to stay in the manor.'

'Right.' I scrubbed my face with my hands. 'I'll get that bag from the cottage and hit the road.'

'Not before you've had something to eat, and a coffee,' Fin said firmly.

'Oh, yes. I suppose so.'

We had a very late lunch in the restaurant by the garden centre. I couldn't help watching the clock, but I had to admit Fin was right. By the time we'd finished eating, my headache was gone. As we went out into the car park, I found the stiffness in my neck and shoulders had eased off too.

'Safe journey. Ring me as soon as you can.' Fin kissed me goodbye and headed back to the manor.

I picked up my overnight bag and checked the cottage was secure before I left. I couldn't see the shuck or any of the dryads around. That cut both ways. One of the dryads might suggest something useful. On the other hand, they might not, so talking to them would be a pointless delay. I checked the time. I had better get moving.

It took me a few miles to adjust to the feel of the Landy without the weight of the trailer. I had to stop for fuel, and I tried not to think what my next credit card statement was going to look like. Still, I made good time on the motorway, and this was my shortest journey since going to the craft fair at the start of the month. Was that really only a fortnight ago? It felt more like four months.

I pulled up outside the house where I'd grown up just before six o'clock. There were no lights on inside. I looked at the front door, then at the woods on the other side of the road. The nature reserve's visitor centre was closed, and that was a relief. I wouldn't have to answer a lot of concerned questions about Dad. Not right now, anyway. I hoped I'd have some answers before whoever opened up tomorrow morning saw the Landy parked beside my dad's car. They'd be straight over to knock on the door and ask what was going on.

I thought about searching the woods first of all. With any luck, one of the younger dryads living here now could tell me what the hell was going on. By my count, there should be at least four of them. Perhaps they could explain why Dave Fulbrooke had said my mum had been visiting some cousins. What was that about?

On the other hand, I found it hard to believe Dad hadn't left me a message inside the house, even if he'd had to leave in such a hurry he'd forgotten his phone. It wasn't a note, because Dave would have found that, but it could be a clue Dave wouldn't see as significant. Dad probably guessed Dave would be concerned and would use the spare key to check the house. He also knew I'd be the first person Dave would ring. Dad knew I'd come home straight away. So I'd check the house first. There were a few hours of daylight left. That would give me long enough to check the woods if I had to.

I unlocked the front door and went in. 'Hi, Dad? Anyone home?'

That's what I always called out when I came home. This stillness and silence unnerved me. I honestly couldn't remember when I'd last been in this house on my own. Not since I was a kid, and Dad had gone out to the shops or something. When I knew how soon he would be back, roughly anyway. Even then, even if she wasn't in the house, my mum would be around.

Nobody answered. I went into the kitchen. Dave had washed up that soup pan he'd mentioned and left it to dry by the sink. There was no sign of a struggle. Nothing was broken or knocked over. If there had been, I realised, Dave would have called in his former colleagues before he rang me. That was a good thing, wasn't it?

Maybe. I'd be a whole lot happier if I could find out what the fuck was going on. I drank a glass of cold water standing by the sink. Then I searched the house, upstairs and down. That didn't take very long. Downstairs there's a small entrance hall, a kitchen diner, the living room and a cloakroom. The upstairs has two bedrooms and the bathroom, an airing cupboard on the landing, and that's it.

I'd lived here until I went to university. Nothing much changed, not really. Dad was an only child, and most of the furniture had come from his parents' house. They had died a few years before I was born. A lot of our everyday kitchen stuff had been his mother's. We replaced pans when they wore out and bowls and plates when they got broken, not just for the sake of an upgrade. Dad only bought a new washing machine or boiler when he couldn't get the parts he needed to mend the old one. There hadn't been much spare cash, but I didn't care. I didn't know any different. I was always warm and fed and safe, and that's what mattered.

We weren't quite as hard up as some people assumed. Dad had his works pension as well as his government one. We were a family of three, but dryads don't run up bills. When I needed new rugby boots or outgrew my winter coat, Dad could find the money. For one thing, he didn't have a mortgage to pay. This old house out by the nature reserve had been so run down that no bank would have loaned Dad the money to buy it. It didn't matter that he had the skills to do it up. That wasn't a problem though. He had bought his first house near the factory before prices went insane. He sold it for more than he could have afforded to pay for it if he had been a first time-buyer.

Usually, coming back and seeing everything was the same as always reassured me. Not today. The house felt wrong without my dad in his chair, watching the telly or listening to the radio. I had better go to see what I could learn in the woods. I locked the front door behind me. I also turned off my phone and zipped it into the pocket with my keys. I didn't even just switch it to silent or vibrate. I didn't know if a dryad could still sense a call coming through, or what else might be able to do the same. Better safe than sorry. If there was something unfriendly out there, I didn't want to risk anything letting it know I was coming. If I ended up dead, Fin would skin me alive.

Crossing the road, I walked past the closed visitor centre. A five-barred gate keeps teenagers on mountain bikes off the main tracks out of hours. As soon as I reached it, though, I wanted to turn back. I absolutely didn't want to go on. This wasn't a nice place for a walk, not this evening. I should go somewhere else.

This was unexpected. It wasn't dryad radar. For a start, I wasn't touching a tree. This was more like sharing someone's thoughts. I didn't feel scared or upset. Nothing was threatening me. I simply didn't want to go into the woods. Why didn't I get back in my car and drive somewhere else?

Because I was here to find my dad. If something was trying to keep me out of these woods, that just made me more convinced that this was where I'd find answers. I climbed over the gate. The sensation of someone or something trying to convince me I didn't want to be here grew even stronger. I ignored it and walked towards the trees.

The feeling vanished when I laid a hand on the first oak I reached. It knew me. I felt recognition spreading. I'd grown up exploring every corner of this nature reserve, and most of the countryside around here. I realised the trees were trying to keep everyone out of the woods. So that was one good thing. I didn't have to worry about meeting stray dog walkers on the public footpaths crossing the site.

Before I could be relieved about that, dryad radar kicked in hard. I didn't sense any dryads. A single presence lurked in these woods. It was evil. The trees were certain about that. I wasn't going to argue. I was assuming Mum and Dad had run as soon as they knew it was coming for them. Hunting one of them or both? Did that matter? I could only hope to hell they had run, and they had got away. After all, the trees would know if they had been hurt or worse. I waited for some sort of reassurance. I couldn't feel anything.

The trees were focused on this intruder. It was something I hadn't met before, otherwise I would have been able to tell what it was. That meant it wasn't a kelpie. It wasn't moving either. It took me a moment to work out whatever this might be was lurking beside my mother's favourite trees. Waiting for me or for someone else? No, it wasn't just waiting. These trees knew a predator when they saw one. It was waiting to pounce.

Fine, but what the fuck was out there? The trees telling me it was evil was as much use as a robot waving its arms and roaring, 'Danger, Will Robinson!' I waited a few more moments. Whatever it was still didn't move. Did that mean it didn't know I was here? I really hoped so.

'Thank you,' I murmured to the oak as I took my hand away. I went back to sit in the Landy and think through my options.

Ringing Fin was pointless until I knew what I was facing. Once I'd got something definite to tell her, I'd come back and sit here surrounded by metal while she and Eleanor found out more about whatever it was. Then I'd go back into the woods and... do what?

I still had the collection of things I'd taken up to Berwick in the Land Rover. The woodland was damp from so much recent rain. A fire would be slow to take hold if I used a Molotov cocktail. I could run back to the Landy for the extinguisher. And I'd never hear the last of it from Mum. Besides, thinking about setting whatever was out there alight assumed that it was flammable. What if it was something like the nightmare that had attacked Aled?

I got out and opened the back door. I took out the entrenching tool I use if the Land Rover gets bogged down. The heavy-gauge-steel shovel blade is serrated on one side.

A smack with that should give most things pause for thought, supernatural or not. And this wasn't going to be a gang of badger baiters who'd run snivelling to the cops when they got what they deserved for threatening my dad.

A moment later, I put the entrenching tool back and closed the door. Doing some reconnaissance with the added benefits of my greenwood blood would probably go better if I wasn't carrying a big piece of ferrous metal. I went back into the woods. As soon as I was underneath the trees, I concentrated on not being seen. The first few times someone had walked straight past me, the Green Man had been responsible. Since then, I'd realised I could do this for myself. Walking silently through the woods was no problem. I'd been doing that since I started going out to watch birds and wildlife when I was a kid.

Every five metres or so, I stopped and took hold of a tree branch. I knew where I was going, but I wanted to be sure that whatever was out there had stayed put. It didn't move. As I got closer, I went more slowly and more cautiously. I was coming up at an angle from some distance behind the tree where this thing was lurking. I could make out a dark outline by the oak's trunk. It looked human-sized and person-shaped to me, sitting on the ground and leaning back against the rough bark.

I needed to circle around, staying well hidden by the undergrowth. As soon as I had seen this thing from the front, I would go back to the Landy and describe it to Fin. As long as it didn't see me, of course. A bit too late, I realised I hadn't ever tried not being seen by the dryads at Blithehurst, or by anything else non-human.

Right now, that didn't change anything. I had to know what had threatened my parents, and this was the only way to find out. I'd keep my distance. If it saw me, I'd leg it back to the Landy. A benefit of my height is the length of my stride. I'd been useless at running any distance longer than the two hundred metres at school, but I could surprise the other side on a rugby pitch with short bursts of speed.

I started moving around in a wide arc. I stopped as soon as I could see what was lurking. So far, so good. It – she – glanced idly around every couple of minutes, but nothing seemed to snag her attention. She was sitting with her legs outstretched, leaning against the oak tree. Her hands lay relaxed in her lap. She had coarse black hair long enough to reach her elbows, held back from her face with combs or clips or something. Her clothing was dull black, and I couldn't work out if she was wearing a long coat over tight trousers or a dress and thick tights. Her flat-soled black boots were muddy from her walk through the woods.

I crouched down low behind the thorn scrub. Her face was... wrong. I don't mean she was scarred or anything obvious like that, though her forehead was lined and I could see deep creases around her hooded eyes. If I focused on her mouth or her nose individually, they looked ordinary enough. As a whole, though, her face was unnerving. Even without the trees' warning, if I'd met her walking in these woods, I'd have hurried to get away, pretending not to hear anything she might say.

She blinked. Dull darkness replaced the whites of her eyes for an instant. At this distance, with the daylight fading, I couldn't see the true colour of her gaze. Never mind. She was evil and she wasn't remotely human. The wyrm must have sent her here. This couldn't be a coincidence. There was only one of her, but that wasn't necessarily good news. The wyrm must be sure she could handle whatever she'd been sent to do without needing help. So she was evil and she was dangerous. I rubbed my forearm where my itching scars confirmed that.

I hoped Fin or Eleanor would remember something they'd read or seen online, to tell us what she was. Keeping low, I edged away backwards into the denser shadows beneath the trees. I willed the unwelcome visitor not to see me twice as hard as I'd done before. I followed a wider circle to get back to the gate. Using dryad radar, I made sure she hadn't moved. I wondered if she'd been waiting for her prey to appear since Mum and Dad had run. If so, she'd been sitting there for at least three days.

I stopped several times to turn around and look behind me. I had to be certain she wasn't following. By the time I got to the Landy, the skin on the back of my neck was crawling. I felt a whole lot safer once I was back in the driver's seat. I made sure the doors were locked, called Fin and told her what I had seen.

There was a moment's silence, then she spoke. 'Is that it?'

'What do you mean?'

'Is there anything else you can tell us?' Eleanor asked. Fin had put her phone on speaker.

'No.' If there was, I would have said so.

'She's just sitting waiting?' Fin persisted. 'Not doing anything else?'

'Not that I saw.'

'How long were you watching?' Eleanor sounded as if she was moving away from the phone.

'Five minutes, maybe.' This was getting irritating.

'We'll phone you back.' Fin ended the call.

I waited. I waited some more. The daylight faded towards dusk. I got out of the Landy and crossed the road to the nearest tree. As soon as dryad radar told me this new enemy was still sitting by Mum's trees, I ran back to safety with my heart pounding. I must have checked my phone's battery and reception were okay five times. When Fin eventually called, her ringtone was deafening.

'We can't find anything.'

I could hear she was frustrated. So was I.

'Can you make a guess?'

'I'd really rather not,' Eleanor answered. 'That could be worse than no help if we get it wrong.'

She had a point. 'Okay, leave it with me.'

I switched off my phone again and stuck it in my pocket. Then I went round to the back of the Landy and took out the entrenching tool.

Chapter Sixteen

I took the most direct route to confront the woman in black. There wasn't much daylight left and I wanted to get this done. I stopped once to use dryad radar to check she was still where I had seen her. When I arrived, she stood waiting for me with her hands clasped behind her back. Up on her feet, she was around five foot six or seven, not skinny, not fat. Not human. Not right.

She smiled with vicious satisfaction as soon as she saw me coming. Her teeth were crooked and discoloured, with gaps where some had rotted away. She blinked, and I saw her true gaze was the dull dark red of dried blood. I stopped when there was still a good three metres between us.

She ignored the threat of the green-painted steel as she looked me up and down. 'They said you were a prize specimen. They were right.'

As she took a step towards me, I let her see the entrenching tool. 'That's close enough. Who are you and what do you want?'

She ran her tongue along her repulsive upper teeth. 'Plenty of meat on your bones. Plenty to share around.'

Her eyes never left my face. She was looking for some reaction. Tough luck.

'I said, who are you and what do you want?'

After a long moment, she shook her head and sighed. 'You truly are your mother's son.'

I wanted to know what she meant by that. I could see she wanted me to ask. No sodding chance.

'Who are you and what do you want?'

She heaved a sigh. 'You humans are so obsessed with your names. So free to share your own. Knowing mine will do you no good. Not when you have so little time left.'

Now she was taunting me. I ignored that. 'Where are my parents?'

She wasn't getting the reaction she wanted. She got annoyed. 'I have no idea. Not that I care. Killing them was only ever the means to this end. To bring you here to meet your end.'

If the usual rules applied, she couldn't tell me outright lies. If she didn't know where Mum and Dad were, that meant she couldn't have killed them. I really hoped I'd got that right.

'Not that the old man would have made much of a meal,' she said, mocking. 'You, though, you'll keep us fed for weeks.'

'Stay where you are.' I raised the entrenching tool as she casually slid a foot forward to edge half a pace closer. 'Who sent you here?'

'You don't think we talk to each other?' Her spitting hatred startled me as she took a quick step closer. 'You and your friends who cause me and mine so much pain. You care nothing for our hunger.'

'Stand still!' I moved quickly backwards.

She angled her head. Now she was calm and thoughtful. 'I will drink your blood first of all. That's a trick I learned long ago, to save myself from fading. Your kind get so upset when they find a loved one dead and skinned and jointed. But if you can convince yourselves that some cruel accident befell them, you surely will. Finding some unfortunate who tragically bled to death, no one suspects my kind had a hand in their demise. You humans have such a talent for deceiving yourselves. We have always found that so helpful.'

'Who's "we"?' I was getting tired of this horror movie bollocks.

'You'll know soon enough, when we come out of the shadows.' She laughed, harsh and chilling. 'Oh, no, forgive me. You won't. You will be dead.'

She tried to rush forward, but I'd been watching her body language, not listening to her supervillain bullshit.

'Shuck!'

The massive black shadow appeared between me and her. It growled, deep and menacing. I had started picturing the spectral hound in my mind when this bitch started talking about eating me.

'My, my.' She began circling sideways. 'You are more resourceful than you look.'

The shuck moved too, and I shifted my feet to stay behind it. The great black shadow's hackles bristled along its hunched neck and shoulders. I couldn't see its head, but I could hear it was snarling. Strings of shining drool from its open jaws hit the leaf litter with a hiss.

Being behind the shuck did make it harder for me to see the bloodthirsty bitch's next move. I'd caught a glimpse of her crooked fingers when she'd tried to attack me. There was something odd about her hands.

I took a quick sidestep to get a better look. 'What are you holding?'

She quickly tucked her hands behind her back. 'Come here and I'll show you. And call off your dog.'

'No chance,' I told her. 'Fuck off back to whoever sent you here. Tell them to leave my family alone.'

The shuck growled and shifted its coal-black bulk as she tried to move towards me.

'Coward.' Her laugh sent shivers down my spine again. 'If you want me to leave, you'll have to make me.'

I tightened my grip on the entrenching tool and seriously considered it. As long as my parents weren't dead, I didn't care what this bitch was. I just wanted her gone. I reckoned I could do enough damage to make her run to save herself. I can't say I liked the idea of attacking someone who looked so close to human, but this bitch had come here to kill my dad.

If I hurt her badly enough, that should warn the wyrm to leave my family alone. Though I'd take Dad back to Blithe-hurst with me, just to be on the safe side. As soon as I knew where he—

The woman in black sprang at the shuck. She clawed at its face and neck with both hands. The shadowy beast howled with agony. As it reared up and twisted away, I saw deep gashes on its muzzle and throat. Five wounds torn by parallel claws glowed red like its eyes against its black fur.

The bitch darted past the shuck, coming for me. I swung the entrenching tool at her outstretched hands. I heard the clang of metal on metal. She caught the shovel blade and held on tight. She wasn't using her hands though. Metal claws stuck out between her fingers and on either side of her clenched fists. Like someone using a bunch of keys as a weapon, only ten times worse. I wasn't surprised the dryads had disappeared now. They can live for centuries, but that doesn't mean they can't be hurt or killed. The thought of one of them being shredded by those claws was too horrible to imagine.

The shuck disappeared. Shit. I pulled against the woman's grip. She was frighteningly strong. That serrated edge on the shovel blade was doing me no favours. The indentations gave her metal claws a more secure hold.

What now? If she let go, I'd drive the shovel through her face. I could see that she knew it. If I twisted the tool out of her grasp, she'd have a split-second to attack me before I could bring the shovel back to hit her. Stalemate. Fuck.

She tried to rip the entrenching tool out of my hands. No chance. But she was powerful enough to drag me forwards.

My boots skidded on the leaf litter. She hauled on the shovel blade again. It took every bit of my strength to resist her.

She didn't get the tool away from me, but I had to fight to keep my balance. Worse than that, as I instinctively tightened my grip, my own biceps and forearms worked against me. I was actually pulling the bitch closer. That meant I got a closer look at those claws. Withered scraps of skin clung to rusty iron hooks that nevertheless had gleaming, razor-sharp tips. Fresh dark smears glistened. Tetanus would be the least of my problems if she cut me with those.

She wrenched again. I let go of the handle. She wasn't expecting that. As she staggered backwards, I darted forward and grabbed the entrenching tool before it could fall to the ground. Her arms were still flailing as she fought to stay on her feet. Without taking a backswing, I smacked the side of her head with the shovel as hard as I could. I couldn't give her a second to recover.

She fell to the ground, stunned. I dropped the entrenching tool. Before she could know what was happening, I was on the bitch. I grabbed one elbow and flipped her over to lie face down in the dirt. I planted my boots on either side of her waist and dropped down to land in the small of her back. I could feel her legs thrashing as she tried to kick me in the arse or the kidneys, but her feet couldn't reach. To get onto her knees, she'd have to lift her hips. She had no chance with my weight crushing her. She might be stronger than me, but I was heavier. That's what counted now.

I leaned forward. I had my knees on the ground, on either side of her ribs. Gripping just above her elbows, I pressed her outspread arms down. Her fists were knuckles up, still clenched around those iron claws. I had to disarm her before I did anything else. I moved my left knee to pin her upper arm down. She twisted under me as soon my weight shifted. I willed myself to relax, to make myself as heavy as I possibly could. She gasped, and struggled to draw breath.

Now I could use both of my hands. I wrenched her right wrist to turn her fist over. She screamed. Her breath was truly disgusting, like the stink of a dead animal heaving with maggots. Leaning over to force her fingers open, I couldn't escape it. If I'd eaten anything since lunch, I'd have thrown up in her hair.

I got her hand open and pressed her fingers back. A thick iron bar crossed her filthy, rust-stained palm, with an iron ring around her thumb to make sure she couldn't drop the weapon. I reached for the crosspiece. It didn't move. I tried to slide my fingertips underneath it. The sodding thing still didn't budge. I realised the metal was stuck to her skin.

She was screeching now, lying limp beneath me. I hoped to fuck the trees were still keeping dog walkers out of these woods. Anyone hearing this unholy row would be ringing 999 to report a rape or a murder. There was no going back now though. I gripped the end claw that stuck out by her little finger as tightly as I could and pulled hard. The metal came loose with a rush of hot dark blood as I felt her flesh tearing. Her shrieks and the stench of her breath were making my head spin.

The bloody weapon slipped out of my grasp and flew through the air. It spun off to land in the undergrowth somewhere. I didn't care. I tore the second set of claws off her other hand. I managed to keep hold of those. Now I scrambled to my feet and retreated. I had to get away from that awful noise and that smell.

She sprang up, lithe as a gymnast. As she spun around and roared at me, I saw dirt on her face, leaves in her hair and murder in her eyes. She flung herself at me with her hands raised and her fingers crooked to tear at me with her ragged nails. Twisting streams of blood ran down her pale wrists.

I dodged sideways, dropped the iron claws and snatched up the entrenching tool. Before she could swerve to attack me again, I got both hands on the handle and swung the shovel sideways as hard as I possibly could. The steel edge hit her between wrist and elbow. I heard bone snap. She dropped to her knees with a gasp. She looked up at me, cradling her broken forearm with her wounded hand. She bared her revolting teeth.

'Just fucking stop,' I spat at her. 'You're beaten.'

'You wish,' she hissed.

I braced myself for whatever was coming next. I still had a weapon and she didn't.

She turned into a hare and raced away on three good legs. As she disappeared into the twilight, I stood and stared. I hadn't expected that.

The adrenaline that had kept me fighting ebbed away fast. I was shaking. I forced myself to take deep breaths, in through my nose and out through my mouth. I stuck with it until the familiar warm smell of the woodland drove out the vile memory of the evil woman's stinking breath.

My hands were still shaking as I used the shovel to scrape leaves and earth over bloody patches of ground. I found sticks to mark where they were, in case my mum wanted these stains dug out and the soil taken away. I went looking for both sets of those iron claws. I wasn't going to leave them for the woman in black to come back and pick up. I didn't think my mum and the other dryads would want them here either.

I found the claws I'd dropped to grab the entrenching tool easily enough. After searching for the other set without any luck for what felt like half an hour, I stopped and looked around. Why hadn't the dryads come back? I'd got rid of the evil invading their woods. If they couldn't pick up her bloodstained iron weapon, they could at least show me where to find it. I glanced at the closest oak tree. Dryad radar might show me where they were, but I didn't want to touch anything that belonged here with that evil creature's blood still on my hands.

The shuck appeared and growled to get my attention. I couldn't see any sign of those vicious wounds on its neck. That was a huge relief.

'Are you okay?' I asked the beast anyway.

The shuck walked away. I followed. Apart from anything else, if another monster turned up to attack me tonight, I wanted an ally at my side. The shadowy beast walked around a few trees and stopped by a tangle of brambles. It thrust its ferocious head forward, ears pricked. As it scraped at the brambles with a massive taloned paw, its fiery eyes blazed.

I saw red light glint on sharp hooks, caught on a thorny spray. Swallowing my revulsion, I carefully retrieved the weapon.

'Thanks. For everything.' But when I looked over my shoulder, the shuck had disappeared.

Now I had both sets of the iron claws in one revoltingly sticky hand and the entrenching tool in the other. First things first. I had a tub of heavy-duty cleanser in the back of the Landy, for getting grease and worse off skin. This evil creature's blood definitely qualified as worse. I started walking along the path to the gate. I'd still have to get my keys out of my pocket, but that couldn't be helped. If my trousers got stained with this stuff, I'd burn them.

I reached the visitor centre and looked across the road. My dad's car was still parked in front of the garage and the house's windows were still dark. That was a punch in the guts. I hadn't realised how much I'd been expecting to see Mum and Dad had come home. Where the hell could they be?

I sniffed and realised my eyes had filled with tears. Fuck that for a game of soldiers. I raised an arm to scrub my face dry on my shoulder as best I could. I crossed the road to the Landy and dropped the entrenching tool and the iron claws onto the tarmac. Crouching down, I scooped up a double handful of dust and grit. As I rubbed my palms together, I realised my sweatshirt's cuffs were crusted with dark blood. That was going into the incinerator too then.

The dirt from the road didn't get rid of the blood on my hands as much as cover it up with a layer of grime. That was better than nothing. Using my fingertips to unzip my trouser pocket, I managed to get my keys out without touching very much else. I opened the back of the Landy and found the tub of orange gel cleanser. As I scrubbed my hands as clean as I possibly could, I thought about what I should do with the weapons at my feet.

A rag and a bit of the cleanser wiped every trace of blood or anything else off the entrenching tool. So that was okay, and I put it back where it belonged. I couldn't decide what to do with the claws though. I didn't even want to touch them, much less try to clean them. But I couldn't leave them here, and slinging them in a metal-recycling skip didn't seem like a good idea.

I used the rag to pick them up. I was going to put them in the old toolbox I'd taken to Berwick, to put another layer of metal between them and anything that wanted its weapons back. Then I had an idea. I walked a couple of metres away and dropped the claws on the road. I came back and got the can of petrol. I poured a small puddle over the claws and lit it with a careful match. It didn't burn for long, but I felt a lot happier about handling the vicious weapons after that. I still padlocked them inside that toolbox, just in case.

All the time I was doing this, I'd been looking back at my dad's house. My stomach hollowed every time I saw the windows were still dark. If Mum and Dad came back, the first thing he would do was switch on a light.

It was no good. I couldn't go back in there on my own. I just couldn't. There was no way I would get any sleep lying in the bed I'd had as a kid, wondering if my parents were alive or dead. I wouldn't possibly be able to hold it together when someone from the visitor centre came knocking in the morning.

I closed the back of the Landy and got into the driver's seat. I'd get a room for the night in a chain hotel at the nearest motorway services. I'd shower and ring Fin and tell her everything that had happened. She could tell Eleanor. In the morning, we'd see who could come up with some bright ideas. I didn't think that was going to be me.

I made a three-point turn that was more like four and a half and started driving. I sped up. The waxing moon was just past the half and the road in my headlights was familiar. Then a whole lot of things happened at once.

A hare darted out from the hedgerow. It bolted across the road right in front of me.

I instinctively stamped on the brake.

The hare stopped in the middle of the tarmac.

I saw its front paws were soaked with blood. It held a damaged foreleg close to its chest.

I hit the accelerator. As soon as I did that, I wished I hadn't. I lifted my foot off the pedal.

The hare leaped back the way it had come. If it had kept on going across the road, it would have been okay. For a split-second, I still thought it would escape. Then I felt that stomach-churning jolt and the muffled crunch under a wheel that says whatever you've just hit is roadkill. Now I stamped on the brakes for real.

I steered out of the skid and switched off the engine. My rapid breaths were deafening in the silence. I wondered what I was going to find when I walked back up the road. I could sling a dead hare into a ditch and hope the local foxes solved that problem. Leaving a body that looked like an ordinary person was something else entirely. The next driver who came down this road didn't deserve that, for a start. The police would have no chance of identifying the corpse from dental records or anything else, but they'd be asking a lot of questions. Dave Fulbrooke would want to know if there was any connection with my mum and dad's disappearance.

How much damage had that impact done to the Landy? It hadn't sounded like much, but I needed to check. I could also do with knowing if any blood on the bodywork would test as hare or human. How the hell was I going to find that out?

I saw movement in my wing mirror. Something was out there in the darkness. I froze. I couldn't think straight. Then four dryads walked up to stand by the Land Rover's windows, two on either side. The closest one waved to me, and the one beside her smiled, excited. I managed to open the driver's door and they stepped back to let me get out. The other two had walked back to peer at something on the road behind the Land Rover.

The first dryad congratulated me. 'Well done, Daniel!'

'Sorry, what?'

'Did you see us?' her friend asked eagerly. 'Did you see us help?'

'Did you...?' I realised they had driven the hare under the Land Rover's wheels. That's why it couldn't escape. Dryads had been chasing it on both sides of the road. I had no idea why the evil thing was so afraid of them, or what they would have done if they'd managed to catch it. I didn't ask. I had a much more urgent question.

'Do any of you know how to contact my mum?'

Chapter Seventeen

The closest dryad nodded. 'Fega has gone to fetch her.'

I assumed that was the other new dryad. I didn't know any of their names. 'And my dad?'

'Him too.' She smiled.

That wasn't as reassuring as it might have been. These dryads wore short green tunics, showing muscular arms and legs. Dark hair curled to their shoulders, tangled with strands of ivy. Their eyes gleamed vivid green. They looked more... feral than the dryads I was used to.

'I should get back to the house.' I glanced at the pair who were crouching by the gory mess on the road. As far as I could see, that was much more hare-sized than human. That was a relief.

I waved a hand. 'What about—?'

'We will get rid of it.' The dryad who was doing the talking shooed me away. 'Go and greet your mother.'

I didn't need telling twice. I drove back the way I'd come, focusing on the road ahead to avoid seeing whatever was left smeared on the tarmac. Now I really put my foot down. Rounding the bend, I saw lights were on in the house. I pulled up and raced through the front door. Dad was in the kitchen, filling the kettle at the sink.

'Are you okay? Where have you been?' I wanted to hug him, but I wasn't going to touch him with bloody traces of that evil dead thing still on my hands and clothes.

'I'm fine.' That wasn't a lie, but it wasn't the whole truth. Dad managed a smile as he switched on the kettle. 'I've spent however long I've been away in a pleasant sunny woodland with your mum. That's as much as I can tell you.'

'What happened?' I had to sit down. I barely made it to a chair at the kitchen table.

'You tell me. You can tell me what day it is, for a start.' Dad sat down opposite. 'The last thing that happened here, as far as I am concerned, is some woman in a black coat came to the front door. I thought she must be selling some sort of religion to bother coming all this way outside the village. I was going to tell her I wasn't interested, to get rid of her before she started talking. Then your mum appeared and shoved me back inside the house. She told me to lock the door. As soon as I'd done that, she swept me away.'

'Where is she? Mum, I mean.'

'She said she had things to do.' Dad rested his elbows on the table, lacing his fingers loosely together. 'So what's happened to you? Why are you here?'

'Dave rang me. He said you'd gone missing. He told me you didn't take your phone, and after you'd been away for three days, he was getting worried.'

'Is that all?' Dad was relieved. 'Just three days?'

I remembered him telling me he'd lost an entire week once, before he realised dryads can change their experience of time passing, and that can happen to humans who are with them. Dryads are by no means the only ones who do that. That's why there are so many stories about people meeting someone strange on a path, waking up some time later from a deep sleep and going home to find their grandchildren are grandparents.

'So who was she, and what did she want?' Dad was talking about the woman in black.

'She...' I couldn't think where to start. I'd done a stupid amount of driving today and then had to fight for my life in the woods. Now the relief of finding out that Dad was okay overwhelmed me.

217

'I have no idea. She was here to kill us though, you and me. Can we talk about it in the morning? When Mum can tell us what she knows? I really need a shower, and some clean clothes.'

'Fair enough.' Dad got up and took the teapot and teabags out of their cupboard. 'Come back down when you're ready.'

If in doubt, brew up. I'd bought him a fridge magnet saying that when I visited an army museum on a school trip. I could see it from where I was sitting.

'Thanks.' I went to the sink to wash my hands first. I ripped my sweatshirt off over my head and dumped it on the floor.

Dad went to pick it up. 'I'll get that in the wash.'

'No!' I could see he was startled, but I couldn't think how to explain. 'Just don't touch it. Please.'

'If you say so.' Dad watched me turn on the tap and found the chunk of green soap he uses after he's been gardening.

I lathered my hands up to the elbows. Finding the nail brush, I started scrubbing. I didn't stop until Dad reached over and took the brush out of my hand. He moved my arms under the running water to wash away the soap.

'I think that's enough. Take your tea upstairs, have a shower and go to bed. We'll sort out everything else in the morning.'

I'd scrubbed my arms and hands nearly raw. I took the towel he handed me and patted the tender skin dry. I hadn't even noticed the kettle had boiled and Dad had made the tea, but the pot was standing on the table with a wisp of steam coming out of the spout.

'I'll get my bag.'

When I came back, Dad was sitting at the table, eating a slice of fruit cake. There was a slab on a plate for me, and he poured me some tea.

'Thanks.' I took the plate and mug upstairs. I showered until the water started running cold. Then I sat on my bed, wearing a towel, and rang Fin.

'Dan?'

'It's fine. He's fine. I mean, Dad's fine, but it's complicated.'

'Isn't it always?' Fin sounded relieved regardless. 'Is it gone? The thing you saw in the woods?'

'Yes. It— The dryads chased it into the road and I ran over it with the Landy.'

'They did what?' Fin was startled.

'It's a long story.' I drank some tea, but that didn't help me work out what to say. 'Mum's not here at the moment. Can I ring you in the morning when I've found out what she knows?'

'Of course. As long as you're all right?'

'I am. Completely knackered, but fine. Now I know Dad's okay.'

'Talk to you tomorrow then. Sleep well. Love you.'

'Love you too.' I ended the call, drank the rest of my tea and ate my cake. Then I went to bed. I don't think I even moved in my sleep, and I didn't dream of anything.

When I woke up, I could hear Dad moving around downstairs. That made me weak with relief all over again. I got up, dressed in the clean clothes Fin had packed for me, used the bathroom and went downstairs. As I went into the kitchen, I realised I was absolutely ravenous.

Dad was leaning against the sink, talking to someone on his phone. He waved to me with his free hand and waited for whoever was on the other end of the call to pause for breath.

'Yes, I know. By the time I realised I'd left it behind, we were over an hour away. There was no point in coming all the way back here. I could always borrow a phone off somebody if I needed to make a call.'

Not having any greenwood blood, Dad's got very good at telling plausible lies to keep our family's secrets. He listened to whoever was answering him. I recognised Dave Fulbrooke's voice.

'Yes, thanks for dealing with it. I meant to put it in the freezer when it was cold, but I forgot.' Dad looked at me and grinned. 'What can I say? Do they still call that having a senior moment?'

He listened again. 'No, I appreciate that. Believe me, if I had been lying at the bottom of the stairs, I would have been very glad to see you.'

Dave started talking again. Dad interrupted. 'Sorry – sorry, I've got to go. I think Dan's just arrived. Yes, I'll tell him. No, no apology necessary. I'm just sorry I had you worried. I will definitely let you know if I'm going away again. Yes. Thanks. Bye.'

He ended the call and put his phone on the table. 'Dave's heart's in the right place, but he does go on.'

'He's a good bloke.' I realised I would never have found out what was going on if Dave hadn't called me. We needed to talk about that.

'I told him your mum and I got back home late last night, in case that ever comes up.' Dad opened the fridge. 'Shall we have bacon and eggs? I'm starving.'

'Yes, please. How much toast do you want?'

'Two slices for me.' Dad turned the heat on under the frying pan. 'About your sweatshirt, your mum told me to burn it, as well as anything else you've got that has blood on it.'

I looked up from slicing the loaf on the bread board. 'That means the trousers I was wearing have had it as well.'

'Bring them down and I'll throw everything in the garden incinerator.' Dad cracked eggs into a saucepan and started whisking.

'Is Mum around?' I put down the bread knife.

'She said she'll be back a bit later on.' Dad added butter and salt to the pan. 'Now, what's this all about?'

'Well, there was this craft fair over the May Day bank holiday weekend...'

By the time I'd told Dad about everything that had happened before Dave Fulbrooke rang me and said he'd gone missing, we'd cooked our breakfast, eaten it, washed up and made a fresh pot of tea.

Talking about Dave reminded me of something. 'He said he was worried you might be here on your own because Mum's been going away to visit cousins. What did he mean by that?'

Dad carefully put the salt and pepper in the exact centre of the table. 'I'm not going to be here forever, Dan. We need to think ahead. As far as Dave and everyone else in the village is concerned, your mum's twenty-odd years younger than me. It's not fair for us to expect her to carry on here, pretending to be human, after I'm gone. We've been getting people used to the idea that she's got family elsewhere.'

He grinned. 'We said her mother fell out with her sisters when she insisted on marrying a man they disapproved of. Her family cut all ties. But recently one of her cousins got in touch after getting a profile from one of those DNA-testing companies who let you look for relatives on their website. Anyway, when I'm gone, once everything's been sorted out with probate and so on, your mum will decide to move away, to live closer to her relatives. As far as anyone else is concerned, anyway.'

'So you've got everything worked out.' I couldn't decide how I felt about this.

I could see it made sense, though I hadn't thought about it before now. Trying to pretend my mum was an ordinary woman growing old and eventually dying would be a total nightmare. I shouldn't be surprised Dad had worked out a way around that. I knew he'd had plenty of practice dealing with official paperwork while I was growing up. These days it seemed anything involving the government got more nosy and complicated every year.

'I've paid for one of those direct cremations,' Dad went on. 'And I've got permission from the wildlife trust for you to bury my ashes beside your mum's trees.'

I wasn't ready to think about that. 'Did she give you some idea when she'll be back this morning?'

I'd barely spoken when she knocked on the back door. 'Dan?'

'Mum?' I'd bet good money she'd been standing on the step listening and waiting for Dad to tell me about their plan.

She was in the jeans and old sweatshirt guise everyone at the nature reserve was used to seeing. She wrapped her arms around me and tucked her head under my chin. 'Fighting off a hag. My brave, clever boy.'

'A hag? Is that what it was?' I had to call Fin and tell her, but right now I didn't want to let go of Mum.

She loosened her hold and took half a step back to look up at me. 'I haven't seen one of that foul sisterhood in an age. What brought her here? Why now?'

I hesitated. Looking over Mum's head, I could see the five younger dryads in the back garden. They looked like a bunch of sixth-formers ready to set off on a Duke of Edinburgh Award hike or something, wearing walking boots, tan cotton trousers and T-shirts in assorted colours. One even had an anorak tied around her waist. They were looking at me with bright curiosity.

They would hear every word I said. I had no idea who they might talk to, or what they might say, even if I asked them to keep this news to themselves. That meant I couldn't risk telling Mum everything. I tried to work out what she absolutely needed to know.

'There's a wyrm up to nothing good. We don't know what it's planning, but it's been using kelpies, and now we know this hag was involved. Whatever it's doing, the Green Man wants it stopped. The wyrm's not about to give up. So far it's sent kelpies after Fin and her sister, and made trouble for Eleanor at Blithehurst. Now it's tried to get to me through Dad. That's why that hag came here.'

'She won't get another chance,' Mum said with vengeful satisfaction.

'It – she really is dead then? The hag.' I'd been worrying that I'd made a mistake last night. Not taking a good look to make absolutely sure the monster is dead never goes well in horror movies.

'Oh yes, and more quickly than the vile creature deserved. If any of her sisters venture this way, they will not be so fortunate, when we get our hands on them.'

Looking over Mum's head, I saw the young dryads liked that idea. I decided not to ask.

'I will keep watch for this wyrm,' Mum went on. 'As well as any other threat it sends us. But do you have some plan to defeat the creature?' Mum looked up at me again. 'Do you, Daniel?'

'He does,' Dad said firmly.

'I promise.' I hugged Mum close to stop her asking any more questions. I'd told Dad that we had a plan, and explained why we had decided we had to keep the details to ourselves. He understood.

'We still need to work out what this sodding wyrm is planning though,' I said. 'We have to know that before we can work out where and when to stop it.'

Mum let me go and waved a hand at the small patch of lawn in the back garden between the vegetable patch and the fruit canes. 'Shall we talk outside?'

Dad nodded. 'If you like.'

The young dryads looked relieved. Clearly, they weren't comfortable coming into the house. I couldn't say that was a bad thing. They sat on the small patch of lawn that had just been big enough for a swing and a slide when I was little.

Dad opened the shed and got out two folding chairs. I sat next to him on the paving slabs under the kitchen window. Mum sat between us and the dryads, perched on the edge of the old wooden table which stayed out here in all weathers.

'This wyrm cannot make a move without giving something away.' She looked at me, swinging her feet. 'What do you know today, Dan, that you didn't know before? What did the hag say to you last night?'

'That she really likes – liked to eat people.' I barely managed not to shudder at the memory of her taunts.

'So do wyrms,' the talkative dryad pointed out.

'And kelpies,' Dad said thoughtfully. 'From what you said.'

I saw Mum's swift, curious glance, but she didn't ask him how he knew that.

'How did the wyrm persuade this hag to do its bidding?' the young dryad sitting beside the chatty one wondered.

'A gift would buy her loyalty,' the one sitting on her anorak suggested. 'Or perhaps she had been promised some reward yet to come?'

I remembered Fin saying the exact same thing about the wyrm enlisting the kelpies. Maybe. Maybe not. 'Unless it just

224

told her it would bite off her head if she didn't do as she was told.'

'Even a wyrm would hesitate to menace a hag.' The gleam in my mum's green eyes said she would have questions for me once the three of us were alone. 'They are few and far between these days, but they are powerful in their own right. More than that, the bonds between them are strong. Make an enemy of one hag and you'll have earned the hatred of the whole sisterhood.'

That was news to the young dryads. They looked wide-eyed at each other.

'What could the wyrm offer?' the talkative one wondered. 'To buy a hag's loyalty.'

'It must be a significant gift. Those few hags that survive always balance their likely gains against the risks before they make any move. They are never reckless.' Mum looked at me. 'Daniel? Did the hag say anything that could hint at a deal it had made?'

'Sorry. Give me a minute.' I was quickly texting Fin.

Thing last night was a hag. Busy now. I'll call asap

'What about food?' Dad had clearly been thinking about this since before Mum and the young dryads turned up. 'That's the most basic reward, surely?'

'Well, yes.' I put my phone away. 'The wyrm promised her she could eat you and me.'

But the woman in black had talked about my dead body feeding more than just herself. She'd said they would be coming out of the shadows, when I asked who she meant by 'we'. Did she mean more hags or other creatures? I wouldn't need convincing the kelpies had left their remote rivers for the promise of an all-you-can-eat human buffet. Could it really be that simple?

'If that's the reward the wyrm has offered its allies, some-one somewhere is in mortal danger.' Mum looked at me. 'More than one person, most likely.'

She was right about that.

'How many kelpies have you seen?' a dryad who hadn't spoken yet asked me.

'A dozen. There could easily be more.' Plus however many hags added up to 'we', not forgetting the sodding wyrm itself. Even just one dead human apiece would mean what the news called a mass casualty event. Everything we learned just made things worse.

I stood up. 'I have to get back to Blithehurst.'

Visitors wandering around the estate's gardens on this nice sunny day would make tasty monster food. Could the hag have been sent to draw me here, to give the wyrm its chance to strike? I fumbled my phone out of my pocket and rang Fin.

'Hi there,' she said cheerfully. 'So, we've been looking up hags—'

'Is everything okay? Please, get hold of the dryads as soon as you can. Tell them to keep watch for hags and anything else the wyrm might send to attack you. Get Blanche to join you, just to be on the safe side. See if Zan or a local sylph can search for any sign of kelpies anywhere close? Has Kalei shown her face at all?'

Where the hell had the naiad got to? I really hoped the wyrm hadn't somehow hurt or killed her without any of us being any the wiser. We'd have to come up with some way to find out—

'What's going on, Dan?' Fin was alarmed. 'Have we still got time to – to do – you know?'

The young dryads were staring at me, startled. Mum's and Dad's expressions told me they understood why I was afraid, though they thought I might be overreacting.

'If this wyrm was planning to attack Blithehurst all along, why put this effort into distracting you? It could just have turned up,' Dad pointed out. 'You'd never have known what hit you.'

'It would have had a fight on its hands,' Mum said, thoughtful. 'There must be easier targets than ancient woodland which is loyal to three dryads, and which shelters a shuck.'

'Dan?' Fin asked. 'Are you still there?'

'Yes, sorry.' I took a breath. 'No, I still don't know what the sodding wyrm has got planned, but we've come up with some nasty ideas. We have to be ready for anything.'

'No argument here,' Fin said with feeling. 'And talking about nasty, we've been reading up on hags.'

'You can tell me when I get back.' I was in no hurry to know what promised to be thoroughly unpleasant details, but I didn't have a choice.

'When will that be?' Fin still sounded uneasy.

I looked at Dad, and at Mum.

'We'll be fine,' Dad assured me.

'We were fine, even before we knew any danger sought to threaten us.' Mum was unconcerned.

'We will guard these woods.' The talkative dryad glanced at the others.

I saw that feral gleam in their eyes again. 'Thanks.'

'Come on.' Mum slipped down from the table. 'Let's tell the trees what's amiss.'

The dryads vanished in the blink of an eye.

'We will be careful. Trust me on that.' Dad got up and folded his chair to put it back in the shed. 'You make sure you do the same. You and Fin.'

'We will.' I handed him the chair I'd been using. 'Fucking hell though, I wish this was over and done with.'

Dad closed the shed door. 'When it is, you can come down here with Fin for a nice relaxing weekend.'

'As soon as we can.' I liked that idea. I liked the idea of being on the other side of all this even more. I didn't say so. That might be tempting fate or something else that could be lurking close by, unseen.

We went back into the house. I got my things together and brought the combat trousers I'd worn last night downstairs for Dad to burn. Sodding hag. I could order more clothes online easily enough, but that wasn't the point.

Dad was wearing heavy-duty rubber gloves. He bundled the trousers up with the sweatshirt. 'I'll get rid of these.'

'Thanks. I'll call you when I get back to Blithehurst.'

'And I'll let you know if your mum and the girls come up with any bright ideas. Safe journey.' He went out into the garden through the open back door.

I went out the front to the Landy. Someone waved at me from over by the nature reserve visitor centre. I waved back, though I didn't recognise them. The paths were already busy with people today. That was reassuring.

I'd just pulled onto the M40 from the slip road when I realised I hadn't asked Mum what she might know about that dead hag's metal claws. Never mind. I'd ask Dad to ask her, when I talked to him later on.

A bit further, and I remembered when Fin and I had encountered something else uncanny and evil that liked to eat people.

JULIET E. MCKENNA

*Fee fi fo fum, I smell the blood of an Englishman. Be he alive, or
be he dead, I'll grind his bones to bake my bread.*

Giants. Once upon a time, there had been plenty of those
who were solid enough to cause death and devastation, if
local folklore was to be believed. I fervently hoped the wyrm
hadn't enlisted any of them.

A few miles after I left the M6 for the last leg of my
journey, I thought of something even more worrying. Like
I'd said to Eleanor, every county across Britain has at least a
couple of stories about a dragon or a wyrm making a nui-
sance of itself until some bold knight killed it or died trying.
Where did they all go? Had they starved until they faded
away to no more than terrifying shadows? That's what Peter
had said happened to kelpies who couldn't get fresh meat.

I had two questions for him now. Could those kelpies
who had faded away into the darkness come back, to be as
solid and as dangerous as they had been before, if someone
fed them a freshly dead human? If that was the case, did that
mean serpent dragons and wyrms could come back from the
shadows as well?

Chapter Eighteen

I had a thankfully easy drive back to Blithehurst. I parked in the dairy yard and called Fin's mobile. 'I'm here. Where are you?'

'In the house. Upstairs.'

'See you in a few.'

The trailer was still where I'd parked it. I went to check on the bog oak. It wasn't there. For one heart-stopping moment, I couldn't think what could have happened. Then I noticed drag marks on the cobbles. Those led to the outbuilding where I'd told Fin I would work on the ancient tree trunk. I cupped my hands to the glass to look through the window. The black wood lay on the cracked and dusty tiled floor. What looked like broken bits of old horse-drawn farm machinery surrounded it.

I went up to the manor, making sure to rehang the 'No Entry' sign across the gap in the yew hedge. A few visitors admiring the ornamental orchard looked inquisitive. I stared back, unsmiling, until they went away. When I went into the house through the side door, Fin was waiting in the staff break room. We hurried up the back stairs.

Eleanor was in her sitting room. She looked up from turning the pages in a big leather-bound book. 'Late lunch break.'

'Does that say anything about hags?' I hoped so.

'What? Oh, no. I've been looking up maenads.'

'Which are what?' I really hoped we didn't have some other fucking thing to worry about now.

'That depends on what you're reading.' Eleanor closed the book. 'Overall, they were female devotees of Dionysos, also called Pan, the god of forests and wild places, as we know.

230

They're human in some myths, and supernatural in others. They're violent and dangerous, and some sources say they tore their enemies to pieces with their bare hands.'

I stared at her.

'I think we can guess where the ancient Greeks got that idea,' Eleanor said briskly. 'I had a chat with Etraia after Fin told me about those young dryads chasing that hag before it went under your wheels. They must be a real threat if something so dangerous was running away.'

I supposed that was good news, as long as the young dryads were on my dad's side. 'What have you found out about hags?'

'Not a lot, unfortunately.' Fin sat on the sofa and picked up a notepad. 'A few have names. Jenny Greenteeth, Peg Powler and Nellie Longarms were known to drag people into rivers and ponds. They'd get on well with the kelpies. Black Annis was a witch with iron claws who liked to skin children and eat them. Beyond that, it's gingerbread houses, generic ugly old women with warts, and stories warning kids to stay out of the woods. Or stuff about crone power and the three-fold goddess. Are we going to ask the wise women what they know?'

'We should hold off on that.' I realised I hadn't mentioned a significant detail last night. 'Before the dryads chased this hag into the road in front of me, she changed into a hare.'

'Bloody hell.' Eleanor checked her watch. 'Let's hear the whole story. Quickly. I'm leading the next guided tour.'

I told them what had happened. They were both appalled.

'That explains Black Annis's claws,' Fin observed.

'If a hag who has those won't hesitate to attack a shuck, I can't see them backing down from anything else.' Eleanor shook her head and stood up. 'Sorry, I have to get back to work.'

'One more thing.' I quickly ran through the conversation I'd had with Mum and Dad and the young dryads. 'Can you think of any way the wyrm and these horrors could kill a whole load of people at once? Some time soon.'

Eleanor looked blank. 'I'll give it some thought.'

She left and I locked the door behind her. Fin was staring at her notepad.

She looked up. 'If they are planning some sort of mass murder, that could happen any time. You had better get to work on that carving.'

'Right. Who got the bog oak off the trailer? Did Mark get someone else to help him?' I needed to know who might be asking questions.

'Seriously?' Fin raised her eyebrows. 'Eleanor and I managed. We are perfectly capable.'

'Right. Sorry. I'll get started.' I heard Fin laughing quietly as I left.

I made a quick detour to the cafe to grab a packet of sandwiches and a cold drink. When I arrived in the dairy yard, Etraia was looking at the buildings. She wore a long skirt and a floaty top, and could have been a tourist who'd got lost.

'Eleanor told me you might need my help with a project.'

'Yes. Thanks.' I opened the outbuilding door to show her the bog oak. 'Give me a minute.'

I moved rusted pieces of a Victorian harrow and a hay-rake to the far end of the room. I was all in favour of precautions, but I didn't have time for an unplanned trip to A&E.

When I was done, Etraia came in and studied the thick log. She crouched down and ran a careful finger along a bare patch where the bark had flaked off. 'Will you tell me what you're doing if I ask you?'

'No.' I wouldn't have lied about that, even if I could.

'Can you tell me your purpose?' She glanced at me. 'So I know how best to help.'

'I want to kill a wyrm.' I hoped that was enough. 'I need this log to do that. A sylph started getting the water out, but the wood is still too damp for me to work on. Can you dry it out just enough so I can carve something without it cracking or splintering?'

'If I do this, you must give me whatever you discard.' Etraia stroked the log as if she was soothing an animal. 'I want your promise that you will not throw a single splinter away.'

'I promise.' No problem. That was one less job for me.

The dryad closed her eyes. The outbuilding filled with the dark brown scent of the fens. A moment later, Etraia looked at me and stood up. 'That should serve.'

Her knowing smile made me uneasy. I didn't think she would guess exactly what I planned, but Asca or Frai might come close to some part of it. I'd just have to hope these three dryads kept their mouths shut. 'Thank you.'

'You are welcome.' Etraia gave the bog oak a last lingering look and walked out into the yard. I was only a few steps behind her, but she had already disappeared.

I fetched everything I'd need. I started very cautiously. You can always chisel more wood away. It's hard to put wood back without making a complete mess of a project. Even if you can glue something cleanly, anyone who knows what they're looking at can tell. If you're too heavy-handed, a sudden split can catch you by surprise and wreck a piece completely.

By the time I'd stripped the remaining bark away, I didn't think that was likely to happen. Apart from the splintered sections at either end, this log looked and felt solid. There weren't any fibrous soft spots, and when I tapped a chisel all the way along the length of it, nothing rang hollow.

I used the chainsaw to cut the useless ends away, and found out everything I'd read about carving bog oak was absolutely true. By the time I'd cut off the slice I was going to need later, I was surprised I hadn't burned out the chainsaw's motor. I'd never worked with such hard, dense wood. It made teak feel like pine. I could also see the log was pure black all the way through. That told me this long-dead tree was truly ancient. Since Fin and I had first come up with this idea, I'd done my homework.

At least the log was considerably lighter now that Etraia had dried it out. Even so, every time I had to move it, I was glad I wear boots with steel toecaps. I still wasn't completely convinced the old kitchen table was going to hold it, even though I hadn't found signs of woodworm and I'd tested the joints for weakness.

Since I really didn't want to do this job on my knees with the log on the floor, I had better find out. I have no idea what the white-painted hooks on the beams above my head had originally been used for, but they held when I threw a loop of rope over them and used it to pull myself up off the floor. So far, so good. I set up a four-pulley rig and knotted the ropes tight around the log. That much mechanical advantage made it easy enough to lift.

There was nothing in this empty room that I could use to tie the rope off. I shoved my would-be workbench under the hanging log with one foot. As I lowered the bog oak gently down, I would have crossed my fingers if I hadn't needed both hands for the rope. The solid old table held. I breathed easier as I drilled holes in the top and fixed thick dowels to hold the log still. Now I could start roughing out the shape I wanted.

My chisels were getting blunt before I'd done a quarter of that. I put the broken bits of rusting iron around the table and locked the door behind me as I crossed the yard to my workshop. I was having second thoughts about using the

234

specialist power tools I'd bought for wood sculpture commissions. They hadn't been cheap, and if I wasn't careful I could wreck them on the bog oak.

On the other hand, Fin was right about us needing to get this done fast. Doing the whole piece by hand would take weeks. No, it would take months. I'd have to risk it. I'd use the power tools for the fine detail and go as carefully as I could. I found my whetstone and started sharpening my chisels. When I'd got them to a razor's edge, I went back to work.

Someone knocked on the outbuilding's door. I looked up and saw Fin and Eleanor peering through the window. Since anyone passing through the dairy yard could do that, I'd brought an old dust sheet over to cover up the carving when I wasn't working on it. I checked the time on my phone. Five o'clock. The manor would be closed, and the restaurant and garden centre would be shutting up shop.

I got up and opened the door. 'Come in.'

'I've been thinking,' Eleanor said grimly. 'If the wyrm's looking for a chance to kill plenty of people, there's an event that could have caught its eye. It could have found out that I know about it.'

I stretched my cramping fingers. 'How about you tell me over a cuppa?'

They gave me a hand covering up the bog oak. I locked the door and we went over to the workshop.

Fin picked up the kettle. 'Tea? Coffee?'

'Nothing for me, thanks.' Eleanor drummed her fingers on the scarred wood. 'An estate in Leicestershire will be holding a brand-new music festival over the bank holiday weekend.'

I sat down across the table from her. 'Next weekend, you mean?' Shit. That gave me, what, ten days to get the carving done? No, better call it eight, including today. There was no reason to expect the wyrm would wait for the Bank Holiday Monday to strike.

Eleanor went on. 'This is their first time hosting a big event, and bluntly, Lysander Repton, the man trying to run it, is completely clueless.'

'Lysander?' I tried to think where I'd heard that name before. I remembered a fellow rugby player at school who'd been obsessed with joining the Royal Air Force. 'His parents called him after a Second World War plane?'

'I imagine they were thinking of the character in *A Midsummer Night's Dream*.' Eleanor couldn't help a brief smile. 'The family seem to lurch from one disaster to another. His father tried and failed to set up a safari park about twenty years ago. That was a complete fiasco, and he's still an undischarged bankrupt, so Lysander has been lumbered with running what's left of their other business interests. Unfortunately, lack of financial acumen seems to run in the family. The Reptons' money had always come from coal, but that stopped when the mines were nationalised after the Second World War. By the end of the 1960s, his grandfather had gambled away the last of the compensation his father had been paid for that. Unfortunately, the mines themselves are still there, and the mansion has been badly damaged by subsidence. It's Grade One Listed, and there's no money to fix it, but Lysander refuses to sell. Though I doubt he could find a buyer, to be honest.'

'How do you know this?' I was curious.

Eleanor sighed. 'I met him at that landowners' conference I went to back in February. He was telling everyone he was broke and asking for help.'

'And someone suggested he put on a music festival?' Fin was as dubious about that plan as I was.

'Somebody had already put the idea in his head. He was convinced he'd be rivalling Glastonbury or Donington in no time.' Eleanor's sarcasm told us what she thought of that. 'He just needed someone to do all the work.'

'Seriously?' Even thinking about the basics, I could see running a festival would involve months of planning and organisation and a fair amount of upfront costs. 'Did he have any sort of budget? Where was that money coming from if he was broke?'

'That was one of the first things I asked. I never did get a straight answer, but he seemed to think if he was sufficiently charming and helpless, I'd take on the whole project for him.' Eleanor shook her head. 'He pestered me for the whole weekend, and he emailed me nine times over the next two days. He even got my mobile number from somewhere and left messages virtually begging me on his knees. Then he stopped completely. I haven't heard another word. But this festival is definitely going ahead.'

'So who put that idea in his head?' Fin spooned instant coffee into one mug and dropped a teabag into another.

'You think the wyrm could be involved?' I went to get the milk out of the fridge.

'We know it's good at manipulating people. Plus, there's one very interesting thing about the estate,' Eleanor said. 'The park around the house was landscaped by someone who supposedly trained under Capability Brown. He dammed a stream to create a spectacular artificial lake.'

'Ideal for kelpies.' The kettle had boiled. I poured hot water into the mugs. 'We have to rule this out as a possibility, if nothing else.'

'How do we do that?' Fin wondered. 'If the wyrm is behind this, it'll be sticking close to Lysander Thingummy, so he doesn't come to his senses.'

'At the very least, it'll be in and around the park, especially if it needs to keep the kelpies where it wants them.' Eleanor looked at me. 'You're the only one who would recognise it, but if it sees you, the game is up.'

'It's a safe bet it knows what all of us look like.' I didn't want to imagine what the wyrm's next move would be if it realised we were on to it. 'Checking this out is an ideal job for a naiad. Isn't there any way we can contact Kalei?'

'I must have asked the dryads if they know where she is a dozen times by now.' Eleanor was as frustrated as me. 'They say she'll come and see us when she chooses to.'

'What about Zan? We'll need them here for...' I jerked my head in the direction of the outbuilding. 'And they said they could find the kelpies, wherever they went. If Zan sees they're in that lake, that needs dealing with regardless.'

Fin nodded. 'Blanche will want to help, after what those kelpies did to the beavers.'

'As long as the two of you can spare her time.' Eleanor knew Blanche had gone back to their flat near Bristol. Their business had clients, contracts and deadlines. They had bills and a mortgage to pay.

'I'll give her a ring.' Fin already had her phone in her hand.

I fetched my tea, and Eleanor got herself a glass of water. Fin explained what we needed to Blanche. I watched her nodding as she listened.

'See you soon.' She put down the phone and picked up her coffee. 'Zan's on their way. Blanche has some things she needs to finish. She'll drive up here tomorrow.'

Eleanor nodded. 'She can have the guest room you've been using.'

'Where is this festival happening?' I asked her.

'Chadbourn Park.' She passed me her phone to show me a map. 'The original owners were the ones with brains. The Reptons married into the family later on.'

I saw the estate was in Leicestershire, but only just. Go a few miles north, south or west, and you'd be in Derbyshire,

Warwickshire or Staffordshire. It was maybe an hour and a half's drive from Blithehurst. Lysander Repton must have thought his problems were over when he realised a proven businesswoman like Eleanor lived so close by, relatively speaking. If we were right, and the wyrm had already got its claws into him, it must have been spitting furious when it found out what he'd done.

'I've never heard of any of these bands.' Fin was looking at her own phone. 'This festival website's pretty rubbish too. Still, the tickets are cheap, as these things go. If each of the bands has their own following, that should add up to a decent audience.'

'And a decent feed for these monsters, if we're right.' This was looking more and more likely to me.

'When do you think Zan will get here?' Eleanor glanced out into the yard.

'Any minute now.' I drank my tea and went back to sharpening my chisels. 'Have you ever met a sylph before?'

'No. I'm curious,' Eleanor admitted.

'They're... unpredictable.' I concentrated on getting the best edge I could on my chisels.

Fin washed up the mugs we'd used and dried them.

Zan arrived about five minutes later. That's to say, a nondescript middle-aged man with greying hair appeared out of thin air in the dairy yard. He wore loose blue trousers and a garish tropical shirt. He saw me through the door and waved. 'Daniel! Finele!'

I'd know Zan's voice anywhere. We walked out into the yard.

'That's a new look for you.' I didn't think Blanche would be a fan.

'I'm trying out a few things.' Zan must have noticed Eleanor was unimpressed. They transformed themselves into an athletic man with fair skin and golden hair.

'No? Is this more to your taste?' The sylph became a petite woman with dark curls and a tanned complexion.

Eleanor laughed. 'No, but thank you.'

Zan turned back into the middle-aged man. 'Blanche said you need me to search a place where our enemy might be hiding?'

'That's right.' Fin held up her phone so Zan could see where Chadbourn Park was on the map. 'Can you—?'

The sylph had already gone.

'I see what you mean,' Eleanor commented. 'Do you have any idea when they'll come back?'

I shook my head. 'No clue.'

'There's no point in hanging around.' Fin put her phone away. 'I'll get my stuff out of the guest room and change the sheets.'

'I'll come and help. Call us when Zan gets back?'

As I nodded, Eleanor and Fin headed for the house. I picked up my chisels and went back to work on the bog oak. If this music festival was the wyrm's target, I had a hell of a lot to do if we were going to have any chance of trying our plan.

Zan knocked on the outbuilding window while I was wondering what we were going to do for dinner, and if I had time to sharpen my chisels again before Fin called me to ask the same question. I went to open the door.

'What are you doing with that?' The sylph looked like Blanche's boyfriend again, wearing jeans and a T-shirt. They grew a few inches taller, to see past me and get a better look at the bog oak.

'Something I'm going to need your help with. You're the only one who can do it, but I can't tell you about it just yet.'

Zan's grin broadened as they returned to their usual height. 'Very well.'

Their eyes glittered. I realised the sylph wasn't only excited about sharing in some secret.

'What did you find?'

'Kelpies,' Zan confirmed. 'The wyrm was in the lake as well.'

'Did you see anything else? Anything at all? Did Blanche tell you I had to fight a hag?' I was assuming Fin had told her sister.

'I didn't see any such menace. I stayed high above the lake, riding currents in the air. If the wyrm or the kelpies saw me, I would simply seem to be passing by.'

I was relieved to see Zan was taking this seriously.

'You should know what I didn't see.' The sylph looked at me, unblinking. 'There are no dryads in those woods. I do not think any have dwelt there for centuries.'

'Right. Thanks.' Finding allies on site had been too much to hope for. 'Let's go up to the house and tell Fin and Eleanor.'

Zan walked to the manor beside me, looking like an unremarkable tourist. We went in through the side door, and as we reached the kitchen, Eleanor called out from the library.

'Dan? In here!'

Zan immediately looked up at the ceiling. I glanced at the maps and computer printouts covering the coffee table.

'We're finding out what we can about Chadbourn Park.' Fin stood by the shelves, carefully putting an old book back.

'It's there,' I confirmed. 'With the kelpies.'

241

'Show me exactly what you've seen, and where.' Eleanor beckoned Zan over. She picked up a pencil and found what had to be a plan of the estate. 'Are they setting up anything for the festival yet?'

'I saw some preparations.' Zan sat on the sofa beside her and started pointing at places on the plan.

Fin walked around the room to join me by the door. 'So it's game on,' she said quietly. 'What about the centrepiece of our plan?'

'I still haven't come up with anyone we could ask,' I admitted.

'Then we need to ask the wise women, and the cunning men. We haven't got any other options, and we can't risk running out of time.'

I didn't need to look up to see the emerald glint of confirmation from the carved foliate faces in the corners of the room as the Green Man agreed with her.

Chapter Nineteen

Fin rang Hazel. She was the wise woman we knew best, and the one we trusted most. Fin explained we needed a massive favour, that this was really serious, but it wasn't something she could discuss on the phone. Hazel said she was busy. I called Peter and he told me the same. Neither of them could possibly get to Blithehurst before Wednesday. That wasn't good news.

After a bit of debate, we asked them both to come. If whoever we asked first couldn't give us the answer we needed, getting in touch with the other one would mean a delay we just couldn't afford. As it was, we were going to be uncomfortably tight for time.

On the other hand, that did give me three more days to work on the bog oak. Three and a half days, really, since Peter and Hazel both said they couldn't get here until the early afternoon. I have no idea what Eleanor told the rest of the staff I was doing, shut away in the dairy yard. I barely saw anyone else. I was getting up at six to start work, and I kept going into the evening until I couldn't trust my eyes or my hands any longer. I kept the bog oak covered up as much as I could now, apart from the bit I was working on. There was always the risk someone could turn up and look through the window.

Wednesday arrived. Fin brought me a pack of ham salad sandwiches and a can of fizzy orange for my lunch just after one o'clock. 'They're here. They're having a bathroom break, and Eleanor will bring them up to date over a coffee.'

'How did they react when they realised we were going to ask them both for help?' I ate the sandwiches in big bites.

'They didn't look thrilled, but then Eleanor asked if either of them had ever encountered a wyrm.' Fin grinned. 'There was no way either of them was going to go off in a huff after that.'

I hoped Eleanor remembered to swear Hazel and Peter to secrecy, until Saturday at least. After the weekend, all bets were off, especially if we tried our plan and it failed. Then it would be everyone for themselves.

Fin fetched the broom from the corner, but there wasn't much for her to sweep up. 'I take it Etraia's been by?'

I nodded as I popped the top on the can of orange and took a swallow. The dryad came every morning and evening, to take the increasingly fine bog oak shavings away. She didn't say what she was doing with the debris, and I didn't ask.

'What does she reckon?' Fin nodded at the shrouded carving.

'She says it's good.' I didn't want to talk about that. 'Is there anything new from Zan?'

The sylph was keeping watch on Chadbourn Park every day now, soaring invisibly high overhead. They were reporting every detail of the preparations for the music festival to Blanche. She was drawing up detailed plans. It turned out she did a lot of that sort of work for her and Fin's business, as well as painting artistic impressions for their clients. She'd got an A* in A level art.

'The kelpies' headcount looks to be the same as yesterday.' Fin shook her head. 'Zan hasn't seen the hags again though. We can't tell if they're still there, or how many there might be.'

I'd eaten those sandwiches too fast. I drank the rest of the orange trying to wash down a painfully tight feeling behind my breastbone. 'We can start talking tactics tonight. Now we know where everything is—'

A knock on the door interrupted me. Eleanor came in, followed by Peter and Hazel. There was no point in pissing

JULIET E. MCKENNA

about. I pulled the dust sheet off the bog oak so they could see what I'd been working on. The carving was very nearly finished.

'Good grief!' Peter was startled.

'What on earth...' Hazel walked around the table to study my work from every angle. 'I take it you've been helping with this?'

She glanced at Fin, who was standing by the rusted metal we surrounded the bog oak with every night. Fin nodded.

'I couldn't have done it without her.' I was watching Peter. He was looking very dubious.

He met my gaze. 'I can see why you wouldn't discuss this on the phone. What is it you're wanting from us, exactly?'

'A glamour?' I hoped that was the right word. 'Magic or whatever you call it that can make this thing look real. Alive enough to fool a wyrm. Just for long enough to get its attention.'

'We need it to move about,' Fin added quickly. 'On its own two feet.'

'Walking should be possible.' Hazel stooped to look closer. She clasped her hands behind her back to stop herself touching the carving. 'But talking?' She shook her head.

'We don't need it to speak,' I assured her.

'I'm glad to hear that,' Peter murmured. He was still standing by the door. 'What on earth are you planning to do with this?'

'Sorry, I can't say.' I hoped Eleanor had explained why we were keeping that to ourselves. I looked her way and saw her slight nod.

'Well, it's a decoy, obviously.' Hazel stood up straight and stepped back. She looked from me to the carving and back again. 'This really is remarkable.'

'Thanks.' I was proud of what I'd achieved with the bog oak, and I never wanted to do anything like this ever again.

Carving a life-size replica of myself had become more and more unnerving. Doing the clothes had been bad enough. The hands were worse. At least I could look at those and take a few reference photos on my phone when no one else was around. When I got to the head and face though... I'd had to call Fin yesterday, and ask her to come over from the manor. As far as anyone else was concerned, I needed her to tell me what the back of my neck looked like. Truthfully, I didn't want to be on my own with this thing any more, not unless I absolutely had to.

Fin had told me to make a few changes around the closed eyes and the chin. Hand on heart, I couldn't see what she meant, but I'd done what she'd said. I'd done the same when I was working on the wood sculpture of Sir Graelent by the castle, when Frai had given me her advice. I'd have been a fool to ignore the old dryad's opinion, and not just because she'd known Sir Graelent when he was alive. Anyway, earlier today, Etraia had confirmed this carving was a good likeness of me. Good enough for what we needed, at least. That had to be true, because a dryad couldn't lie to spare my feelings.

'You need this thing up and walking aboot for Sat'day?' Peter was chewing his lower lip. 'That disnae give us much time.'

He sounded very Scottish. I wondered why. We had agreed Eleanor was going to tell the two of them about the music festival at Chadbourn Park, and what we thought was going to happen there. Though we had agreed no one was going to mention hags. Starting that conversation might lead to questions about their links with wise women. That wasn't a can of worms we wanted to open, especially not in front of a cunning man.

'We don't think the wyrm will strike before then. Not if it wants as many people as possible to get there.' Fin looked for Hazel's agreement. 'The site opens on Friday afternoon, but the bands don't start playing until noon the next day. It might wait until Sunday, or even Monday, though. There's no way to know, so we have to be ready.'

Hazel nodded, thoughtful. 'I'd say the wyrm will most likely wait until dusk, whatever day it chooses to strike. The kelpies and whatever other horrors it's enlisted will be able to see in the dark, and the people they're hunting won't. They won't dare make a move before the wyrm does, which is one thing in our favour.'

'You're cutting this awfu' fine.' Peter looked at me. 'Did ye no—?'

Eleanor's phone rang. 'Excuse me.'

'I thought we'd have more time,' I admitted. 'I was going to ask an old Welsh woman who used to be a fairy—'

'Just a moment.' Eleanor interrupted whoever was calling and snapped her fingers a couple of times to get my attention. She put her phone on speaker. 'Sorry, Sarah, could you say that again, please.'

'I said, Denise is here. Bold as brass. I've just seen her by the rock garden.' Sarah was cross enough for everyone to hear her outrage.

'Thanks for letting me know. For the moment, can you just keep an eye on her, please? I'll call you back in a few minutes.' Eleanor ended the call and looked around the workshop. 'This can't be a coincidence.'

'No fucking chance,' I agreed.

'Excuse me.' Hazel raised a hand. 'Who is Denise? Other than bad news, I assume?'

I looked at Fin. We both looked at Eleanor. Calmly and coldly, she told Hazel and Peter about Denise's behaviour when the bitch had worked here. She explained about the fake bad reviews and that horrible website trying to stir up suspicion about Robbie's death. She didn't mention Sophie's wedding or the stalking photos, but even without that, Peter and Hazel could see she had every right to be furious.

I spoke up as soon as Eleanor stopped talking. 'This is a private business. You can tell her to get lost and not come back.' I was pretty sure I was right about that, legally speaking.

'Follow it up in writing,' Fin added. 'Tell her she's banned from any and all Blithehurst Estate property, and send a copy to the police, so they've got a record on file.'

'I don't see how that helps this poor woman,' Hazel objected. 'If this wyrm has got her under its influence.'

'I don't see how that's our problem.' Besides, if my plan worked, the wyrm wouldn't bother Denise again.

'Obviously, she's no a nice person,' Peter said mildly, 'but do you only help folk you like?'

I bit back the urge to confront him with a few of the things I knew other cunning men had done. They were hardly ones to talk. I was also relieved Eleanor hadn't mentioned Sophie's wedding now. Somehow, I didn't think Hazel or Peter would be too impressed if they knew I'd left Denise unconscious by the side of a road for an ambulance to find. Even if the wyrm hadn't been responsible for her being a pain in the arse back then.

'Let's assume she's here to snoop on the wyrm's behalf.' Hazel broke the awkward silence. 'If you throw her out on her ear, that's as good as saying you have something to hide. But if we can get her away from here and well beyond its reach fast enough, it'll have no idea where she's gone. Trying to find her could very likely distract it for a day or so.'

'That could be useful,' Eleanor conceded.

'How long will getting rid of her take you?' I picked up the dust sheet to cover up the carving again. 'Getting this ready to go has to be our priority.'

Peter shook his head as he looked at the bog oak. 'We cannae do that for you. Cast the glamour you need, I mean.'

'Can't, or won't?' Before he answered, I looked at Hazel. 'Can the wise women help?'

'No. We can't,' she clarified. 'Any more than the cunning men could.'

Fuck. Fin looked as if she was going to say the same, and she doesn't often swear.

'Fine. I'll call Aled. Let's see if he knows where I can find one of the Tylwyth Teg.' Though I hated to think what sort of price a scary Welsh fairy would ask for in return for this sort of favour. Assuming we could find one of them in time. Assuming they would agree to do this. The Welsh have different myths about dragons. Shit. We were in serious trouble now.

'No need for that,' Peter said quickly. 'We cannae do it, but we know who can. As long as everything you see and hear stays strictly between the two of us, Dan. As long as no word that I'm doing this for you leaves this room.'

He looked warily at Hazel. She spread her hands as if she was surrendering.

'I won't say a thing to anyone. In return, I'd appreciate you not telling your associates that we're unable to help with this.'

Peter nodded. 'Aye, that's fair.'

'Let's go then.' I was more relieved than I could say.

The cunning man shook his head, stubborn. 'After we've dealt with Denise.'

'Can't you do that on your own?' I asked Hazel.

'I could,' she agreed, 'but I see no reason why Peter shouldn't help, since he's offering.'

They shared a glance. Some unspoken negotiation was going on between them. Fine. That was none of my business. My priority was getting rid of Denise.

'What are you going to do with her?' Fin wanted to know.

'Ideally without any sort of fuss.' Eleanor looked tense. 'We don't need videos from visitors' phones going viral.'

'That shouldn't be an issue.' Hazel sounded confident, which was reassuring. 'First things first. Peter and I will need to get close without her noticing us.'

'Shall I see if one of the dryads can lure her into the woods?' Personally, I'd be fine with whistling up the black shuck to scare Denise into running for cover, but that would probably cause the uproar Eleanor wanted to avoid.

'I was thinking more of luring her into the garden centre.' Hazel looked at me, exasperated, as if she knew what I'd been thinking. 'If we can find out where she is now, I want the three of you to meet up where she can see you. Then you can hurry off, as if you've got something important to do. That should be enough to get her to follow, don't you think?'

'And we lead her into the garden centre?' Fin didn't understand this plan any more than I did, but she was ready to do what the wise woman asked.

Eleanor was already on her phone. 'Sarah? Can you still see Denise? Do you know where she is right now?'

'Sitting here having a cuppa and a scone, calm as you like.' Sarah sounded like she'd have happily stirred poison into the teapot.

'Thanks. You can leave this with me now.' Eleanor put her phone away.

'Right,' Hazel said briskly. 'Fin, you go down to the castle cafe and buy yourself a coffee. Sit down, relax, look as if everything's just fine. Eleanor, you go in a few minutes later, and whisper in Fin's ear. Then the two of you come hurrying out. Dan, I want you waiting somewhere visible, so Denise will see you as soon as she comes out of the cafe. You two, join Dan as quick as you can. Then the three of you get to the garden centre as fast as possible.'

'What happens there?' I demanded.

Peter grinned. 'You three have a wee chat about the weather, and we do our thing.'

'Which is what, exactly?'

'Never mind,' Eleanor interrupted. 'Fin, let's go.'

The two of them left the outbuilding and Hazel went after them.

I decided not to say what I was thinking. 'Help me cover this up.'

I tossed the other end of the dust sheet to Peter. He caught it and we spread the grubby cloth over the bog oak carving.

'Man, that's better.' He shivered as he looked at the shrouded effigy.

'Tell me about it.' I fetched some broken bits of rusted farm machinery.

Peter helped me with the rest, and we ringed the thing with old iron. I was relieved to see he was as uneasy around the carving as me, but I still wasn't going to leave him alone with it. If he rolled the bog oak over to look at the back, he'd have questions I didn't want to answer just yet.

'After you.' I gestured towards the door. Peter went out into the dairy yard, and I locked the outbuilding door. 'Can you find your way to the garden centre from here?'

'I can.' The cunning man walked away.

I watched him leave the yard, then I hurried up to the manor house and followed the path down towards the castle. I'd only just passed the rock garden when I saw Fin and Eleanor come out of the gatehouse. They crossed the footbridge over the moat so fast, you'd think the shuck was stalking them. I stayed where I was and pretended to check my phone. Looking down at the screen hopefully meant it wasn't too obvious I was watching for Denise.

The slope of the path up the valley is more noticeable coming back. Eleanor stopped to catch her breath as they reached me. 'Is she—?'

'Yes.' Denise was coming up the path more slowly than Eleanor and Fin. The nosy cow was looking wary. She also looked thinner and a lot older than I expected. If I didn't know better, I'd think she'd been ill. Being in a wyrm's thrall couldn't be healthy.

I put my phone away and turned my back on her. I didn't like doing that, but if Denise realised we were on to her, we were screwed. I had no idea what would happen then, but I knew we couldn't risk anything that delayed Peter taking me to whoever he could ask to cast the glamour we needed over the carving.

I walked towards the house, trying to work out how fast I needed to go to keep Denise hooked, without going so fast that she lost sight of us in the crowd. There were a whole load of visitors here today, just to be sodding inconvenient.

Eleanor was on my right as we crossed the gravel in front of the manor house. She turned left to take the wide central path through the knot garden towards the gate and the ticket office. 'Is she still following us?'

'Give me a minute.' Fin found her phone and flipped the camera around as if she was going to take a selfie. She moved the phone so she could see behind us. When we paused by the gate to let a group of new arrivals in, she nodded. 'She's there.'

We went out through the gate and took the path to the car park. The skin on the back of my neck was crawling. I really hated this. 'Can you see Hazel anywhere? Is she following Denise?'

Fin tilted her phone in a few different angles. 'Not that I can tell.'

'Put that away. Let's get this done.' As we reached the car park, Eleanor walked faster.

People stopped to stare as they noticed us hurrying past. I could see them wondering if there was some emergency. I didn't say a word. Eleanor's expression told me she was in no mood to slow down right now.

'Where should we go?' Fin looked around as we went through the garden centre door.

'This way.' I have no idea why this particular old stable building originally had big doors on both sides, but they make it easy to walk out to the rows of plants that Blithe-hurst's team of gardeners grow for sale.

We went past the displays of fancy gardening gloves and shelves holding everything from secateurs to bird food. Out-side, in the stable courtyard, a gazebo in one corner shelters a circle of the oak benches I make for sale. I sat down on one of those and leaned forward with my elbows on my thighs. Fin and Eleanor did the same, sitting on the benches to ei-ther side. With our heads close together, anyone would think we were talking secrets.

'Can either of you see her?' Eleanor asked urgently.

'I can see Peter.' I'd taken the bench facing back the way we had come.

'What about Hazel?' Fin spread out her hands and flexed her fingers. I knew she never liked feeling pursued.

'No. Wait – no, sorry. That's someone else.' Trying to see what was going on while I was apparently looking down at the ground was sodding annoying. I was itching to just stand up and get a clear view of everyone else's position.

'What about bloody Denise?' Eleanor hissed.

'Hang on.' I waited a moment to be absolutely certain. 'She's over by the bird baths. She's – yes, Hazel's talking to her.'

I had no chance of hearing their conversation. I also realised the three of us were getting curious glances from customers and staff. Any minute now, someone was going to come over and ask what we were doing.

'How long are we supposed to sit here like this?' Now Fin was getting frustrated.

'No idea – no, wait, Peter's coming over.' I had to force myself to stay on the bench.

He grinned as he reached the gazebo. 'You're okay now. You can get up.'

Eleanor was on her feet so fast you'd think she'd been sitting on a springboard. 'Well?'

'She's under a compulsion.' Peter led us over to a cluster of bay trees for sale in decorative pots. '"Geas" is as good a word as any, if you want to look that up. It's a nasty one, right enough.'

'And?' Eleanor was still more wound up than I'd ever seen her.

'And we've overrode it,' Peter said quickly. 'Hazel will take her away, and the wise women will make damn sure that wyrm can't find her. They'll lay a few false trails as well, to keep the beast guessing.'

I don't think Eleanor heard that last part. She was already heading for the car park. Fin and I followed. We saw Hazel guiding Denise towards a dirty white Fiesta with a firm hand gripping her elbow. I couldn't see Denise's face, but something uncoordinated about the way she was walking remind-ed me of seeing her mazed by Frai and Asca.

'These aren't the dryads you're looking for,' Fin murmured.

'Sorry, what?' I was sure I'd misheard her.

'Never mind.' She turned to Peter. 'What now?'

'Another road trip for me and Dan.' He didn't sound thrilled about that. 'Let's get your Land Rover loaded up.'

'Where are you parked?' I looked around for his 4x4.

He hesitated. 'We'd better just take the one vehicle. Is it okay if I leave mine here?' he asked Eleanor.

She nodded. 'Whatever you need.'

Chapter Twenty

We drove north until well after midnight. We stopped for fuel near Perth just before seven. When I came out of the garage shop after paying, I saw Peter was on his phone. He put it away as I got back behind the wheel.

'Do you want me to drive for a bit?' he offered.

'I'm fine.' Concentrating on the road stopped me thinking about the carving wrapped up in dust sheets in the back. 'I could go for a burger and chips though.'

'Good idea,' he agreed.

We stopped at the next place we saw at the side of the road. We didn't say much as we ate. What did we have to talk about? We reached Inverness just after nine.

'Let's get a coffee. Take the next exit.' Peter wasn't suggesting we make a stop. He was telling me.

'Okay.' I'd been about to say I needed a piss.

I turned off the A9 and followed his directions to a half-way-decent pub. We both headed straight for the Gents.

'I'll get the coffees to go,' Peter offered as we washed our hands. 'See you back out there, okay?'

'Fine.' I can take a hint. I'd also seen two blokes sitting at a table with half-finished pints look at him as soon as we walked in.

Out in the car park, I waited by the Landy, enjoying a bit of fresh air and the chance to stand up for a while. Peter came out of the pub carrying two takeaway cups. Either the barista in there was on a serious go-slow or he'd been talking to someone.

'Latte with two sugars. Did I get that right?' He handed me a cup.

It took me a moment to remember we'd had a coffee together at Durham services on our way to Berwick. 'That's fine.'

'You've done enough driving today.' He sipped his own drink. 'I'll take it from here.'

Again, that wasn't a suggestion. Whatever. I wasn't going to argue. Apart from anything else, I was knackered.

The A9 took us across an impressive bridge. When I saw Peter get comfortable with the feel of the Landy, I could relax a bit. He soon turned off the coast road though, and he switched off the satnav without asking me. I thought about saying something, but he obviously knew where he was going. Equally clearly, he didn't want me to know where that was.

Soon we were driving through mountains that cut stark black outlines against the endlessly twilight sky. I'd never been this far north before. I caught sight of a few names I vaguely recognised on road signs to places like Ullapool. That didn't help me work out where we were. Ullapool was miles away, for one thing, and for another, I couldn't have found it on a map if someone had offered me a hundred quid.

Peter carried on driving. He didn't say anything and neither did I. The roads were getting narrower and steeper, and I didn't want to distract him. More than anything else, I wanted to get this done and get home. At long last, the cunning man pulled up on the grass verge between the road and a long narrow stretch of water that shimmered silver beneath the full moon. I couldn't tell if that was a freshwater loch or a sea inlet reaching this far inland. I wondered what might be hiding under the glassy surface, and I wasn't thinking about seals or fish.

'Here we are.' Peter left my keys in the ignition as he opened the door and got out.

As I leaned over to take them, I checked the mileage for this trip and how much diesel was still in the tank. Dad taught me a sudden drop-off in miles-per-gallon can be an early sign of trouble, and I sure as hell didn't want to break down way out here. Wherever 'here' might be. We had driven for something like five hundred miles. And if we drove five hundred more? The last thing I needed was that song stuck in my head, so I grabbed the keys and got out of the Landy.

Peter was opening up the back. He grabbed the bog oak carving's feet and started dragging it out. 'Give me a hand, will you?'

I waited until I could get hold of the effigy's shoulders. Between us, we carried it to an open space between the clumps of bracken, halfway to the water's edge, where Peter put the feet down. It was nowhere as heavy as the original log, but this was still a two-man job.

'What now?' I made sure the dust sheets were tucked underneath the effigy's head and feet to defeat any curious gusts of wind.

'We wait.' Peter went back to the Landy to close the doors.

I should have expected that. At least I didn't think we'd have to explain ourselves to passers-by. Somebody must have had some reason to build a road on the narrow ledge of level ground that ran alongside the water here, but I couldn't see squares of light in any direction that might identify some distant house. No hint of headlamps warned me that another vehicle was coming this way. We were on our own out here.

Peter sat down cross-legged on the coarse grass, looking towards the west. I sat down not far away. The night was none too warm, but my sweatshirt was thick enough to keep the breeze off. It must have rained earlier, because I could soon feel dampness seeping through to my backside, but for the moment, the wind was keeping the clouds moving overhead. Their dark shadows swept across the silvery water.

The quietly rippling lake or loch, or whatever it was called, was dotted with lumps of rock. Some of them were probably big enough to be called islands. The hills that surrounded us were dark outlines against the night sky. The land sloped upwards, gently at first, and then more steeply before levelling off. Close by, a few scrubby saplings had claimed a foothold close to the water. I could smell damp pebbles and fresh summer growth. An idle breeze whispered through the bigger trees hidden in the shadows behind me. My eyes grew used to the low light, and I realised pale green radiance was shimmering in the sky above us.

'She's here.' Peter sprang to his feet.

The cunning man was looking westward. I stood up and did the same. At first, I was convinced there was nothing to see. A moment later, I saw movement. I'd been looking in the wrong place, down by the water's edge and along the road. Far away on the horizon, a huge dark figure had paused, silhouetted against the eerie sky. I couldn't say if it was male or female, but I had seen something like this before. That had been an ancient earth spirit, stirred up when I'd first met Peter. I reminded myself that Iain and the other cunning men had known how to put the fearsome shadow back to sleep.

This massive figure was coming closer, stride by giant stride. With its broad shoulders hunched, it walked along the edge of the water. By that I mean it was walking on the shifting surface, not on the pebbly shore. Whatever this was, it was getting smaller, though it was at least three times my height right now. As the approaching outline shifted and reshaped itself, I remembered the murderous giant I had faced with Fin, hundreds of miles south of here on the ancient Ridgeway. As far as I could tell, this apparition wore a long skirt, with some sort of shawl or blanket wrapped around its shoulders. Her shoulders. That didn't reassure me.

Overhead, the northern lights grew brighter. An old woman was coming towards us now, still walking on the water, and not leaving a ripple behind. An apron around her waist was a pale rectangle against her long dark dress, and the moonlight showed me her woollen shawl was woven with a mossy chequer pattern. The fringed ends crossed over on her chest and were tied behind her back.

That left her hands free. One long-nailed hand gripped a staff. The sheen told me the wood had been oiled or waxed after the bark was stripped off, but no tool had shaped it. She wasn't using it as a walking stick, even though she stooped as she came closer. Stood up straight, her head wouldn't have reached my elbow. I wasn't fool enough to think that could give me any sort of advantage. Her weathered, wrinkled face was as old as the hills surrounding us. One of her eyes was closed, half hidden by strands of long silver hair that slid free of a square of pale cloth that covered her head, knotted at the back of her neck.

She halted where the water met the land and tucked a stray wisp behind her other ear with her free hand. Her open eye shone bright as the moon overhead as she studied me. I was chilled to the bone, and not because the weather had turned. Whoever this ancient being might be, she was some sort of kin to the hag I'd met in my mother's wood. Don't ask me how I knew that, but I had absolutely no doubt. She was also infinitely more powerful. One wrong move and I'd be dead. I stood still and focused my attention on her staff, trying to decide what that wood might be.

Peter was talking to the ancient spirit, or fairy or whatever she was, in what had to be Gaelic. I had no clue what he was saying, but I could hear the respect in his voice was edged with fear. That wasn't reassuring. She nodded, frowning, though I didn't think she was cross with him. I hoped so anyway. I hoped he was telling her what had happened after the wyrm had lured those kelpies south.

His tone changed and he spoke more quickly. He was clearly asking her something. So far, so good? Maybe not. Peter broke off when the old woman sniffed with sudden irritation. Now she was scowling. Had he said something wrong and landed us in the shit? I didn't dare open my mouth in case I made things worse.

The ancient spirit came onto the shore. I quickly stepped back out of her path. She ignored me as she walked over to the shrouded carving and pushed at the dust sheets with the end of her staff. Finding she couldn't unwrap it, she snapped withered fingers at Peter. He hurried over to uncover the bog oak.

She bent down to study it, then glanced over at me. As she cackled with laughter, I saw she had a single tooth left in her gummy grin. She hit the bog oak effigy with her staff three times. The hard, sharp sound rang out across the water. It echoed back from the hillside opposite. I heard a splash somewhere out in the moonlight and tried to see what that was. No luck. When I looked back, the old woman had gone. Something that looked exactly like me was lying on the grass. The old fairy had left her staff beside it.

Peter was saying something fervent in Gaelic under his breath. I forced myself to go closer and look more closely at this thing I had made. Its brown boots looked like leather now, and I could even see the loops of their laces stir in the breeze. The combat trousers and T-shirt I had carved draped like green cloth. I guessed we had the old woman to thank for that colour. Its skin looked like, well, human skin. I could see fine hair on its forearms that I sure as hell hadn't carved as a detail.

This had seemed like a good idea at the time. No, it had seemed like a great idea. I told myself it still was, even if I was starting to realise I should have asked a hell of a lot more questions and got some crucial answers before we ever

261

started this. I trod on a twig hidden in the grass. The effigy opened its eyes at the snap. It turned its head to look at me.

Peter stumbled backwards so fast he nearly fell on his arse. 'Man, that's creepy.'

'Fuck, yes.' I had to look away. The last thing I wanted to do was meet the sodding thing's gaze.

'So how's this supposed to work?' Peter's voice was shaking.

That was another of the things we should have discussed earlier. 'What did you say to her?'

'I told her you wanted a glamour on the thing, to fool people into thinking it was you. Not just people,' he added hastily. 'Everything, up to and including the wyrm.'

'Did she say anything about how we get it to do what we want?' I was grasping at straws. I hadn't heard the old woman say a single word.

'Nothing,' Peter confirmed.

I saw the effigy's head turn towards his voice. He backed off a few more steps.

I took a breath. 'Okay, let's think this through.'

We'd got what we had come here for. We should definitely have asked for instructions, but it was too late for that. We could stay here until the sun came up and went down again, and that wouldn't change.

I bent down to pick up the wooden staff. 'Why do you suppose she left this?'

Peter chewed his lower lip. 'Let me see that?'

As I reached across the effigy to hand it to him, I saw the thing's gaze was following the staff. Whether that distracted me or Peter fumbled the catch, between us we managed to drop it. The instant it landed on the effigy, the thing was a bog oak carving again.

262

If we hadn't been standing there in the small hours of the morning, I could have sworn I heard a raven's caw. It sounded like mocking laughter. I looked around and saw the northern lights had gone from the sky. When had that happened?

Peter poked the carving's leg with the staff. Nothing changed. He hit it quickly, three times. Still nothing.

I held out my hand. 'Let me try?'

He tossed me the staff. I caught it and tapped the effigy's chest where the old woman had hit it. Once, twice, and the third time was the charm. My silent, creepy twin lay on its back at our feet. Seeing it again was even worse than the first time. I smacked it once on the thigh before I realised what I was doing. It was just carved wood again. Three quick thumps on the closest boot, and the eerie thing was life-like enough for someone to ring 999 when they realised this motionless stranger wasn't breathing.

I hadn't noticed that before. Would it give the game away? I could only hope not. Besides, that didn't matter right now. I needed to work out the ground rules if this thing was going to be any use at all.

I retreated a few metres. 'Tell it to stand up.'

'Right enough.' Peter cleared his throat. 'On your feet – whatever you are.'

The thing turned its head towards the sound of his voice, but it didn't make a move to do what he said.

I tightened my grip on the staff and looked down at the effigy. This time, I did look into its blank, unthinking eyes. 'Stand up.'

It sat up first of all. Then it bent its legs to kneel before it got to its feet, just like a normal person. I'd like to say we both stepped back to give it plenty of room. I can't speak for Peter, but that's not what I was thinking. As soon as it moved, I nearly pissed myself.

'Okay. Let's try something.' I offered the staff to Peter.

He didn't reach for it. That would have meant getting closer to the thing. 'Try what?'

'Just work with me.' I held out the staff horizontally so he could take the end.

He muttered something under his breath, but he stepped forward to grab it before quickly retreating.

'Turn around,' I ordered the effigy.

It didn't move.

I nodded at Peter. 'Your turn.'

He pointed the staff at the thing. 'Turn around!'

It still didn't move.

'Here.' Peter tossed the staff back to me.

I caught the smooth wood. 'Turn around.'

The effigy did a quick one-eighty degrees and stood staring straight ahead. That meant I could see its back for the first time. There was nothing but the cloth of its T-shirt. Good. I hoped Peter didn't notice my relief.

He had other things on his mind. 'Yon cailleach knows what she's about, even if we don't.'

'Right.' I wasn't sure what he meant, but this wasn't the time to discuss it. 'Okay, let's get back to Blithehurst.'

Peter managed a crooked smile. 'My apologies. I'll have to leave that to you.'

'Oh, come on!'

But the cunning man was gone. A black panther raced up the hillside to disappear into the shadows beneath the trees.

'Well, that's just fucking marvellous.'

The effigy turned its head at the sound of my voice. Its expression didn't change. Did I seriously look that unfriend-ly to other people? I would be so sodding relieved when this weekend was over and, one way or the other, this thing would be out of my life. Tuesday morning couldn't come soon enough.

'Stay there.' I gathered up the dust sheets and opened up the back of the Land Rover. There was absolutely no fucking way I was driving for ten hours with that in the passenger seat beside me.

'You. Come here.' I kept tight hold of the staff as it walked over. 'Get in.'

As soon as the thing had climbed inside, I tapped it between the shoulder blades. Now all I had to do was throw dust sheets over an awkwardly poised wooden carving. As I locked the door on it, I was really, really glad we had told Peter this thing didn't need to speak. I was even more relieved that old woman hadn't decided it should regardless.

I looked up at the paling sky. There really was sod all night worth the name so far north at this time of year. I checked my phone and was unsurprised to find no trace of a signal. I looked up and down the narrow road. Peter had pulled the Land Rover far enough off the tarmac not to cause an obstruction. I wanted to get home, but I wanted to get back in one piece. I needed a few hours' sleep before I headed south. Everyone's efforts through this seemingly endless month would be wasted if I dozed off at the wheel and totalled the Landy, myself and the carving I had spent so many hours on.

I tried to make myself comfortable in the passenger seat. That wasn't easy, and not just because I found I was sitting on Peter's car keys. Wondering when he had left them there didn't distract me for long. I couldn't stop thinking about the thing shut up in the back. Back when I'd been a cocky teenager, I'd made the mistake of watching some horror film about a cursed doll that had come to life. Or had it been an evil puppet? Maybe it was a possessed ventriloquist's dummy? Never mind. The problem wasn't so much the movie as the dreams that scared me shitless for weeks. When I opened the back of the Landy again, would I find the effigy had been moving around while I wasn't looking? I had the old woman's staff here in the front seats with me, but even so...

A tractor rumbling past woke me up. I really had been knackered. Right now, I was stiff, cold and thirsty, as well as desperate for a pee. I opened the door, got out and took care of that. The sky was grey with clouds and drizzling. At least cold rain on my face helped wake me up. I checked the time on my phone. Six-thirty in the morning. Good enough.

I knew I had some bottled water in the back of the Landy, but I decided I could wait for a drink. I got into the driver's seat and switched on the satnav. I didn't bother zooming out to find out exactly where we were. Peter wouldn't want me to know, and honestly, I couldn't be arsed. I just wanted to get home. I turned the key in the ignition and set off. I followed the little blue car on the scrolling map until I hit a decent-sized road, and I stopped at the first truckers' cafe I found. While I was waiting for a full Scottish breakfast, sipping tea strong enough to make my eyes sting, I called Fin.

'Dan? Is everything okay?' She sounded tense, which was hardly a surprise.

'I'm fine. We – we've got it done. You'll see when I get back.'

'Okay. When will you get here?'

A quick calculation told me this was going to be a pig of a day. I'd have to make more stops than usual to stay topped up with caffeine. That would mean more bathroom breaks as well.

'Not before five this afternoon. Later, if I hit bad traffic.' Which was pretty much guaranteed, given the time of day

I'd be reaching Manchester or Leeds, whichever route I took. 'Can you do me a favour?'

Fin had got there ahead of me. 'You want me to ring Conn?'

'Please.' From everything Iris had told us, we knew he could bring us the last thing we needed. Once he knew why, we were certain there was no way he'd refuse.

I saw my breakfast approaching. 'I've got to go. I'll get back as soon as I can. Love you.'

'Love you. Drive safe.'

Fin ended the call. I put my phone down and ate as fast as I could without risking indigestion. By the time I got back to Blithehurst, we'd have less than twenty-four hours before Chadbourn Park opened its gates for its first and most likely its last ever music festival.

Chapter Twenty-One

Conn's Mercedes pulled into the dairy yard just after half past eight on Friday morning. I'd been tidying my workshop since just before seven. Fin had said she'd told the Irishman the back gate would be open for Blithehurst employees coming to work, so he could just follow the estate road and go left where it forked. Conn got out and looked around. He was wearing jeans and the same leather jacket over a black T-shirt.

I went out to meet him. 'Thanks for getting here so fast.'

'Night ferry.' He nodded at Peter's Toyota. 'Who else is here?'

'No one.' I'd brought the 4x4 down from the main car park to avoid awkward questions. I'd rung Peter to ask when he planned to collect his car, but my call had gone straight to voicemail. No one was answering Iain's phone either.

Conn opened the back of the Merc. 'There you are. Cut, dried and ready to go. Just don't tell Bord na Móna.'

'I won't.' That was an easy promise, since I didn't know who she was.

'Do you know what you're doing with this?' Conn glanced at me, curious.

'Not really.' I looked at the wooden box stacked with what looked like dried clods of earth. The dark brown lumps were roughly rectangular and threaded through with fine pale roots.

'But you have to use a turf – a peat fire – for this thing you're going to do?'

'That's what the stories say.' Like the bog oak. I wasn't going to try anything else and risk failure.

'So what exactly is this plan of yours?' He shut the SUV.

'It'll be easiest to explain if I show you. Hang on a minute.' I went back into the workshop and fetched the staff from the corner where I stack spare lengths of dowel and architrave.

'What's that?' Conn asked as soon as he saw it. That line between his eyebrows deepened.

'Alder, finished with beeswax.' I'd recognised the colour and grain of the wood as soon as I saw it in daylight.

Conn shot me a look which I knew I deserved. 'Where did you get that, and what does it do?'

'I can't tell you, and I'll show you.' I walked over to the outbuilding and unlocked the door.

As soon as Conn was inside, I locked the door behind us. Conn was staring at the shrouded shape in the circle of rusted iron. I'd fetched a chair and made the effigy sit on it last night. Then I'd turned the thing back to bog oak and covered it with the dust sheets. I'd nailed another sheet over the window as well. I uncovered the carving and saw his eyes widen. I gave the effigy three quick taps on one shoulder with the alder staff.

Conn took a step back. 'Loscadh is dó ort!'

I guessed that meant he was surprised to see my eerie idiot twin. That was fair. I didn't think I would ever get used to it.

'Stand up.' The effigy got to its feet. I tapped the side of its leg and it was a wooden statue. 'You need to see the back while it's like this.'

Conn walked around to join me, keeping an arm's length away from the iron circle. I showed him the panel I had made from that first slice I'd cut from the bog oak. That closed up the hollow I'd carved into the effigy's back. Doing that had been a job and a half, but I was pleased with the result. The panel fitted so tightly I had to use my penknife blade to get it out.

'We put some burning peat in here, before we let the wyrm see it. Before I make it look like me.'

'Then what?' Conn didn't come any closer.

'Then we send it for a walk where the wyrm will see, and we hope to hell the bastard eats it whole.' When Fin and I had put this plan together, that had seemed the obvious outcome. Now I was telling somebody else, I wasn't quite so confident. 'It's seen me before. It'll recognise me. It must know I'm who's been fucking up its plans.'

'So it'll want to kill you itself. Get the job done.' Conn nodded. 'I can see that. So it swallows your mannikin here and gets a turf fire in its belly. Then what?'

'Then it burns to death from the inside out because it can't heal itself with a quick dip in the nearest lake.'

Eleanor and I had seen for ourselves that those legends about wyrms and water were true. No matter how badly we hurt the one we'd fought here at Blithehurst, the bastard creature dived into the castle moat and came back as good as new.

'That's bog oak.' Conn didn't need me to tell him what I'd used to make the effigy. 'You've dried it out, I can see that, but you're expecting a few sods of burning turf will set that whole thing alight? When it's inside a wyrm's guts?' He was doubtful.

'Burning turf with a bit of help,' I admitted.

'Such as?' Conn asked.

'Hexamine fuel tablets, for a camping stove.' That was the first thing I'd thought of when we had discussed using some sort of accelerant to guarantee the bog oak caught fire.

I'd always taken a little hexi burner when I went hiking. It was great for making a cup of tea and even frying a quick breakfast. The burner folded up into a neat, small rectangle and the tablets barely weighed anything.

'You do know that's a controlled substance these days?'

'I do now.' When I'd got online to buy some, I hadn't found any for sale. What I couldn't find out was why. A bit of lateral thinking with search engines took me to a very pissed-off model steam engine maker's website. Thanks to other uses for hexamine allegedly circulating on the dark web, possessing it now required an official licence, to be paid for and renewed every three years. The penalties for not following these new rules were serious.

'I knew I'd left a nearly full box in my dad's shed. So Fin went to visit my parents and brought it back here yesterday.'

I wondered how Conn knew the UK regulations on hexamine had changed, but he had already moved on.

'What bright spark came up with this mad idea?'

'Well, you wouldn't believe how many stories we had to read before someone killed a wyrm without hacking it into pieces. Someone supposedly poisoned one, but when he cut its head off, he got the concoction on his hand. He went out drinking with his mates to celebrate, licked the poison without realising and dropped dead. He hadn't written down the recipe.'

'Thoughtless of him,' Conn said dryly.

I nodded. 'Then we read about several knights in different places who had skewered wyrms with lances covered in burning pitch. So it looked as if that worked well enough for word to spread. We went searching for stories about killing wyrms with fire and found a couple of stories where they'd been burned from the inside out with peat.'

'And one of you knew what fairies can do with bog oak.' Conn shook his head as he stared at the effigy. 'Ní rachainn i bhfoisceacht scread asail...'

He turned to me. 'What will you do if this doesn't work?'

'Go back to plan A. Try to chop it to bits.'

I hoped it didn't come to that, but Eleanor had been collecting every sword and polearm that she could find stashed in family cellars and attics. A few were genuinely medieval, but most were Victorian fakes. As long as they were heavy enough to hurt and sharp enough to cut through wyrm hide, I didn't care. She'd also come up with a better idea than a shotgun loaded with ball bearings, but I decided not to tell Conn about that just now.

'And the kelpies?' Conn demanded. 'What will you do about them?'

'We know the wyrm's been threatening them, and stealing their silver chains if they don't do what they're told. I've promised to help some of the ones I've met – if I can. If we can kill the wyrm, I think there's a chance they'll back off and talk.'

If not, we'd have to see if Zan's threats were more than hot air. That was as far as Eleanor, Fin and I had got, discussing how we might tackle the kelpies last night. I couldn't stay awake, so I'd gone to bed.

Conn frowned. 'Turf's not that hard to light, but where do you plan to do that? How will you stop some kelpie, or even the wyrm itself, seeing what you're up to?'

Before I could answer him, someone knocked on the door.

'Dan? It's us.' Eleanor had booked a long weekend off as soon as Zan had confirmed the wyrm was in the lake. She told Sarah and Janice she needed a break before the peak summer visitor season. She'd said she might go and visit some friends, without being specific about her plans.

She was surprised to see Conn. 'Oh, you're here already. Were you able to bring us some peat? I read something about it being banned as a fuel.'

'Commercially, yes. It's discouraged for private use, but if you know a family who own a bog, you'll be grand.' He grinned.

I was glad Eleanor hadn't mentioned that earlier. I didn't need anything else to worry about. I was surprised to see Iris with Eleanor and Fin. Blanche was with them too, as well as Zan. I was even more surprised when Iris walked over to Conn and slid a hand around his waist. He put an arm around her shoulders. I guessed they'd got over whatever they had argued about.

'Did you know about this yoke?' he asked her as he gestured at the effigy.

'They told me just now.' Iris stared at the thing.

'What do you think of this plan?'

'I'd say it's a thousand – million – whatever – to one shot, but it could just work.' Iris grimaced. 'Don't take this the wrong way, Dan, but bloody hell, that's horrible.'

Fin shuddered. 'Wait till you see it walking about.' She'd kept watch at the yard entrance yesterday evening while I got the thing out of the Landy and into the outbuilding.

'Daniel,' Conn said. 'Are you the only one who can wake it?'

'I don't know.' I offered him the alder staff. 'Want to try?'

Zan had been standing at the back by the door, uncharacteristically still and quiet. This was too much for the sylph to resist, even though the effigy was ringed with iron. They were grabbing the staff out of my hand before I realised they had moved.

'Let me! What do I do?'

'Tap it three times.'

Zan smacked the effigy's arm so hard that everyone winced. I expected to see dents in the bog oak. To my relief, there wasn't a mark, and the alder staff was still in one piece too. Most importantly, the carving was still solid, silent wood.

'What use is that?' Annoyed, the sylph threw the staff to the floor.

Blanche quickly picked it up. 'Never mind. You've got much more important things to do. That's right, isn't it, Dan?'

'Absolutely.' I hoped Blanche was right when she assured us Zan would do what we asked without getting too creative and wrecking everything. 'As soon as there's any sign of the wyrm, we need you to raise a few small whirlwinds or something like that, to drive people away from the lake. Can you get a barrier between the kelpies and whoever they're hoping to eat?'

'Of course.' The sylph liked that idea.

'Be careful no one gets hurt,' Fin said quickly.

'Freak weather in Leicestershire will make headline news.' Conn looked at Iris.

She would know. Iris was a commercial meteorologist, working for a company that prepared weather forecasts for ships and aircraft.

'A tornado hit Birmingham a while back.' She shrugged. 'Climate change.'

That wasn't so far from the truth. Frai insisted these wyrms were stirring because the world was getting warmer and wetter.

'Zan?' I got the sylph's attention. 'What matters is scaring people who just came to a music festival away from danger.'

'If Zan's going to be busy, we'll have to keep watch up above.' Iris looked at her sisters.

'Are you going to stay and help out?' Blanche asked Conn.

'I wouldn't miss this,' he assured her.

Because if I fucked up, someone was still going to have to deal with the wyrm. Conn's glance told me he'd be getting the others safely away, then leaving to warn whoever he could find who might be able to help. That was reassuring, in a grim sort of way.

Iris was staring at the effigy again. 'You try,' she suggested to Blanche.

'If you like.'

I was pretty sure Blanche didn't want to, but she wasn't going to back out with her sisters watching. As it turned out, nothing happened. The three of them looked relieved.

'Your go.' Blanche handed the staff to Eleanor.

She didn't look at the effigy as she tapped it on the knee. 'Dan, I came over to tell you—'

The third tap was the charm. My eerie idiot twin was standing there. Blanche yelped and Zan turned translucent, instantly standing in front of her. The sylph's eyes flashed, as menacing as lightning.

'Swans and sylphs zero, greenwood two.' Conn tried to make a joke of it, but he was ready to get between the effigy and Iris if it showed any sign of moving their way. They backed off as far as they could. Iris was as pale as the whitewashed brick wall behind her.

'Bloody hell!' Eleanor took a step closer to study the effigy. When it looked her way, everyone froze, including me.

'It was a remarkable piece of work before, Dan, even if it gave me the creeps.' She screwed up her face. 'But now, whatever's been done to it... I'm sorry, but this is just *wrong*.'

I knew what she meant, and I wasn't going to argue. 'But it's what we need.'

'How wrong?' Fin demanded. 'Wrong enough to warn the wyrm it's a fake?'

'No.'

I don't know about anyone else, but I was startled when Zan answered her. The sylph was still in their simplest form, but they didn't look ready to blast the effigy into splinters any more. Not just yet, anyway.

'Dan is the one who shaped it with his tools and his intent,' the sylph said, as if that explained everything. 'The beast will be deceived.'

'Good to know.' Conn relaxed his hold on Iris. 'Does the same person have to—' He gestured, trying to find the right words. 'Turn it on and off again, as you might say?'

'Let's see. May I?' I took the staff from Eleanor and stepped into the effigy's line of sight. 'You, sit down.'

Everyone tried unsuccessfully to hide their unease as the thing did as it was told. Relief filled the room when I tapped its shoulder and a lifeless wooden carving was sitting on the chair.

'So that works for either one of you,' Conn commented. 'That could be useful, I suppose.'

'Maybe. Let's cover it up.'

As I picked up the dust sheets, Eleanor looked relieved.

'What I came here to tell you was I've had a call from Hazel.'

'About Denise?' I made sure the cloth wasn't going to slip off the effigy.

'I don't know where they've gone, but Hazel said they've begun to deprogramme her, which sounds more like rescuing someone from a cult to me, but never mind. The thing is, do you remember she said the wise women would lay a few false trails?' Eleanor went on before I could answer. 'Her colleagues have seen several hags following those scents.'

'Hags?' Conn interrupted. 'There are hags working with this wyrm?'

'A few, we think,' I admitted.

'Can the wise women deal with them if they try to snatch Denise?' Blanche asked the room in general.

Eleanor answered. 'I got that impression.'

That was another conversation I should have had before now. Sod it.

'If there's any chance of hags about, we have to watch each other's backs,' Conn insisted to Iris, Blanche and Fin.

'They can fly?' Fin didn't like that idea.

'Some can,' Conn said grimly. He looked at me. 'This festival, the music doesn't start till tomorrow, but the gates to the site will be open this evening? So people can set up tents and such?'

'That's right. From five o'clock onwards.'

The Irishman looked around the room. 'We should get over there tonight. I know you're thinking this wyrm will wait until more folk arrive tomorrow, but I'm not convinced it'll be able to hold back those kelpies. Not once they see warm bodies there for the taking. If those hags have gone off to chase after your wise women, why don't we see if we can't be done with this today?'

'The sooner we do, the sooner we're rid of that thing.' Fin looked at the shrouded effigy with loathing.

I chose not to point out that I'd been saying we needed to be ready for trouble to kick off as early as Friday evening. 'That's fine with me.'

'Then let's go!' Zan was closest to the door, looking like Blanche's boyfriend again.

No one argued. The sylph left and the others followed. I came last, making certain the outbuilding door was locked. When I turned around, I saw everyone was standing in the yard. The three dryads and the shuck stood in their way.

Frai could have modelled for a statue of an avenging goddess. Asca and Etraia looked more than capable of backing her up, with or without the shuck's help. The great shadowy black dog's hackles bristled as its smouldering eyes fixed on the outbuilding's window. It growled at the lowest edge of human hearing.

'We know what you have done and why. We cannot say you are wrong.' Frai sounded as if she'd like to, even so.

'If the beast does not take this bait, that stock – the carving – it must be destroyed.' Asca must have seen that what she had called the effigy confused me.

Then I realised she wasn't only talking to me. She was telling everyone.

'If the wyrm does not swallow it, you must bring it back here,' Etraia insisted, looking at Eleanor. 'We will destroy it for you. It cannot fall into any other hands.'

So the dryads didn't expect to see me again if our plan didn't succeed. That was a cheery notion. I didn't ask what they thought could go wrong. Fuck it. There were no dryads at Chadbourn Park, so they didn't know anything about the place. This was the only thing we could do. Hope for the best and plan for the worst, even if no plan survives contact with the enemy.

I shoved my keys into my trouser pocket. 'Let's get on with it.'

Chapter Twenty–Two

We finally set off just before four o'clock that afternoon. For no good reason I could see, getting everything together took far longer than it should have. I had just about run out of patience by the time we stood by the cars and Blanche arrived with the final map she had marked up with everything Zan had seen at Chadbourn Park today.

'The line-up of bands on the website has changed again,' she commented as she handed out copies.

Eleanor studied the sheet of A4 and looked around. 'I know we won't arrive until after the gates are open now, but there's no need to break the speed limit and risk getting pulled over. There'll be plenty of daylight left when we get there.'

I wondered if she was trying to convince herself or the rest of us that our plan wasn't already going off-course.

'Come on then,' I said. 'Let's go.'

Zan gave Blanche a quick kiss and vanished. Iris, Blanche and Fin got into Blanche's dark blue Honda. They weren't carrying anything, and they wore leggings, sweatshirts and thin nylon waterproofs. Swan maidens need to travel light. As Blanche pulled away, I realised that she or Fin must have tipped Iris off about what to wear before she got here and found out what was going on.

Conn watched Eleanor drive away. 'Let's hope she doesn't get stopped by the cops. That load of swords in the back will be a bit hard to explain.'

We'd given up on the idea of taking the halberds. They wouldn't fit into Eleanor's new Golf, and strapping polearms to a roof rack would definitely get a policeman's attention. We'd picked the dozen most effective-looking swords and put them in the Golf's boot. None of us had any particular skills, so we'd need to do as much damage we could, as fast as possible, with a blade in each hand. I hoped it didn't come to that.

Conn looked sideways at me. 'How long are we going to give them?'

We'd agreed not to take any chances that we absolutely couldn't avoid. Like driving in a three-vehicle convoy.

'A few minutes should do it. Let's load up.'

Conn followed me back into the workshop. The box he'd brought here filled with peat was on the table. It sat beside a rough wooden tray I'd knocked together out of 'that could come in useful' offcuts. The high-sided tray held an ancient biscuit tin Eleanor had brought down from the manor. I'd punched holes in the sides.

Conn scrunched some of yesterday's maps into tight twists and piled wood shavings into the tin. 'We might as well be ready to go as soon as we get there.' He scooped dark, crumbly bits out of the box of peat and trickled them into the corners.

'Okay.' I picked up the wooden tray. Conn got the bag holding the peat bricks he had carefully selected, along with a thick pair of work gloves and some conveniently small fire irons. Eleanor had found a load of those dumped in a cellar when the Beauchenes had installed central heating.

Conn opened the Landy's passenger door, put the bag in the footwell and got in. When he'd fastened his seatbelt, I handed him the tray, closed the door and went around to get behind the wheel. The effigy was already sitting in the back. That had been the first thing we had done. I'd put the alder staff behind the seats in the front.

The estate's back gate was open, so I didn't have to stop. Outside, I put my foot down. Neither of us said anything as I concentrated on following the route we had agreed. I didn't see Blanche's Honda or Eleanor's Golf anywhere ahead of us.

When we'd been driving for about an hour, the traffic started getting heavier. Cars waiting at side junctions had passengers in every seat. I let a rusting Ford Focus join the main road and saw sleeping bags and rucksacks filling the back window. I hoped the driver was using his wing mirrors.

Everything was slowing down now, though I couldn't see any obstruction ahead. A couple of VW camper vans had turned up from somewhere to block my view of the road. Ten minutes later, we were crawling along. 'There is heavy traffic on your route,' the satnav helpfully explained. 'You are on the fastest route.'

'Looks like most folk are turning up this evening,' Conn said uneasily.

I remembered what he'd said about the wyrm losing control of the kelpies once they saw dinner strolling past. 'Best way to get a decent pitch for a tent, I suppose.'

I tried not to tense up as the Focus in front stopped completely. Nothing was moving as far as I could see down the road.

Conn stiffened in his seat. 'There. Over there. Isn't that our turn?'

I saw a yellow rectangle edged with black cable-tied to a road sign. 'This way to Chadbourn Park.' I checked the satnav and managed to resist the temptation to shunt the rusty Ford out of our way with the Landy's solid bumpers. Conn was right.

The Ford started moving, infuriatingly slowly. I gripped the steering wheel until I could take the next left. We weren't following the arrow directing everyone else to the festival. There was no way we were going through the front gate.

Conn leaned forward to take a couple of smaller, paler lumps of peat out of the bag by his boots. 'Drive steady, will you?'

'What are you doing?' This narrow road twisted and rose and fell far too abruptly for me to take a look.

'I'll get these first pucks lit. We want to be ready to go as soon as we stop.' He took the lid off the tin on the tray in his lap.

I wanted to tell him to wait, but time was getting away from us. I kept my mouth shut and concentrated on the road. Conn took a box of long cook's matches out of an inside pocket. He struck one and burning paper crackled inside the tin. He studied the little fire for a few minutes, then carefully laid some darker, larger turfs on top of the ones he already had burning. He put the tin's lid on tight. 'Let's go.'

'We're nearly there.' I was relieved to see an old stone estate wall up ahead. Even better, this route alongside the crumbling masonry didn't see much traffic. The verges were overgrown and the more level stretches of road had grass growing down the middle. We even startled a few rabbits out for some early grazing.

I kept an eye out for deer. This was an ideal habitat for them, and a likely time of day for one to come bounding out of the undergrowth. They're worse than bloody sheep for testing a driver's reflexes, brakes and air bags in the same two seconds. I didn't want to imagine what could happen if I had to make an emergency stop right now.

The burning peat didn't give off a lot of smoke. I still opened my window a crack so I didn't get kippered. The scent was quite unlike a wood fire, and nothing like coal. I tried to think what it reminded me of. After a moment, I remembered. Years ago, when I was a kid, Dave Fulbrooke had smoked a pipe. His tobacco had burned with a vaguely similar, sweetish smell. I remembered how that lingered in my hair and my clothes when Dad took me around to Dave's house. The Landy's seats were going to be full of this for months.

Turning one last corner, I saw two familiar vehicles with Zan and the others beside them. 'There they are.'

'Grand.' Conn sounded as relieved as I felt.

I stopped beside Blanche's Honda. She had pulled right off the road. Eleanor had as well. I kept the Landy's four wheels on the tarmac. If anyone else drove down this road and had trouble getting past, that was their tough luck. I had no idea how soft these verges were, and I wasn't going to risk getting stuck. The swans could fly out of here if they had to, but Eleanor and I needed a guaranteed get-away vehicle. I was determined get away from this, whatever the Blithehurst dryads thought of our chances.

Fin walked over as I opened my door. She coughed as a gust of peat smoke reached her. 'You'll need a shower to get that off you before you come to bed.'

'You're telling me.' I took the car keys she was offering and zipped them in my pocket.

Blanche handed me the box of fuel tablets. She'd brought those in the back of her car in the bottom of a plastic bag full of Eleanor's old Girl Guide camping stuff.

The chances of any of us being stopped by the cops on our way here were miniscule, but they weren't zero. We had decided not to put a substance banned on anti-terrorism grounds in the same car as an Irishman and an Englishman with a criminal record for violence. If Eleanor had been stopped, she already had a bootful of offensive weapons to explain, though she did have the Beauchene family solicitors on speed dial. So the Wicken sisters would plead ignorance of the new hexamine regulations and play the blonde card for all it was worth. Fin's words, not mine.

She gave me a quick kiss. 'We'll go and see what's happening while you're making your way through the woods.'

A minute later, she and Blanche and Iris were running along the road on flat black feet with their long white wings stretched out until they could get airborne. Eleanor tried not to smile.

'It's all right,' Conn assured her. 'We do look ridiculous.'

I got the alder staff out of the Landy, handed it to Eleanor and went round to take the wooden tray with the fiery tin. Zan came closer as I put it on the ground. As Conn got out of the Landy, I took the staff from Eleanor and opened up the back door.

'Come out. Walk that way.' I showed it where I meant with the alder wood. 'Stop. Turn around. Stand still.' I turned the effigy back into bog oak and propped the staff against the Landy.

'This'll be ready soon enough.' Conn put more peat into the burning biscuit tin. There were no flames to speak of, but the heat was definitely building.

We waited. I used my penknife to prize the panel in the carving's back loose. Eleanor checked her watch a couple of times. I managed not to look at my phone. That wouldn't change anything. After what felt like half an hour but was probably nowhere near that, Conn used a bedroom fireplace shovel to scoop up a clod of smouldering peat. The swirling breeze caught the pale ash as fine as dust that came with it. Zan watched, fascinated, as Conn carefully put the peat into the hollow in the effigy's back.

I took the battered cardboard box and showed it to the inquisitive sylph. 'Can you stop the fire reaching this until the wyrm has taken the bait? Without smothering the peat? Then can you make everything burn as hot as possible? We want to set the bog oak alight once it's inside the wyrm.'

Blanche had been certain the sylph could do this as well as everything else, but I was still worried we were asking too much. I couldn't risk the effigy going up in flames too soon because they got distracted.

'Of course,' Zan said confidently.

Cold, dense air wrapped itself around the box. A moment more and my fingernails were turning blue. I put the box on top of the glowing turf inside the effigy. The searing heat I could feel didn't change. Conn put another smouldering block on top of the hexamine. The peat carried on burning but the cardboard didn't even char. Sylphs. An arsonist's best friend.

I pushed the tightly fitted panel into place as hard as I could. Grabbing the staff, I turned the carving into my eerie idiot twin. Looking at its back, all I saw was a smooth green T-shirt. Hopefully that meant there was no chance of the fire spilling out before we reached the lakeside and the wyrm.

'Are you set?' Conn asked.

I'd barely nodded before he turned into a swan and flew after the others. Zan didn't even bother to ask before disappearing.

Eleanor was pouring a bottle of water into the biscuit tin. Steam rose with a hiss to mix with the smoke and then subsided. 'What shall I do with this?'

'Just get it out of sight.'

She used a foot to shove it into the tall grass around a sprawling blackthorn hanging over the road. Given she'd doused the peat, and the wet recent weather, that didn't risk starting a bigger fire.

'Let's go.'

We weren't using the front entrance. We hadn't come to a back gate either. Trees felled by storms had smashed Chadbourn Park's boundary wall in at least ten places. A hollow

285

beech had brought down three or four metres conveniently close to the road here, and not too far from the festival site.

'Let's be grateful Lysander Repton is too cheap to pay for fencing to stop people sneaking in without a ticket.' Eleanor climbed carefully over the heap of weathered, moss-covered stones. 'I'll be sure to mention that if I have to.'

Unfortunately, Eleanor's greenwood ancestry must be too far in the past for her to do the 'don't see me' trick. She had experimented earlier today with Fin and Blanche's help. If anyone asked what she was doing here, she was going to say she was assessing the festival so she could offer her professional advice.

Eleanor was confident she could talk her way past anyone who expected her to wait while they got hold of Lysander Repton to check her story. I wasn't sure how she planned to explain why she was walking through these woods in dark grey clothing, wearing a lightweight ski-mask and carrying a sizeable backpack. If anyone got a look inside that, they'd have even more questions, starting with 'Can someone call the police?'.

We needed to get this done fast. Then no one would have time to demand answers.

'Follow me,' I told my eerie idiot twin, and walked towards the gap in the wall.

I concentrated very hard on not being seen. From now on, anyone we met must only see Eleanor and the fake version of me. Something else that had delayed us was finding out if the effigy could still see me when I opted to fade into the trees. That possibility hadn't occurred to any of us until Iris asked the question.

It turned out the thing's unblinking gaze stayed fixed on me and followed me wherever I went. It still did whatever I said, even when no one else could see where I had gone.

That was useful to know, and I reckoned I'd have nightmares about it for weeks.

Even so, I kept checking the effigy was still following as we made our way through the woods. Every time, it was exactly the same distance behind me. I found its expressionless face more and more unnerving, but no one else had seemed to think the wyrm would notice that.

After looking back and nearly tripping over a fallen branch, I concentrated on getting to the festival site without breaking an arm or a leg. This woodland had been as badly neglected as the boundary wall. Oaks planted generations ago had been left to grow crowded together. Timber intended for shipyards or house building had never been harvested. The trees were fighting each other for sunlight.

Under the dense canopy of smothering leaves, this wood was a sad and barren mess. Dead wood lay everywhere, far more than the animals or insects who benefit from it could cope with. I didn't see deer tracks or other signs of wildlife. No birds were settling to roost in the branches overhead. The wyrm or the kelpies might have scared them off, but I didn't think so.

Eleanor was some way ahead of me. Stopping at the edge of the trees, she glanced over her shoulder. I nodded to show her I could hear the noises ahead telling us we were getting close to our agreed target. Then I realised she couldn't see me. I saw her eyes slide past me to find my eerie idiot twin hidden in the shadows. She quickly looked away. She couldn't know how clearly I saw she hated it. I turned my head and told the thing to stand still.

Eleanor jumped. 'Dan? I swear, if you ever pull a stunt like this back home, I'll make you regret the day you were born.'

'I won't.' I stood beside her and looked out over the parkland. Out from under the trees, there was enough daylight for us to see all the way to the lake and across to the other side. That was the only good news.

'What the hell's happened here?' Eleanor wondered.

From everything Zan had told us, plus the information on the website, the layout for the festival had been clear. However badly subsidence had damaged walls and floors inside the house, the broad steps and the tall pillars of the massive Palladian front still looked intact. The black-draped stage had been set up on the edge of the front lawn where the audience would stand. The fans would have plenty of space. You could paint two rugby pitches side by side on the grass and leave room to spare.

That would give the bands a dramatic backdrop as well as making it easier to run power cables from the mains. In theory, anyway. I couldn't see a single light on inside the huge building, or anywhere around the stage. Two power company vans and a scissor lift were parked next to the security-fenced enclosure that would be 'back stage'. Over on the gravel drive by the house's steps, people in overalls, hard hats and power company hi-vis vests were talking to a group dressed in black with red hi-vis.

Whatever they were talking about involved a lot of waving arms interrupted by sharply pointing fingers. I could hear shouting, but that came from another team in black-and-red hi-vis who were chasing people off the stage. Laughing and jeering, the trespassers sounded like teenagers. The security people would have more chance of stopping them if they'd had walkie-talkies or some other way to talk to each other, but there was no sign of that.

The strident beep of a reversing lorry straight ahead drowned everything else out. On this side of the lawn, Lysander Repton's father had built a sizeable cafe and a gift shop for his failed zoo, with toilets at either end of the ugly concrete block. From what the website said, these facilities were supposed to be catering to the festival-goers' needs this weekend. Zan had reported electricians and plumbers and painters were busy here all week.

Right now, those windows were as dark as the big house. The flat-bed we'd just heard reversing was stacked with Portaloos. The driver got out of his cab and looked to be having an argument with a woman with a clipboard. The roar of a diesel generator was cheered sarcastically by the ragged queue waiting by a fish and chip wagon. A couple of other food vans were getting ready to start serving, and several more were pulling up.

'This is an absolute shambles.' Eleanor didn't sound remotely surprised. 'The refunds will probably bankrupt him if his insurers can prove negligence. I bet they'll be able to.'

'We have to get over to the lake.' I didn't give a toss about Lysander Repton's finances. We were here to stop the festival-goers getting eaten.

That was going to be a fucking sight more difficult now. The punters were setting up their tents on the other side of the lake. They were supposed to be camping close to these woods, near the cafe and gift shop and close enough to the loos for a reasonably short walk for a pee in the night. Instead, a small team in jeans and sweatshirts were waving chemical light sticks and trying to get cars and vans to park in straightish lines in front of us. Whether they were official stewards or just people showing some initiative, they were fighting a losing battle.

Vehicles were arriving thick and fast, and most of them stopped wherever they saw some space. As soon as everyone was loaded up with their gear, they joined the column trudging towards the lake. They would get to the campsite by crossing the ornate stone bridge on top of the dam that held back the water. Eventually, when they got through this choke-point.

The lengthening queue didn't stop the ones who couldn't be arsed to walk from driving along the wide flat path, flashing their lights and honking their horns to force everyone else out of their way. A stocky man in a sleeveless vest and a sharp black mohawk was pissed off by this. He stood with both hands planted on some wanker's bonnet, leaning forward to yell at the driver. Other people stopped to see what was going on. Most were getting their phones out to video whatever might happen. Everyone else kept on walking.

A swan landed on the lawn in front of us. A moment later, Iris appeared.

'Over here.' Eleanor barely raised her voice.

Iris hurried over. She shuddered as she saw my eerie idiot twin and spoke quickly to Eleanor. 'The car park they were supposed to be using? For the old safari park? One of the stage-set-up lorries fractured a water main when they drove over it this afternoon. There was a weight limit on the access road that nobody thought to mention. No one realised what had happened until the first cars to arrive got bogged down. The ground is saturated. So they're sending vehicles over here to park and telling people to camp around the lake.'

I didn't care about that. 'Have you seen the wyrm or the kelpies?'

Hearing my voice startled her as much Eleanor. 'Dan? No,' she went on, before I could ask who else she was expecting. 'There's been no sign.'

'There's every chance the police will turn up to shut this fiasco down,' Eleanor said thoughtfully. 'I bet people are already making calls to the local council as well. Health and safety. Trading standards. Food hygiene. Event licensing. You name it, their phones will be ringing.'

That was a thought. 'It wouldn't be the worst thing to happen, if people started going home. Iris?'

She looked vaguely in my direction. 'Yes?'

'How about you and the others go to the main gate? Start knocking on car windows. Tell everyone stuck in the queue there's no power and no water here, and the whole event looks like a disaster.'

Before I could say anything else, the screaming started. We ran towards the lake.

Chapter Twenty-Three

Eleanor reached the path around the lake ahead of me. She must have been a runner at school who reckoned four hundred metres was still a sprint. She ran towards the bridge across the dam. I stopped for a moment to see what was happening on the other side of the lake.

Shaggy black horses stampeded through the tents. Shouts of alarm rose louder than the thunder of hooves. As people tried to get out of the animals' paths, they stumbled into each other. The tents hadn't been pitched in anything like straight rows, which made this bad situation worse. Festival-goers were knocked off their feet. Yells and cries of pain floated over the water.

The kelpies reached the open grass on the far side. They wheeled around and came straight back. Charging shoulder to shoulder, they chased panicked people towards the lake's shore. Fuck. Someone was going to wonder why a herd of ponies without any riders was acting like a sodding cavalry unit.

A translucent greenish wall rose up to block my view. The water surged past me, moving outwards from the shoreline. I turned to see where half the lake was going, surprised to realise I was still on my feet. A cold wind stuck my sodden clothes to my skin. It whipped the water into dense mist. I couldn't see the lawn now, never mind the house. The air around me was calm though. I could have been standing in the eye of a very small and localised hurricane.

No one else was left on the lake path. I was alone with my eerie idiot twin. Everyone else at risk had been swept away from the water's edge. I owed Zan and Blanche an apology. I had underestimated the sylph.

I'd do that later. The stillness on this side of the uncanny squall was humid and oppressive. I was convinced a storm could break at any moment, with or without Zan's permission. I didn't want to find out if lightning could find me while I was trying not to be seen, and we would be completely screwed if my eerie idiot twin got struck before the wyrm could see it. Right now, the thing looked like a drowned rat, but it still looked like me and it was still staring in my direction. I could only hope the panel in its back had stayed watertight. I really hoped Zan had remembered that.

I saw Eleanor had reached the elegant stone arch that crossed the dam. She stopped halfway, at the highest point of the bridge. As she assessed the chaos on the other side, she tore off her ski-mask and slipped her backpack off her shoulders.

Festival-goers still on their feet had presumably been driven back behind the swirling grey wall that now circled the lake. I hoped the ones I saw left behind, sprawled on the ground and not moving, hadn't been too badly hurt. On the other hand, I also hoped they were properly unconscious. If they weren't, they were going to have a hell of a story for their social media.

The horses were under attack from big black cats working in pairs. The first cat leaped onto its target's back, sinking its claws in deep. As the shock and the sudden weight hitting its spine sent the kelpie staggering, a second cat went for its head. If it could, it wrapped its forepaws around that shaggy black neck and fastened its jaws behind the kelpie's ears. A leaping cat that missed its mark could still cling to the pony's chest and shoulders with those murderous talons and try to seize its throat with a crushing bite. I watched a kelpie's thick legs buckle under the weight of an attack. It sank out of sight behind a wrecked tent. Now I just saw two lashing black furry tails.

Not every skirmish went the cats' way. One pair really fucked up their timing. The kelpie reared up fast enough to escape the attack from the front. Its hooves came down hard on that cat's head. The black shape collapsed and lay still. As the kelpie kicked out backwards, it caught the second attacker under the jaw. That cat went tumbling through the air like a kid's toy chucked away in a tantrum. As another kelpie bucked, the cat on its haunches lost its grip and flew straight over the kelpie's head. It hit the ground and the kelpie was on it, stamping and biting.

Even with the lake between us, I could hear shrill neighs of fear and outrage. Cats yowled with pain, threatening mayhem in retaliation. Could this uproar rise above the howl of the swirling mist to terrify and confuse the festival-goers? Then I realised we had bigger problems.

Something thrashed in the depths of the lake. It surged upwards, churning the water into filthy foam. The wyrm's pointed snout broke the surface. The beast soared into the air, trailing its lashing tail. It was white, which surprised me. This was supposed to be a creature of shadows. Then I realised this wasn't the bright, vibrant white of, for instance, a swan's wing. The dull absence of colour reminded me of those pale crabs and insects and weird scuttling things that I'd seen on TV, living in caves hundreds of metres underground, never knowing daylight even existed.

At first glance, the wyrm looked like an enormous snake. The other name for these monsters is serpent dragon, after all. Though its scales didn't lie smooth and flat. They bristled with jagged edges that caught the light like broken glass. Anyone caught in those glistening wet coils would be ripped to shreds before they got crushed to death. Unless they were bitten in half first. The wyrm's merciless jaws were filled with dagger-sharp teeth as long as my hand.

The fucking thing was enormous, but gravity was still going to win. The pale wyrm crashed back down into the water.

That didn't matter. Those great pale eyes had seen what was going on. Seconds later it reappeared, and fresh waves swept over the path to run over my already sodden boots and soak my socks.

The wyrm shot towards the churned-up shallows where cats and kelpies were tearing into each other. Before it reached the shore, a shudder ran through the monster. I saw a black splotch of blood on its scales for barely a second before the water washed it away. I looked over to the bridge. Eleanor was watching the wyrm and she had her crossbow ready. That's what she'd brought in her rucksack. Folded up, it was a surprisingly compact weapon.

While Fin and I had been searching for ways to kill a wyrm, Eleanor had been thinking about the one we had fought. About the wyrmling I had killed with a halberd. About how tough its hide had been. What really counted, she had decided, was penetration. Pounds per square inch. Newton metres. That, and being able to hit the bloody thing from as far away as possible.

Eleanor is a historian. She did some research into crossbows. The weapon in her hands was nothing like the illustrations in any book from Blithehurst's library. It had a pistol grip and a telescopic sight and was made from fibreglass, polymers and who knew what other space-age materials. Forget using a stirrup or a goat's foot lever to crank it. A battery-powered system cocked this killing machine. I had been surprised by the weight, but it wasn't actually much heavier than a shotgun. Eleanor was fine with that. She had been shooting clay pigeons for years. She had a licence for the twelve-bores in the gun safe at Blithehurst, issued by the police.

She had only needed to prove she was over eighteen to buy the crossbow. That and have three to four grand to spare. It had come with wood and aluminium bolts. I'd used those as a pattern to make as many as I could, using the longest iron nails I could find.

The wyrm writhed, trying to work out where it had been hit. If it could pluck out the bolt, the water would heal it in seconds. If the bastard could get the bolt out. Good luck getting a grip on the end of that narrow shaft with those teeth. Fingers would come in handy right now, but the dryads had assured us a wyrm couldn't change shape with that much iron sticking into it. Or if it could, they said, it surely risked bleeding to death in its human form.

The wyrm wasn't looking Eleanor's way. It hadn't heard a gunshot. Besides, it could kill whoever had done this later. Right now, the monster wanted the searing metal out of its flesh. It bent itself double, searching for the source of the torment. Eleanor settled the crossbow's stock into her shoulder and fired again. She'd spent hours practising in Blithehurst's woods without telling anyone. She was deadly accurate.

I didn't see where the second bolt landed, or the third. That didn't matter. I could tell she'd hit the monster from its spasms. Though this wasn't going to kill it. The wyrm might die slowly if Eleanor could skewer it with enough iron, but we had no idea how many bolts she would need or how long that would take. Her chances of a lethal shot through an eye or its mouth weren't worth considering. But she could sure as hell distract it while I got the bait in place.

Before I could send my eerie idiot twin strolling along the lake path, someone else appeared on the bridge. Even at this distance, I knew it was a hag. This one was bare-legged and bare-armed, draped in layers of ragged reddish-brown. Spikes jutted from its fists as its repellent face twisted with malicious anticipation.

'Eleanor!' I had no idea if she could hear me yelling over the deafening wind. 'Behind you!'

Something alerted her. She spun around and loosed the crossbow at point-blank range. The hag staggered backwards. Halfway down the far slope of the bridge, it stopped. It ripped the crossbow bolt out of its chest and hurled the iron spike into the water. It charged towards Eleanor with its crooked arms raised, ready to tear her to shreds.

Someone else got there first. A festival-goer with long blonde hair appeared between them, in sodden jeans and a light blue sweatshirt. Where had that unlucky sod been hiding? Behind the bridge's parapet on the other side? They'd picked the worst possible time to come out to find help. Worse than that, they stopped right in Eleanor's line of sight. She couldn't get another shot at the hag.

It tried to tear off the newcomer's face. No such luck. The hag's murderous metal claws passed right through the blonde woman's head without leaving a mark. A splash of water flew through the air, not some gush of blood. The naiad wrapped both arms around the hag, pinning its hands to its sides. She forced it back towards the carved stone balustrade. The hag was trying to fight, but its feet kept slipping. Water poured off the bridge. The naiad had the hag bent over backwards with its head and shoulders hanging over the lake. The monster's dark hair was plastered to its face, covering its eyes. The hag toppled off the bridge, still tight in the naiad's merciless hold. They disappeared into the depths.

Agony tore through my left shoulder, high on my back. A hag cackled with triumph. I staggered forward and spun around. The bitch had crept up behind me. My eerie idiot twin stood a few metres away, as much use as a limp prick. The hag had ignored it completely.

This one wore tattered layers the colour of mudstone. It stepped forward, sniffing loud enough for me hear over the whistling wind. As it peered from one side of the path to the other, groping with outstretched hands, I realised those blood-coloured eyes couldn't see me. It could smell the peat smoke though, even after the drenching I'd had.

I was still holding the alder wood staff. I hit the hag's forearm as hard as I could. It screeched with pain and snatched its hand back. Backing off, I aimed for the side of its head. That meant getting closer than I wanted. Warm blood was trickling down my shoulder and side, but I had to ignore that.

The alder staff connected with a solid thud. The hag stumbled sideways. It still tried to claw at the empty air where it thought my head must be. Ha, missed me! I dropped into a crouch, using both hands to swing the staff now. This was hurting my torn shoulder even more. Gritting my teeth, I went for the hag's knees. It was already unbalanced and my strike swept its feet out from under it. It fell hard on the gravelled lake path.

The wyrm roared with fury. Fuck. Could it see me? Was it coming to rescue the hag? I snatched a quick glance at the lake. The wyrm wasn't looking my way, but that wasn't good news. It was heading for the bridge, cutting a foaming furrow through the surface of the water. With its head held high and its forked tongue flickering through the air, its curved neck made me think of a Viking warship.

Eleanor raised her crossbow. The wyrm flinched and bellowed as more iron bolts hit it, each one marked by a momentary dark smear of blood. The bastard thing didn't slow down though. Eleanor started retreating down the slope on this side of the bridge. She kept firing, but now she was on the move, she missed most of her shots. The monster kept coming for her. Its underside looked dark now, reflecting the surface of the lake. Those translucent scales would take on the colour of whatever surrounded this wyrm, making it hideously hard to see in a forest or a cave or wherever it was lurking.

The hag lay still, face down. I looked over it to my eerie idiot twin and jabbed the alder staff towards the bridge. 'Get between that wyrm and Eleanor!'

The effigy moved fast. Its boot left a muddy footprint between the hag's shoulder blades. I barely had time to get out of its way. I pinned the hag down with the alder staff as I turned to see if our plan would work.

The effigy was still running along the lake path. Eleanor was still retreating towards me. The wyrm was still dead set on killing her. There was nothing I could do. Where the fuck was that naiad? Could she do anything to help?

My eerie idiot twin drew level with the wyrm. It must have caught sight of him in the corner of its pale, lidless eye. The monster turned so fast that a massive muddy wave washed right the way up the stone face of the bridge. The gigantic sinuous shape reared up out of the water. Its neck bent as its eyes fixed on the running effigy. The wyrm's jaws gaped wide.

It struck so fast I didn't see what happened. The wyrm twisted away and sank back into the lake. The effigy was gone from the path. Had the monster eaten it or smashed it? I couldn't see pieces of bog oak or charred peat floating on the water. There was barely a scuff on the gravel. It must have swallowed it whole, surely?

The surface of the lake grew calm surprisingly fast. On the far side, I could see kelpies standing on the shore. Some looked like horses. Others stood on two feet. They were all frozen with shock. Crouching black cats surrounded them, equally stunned. A few dark shapes bobbed in the shallows. I couldn't tell if they had been enemies or allies.

The hag's claws raked down my shin, ripping through my trousers. It had been lying still, waiting for its chance. As I backed off, it scrambled to its feet. This hag could definitely see me now. I gripped the alder staff with both hands. My left hand was slippery with blood running down from my shoulder. I wiped it quickly on my T-shirt, feeling the cloth stick to the cuts on my back.

The hag spat at me, snarling. 'Some whore of a dryad's by-blow? If you—'

A brutal surge of water drowned out the rest. The wave swept the hag into the lake and a naiad appeared. She rose out of the water as far as her waist, planting both hands on top of the hag's tangled head. The naiad used her weight to force the struggling hag under the surface and they both disappeared.

Eleanor reached me, still holding her crossbow. 'Did you see it? Did it eat it?'

'Let's hope so.' Unless someone could show us a slow-motion replay, there was no way to know. 'What's that out there?'

I hardly expected her to answer me, but something was happening in the centre of the lake. The water bubbled like a boiling pot and white-capped waves twisted into a whirlpool. If the wyrm was somewhere in there, I couldn't tell where the foaming water ended and those pale scales began. The maelstrom spun faster and faster and deepened into a spiral. Standing on the path, we could see the top of the widening hollow, but there was no way for us to know what was going on at the bottom.

Lithe dark blue shapes sprang out of the lake's shallows to stand along the path. The naiads weren't bothering to hide what they were. Like Eleanor, they watched the seething water. I was on the lookout for any sign of those hags. They didn't reappear.

Zan turned up next, with a handful of other sylphs, translucent and ethereal. 'You have to go.'

'Is it dead?' I demanded. 'The wyrm. Did we kill it?'

Before I got an answer, the vortex collapsed. A column of dark water erupted, rising high into the air. As that crashed back down, an indescribable stink swept over the lake. An oily slick was spreading, dotted with the pale bellies of dead fish.

That was good enough for me. 'Do you know where Fin is? And the others.' I had no idea how long we'd been hidden by the mist. I'd lost all sense of time. The sylph was right though. We needed to leave.

'They are back with the cars.' Zan reached for my hand.

'Wait.' Eleanor stepped away and pulled me with her. 'What's happening over there?'

The naiads started diving back into the lake. They skirted the wyrm slick, swimming impossibly fast towards the far shore. Some of their sisters were already there. Now the cats surrounding the kelpies were looking outwards and roaring. A naiad strode out of the water to confront them. The closest cat shifted back into a cunning man. I thought it was Peter, but at this distance, I couldn't be sure.

'Come on.' I started running, and Eleanor followed me.

By the time we crossed the bridge, more naiads had appeared. More cats turned back into men. By the time we reached the confrontation, both sides were yelling at each other.

I recognised the naiad who was taking the lead. That was a relief. 'Kalei. It's good to see you.'

'I have nothing to say to you.' She even didn't spare me a glance as she challenged Peter. 'Step aside. We will deal with these vermin.'

'No.' He didn't move. Behind him, a black cat growled.

'Dan.' Zan appeared beside me again. 'They are taking the water away from us.'

He didn't have to explain. The wall of mist was thinning and getting paler. I could hear approaching sirens. We really did need to get out of here.

'Greenwood son!' A desperate kelpie waved a hand. 'You swore to help us!'

Was he one of the gang who'd robbed the craft fair, or from the fight at the beaver pond? I had no clue.

Now Kalei did look my way. Her turquoise eyes flashed with fury. 'You had no right to make a bargain with these filth. Certainly no agreement that binds any others.'

What the hell did she think I had done? I tried to remember what I had said to the kelpies by the beaver pond in the middle of the night weeks ago in Shropshire.

'I only said I would try to find out if someone can remake their silver chains. The wyrm stole and destroyed—'

'Whatever Dan may have done is irrelevant,' Peter interrupted. 'These kelpies are under our protection.'

'You think that impresses me?' Kalei asked with soft menace. 'Pussy?'

Peter's face reddened, suddenly embarrassed. I remembered how easily Kalei could get under a man's skin. Any man's skin, in intimate places, so testosterone washed away rational thought. Naiads didn't hesitate to use their allure as a weapon. One of them blew a mocking kiss at the closest cunning man.

'Kalei!' I stepped forward. 'You want these kelpies out of your rivers? Just let them go home. That's the quickest and easiest way to get rid of them.'

I looked past the cunning men to the cowering creatures. 'I may have found someone who could help you. I'll ask them if they will, but I will only do that if you swear to go back to your home waters and promise to stay there. You must never come south again. Whether or not I succeed.'

The kelpies stared for a moment, muttering to each other. I turned to Peter. 'Give Kalei your word that you'll make sure they leave every river that belongs to the naiads. If this comes to a fight, you will lose, trust me,' I added before he could argue.

'That much is true,' Kalei agreed with smug satisfaction. 'Listen to my greenwood friend.'

'Oh, fuck off.' I didn't have time to waste with this bollocks. 'If you were my friend, you'd have come to see me as soon as you found out about these kelpies. I sent enough messages to try and reach you. Besides, you owe me, and you know it. You couldn't have got rid of this wyrm on your own. We had to kill the last one for you too.'

Eleanor chipped in. 'Isn't this the third wyrm whose death you can claim, Dan? If we're keeping score.'

I noticed the way she phrased that, to imply I was mostly responsible. In reality I couldn't have done anything about those other wyrms without a whole load of help. Just like now. But the fact remained that I was human enough to handle iron, and as my mother's son, I could use it to attack a wyrm. Naiads couldn't do that.

Kalei looked angry enough to argue the toss. Then she noticed what I had already seen. Half of these other naiads clearly had questions about whatever she had told them was happening here. The rest were studying me and Eleanor with curiosity and a little unease.

Before Kalei could say anything, a kelpie called out, 'We will swear to you, greenwood son, come what may.'

They chorused something unintelligible in human and horses' voices. Now Peter looked smug as he folded his arms. Kalei looked mightily pissed off. I was just glad they clearly understood what the kelpies had said, because I didn't have a sodding clue.

Peter raised a dark eyebrow as he stared at the naiad. 'If that's good enough for you, we will swear to do as Dan has asked. As a courtesy to him.'

'Then do so,' she hissed. 'If you break your word, we will have our vengeance on you both.'

Marvellous, but that had to be a problem for another day. I could see red and blue flashing lights through the thinning veil of fog. Somewhere close, voices shouted orders, expecting to be obeyed.

'Get on with it,' I advised Peter. 'Before half of you end up back in prison.'

'You have to go!' Zan seized my hand, and Eleanor's.

'Dan!' Peter shouted suddenly as mist swirled around us. 'You should give that staff back!'

Everything went white. In the next breath, I was standing beside Blanche, Fin, Iris and Conn. One of the other sylphs handed Eleanor her rucksack and her ski-mask.

'Thank you.' She folded the arms of her crossbow so she could put it away.

I held the alder wood staff out to one side so Fin could hug me.

'Tell us—' Her hand on my back found the rips in my T-shirt and skin. 'What happened?'

'Hold this for a minute, will you?' I handed the staff to Conn as I unzipped my pocket to find both sets of keys. 'We really have to leave.'

Conn took the Land Rover keys off me. 'I'll drive.'

Chapter Twenty-Four

Getting away from Chadbourn Park was easier said than done. Even when we left the back lane for a decent-sized road, the traffic was barely getting out of first gear. This time we did stick together. The Land Rover led the way. Fin and Eleanor stayed tucked close behind. No one gave way to anyone who was trying to rejoin the main route from the side roads after their satnav had taken them on some pointless detour to try to escape the gridlock.

Eventually the vehicles ahead began to accelerate. Conn put his foot down. Sirens were still coming our way every few minutes. The cars pulled over as far as they could to let cop cars, fire engines and ambulances speed down the middle of the road. Either someone had rung 999 and said 'all of them' when the call handler asked what emergency service they needed, or a whole lot more things had gone horribly wrong between the naiads, the kelpies and the cunning men after we had left.

I struggled to care, though I knew I should. I felt like shit. I couldn't stop shivering, though I wasn't actually cold and my clothes were drying off. I leaned forward against the pull of my seatbelt to stop my shoulder touching the seat behind me. Mostly to avoid having to get blood off the upholstery. Whatever the hag had done didn't hurt too badly now, though the dull ache seemed to be spreading down my arm.

Every so often, Conn glanced my way. I didn't realise I'd closed my eyes until he spoke sharply. 'Dan! Am I taking you to a hospital?'

'No.' I wasn't about to get in the way of anyone brought in by those ambulances we'd seen rushing to Chadbourn Park. Plus, I couldn't come up with a convincing story to give a bunch of doctors and nurses.

I couldn't find the words to explain that, so I closed my eyes again. Now I was far too hot, even if I wasn't sweating. I must have dozed off. The jolt of Conn pulling up at Blithehurst's back gate woke me up. The gate was locked.

'I'll get it.' I unbuckled my seatbelt and opened the door. I stepped out onto the road and my legs gave way. I hit the ground before I realised I was falling over.

'A Mhuire Mháthair!'

I looked up at Conn and tried to remember what I was trying to do.

'What's wrong?' Fin was there. Someone answered her. Don't ask me who.

The next thing I remember, I was lying on my back in the woods. Asca and Frai looked down at me. The old dryad's knees cracked as she crouched down and put her wrinkled hand on my chest. The gashes in my shoulder burned as if someone had poured acid into them. I heard somebody screaming and realised that was me.

I woke up bollock naked in my own bed in the cottage. The sheet underneath me was soaked with sweat and the empty duvet cover draped over me wasn't much better. Fin was dozing in a chair by the window. I was horribly thirsty, but I didn't want to wake her, so I reached for the glass of water I could see on the bedside table.

Bad move. My shoulder was suddenly agony. My arm jerked. I knocked over the glass and it hit the floor. Fuck.

'What is it?' Fin was awake and on her feet. She came over and picked up the glass. At least it hadn't broken. 'I'll get you some water.'

I wanted to go after her as she left the room. Trying to sit up turned out to be another stupid idea. The room was spinning as I fell back against the pillows.

Fin came back and held the glass so I could sip the cold water. 'Careful.'

I drank about half of it. 'That's enough, thanks. How bad is it?'

She held the glass tight in both hands. 'Asca said we have to get you to a doctor today.'

Eleanor came up with a cover story when she took me to the nearest minor injuries unit later that morning. Something about me tripping over a tree stump which nobody realised was hidden in a big patch of nettles.

I wasn't really listening as I sat shirtless on the trolley in a side room. A friendly nurse was cleaning out the gouges in my shoulder while I gritted my teeth and concentrated on not swearing. I'm sure whatever he was doing hurt twice as much because I couldn't see what he was up to.

At least the doctor sounded happier once he'd finished and she came back to take another look. 'You can put a dressing on that, thanks. I see your tetanus is up to date, Mr Mackmain, so that's a plus, but you're dehydrated and I can see some pain relief wouldn't hurt. We need to take some blood and check a few things, so we'll give you fluids and IV paracetamol while you're here.'

She gave the nurse his instructions and went off to help some other poor sod. The nurse, whose badge said his name was Jesse, got the needle thing, the cannula, into my arm first try. He filled a whole lot of test tubes with blood, put me on a drip fed by a small plastic bottle as well as a big bag of fluid, and went off to do something else.

'How are you feeling?' Eleanor was sitting on a plastic chair on the other side of the glaringly white room.

'Not as bad as I did. What are you going to put in the accident book?'

'Let me worry about that.' She took out her phone. 'May as well catch up with the latest headlines.'

I found my phone and did the same. That was one way to take my mind off things. Freak waterspouts in the Midlands was definitely a story, but it was well down the web pages. Apart from 'What weird weather!', no one had a lot else to say. There weren't any decent video clips to make the story more interesting, and I wondered who we could thank for that. Sylphs can screw with electronics, the same as dryads.

I had to check the regional news before I found a report on the abandoned music festival. That was mostly quotes from the bands who had arrived to find no power, no water and no facilities. I held my phone out towards Eleanor. 'Have you seen this?'

She glanced up and nodded. 'I'm reading it at the moment.'

The story moved on to what the emergency services were calling a crowd crush. I was surprised and relieved to see no one had died, though a lot of casualties were still in hospital. No one's injuries were expected to be 'life-changing', but that left plenty of scope for a nasty few months ahead for some unlucky sods.

No one mentioned stampeding black ponies. I wanted to ask Eleanor what she thought about that, but I didn't want someone to walk in and find us talking about Chadbourn Park. I didn't want anyone to think we had the slightest interest in the place.

A few lines at the end of the most detailed story got my attention. Police were investigating reports of drinks being spiked as well as other drug offences at the festival site. Arrests had been made and enquiries were ongoing.

I wondered if the cunning men had wanted to make sure the cops took reports of giant snakes or big black cats with a sizeable spoonful of salt. I didn't think they'd have much trouble planting convincing evidence. I knew a good few of them had criminal records. I also realised I had no idea how Peter had been recruited to join them.

'Lysander Repton is in trouble.' Eleanor shook her head, still looking at her phone. 'His lake has been polluted by contaminated water suddenly leaking from an old coal mine.'

'That's bad.' I hoped that was the naiads' work, to cover up whatever mess was left by the dead and burned wyrm. I really hoped they'd washed those two drowned hags into some deep flooded tunnel where they'd never be found.

The nurse Jesse came back a bit later to check my blood pressure, my heart rate, my temperature and my blood oxygen levels again. 'That's looking better, and I've got you some antibiotics.' He shot a syringe of something into my arm through the cannula, checked my drip and added another bag of fluid. 'Is there anything either of you need?'

'I'm fine,' Eleanor assured him.

He left us on our own again. I was starting to think I should turn my phone off to save what was left of the battery when the doctor finally came back. She was smiling, which was good.

'We're happy for you to go home with a two-week course of antibiotics, Mr Mackmain, once that drip has finished. Obviously, you should call an ambulance straight away if you take a turn for the worse. Once you've finished the antibiotics, if you have any concerns, contact your GP.'

'Of course. Thank you.' I took the prescription she was offering me, along with a leaflet about symptoms of sepsis.

I tried not to look impatient while she explained why I had to finish the full course of antibiotics, even when I started feeling better. By now I just wanted to get out of there.

309

As soon as Jesse came in to take the needle out of my arm, I grabbed my T-shirt.

He checked whatever it was he had taped over the wounds I couldn't see. 'Is there someone at home who can dress this for you?'

I saw him glance at Eleanor.

'Yes.' Explaining she was my boss would just have held us up. She stood up and found her car keys. 'Thank you for everything.'

We stopped on the way to pick up my tablets, which turned out to be big enough to choke a donkey. I was feeling so much better by the time I got back to Blithehurst, I reckoned I'd be back at work in a few days.

I was off sick for a fortnight. As long as I sat on the sofa doing nothing, I felt pretty much okay. Not brilliant, but okay. I soon found out that five minutes of trying to do anything more strenuous than making a cup of tea meant I started feeling like crap. So I sat on the sofa and watched the least annoying stuff I could find on TV, which was pretty much sod all. I tried reading a few of the books Eleanor brought over, but I found it hard to concentrate. Mostly, I just got very, very bored.

With no Internet out in the woods, I couldn't go online. Going up to the manor to watch something on Netflix would have meant awkward questions from other members of staff. In any case, the house was full of visitors in the daytime, and in the evenings, I was ready for bed before the sun went down. At least I slept well and without dreaming. Until I rolled onto those gashes on the back of my shoulder and the stabbing pain woke me up.

That wasn't the worst thing. After the first week, once Eleanor and Fin agreed the wounds I couldn't see were healed enough not to need any more dressings, Fin and Blanche went back to Bristol to sort out a whole load of work stuff. She called and we texted, because I suddenly had an excellent mobile signal. She forwarded some messages from Iris which were quite funny, because meteorologists around the country were still arguing about what could have happened at the lake.

I swapped a few messages with Blanche, and she admitted knowing before the festival that Zan had asked some other sylphs to help out. She had decided not to tell me because we didn't have time to discuss it. Anyway, Zan had been right. I decided that wasn't worth arguing about now.

I really missed Fin, but that still wasn't the worst of it. Knowing I was on my own and off work sick in the cottage, Sarah and Janice and some of the others decided I must need cheering up. People kept stopping by to see how I was, expecting I'd enjoy a chat. I know they were just being nice and I did my best to be friendly. Honestly though, the last thing I wanted was visitors. I did try to go out for a walk in the woods one day so they couldn't find me, but the shuck was there on the doorstep. It silently stood in my way, so I went back indoors and rang my dad. I did that most days, and talking to him about nothing to do with hags or wyrms or anything else like that was good.

I'd eaten my breakfast and was counting my antibiotics to double-check that I only had three more days of them left to take when the doorbell rang. Bollocks. I was seriously thinking about ripping that sodding thing off. But then ordinary people would still use the knocker, and I didn't want Zan sending another branch through a window.

I went to open the door and found Hazel outside. 'Oh. Hello.'

'How are you?' She didn't wait for me to invite her in, walking past me into the hall. 'I was sorry to hear you'd been injured. Congratulations on killing the wyrm, by the way. I really didn't think that plan would work.'

'Now you tell me.' I followed her into the living room. 'Who told you I'd been hurt?'

'Does that matter? I can see you're well on the mend.' The wise woman walked over to the open window and looked out at the bright June woods. 'I came to talk to you about Denise. So you can tell the others. It's not really a conversation to have up at the house with tourists listening in.'

'Go on.' I really didn't give a toss, as long as the woman was out of our hair, but Eleanor would want to know. At least that horrible website had disappeared.

'She was lonely, Daniel.' Hazel looked at me, critical. 'Have some compassion, can't you? I grant you, she has an unfortunate manner, and she genuinely doesn't understand how offensive she can be, but there's no malice in her. At least there wasn't until that wyrm tracked her down. She had no chance, once—'

Hazel stared past me to the corner by the kitchen door. I glanced over my shoulder and saw she had seen the alder wood staff. That could wait. I turned back to her.

'Where is she now? Denise? Will she be any more trouble?'

'What? No.' Hazel focused on me again. 'She's back at home, but we've got somebody watching her. A friend she thinks she's made at the library. They're going to be in the same book group. Denise believes she had a bit of a nervous breakdown and has been seeing a therapist. We're persuading her to move to the south coast. We can keep an eye on her there. Where did you get that?'

I didn't bother to ask what she was talking about. 'The – whoever she was – who cast the glamour on the bog oak gave it to me. If you want to know anything else about her, you'll have to ask the cunning men.'

'What are you going to do with it?' Hazel asked, tense.

'Peter said I should give it back.' I watched to see how she'd react.

I had so many questions about what the wise women knew about hags and about hares. About dealings they might have had with each other in the past. Fin wanted to know too, and so did Eleanor. This wasn't the time to ask. We wanted at least two, ideally all three of us, to hear whatever Hazel had to say, to catch anything the others might miss.

Right now, Hazel looked relieved. 'I think that would be best.'

Screw it. 'Why?'

'You won't need it again, will you? If you want to try that trick some other time, you'll need a fresh glamour cast.' Hazel was heading for the front door, talking fast so I couldn't ask my question again. 'For now, that wyrm is dead and I can't think anyone else will have worked out how you killed it. That should give anything else with ambitions pause for thought.'

I followed her out of the cottage. 'I'm pretty sure one hag worked it out.'

Hazel pretended not to hear me, walking quickly away. 'I'm parked up by the restaurant. Give my regards to Fin and to Eleanor. I'll be in touch.'

She didn't look back as she waved a brisk goodbye. I would have gone after her regardless, but Kalei was standing under the trees.

I looked around, but there was no sign of the shuck. I looked back at the naiad. 'Hello?'

She smiled briefly. 'I think you mean, why the hell am I here and what the fuck do I want? Two questions, one answer. I came to apologise. I should have trusted you. At the very least, I should have asked you what was happening. I'm sorry.'

This was unexpected. It was also a relief. A pissed-off nai-ad was not an enemy I needed. 'Thanks. What do you want to know?'

She shook her head. 'That's what I came here to say, and to tell you the kelpies have kept their word. They have left our rivers.'

'Good to know.' That was also welcome news.

'Have you spoken to – what was his name? Peter, recent-ly?'

Kalei's question was a bit too casual. So much for not wanting anything else from me.

'No. Why?'

The naiad shrugged. 'I was wondering if you had taken his advice to return that staff.'

'Not yet, but I will.' This morning had made up my mind about that. When I'd shown it to the dryads and asked their advice, they'd told me to burn it. I wasn't going to do that, but hanging on to it seemed an increasingly bad idea.

'Good.' Kalei's turquoise gaze held mine. 'Don't wait too long.'

I wanted to ask why, but I had a more important question first. 'Who told you I'd been talking to the kelpies? Who told you I'd agreed some deal with them, making promises I had no right to?'

She looked at me for such a long time that I didn't think she was going to answer.

'A hag. She is dead now.' Kalei disappeared.

I went back into the cottage and phoned Aled. If the kel-pies had gone home and I was on the mend, there was one thing I still had to do. I was going to do it with someone I knew I could trust.

314

Chapter Twenty–Five

Aled and I drove past Berwick-upon-Tweed late on Mid-summer Day. The timing was just a useful coincidence. Aled had stuff he needed to sort out before he could take a few days off, and I wanted to get a crate of things together. We went in Aled's van, and we timed our journey so we could sleep in before we set off and stop for an evening meal half-way. He'd bought a Transit Connect to replace his Fiesta van that had gone up in flames. I had enough legroom and it was a comfortable ride. Eleanor said she would cover the petrol costs.

Before we went, I spent hours studying the relevant maps from Eleanor's dad's Ordnance Survey collection in Blithe-hurst's library. Checking satellite views online, I was sure I'd found the remote house where Peter had taken me, and the earthwork where we had met the delvers. Ninety-nine per-cent certain, anyway.

On the way there, we talked about everything that had happened after the festival fiasco at Chadbourn Park. Ly-sander Repton was being sued by loads of people. A gang of drug dealers appeared in court. They were charged with ma-liciously administering noxious substances and causing nox-ious substances to be taken by other persons without their knowledge, to intentionally injure and aggrieve. I wondered if the cunning men had been settling some debts we didn't know about. Killing two wyrms with one bog oak effigy.

Aled asked how my shoulder was getting on. I told him it was fine. That was true. I still couldn't see the scars properly though, however awkwardly I twisted in front of the bath-room mirror. Eventually I'd asked Fin to buy me a shaving mirror so I could see the reflection of their reflection. These weren't even useful scars like the pale fading lines on my arm. They were just ugly, ragged and red. Not having to see them every day didn't change that.

Aled brought me up to date with the renovations at Annis Wynne's farm. The place was going to be a residential centre for arts and crafts courses, yoga retreats and things like that. He'd seen a couple of white dogs with red ears sniffing around at dusk and dawn a few times. The Cŵn Annwn had wagged their tails when they'd seen him and then they had disappeared.

Eventually we left Berwick behind us and headed into the Lammermuir Hills. Now we drove along in silence.

'Is that the turning?' Aled had put the grid reference into his satnav, but he asked me anyway.

'Yes.' I recognised this road.

'What do we say if someone's on holiday in the cottage?' He drove up the track regardless.

'That there's right to roam in Scotland, and we have the owner's permission to park here.'

I'd tell any cunning man we found there to mind his own sodding business. He could phone Iain if he had a problem with that. Not that I'd told Iain or Peter what we were planning, but their man doing that should buy us enough time to get set up on the hillside. I didn't think the cunning men would interfere once everything was in place.

There was no one in the house. Aled parked and I got the crate out of the back. He grabbed a big holdall. We walked up to the forgotten earthwork on the moor. The night sky was luminous overhead and I smelled wildflowers on the warm breeze.

I had decided we could offer an improvement on paper napkins and disposable plates. Eleanor had found a linen tablecloth her grandmother had embroidered and a set of those lead crystal tumblers. I'd carved some wooden spoons and a honey dipper. Fin had baked two dozen bread rolls and we'd done the rounds of the farm shops near Blithehurst. The crate I was carrying held organic cream, honey and a free-range chicken which I'd roasted and already cut up. Aled had bought handmade bowls and plates from a potter at Canolfan Meilyr.

He took two bottles out of his holdall once we had set everything out. 'Finest Welsh whisky.'

The first bottle was. The other one didn't have a label. 'What's that?'

'A gift from Conn. Poitín. He stopped by the other day.' Aled tilted the colourless liquid to see how it flowed, leaving thick streaks on the clear glass. 'I didn't ask.'

I hadn't told the Irishman we were coming here. I guessed Iris had mentioned it, and I supposed that didn't matter. I could also see why Conn might want to offer the delvers a show of goodwill, if they could do what we had come here to ask. 'Pass me some salt.'

We worked together to make the circle. We had just about finished when I heard a chuckle behind me.

'That will suffice.' The head delver greeted me with a nod. Six others had come with him. They stared at Aled with curious intensity.

'Please, join us.' I stepped back from the gap in the white ring. To my surprise, the rest of the delvers came in too.

'You may as well close that up,' the head delver said to Aled, who was still holding his bag of salt. 'Cousin.'

The other delvers were already helping themselves to food. Aled smiled nervously and quickly completed the circle.

'You have rid us of the wyrm that menaced us.' The head delver tore a soft white roll in half and scooped up some cream. 'You have our thanks for that.'

317

'We would be grateful if you would be willing to help us restore what that wyrm stole, to settle any grievances that might be used to stir up further trouble.'

Aled and I had debated how best to phrase this request. I'd ended up typing this sentence into my phone so I could memorise it.

'How many kelpies were robbed?' The delver was prepared to be a lot more straightforward now the wyrm was dead.

Though I noted he still didn't want to be overheard. Was there something I couldn't see outside the salt circle, or was he just being cautious on general principles? I answered his question.

'Seven, that we know of.' If there were others, that would have to be a problem for another day.

'This is all you ask?' He helped himself to some chicken. 'That we craft the chains they need?'

'Yes. Please.' I tried to work out if I'd somehow cocked this up. I couldn't see how.

'And you?' He looked at Aled. 'What brings you here?'

'I've brought you some silver. If you are happy to use it, of course.' He'd made the point that it was probably best if we weren't in debt to the delvers for the precious metal they would need. I had agreed, and I was very glad he had thought of that.

'Very well.' The delver nodded towards the bottle of whisky. 'I will try some of that, if you please.'

I saw a couple of his underlings were looking at the other bottle. I unscrewed the metal cap. 'This is a gift from Ireland.'

The delvers were happy to share the crystal glasses, leaving one each for Aled and me. I had a few sips of the Welsh whisky just to be sociable. The delvers were being friendly, but I wanted to keep a clear head in case a big black cat turned up. A circle of salt wouldn't keep a cunning man out.

Aled tried the Irish liquor. His startled expression told me it was as strong as I suspected. The delvers seemed to like it. They appreciated the food as well. It wasn't long before everything was eaten.

'Let us get to work.' The head delver put down his glass. 'Will you join us, cousin?'

'Me?' Aled tried to look surprised.

The head delver laughed and gestured at the big holdall. 'You have come prepared, have you not?' He turned to me. 'We will return before daybreak. I take it you will wait?'

'Is that okay with you, Dan?' Aled couldn't hide his eagerness. 'I did bring some gear, just on the off-chance.'

'Fine.' I wasn't keen, to be honest, but it wasn't my decision. Besides, Aled was an experienced caver. Plus, I should have expected he'd want to see the delvers at work.

What mattered most was getting those necklaces. Knowing they'd be ready before we left here was a relief. On the drive up, we'd wondered how long the delvers might take. We'd had no clue. Would we be better staying on until they were done or going home and making a second trip?

Aled was getting into his pot-holing gear. The delvers were very amused. He pulled on his gloves and picked up a brown cardboard box that held the silver ingots he'd brought. 'Right then. Lead the way.'

'If you would be so good.' The head delver pointed at the unbroken white line around us.

'Oh, right.' Aled scuffed salt aside with his boot. That was good enough, apparently.

'Have fun.' I watched them walk away until they disappeared into a dip in the moorland, way off in the distance.

I stacked the bowls and plates and glasses back in the crate, with the plastic boxes we'd used for the food. There wasn't much whisky left, and even less of the Irish liquor. I screwed the tops back on both bottles. Maybe I'd try the poitín when we got home.

I folded the linen tablecloth lengthways and used it to pad the pottery and the crystal in the crate. The last thing we needed was non-stop clinking in the back of the van. When I looked up, I nearly knocked the crate over. I should have closed up the salt circle again.

A woman was watching me. She wasn't some hiker out here to enjoy the shortest night of the year. I could see her bare feet and ankles below the hem of her flimsy pale green dress. A wide length of cream-and-yellow-checked cloth tied around her waist emphasised the curve of her hips and the swell of her breasts. Long pale hair hung down past her shoulders and half covered her supermodel-beautiful face. She wore a garland of summer flowers on her head, and a soft smile curved her lips.

As she tucked a stray lock of hair behind her ear, I realised I'd seen that gesture before. Her eye, the one not hidden by her hair, shone bright, and I was willing to bet she only had one tooth. That would explain her Mona Lisa smile.

'Hello.'

Her smile widened and she angled her head. Folding her arms, she raised the single eyebrow I could see.

'Would you like your staff back?' As unnerving as this encounter was, I couldn't help thinking we were going to save a lot of time and mileage. Better yet, I wouldn't owe the cunning men a favour. Once we'd settled things with the delvers, we had planned on asking Peter where to go to return the alder wood staff.

The – whoever she was – didn't say anything, but she nodded. I left the crate where it was and forced myself to walk out of the circle. I hadn't expected to be meeting her – whoever she was – on my own. But I had something she wanted, so I told myself I should be okay. I wasn't some halfwit in a fairy story either. I wasn't going to lay a finger on her, no matter how dazzlingly gorgeous she might seem. Somehow, in some way I didn't understand, she was still kin to the hags.

Aled had left his keys in his holdall. I found them and started walking back to the house where we'd parked the van. I left everything else behind on the grass so I had my hands free, though I wasn't sure how much good that might do me. I didn't like having the girl in green, for want of something else to call her, following behind me. When I glanced over my shoulder, just once to be certain she was following because her bare feet didn't make a sound on that short grass, she gestured, irritated like someone shooing away a troublesome fly. Get on with it. I walked faster.

I hit the button on the fob to unlock the van as soon as I could see it. I opened the sliding side door and reached in to find the alder wood staff. As soon as I had it clear of the door, she was right beside me. She took the staff out of my hand.

'Thank you,' I said quickly. 'For the loan. We're all square now.'

I made it clear that was a statement, not a question. Something about her sly half-smile made me hope I was right about that. Was there anything within reach inside the van that was made of metal, if she made a move to use the alder wood on me? To do what? I had no clue.

This not saying anything was an unnerving tactic, as well as an effective one. No one could twist her words to their advantage if the girl in green didn't speak. Meanwhile, whoever was up against her could talk themselves into all sorts of trouble.

Was there anything else I could do for her? Something else she needed? May I be of any assistance? The customer service phrases that everyone at Blithehurst was reminded to use came crowding to the front of my mind. I swallowed hard to keep them out of my mouth.

She looked amused, as if she knew exactly what I was thinking. Then she disappeared.

I was tempted to get into the van and stay there, surrounded by metal. But 'before daybreak' wasn't a time I could use to set an alarm on my phone, telling me to walk up to the moor. Aled would have no idea where I'd gone if he got back and I wasn't there. I took a deep breath and headed up the path.

Nothing else happened for the rest of that very short night. I was sitting inside the earthwork watching the sun rise when Aled turned up with dirt smeared across his face and his overalls.

I stood up. 'How was it?'

'Good.' He was grinning from ear to ear.

'That's all you've got to say?' I picked up the plastic crate.

'Sorry. It's what you might call a non-disclosure situation.'

'Fair enough.' I was curious, but I wasn't going to argue. 'Have you got everything we need?'

'Oh yes.' He patted the front of his overalls.

I saw the bulge of something in an inside pocket. When we got back to the van and he had stripped off his caving gear, Aled handed me a soft leather drawstring bag.

'Take a look. It's okay. I did ask.'

I sat in the passenger seat and loosened the leather thong. As I tipped the bag up, silver chains slithered into my hand. These necklaces were made from solid, sizeable links, engraved with curving, coiling lines. Something about the design made me think of the wyrm. Something else was sending pins and needles halfway up my arm towards the scars on my shoulder. I slid the necklaces back into the bag and put it in the glove box.

'I've got some news,' I said to Aled. 'We can head home sooner than planned.'

While we were getting everything stowed, I told him about the girl in green turning up to reclaim the alder wood staff. Aled agreed that was good news. We drove back towards Berwick, and as soon as I had a decent phone signal, I called Peter.

'We have seven necklaces for the kelpies who need them. Can you deliver them for us?'

We'd been planning to trade them for the grid reference we would need to return the staff, but now we were happy to just hand them over. The kelpies could be the cunning men's problem. As long as they stayed put.

'You've— Where are you? Don't tell me. Lammermuir?'

Peter was angry. I'd half expected that.

'Where shall we meet?' I asked him. 'Somewhere on our way south from Berwick for preference.'

He took a few minutes to answer. 'Can you spare an hour to come to Edinburgh? There's a service station on the Musselburgh bypass where I can meet you.'

I had the phone on speaker. I looked at Aled. 'Well?'

He shrugged, keeping his eyes on the road. 'Can we get breakfast there?'

Peter heard him. 'Sorry, no. There's just a shop.'

Aled shrugged again. 'We'll find somewhere to eat after then.'

So that's what we did. We topped up with fuel to give us an excuse for turning into the petrol station. We had to wait for Peter though, and that made me nervous. Anyone watching the CCTV would be wondering what we were doing. If they watched long enough, they'd see me hand over a small package before both cars immediately drove off. That would look very dodgy, and those cameras would have our number plates.

Peter only had one question. 'Where's my car parked at the moment? Back at Blithehurst?'

'Outside the cottage.'

Before I could ask when he planned on picking it up, he just nodded. 'Leave it unlocked with the keys in the sun visor.'

He turned and walked away. I hoped the black Audi he was driving wasn't linked to any activity that might interest the cops.

That meant I didn't get a chance to tell him about giving the alder wood staff to the girl in green. Since we wanted to get away from there as fast as he did, I only realised that half an hour later. Oh well. Peter hadn't asked. I took out my phone and started looking for somewhere to stop for breakfast.

Since we were on the road so early, we had an easy run back to Blithehurst. Aled stayed for the night in the manor and went home the next day. Peter's 4x4 vanished in the middle of the night the following Wednesday. Whoever had picked the padlock on the back gate snapped it shut on the chain on their way out, so I decided to let that go. I was busy back at work, and Fin came up to stay most weekends. Life got back to normal.

There was one last thing I wanted to do. I took my time and worked out a plan. When I was ready, at the start of August, I texted Eleanor late on a Friday afternoon. I asked if she could meet me in the library after everyone else had gone home. She told me to be there at six.

'Sophie and David are coming over on Sunday,' she said cheerfully as she came through the door. 'Mum's doing lunch for their wedding anniversary.'

'That'll be nice.' Crap. I hoped what I was going to suggest didn't wreck that.

'What do you want to talk about?' Eleanor looked expectantly at the folder in my hand.

I handed it over. 'If we clear the old watermill ruins, we can make a wetland to attract birds and other wildlife. It can be an asset instead of an eyesore.'

Instead of a festering reminder of how Robbie Beauchene had died. I didn't say that. I didn't have to. Eleanor went red as she sat on the other sofa, turning over the pages I had printed out that afternoon in Janice's office behind the restaurant.

Fin and Blanche had helped me work out how to make best use of the mill pond, as well as the old leats that once carried stored water to the wheel to power the grinding stones. Blanche had painted a watercolour of the finished scheme, framed by the willows along the riverbanks.

Eleanor sniffed as she studied my calculations. She cleared her throat. 'These costs look reasonable. I'll have to think about it. We'll see what the rest of the family say. And the dryads.'

'They like the idea.' I wouldn't have started this without asking Frai and Asca. 'But there's no hurry. Discussing it can wait until after you've had your lunch on Sunday.'

Eleanor looked at the ceiling. I saw the faint glint of the Green Man's approval as I stood up. 'That's all I wanted to show you. Have a nice evening.'

Eleanor nodded, still sitting on the sofa. 'You too. See you tomorrow.'

Shit. I really had upset her. But the wetland was still a good idea. I let myself out through the side door and headed back through the woods to the cottage.

I was about halfway there when the shuck appeared on the path right in front of me. Seriously? What was coming our way now? Hadn't we already had our fair share of shit for the year? More than our fair share?

The great spectral black hound walked a little way into the trees. It stopped and looked back at me with smouldering red eyes. It went a few paces further on and looked back again. The woods felt calm to me, and the birds were singing. I didn't feel any hint of a warning from the scars on my arm. I reached out to the closest tree. I sensed the shuck right there and the three dryads by the temple. Nothing else but squirrels, badgers and hedgehogs.

'Has Little Timmy fallen down the well?'

If the shuck understood the joke, it didn't show any sign.

'Okay. Where do you want to go?' I stepped off the path and followed it.

I was careful where I was walking. I knew the ground sloped unexpectedly steeply in this bit of the woods. In places, the wet weather in the spring had swept away the leaf litter and the topsoil, deepening the gullies that carried rainwater down to the river. I watched my footing as well as staying alert for anything out of place.

The shuck stopped beside an old hollow oak. I saw it was split in half. Some downpour had washed away the soil around its roots on one side. I approached the stricken tree carefully. It was a sorry sight, if you didn't understand this final stage of its life. These oaks were some of the oldest trees on the estate. The half that had stayed upright was still flourishing. Come to that, the leaves on the fallen half were barely wilted. This had only just happened.

The shuck was standing guard over the hollow torn up by the tree's roots when half of its trunk fell away. After checking that none of the branches overhead looked likely to come crashing down on me, I knelt and looked into the hollow. Something gleamed in there. I used my phone's camera to take a couple of pictures.

As I zoomed in, I saw what looked like a brooch as well as a couple of bracelets. They were made of gold, like the coins I could see now I looked closer. I zoomed in closer on the bracelets or arm rings or whatever they were. I'd seen that snake-like design engraved on those necklaces the delvers made for the kelpies.

'They said you didn't seek a reward.' Frai stood beside the shuck.

'The sylph told us,' Etraia explained.

'That hardly seemed fair,' Asca commented. 'You did kill the wyrm.'

I didn't bother asking if the dryads had sent Zan to keep an eye on me and Aled or if the sylph had been watching us of their own accord. I looked at the treasure. Blithehurst had held several open days for detectorists who searched in and around every inch of Sir Graelent's little castle. They had explained the legal situation when a discovery was deemed to be a treasure trove to anyone willing to listen. When a museum raised the money to meet a hoard's valuation, half went to the landowner and half went to whoever had found it.

None of the detectorists had come out this far into the woods. They didn't have any reason to think there'd be anything to find. I didn't think there would have been if they had. I remembered the cheerful lady from the portable antiquities scheme telling a bunch of kids that no matter how old a find might be, if it was made of gold, it came out of the ground as shiny as if it was made yesterday.

I reckoned these pieces probably had been, or they were a few months old at best. Not that anyone would ever suspect it. Apart from Aled.

The dryads had disappeared, so I couldn't ask how the delvers had done this. I didn't expect them to tell me, but it would be entertaining to watch them trying to avoid straight answers. The shuck was lying down with its head on its outstretched paws, ears pricked and watching to see what I did next.

I had a good strong signal on my phone. I swiped the pictures away and called Eleanor. 'I've found something you'll want to see.'

JULIET E. MCKENNA

Acknowledgements

In what has been an unexpectedly challenging year personally, I am more grateful than ever to be working with Cheryl Morgan of Wizard's Tower Press, editor Toby Selwyn, and artist Ben Baldwin. Saying 'thank you' feels wholly inadequate, given their hard work as unforeseeable events threw my writing schedule into chaos, landing them with the knock-on effects.

As ever, friends have generously helped me to get key details in this story correct. Any errors that remain are my responsibility alone. Martin Owton and Peter McClean shared their pertinent hands-on experience with turf fires, as did sundry others online. Sabine Furlong helped ensure that police procedures pass muster for fictional purposes. Sue Rumfitt detailed the challenges of driving a Land Rover towing a heavily-laden trailer. Ruby Price offered valuable insights into good and bad organisation at music festivals. Fine writer and man of Mercia, Mark Chadbourn lent me his surname for the site of this story's climactic events. My sincere thanks go to all.

I am indebted to Pádraig, Mícheal and Seán Ó Méalóid, for a wealth of ways in which an Irishman might express various emotions. For those who are curious, the Irish phrases used in this book translate as follows:

Loscadh is dó ort! That you may be burned and scorched!

Ní rachainn i bhfoisceacht scread asail... I wouldn't go within an ass's roar...

A Mhuire Mháthair! Oh Mother Mary!

Not for the first time, in the course of writing this story, I discovered non-fiction books providing invaluable information through passing mentions and longer reviews shared on social media. It's also thanks to readers' enthusiasm continuing to spread the word about Dan's adventures that I can continue writing this series. I am extremely grateful for these and many other benefits of belonging to the online SF and Fantasy community.

2024 has been a busy year for SF and fantasy conventions, in person and online for me, including but by no means limited to the largest which was the World Science Fiction Convention in Glasgow. These fan-run events offer me the chance to connect directly with readers, to meet my fellow authors and to swap notes about this business, to take part in fascinating conversations about myriad aspects of writing, and to listen to other panellists discussing any number of interesting topics. I invariably come away from a convention with new ideas and fresh perspectives which inform and improve my own work. None of this would happen without the hard work of dedicated people who give up a frankly staggering amount of their personal time as well as offering the benefits of their professional expertise, all for the love of this genre. I cannot overstate my gratitude to the committees, staffs and volunteers who make conventions possible.

About the Author

Juliet E McKenna is a British fantasy author living in the Cotswolds, UK. Loving history, myth and other worlds since she first learned to read, she has written fifteen epic fantasy novels so far. Her debut, *The Thief's Gamble*, began The Tales of Einarinn in 1999, followed by The Aldabreshin Compass sequence, The Chronicles of the Lescari Revolution, and The Hadrumal Crisis trilogy. *The Green Man's Heir* was her first modern fantasy inspired by British folklore in 2018. *The Green Man's Quarry* in 2023, the sixth title to follow, won the BSFA Award for Best Novel. *The Green Man's War* continues this ongoing series.

Her 2023 novel *The Cleaving* is a female-centred retelling of the story of King Arthur, while her shorter fiction includes forays into dark fantasy, steampunk and science fiction. She promotes SF&Fantasy by reviewing, by blogging on book trade issues, attending conventions and teaching creative writing. She has served as a judge for the James White Award, the Aeon Award, the Arthur C Clarke Award and the World Fantasy Awards. In 2015 she received the British Fantasy Society's Karl Edward Wagner Award. As J M Alvey, she has written historical murder mysteries set in ancient Greece.

For more, visit www.julietemckenna.com

The Tales of Einarinn

1. The Thief's Gamble (1999)
2. The Swordsman's Oath (1999)
3. The Gambler's Fortune (2000)
4. The Warrior's Bond (2001)
5. The Assassin's Edge (2002)

THE GREEN MAN'S WAR

The Aldabreshin Compass

    1. The Southern Fire (2003)

    2. Northern Storm (2004)

    3. Western Shore (2005)

    4. Eastern Tide (2006)

Turns & Chances (2004)

The Chronicles of the Lescari Revolution

    1. Irons in the Fire (2009)

    2. Blood in the Water (2010)

    3. Banners in The Wind (2010)

The Wizard's Coming (2011)

The Hadrumal Crisis

    1. Dangerous Waters (2011)

    2. Darkening Skies (2012)

    3. Defiant Peaks (2012)

A Few Further Tales of Einarinn (2012) (ebook from Wizards Tower Press)

Challoner, Murray & Balfour: Monster Hunters at Law (2014) (ebook from Wizards Tower Press)

Shadow Histories of the River Kingdom (2016) (Wizards Tower Press)

The Green Man (Wizards Tower Press)

1. The Green Mans Heir (2018)
2. The Green Man's Foe (2019)
3. The Green Man's Silence (2020)
4. The Green Man's Challenge (2021)
5. The Green Man's Gift (2022)
6. The Green Man's Quarry (2023)

The Philocles series (as J M Alvey)

1. Shadows of Athens (2019)
2. Scorpions in Corinth (2019)
3. Justice for Athena (2020)
4. Silver for Silence (a dyslexia-friendly quick read, 2022)

The Cleaving (2023)

THE GREEN MAN'S WAR

Printed in the USA
CPSIA information can be obtained
at www.ICGtesting.com
LVHW041459061124
795876LV00004B/75